... editor ... writing ... farm in ... lue Mountains near Syd... with her ... band, daughter, and lots of pe... ves in love ... first sight and real-life romance—the... ed for her! ... andy loves to hear from her readers. Visit her at ... ndyshepherd.com

fter writing more than eighty books for Mills & Boon, ... ella Bagwell still finds it exciting to create new stories nd bring her characters to life. She loves all things Western and has been married to her own real cowboy or forty-four years. Living on the south Texas coast, she lso enjoys being outdoors and helping her husband care or the horses, cats and dog that call their small ranch ome. The couple has one son, who teaches high school athematics and is also an athletic director. Stella oves hearing from readers. They can contact her at ellabagwell@gmail.com

ONE NIGHT WITH HER MILLIONAIRE BOSS

KANDY SHEPHERD

THE TEXAN TRIES AGAIN

STELLA BAGWELL

MILLS & BOON

First Published in Great Britain 2020
by Mills & Boon, an imprint of HarperCollinsPublishers,
1 London Bridge Street, London, SE1 9GF

One Night With Her Millionaire Boss © 2020 Kandy Shepherd
The Texan Tries Again © 2020 Stella Bagwell

ISBN: 978-0-263-27875-0

0420

MIX
Paper from
responsible sources
FSC
www.fsc.org
FSC™ C007454

This book is produced from independently certified FSC™ paper to ensure responsible forest management.

For more information visit: www.harpercollins.co.uk/green

Printed and bound in Spain
by CPI, Barcelona

ONE NIGHT WITH HER MILLIONAIRE BOSS

KANDY SHEPHERD

To my wonderful, clever and patient editor,
Victoria Britton, who helps make my stories the best
they can be. Thank you!

CHAPTER ONE

NED HUDSON HAD lost count of the times he'd been best man or groomsman for one of his friends. His cousin, Erin, however—one of the bridesmaids in today's ceremony—delighted in reminding him of the specifics of his track record. 'You know what they say, Ned: *five times a groomsman, never a groom*,' she teased before the service in the country town church where generations of his family had taken their vows, been christened, even buried.

Ned tried to laugh it off. 'You make it sound like a curse. Doesn't that saying apply to bridesmaids? Girls, not guys?'

'I can't see why it doesn't apply to men too,' she said. 'You're pushing thirty, Ned. Handsome, wealthy, a great guy. I don't know why you're so determined to stay single. Maybe it's time for the farmer to think about taking a wife.'

Ned gritted his teeth. He wasn't actively avoiding marriage. Far from it. He wanted a wife to share his life on Five and a Half Mile Creek, the historic homestead and vast holdings of land that had been in his family for more than one hundred and fifty years, and which was now in his hands. *Farmer* wasn't really the right word to describe him though—he was more of a CEO of a multi-faceted rural enterprise with a turnover in the multi-millions. It wasn't a role for a single guy. He needed a supportive spouse by his side. And then there was the matter of providing an heir.

But he fell for the wrong kind of women. Women who valued the trappings of his considerable wealth—the penthouse in the most exclusive part of the big city of Melbourne, the private plane, international travel—over the idea of a settled family life. Women who wanted the excitement of the city over the more fulfilling pace of the rural life he loved, but who pretended to like the country until they had him snared. Three years ago he'd fallen head over heels in love with such a woman, had come close to proposing to her, so close he'd been gutted when she'd revealed her true colours. He wouldn't get caught like that again.

Today, his brother Wil was marrying lovely Georgia. They'd been friends at university but never more than friends until Wil had taken custody of his baby daughter, Nina, after his ex-wife had died in an accident. Learning to look after the daughter Wil hadn't known about had brought him and Georgia closer and they had fallen in love.

Love. *Huh.* Wil and Georgia had been lucky in the love stakes. Ned, however, had been working on the wrong criteria when it came to relationships. The roller-coaster ride of infatuation and emotion did not appear to work for the kind of wife required for the boss of Five and a Half Mile Creek. He had seen the way it had torn his parents apart, so he should have known better. It had been a painful lesson to learn.

Never a groom. The curse-like phrase kept reverberating through his mind. He would turn thirty in a few months, and was fed up with putting his personal life on hold. Sooner rather than later, he wanted to get married, to exchange vows at this very altar. And he didn't want to deal with time-wasters like Leanne, the gold-digger who had broken his heart.

So what did he want in a wife?

As the ceremony proceeded, Ned thought about his requirements for the ideal wife and mother of his children. It didn't take him long to formulate a wish-list.

She should be tall, as he was six foot three. Dark-haired, brown-eyed women were his 'type' though he was open to hair colour, eye colour, et cetera.

But there were other, non-negotiable attributes for the future Mrs Ned Hudson:

1. Genuine enjoyment of country life essential.
2. Management experience to help run the business would be advantageous. Accountant or lawyer ideal.
3. Love of animals, particularly horses. A vet or vet nurse would be very welcome.
4. An interest in gardening.
5. A good cook.
6. Conservative, country-focused values.

But how to find her? Living out here, nearly four hundred kilometres from Melbourne, meant he couldn't count on happenstance to deliver him the right kind of wife. That meant a dating site.

He dreaded having to create a profile to sell himself. *Tall, well built, financially secure...* That might work. He was an expert horseman. Piloted his own plane. Liked reading political thrillers in his rare downtime. But above all, he was a man of the land—*his land*.

He never wanted to live anywhere else. His connection to the land came before everything. Any future wife would have to understand that. Five and a Half Mile Creek was more a vocation than a job—he'd been born to it.

He'd been an only child until he was fourteen. Then Wil, aged thirteen, had come to Five and a Half Mile Creek—a troubled foster child, hostile and hurting. Ned had treated the boy with caution and respect, as he did the lost and injured animals he cared for, and had been overjoyed when Wil had been adopted and become his brother.

His parents treated them equally as sons. However, while Wil loved Five and a Half Mile Creek, he had no desire to own it. Ned was destined to inherit the property but when his mother had survived breast cancer, his parents had decided to fulfil her bucket list by travelling around the world. Ned had been in partnership with his dad running Five and a Half Mile Creek before. Now the responsibility was entirely on his shoulders. That left little opportunity to look for a wife.

Never a groom.

By the time the reception at the homestead was in full swing, he'd decided he would not let that happen. A dating site it would have to be. After he'd posed for the last of the seemingly interminable photos where the best man was required, he managed to get away from the celebration and into his private study. No one would miss him for ten minutes or so. He closed the door, sat down at his computer and typed up that wife wish-list.

Perhaps it seemed a tad impersonal, he thought uncomfortably when he reviewed the list. In fact, it read more like an employment ad. But anyone marrying him would have to take on not just a husband but Five and a Half Mile Creek too.

Besides, there was nothing wrong with being practical. He'd fallen head over heels in love before and it hadn't worked out. In fact, each time had ended disastrously. Infatuation was *not* the basis for a lasting relationship. Practicality was the way to go. Mutual values, shared interests, a judicious getting-to-know-each-other period. That was how it could work.

He would make sure of it.

With a sigh of relief, Freya Delaney swung her little purple van into the driveway that led from an imposing set of gates to the Hudson family's historic property, Five and a Half Mile Creek. She hadn't realised just how far away from the city it was when she'd set off from Melbourne the day before. She'd actually crossed the border from the state of Victoria into New South Wales.

This was the real Australian countryside—huge skies, mile after mile of emptiness with only the occasional dwelling. Swathes of rich, productive land were devoted to crops or sheep, interspersed with areas of natural bushland.

She shuddered. How could anyone live in such isolation? The inner city with crowded, buzzing streets and a coffee shop on every corner was more to her taste.

But the landscape was beautiful in its own way and she was glad for the opportunity to visit. Not only was she on assignment for her boss, Hugh Tran, the photographer who had shot the wedding held at Five and a Half Mile Creek the previous weekend, but she was also on a secret, personal mission of her own.

She'd known Wil Hudson—though his name hadn't been Hudson then and her name hadn't been Freya— when they'd both been thirteen and in foster care. Wil had proved a true friend to her when her safety had been threatened. But she hadn't seen him since. Helping her boss edit the wedding shoot, she'd immediately recognised the handsome, dark-haired groom as grown-up Wil.

She'd felt an immense rush of relief that he'd found happiness with a lovely wife and a sweet baby daughter. Things had, thank heaven, turned out well for Wil. But she hadn't shared any of those thoughts with her boss, Hugh. All she'd done was comment on what a beautiful wedding it was. And what an utterly gorgeous location.

'I'm an old friend of Jackie Hudson, the mother of the groom,' Hugh had said. 'She was a well-known interior designer in her day—I first knew her as Jacqueline Travis. She asked me at the wedding could I photograph the newly redecorated homestead. It's a job right up your alley, Freya, would be a good thing for your portfolio. Why don't you take over the shoot?'

A shiver of what she wasn't sure was excitement or trepidation had run up her spine. 'But won't your friend expect you to do it?'

'I shot the wedding purely as a favour. Besides, Jackie doesn't live there any more. Her older son, Ned, is running the place. Good, steady kind of guy.'

Boring kind of guy, Freya translated.

She dated creative, interesting men—much good that they had done her. Her last relationship had been with a rock musician. She'd thought he'd sung to her soul, but in truth he was manipulative and borderline abusive. Freya been left with a bruised heart and hadn't let down her barriers to a man since.

She knew she should say no to the assignment. Wil had found the happy life he deserved. Freya had made something of herself too. Her traumatic past was something to be pushed to the furthest corners of her mind. She had no desire to intrude on Wil's new life. But she loved shooting interiors. And she couldn't deny she was curious about the home her old friend had ended up with after those awful years in foster care and institutions. She'd like to see Five and a Half Mile Creek.

'I'll check with her son to see if it's okay,' she'd said. 'Show me which one he is in the wedding photos.'

She'd flicked through the images of Ned Hudson, the best man. He was good-looking in a rugged, manly way—tall, wore a tux well. Even in the photos, he seemed to have a presence, as if people would take note of what he had to say. He didn't look anything like Wil but, of course, they weren't related by blood.

She'd felt some trepidation about informing Ned Hudson she was replacing his mother's choice of photographer. But when she'd called him, and had a brief, to-the-point conversation, he'd raised no objections. So here she was, ten days after the wedding, at one of the grandest pastoral properties in the country—owned by people who were in the highest echelons of society.

She drove slowly up the long, tree-lined driveway to the house, set in what must be an acre of glorious, well-tended gardens bright with autumnal colour in the early morning sun. It was more mansion than farmhouse, an imposing Victorian-era building with peaked slate roofs and turrets and surrounded on all sides by wide verandas.

She'd seen the wedding photos, but still she was knocked out by the house's classic beauty and elegance. This was serious money. *Old money.* But she wasn't intimidated. She'd shot interiors in some of the finest homes in Melbourne for the glossiest of lifestyle magazines. She could do this one justice.

Freya negotiated the circular gravel driveway and parked the van as close as she could to the house. She swung herself out of the driver's seat, to be greeted by crisp morning air, the scent of roses…and the furious barking of a dog.

The black-and-white border collie stood on the wide veranda just steps away, in front of the double-fronted door. Freya froze, paralysed by her fear of dogs. One of her foster parents had had a vicious mutt they'd used to keep the children in order. It had never bitten her, but its ominous snarling and bared teeth had established a terror she'd never got over.

A man shouldered his way through the door. 'Molly, *stay*,' a deep masculine voice commanded.

Ned Hudson. She recognised him immediately as he strode out onto the veranda. Tall, broad-shouldered, more handsome than the photos gave him credit for. He was totally in charge of the dog. At his command, it dropped to the floor. 'Good girl. Miss Delaney is a friend,' he said, as he scratched it behind the ears.

The dog had ceased its fearsome barking but its pink tongue lolled from its scarily sharp white teeth. As long as it didn't come any closer, Freya thought, she'd be okay. She took a deep breath to calm herself. How mortifying to be cringing in terror at a dog on a farm, where, of course, you would expect a dog to be.

'Don't worry about Molly,' Ned Hudson said. 'She's a sweet old girl. Her days working with sheep are over, so she makes it her mission to guard the house. Now I've told her you're a friend she'll drop her guard.'

'Er, that's good,' Freya said, keeping a wary eye on the animal. All dogs, even fluffy little white ones, terrified her. She felt okay with cats but had never owned one. A pet was too much commitment—and commitment scared her more than even the most ferocious dog.

Ned stood at the top of the steps, towering over her, even taller than he looked in the photos, with a strong-jawed face, light brown hair and clear blue eyes. She caught her breath.

Not boring at all.

As he took the steps in just a few long-legged strides she stood transfixed at how attractive she found him. Not her type, of course. But he was so big, so strong, so *rural*. In his dark blue jeans and a blue-and-black checked shirt he was totally in keeping with his surroundings with the confidence of a wealthy man utterly sure of his place in the world.

Whereas she, scared of dogs, with a wide purple stripe in her hair, wearing skinny black jeans, a flowing black top and ankle boots that were perfectly in keeping with her inner-city Melbourne lifestyle, suddenly felt very, very out of place.

All the old insecurities she'd battled so hard to overcome threatened to come rushing back.

She didn't belong here.

Especially under false pretences—she had no intention of revealing to Ned Hudson that she'd ever known his brother Wil. She would just be Freya the photographer, do her job efficiently and head back down that driveway as soon as she could.

Ned didn't know what he had been expecting the replacement photographer to be like—to be honest he hadn't given her much thought—but Freya Delaney made him look twice. She was about his age, he guessed, petite, slender, arty in the way she dressed and quite lovely—wide cheekbones and a determined jaw saving her from doll-like prettiness. Her pale blonde hair was streaked with purple.

She took a step towards him. 'I'm Freya,' she said.

'Not Miss Delaney. And I'll try not to be too frightened of your dog.'

A slight breeze lifted her long lavender-coloured scarf so it wafted behind her like wings. She laughed as she tried to bat it back into place, twisting and turning as she did so. Her hair shone like a pale gold halo in the morning sun and her eyes gleamed a brilliant shade of blue. Ned wasn't a fanciful man but for a moment she seemed like some fey, other-worldly creature who had flitted in from the rose garden behind her.

He shook his head to clear it of the ridiculous thought. *Where in hell did that come from?*

He held out his hand, ready to begin his 'welcome to Five and a Half Mile Creek' spiel but the words choked in his throat and something disconcertingly different came out.

'You like purple,' he said, indicating the purple van, the streak in her hair, the tiny purple stone in her eyebrow ring, more purple glinting at her earlobes.

He knew the comment was inane the second that it slipped out. *Damn.* He could be cursedly awkward when it came to chit-chat. Her eyes widened but she politely shook his hand in a firm grasp for just the required amount of time.

'Yes, I love purple,' she said with a delightful curving of her lips. 'It's the colour of creativity.' Her voice was slightly husky in an intriguing contrast to her very feminine appearance.

'You're a photographer—that makes sense.'

She gave a small, self-deprecating shrug that he found charming. 'Not all my photography is creative,' she said. 'Most of it is commercial, the highlight being a Christmas tree decorated with small cans of cat food instead of baubles.'

He laughed. 'Really? That sounds creative to me.'

Again, that little shrug. 'It did look rather cute. And I believe it sold a lot of cat food. But the shoot was hardly the highlight of my career. I hope wearing purple will better channel my creativity for my own, more artistic photography.'

If anyone else had said that, Ned would have snorted his disbelief. But from this woman it seemed to make a curious kind of sense. She put her left hand to a purple-stoned earring without, he thought, realising she was doing so. He noticed one thing she didn't wear was a purple-stoned ring. Any ring, in fact, on her pale, slender fingers.

'Also my birthday is in February and amethyst is my birthstone.' She paused, flushed high on her cheekbones. 'But you don't want to hear all that.'

But he did. Suddenly Ned wanted to know more about Freya Delaney. 'My mother is very creative,' he said.

'What's her birthstone?' Freya asked.

Now it was his turn to shrug. 'No idea,' he said. It wasn't part of the knowledge bank of a man running thousands of acres devoted to sheep and mixed grains, handling multiple high-stakes investments.

'Your mother is a big name in her field. I looked her up.'

'She's pretty much retired these days.'

Ned was proud of his mother's achievements, the beautiful home she had created for her family on the bones of the historic property. But his mother's creative drive had not come without its demands. Jacqueline Travis had been a city girl at the top of her career game who had fallen for a country guy—and settling down on Five and a Half Mile Creek hadn't been without its problems. Ned knew from painful experience how difficult that had been for her, his father, and him as his mother had battled to both keep up her career and make a home out here. Periodically, she had packed up and headed back to Melbourne for weeks on end—leaving her young son torn between his mother and the home he loved.

Finally, when Ned was nine years old his mother had left his father and wrenched her son away from everything he'd loved to live with her in the city. He could still remember how utterly miserable he'd been away from his pony, his dog, his pet chickens. How impossible it had seemed to have to choose between his mother and his father, both of whom he'd adored.

'According to my boss, Hugh, this house is a wonderful showcase for your mother's talents. It's a shame she can't be here to show me her work.'

'My parents don't live here any more. They moved to Melbourne. But right now they're in Tuscany,' he said.

'Nice,' Freya said with an undertone of longing in her voice.

Ned could have just agreed with her, skated over the truth, but he believed in being straightforward. 'My mother is a breast cancer survivor and—'

Freya gasped and her hand flew to her mouth. 'I'm so sorry,' she said. 'Well, not that she's a survivor but that—'

He had to clear his throat. 'She's been incredibly brave and strong. But she's in remission, thankfully. Now she and my dad are off to see all the places they couldn't see when Five and a Half Mile Creek was their life. No opportunity for extended vacations when you're running a property this size.'

'So now you're in charge.'

'Yes. I took over from my parents so it's all on me now. Not that I'm complaining. I love this place.'

He watched as she looked around her with wide eyes.

This was just the house and garden—impressive enough. It was unlikely he'd get the chance to show her there was so much more—the tennis court, swimming pools, an administration office, staff accommodation, historic shearing sheds, horse arena and stables, an airstrip. Thousands of acres of land and the actual creek—really more a small river—from which the property took its name.

'It must be a big job,' she said.

'Yes,' he said. 'But nothing I can't handle.'

The steady hands on the reins.

That was him: steady, reliable, you-can-count-on-me Ned. No one had ever imagined he would say no to the job of running Five and a Half Mile Creek—even if it meant more time spent behind a computer with spreadsheets than on horseback. Ned had known from an early age that his destiny was to run it. There'd been no choice of career for him. He'd excelled at violin but a role in an orchestra had never been an option. Neither had studying to be a veterinarian. When he'd been asked to step up, he'd said *yes*.

He'd only ever strayed from his predestined path once—that crazy time when he'd been so infatuated with Leanne and spent more time in Melbourne with her than he should have. He'd been too blinded by his so-called *love* for her to notice his mother getting frail, his father anxious. His father had actually had to beg him to spend more time at home. When, to Leanne's intense displeasure, Ned had dragged himself unwillingly back from Melbourne, his parents had sat him down and told him about his mother's diagnosis.

Shattered at the news, horrified at his neglect of his duties, he had immediately agreed to move back full-time to Five and a Half Mile Creek while his mother underwent treatment in Melbourne. Foolishly, he'd thought

Leanne would come with him, help him heed his wake-up call.

But she hadn't seen his mother's life-threatening cancer as enough reason for her to turn her own life upside down. Certainly not to give him the support he had expected would come freely from the woman he was about to ask to become his wife. He'd never noticed how cold Leanne's eyes could be until she'd told him to hire someone to run his property because she had no intention of leaving Melbourne. He had ended it with her immediately. It had cut deep when he'd realised she wouldn't mourn the loss of him as a boyfriend so much as the lavish expenditure she'd seen as her right.

Ned had regretted that relationship, but had never regretted his decision to do the right thing by his family. Looking back, he wondered whether, when he was a child, his unquestioning acceptance of his destiny was because he had so desperately wanted to please both parents so he could keep them in his life—right here.

But lately he was beginning to feel constricted. Even his wish-list for a wife put Five and a Half Mile Creek's needs first. It wasn't that he wanted to be wild and throw his wonderful life away but sometimes it irked that people seemed to find him so *predictable*. When had he become like that?

'So you took over from your parents,' Freya said. 'Is that why your mother redecorated the house? To mark the new order?'

'It's a family tradition that when the son—and it's always been a son—takes over from the father, he puts his own stamp on the place. My mother met my father when he employed her to redecorate. She came out here and—as Dad says—"captivated" his heart.'

'Aww, that's so romantic,' Freya said with what seemed like genuine appreciation.

'Love at first sight, according to them both.' Another reason for him to avoid relationships based on infatuation.

Head over heels in love.

He'd learned that expression from the story of his parents' 'romantic' meeting. It had never sounded particularly comfortable to him as a child. And it hadn't worked out well for his parents; they'd always seemed to be arguing. He would stick his fingers in his ears so he didn't have to hear their raised, angry voices.

'But it must have been a shock for your mother moving here from Melbourne,' Freya said. 'It's so far away from the city.'

He detected a little shudder of what could be distaste but might have been trepidation. His mother's voice echoed in his ears. *This place is so far from civilisation.* It had been a familiar refrain in his earlier years. One he had grown to fear, as it had usually heralded one of his mother's departures.

How he'd hated those times. When he was pre-school age, she had taken him with her. That had meant time spent with her parents, who'd had their grandson in their house under sufferance. He could clearly remember how he'd felt like an unwelcome intruder in their house in the upscale suburb of Kew, stuffed with china ornaments just waiting to be knocked over by a lively little boy. Once he'd started school in Hilltop, the nearest town to Five and a Half Mile Creek, he'd been left with his father when his mother went to work in Melbourne.

While he loved his father, and knew his father loved him, he'd rarely seen him. Running the property was not a nine-to-five job—especially during the years-long drought that had devastated the land. Ned had been placed in the care of a series of nannies ranging from fun and caring, to indifferent, to outright incompetent—none of whom had stayed long. His animals had become his trusted friends and companions. Dogs and horses were so much more reliable than the humans in his life.

But his mother had eventually come to terms with life on the land and his father had learned to delegate and spend more time with his family. When Ned had grown up, his father had tried to explain to him that his enduring deep love for his mother and hers for him was what had driven them to reach the compromise. Ned had felt uncomfortable discussing his parents' love life and had wanted to put his fingers in his ears against that too. More recently his dad had brought the subject up again as the reason why he was handing over the reins—so that two people still very much in love could enjoy every remaining minute of their lives together.

Still, those early painful days when his parents were sorting out their lives were behind much of his criteria for his wife wish-list. Why leave compatibility to chance?

'Without a doubt, it is a long way,' he said. 'You must have left the city very early to get here at this time.' When he visited the city, he cut down the travel time by flying his helicopter or light plane.

She shook her head and her fine hair fell softly around her face. He decided he liked the purple. 'Too far for me to drive all that way in one hit and get here ready to work. I left Melbourne yesterday, then stayed last night at a pub in Hilltop.'

He frowned. 'You should have let me know. We have a guest cottage. You could have stayed here. It's very comfortable.'

She shook her head rather more fiercely than his question warranted. 'I wouldn't dream of imposing. The pub was fine. I also have my room booked for tonight as this shoot could run to more than one day.'

Ned opened his mouth to say *next time*, before realising there was unlikely to be a next time. Instead he nodded with a non-committal sound.

'I like to work with available light. So I need to get started.' Her voice was brisk and efficient, with that appealing edge of huskiness.

'Do you need a hand with getting equipment in from your van?'

'Thanks, but not yet,' she said. 'I need to assess the shoot first.'

'Then let's get going,' he said. Looking after the photographer had seemed like an intrusion on his busy day, but suddenly it seemed it might become the highlight. He realised that these days he could go weeks without seeing anyone other than the people who worked for him. His regular trips to Melbourne to take in a concert or a band had stopped after the Leanne fiasco.

'The house looks amazing. I can't wait to see inside.' Freya looked up at him and smiled.

He was mesmerised. She had a tiny gap between her two front teeth and it made her smile both quirky and sensual. This close, he noticed her eyes were blue with a darker ring around the edge that was almost purple. His gaze held hers for a moment too long yet he found it impossible to drag his eyes away.

She was beautiful.

But it wasn't just that. He had known Freya for all of ten minutes and yet she seemed somehow familiar, as if there was an inevitability about their meeting. Her smile wavered and she frowned, obviously puzzled.

What the hell?

Did she think he was hitting on her? He dropped his gaze, took a step back.

Freya was here to fulfil an assignment on behalf of her boss. She was an employee of both Hugh Tran and of him on behalf of Five and a Half Mile Creek. And he never, ever showed personal interest in an employee.

His role here was to show her the rooms she had been engaged to photograph and then leave her to it. It was completely irrelevant whether he found her attractive or not.

More gruffly than he had intended, he asked her to follow him into the house.

CHAPTER TWO

FREYA HAD TO force her gaze away from Ned Hudson's sensational rear view as he strode across the gravel towards the veranda. She didn't want to appreciate the appeal of those broad shoulders, his athletic stride, his impressive butt hugged by blue jeans. Most of all, she didn't want to acknowledge her instant and unsettling attraction to him.

For a long moment just then her eyes had locked with his and she had seen an echo of the same puzzlement she felt at the thought their meeting was somehow…*significant*.

It was a crazy thought and she had to shake herself mentally to get rid of it. For one thing she didn't feel comfortable around this type of man. Ned Hudson was the heir to property and wealth equivalent to a small principality. The 'squattocracy' they called families like the Hudsons, in a play on the word *aristocracy*.

Their ancestors in the early days of the Australian colony had either been granted or had grabbed vast tracts of land—by squatting on it—that they had tenaciously held onto over the years. There wasn't supposed to be a class system in Australia but people like the Hudsons were considered to be blue bloods, as close as Aussies got to landed gentry.

The young men she'd met from that background had been arrogant, with an overblown sense of entitlement. When she was twenty-four, she'd dated one of their kind. She'd thought Henry had been different, and had fallen for him. His snobby mother had openly disapproved of her. But Henry had stood up for her. Until she'd confided in him about her background: daughter of a seventeen-year-old single mum, brought up by her grandparents until they died, then taken into state care at the age of twelve. Everything she had achieved had come from her own hard work and initiative.

Henry had recoiled from her revelation. That she was a photographer made her cool, but her past made her decidedly uncool. He'd stuttered as he'd made it clear that, while what they had together was fun, it was important he marry a woman from the same background as his. She'd walked away, fun over.

Not that Freya ever intended to get married. She refused to give another person—especially a man—power over her life, and certainly not over her heart. She wasn't ashamed of her past; her grandparents had been good people. But the implication that she didn't meet Henry's standards had stung just the same. From then on she'd stuck to dating her own inner-city, creative kind. At least she knew the possible relationship hiccups she faced with those guys. Being not good enough wasn't one of them.

When her boss had entrusted her with this shoot, she'd gone online to research her new client, Ned's mother. If she did the same for Ned, she reckoned she'd find private schooling for him all the way—every privilege inherited money could buy—family trusts and a very easy path in life. He seemed very much a scion of the squattocracy.

Yet her past had taught her not to instantly judge others. After all, Ned's impossibly wealthy family had thrown the door wide open to their privileged life for her old friend Wil, a rebellious, angry teenager. That didn't fit with the behaviour of the so-called elite she had encountered in Melbourne. She would try to keep an open mind.

She followed Ned towards the steps to the veranda, then stopped abruptly as she realised he was leading her towards where the black-and-white border collie sat. Up close, Freya could see her muzzle was silver and one of her eyes cloudy. As she approached, Molly thumped her tail on the wooden floor in greeting. But a dog was a dog and Freya wanted to keep her distance. She couldn't help glancing nervously at the animal—something that didn't escape Ned.

'Molly is more likely to lick you than harm you,' he said. 'Slobbery doggy kisses are her speciality. But I'll put her on her leash, otherwise she'll want to follow you around the house. I'll take her with me when I go back to the office.'

'Thank you,' Freya said on a sigh of relief. 'I know it's ridiculous, but I had a bad experience when I was young and I'm frightened of even small dogs.'

'Not ridiculous at all. But you really have nothing to fear from this old girl.'

He stroked his dog gently around the head with strong, callused hands. How could such a big man be so tender? He looked at Molly with unabashed affection in his eyes and the dog looked adoringly back. How would it feel to have a man look at her like that—open, honest, not afraid to show his feelings? It was something she had never experienced.

'I want to believe you, but I'm happy to keep my distance from her all the same,' she said.

After Ned attached the dog's long leash to a metal ring

on the wall, he glanced at his watch. 'I know you're keen to get going so we'd better get you started.'

Freya reached into her tote bag and pulled out a sheaf of printouts. 'Your mother sent a detailed room-by-room shoot list. If you could point me in the direction of the rooms she mentions, I'd appreciate it.' There was no need for him to babysit her.

'Let me have a look,' he said, reaching for the papers and flicking through them. 'Okay, so you need a guide through all this.' He smiled. Again she had to stop herself from staring at him. He had the kind of warm smile that reached his eyes; big, white perfect teeth; a generous mouth. It was impossible not to respond with a smile of her own.

'Maybe. The house looks enormous and I don't want to get lost or get the rooms wrong.'

'Just follow me,' he said.

Ned pushed open the grand double doors and ushered Freya through ahead of him. With a sense of anticipation, she stepped into a wide corridor, the walls panelled, the wooden floors covered in beautiful, oriental rugs. She paused to glance up at ornately moulded ceilings, and breathe in the scent of beeswax polish and roses from the enormous vase of red blooms on the entry table. As she followed Ned down the corridor, he flung open doors that led into a grand, formal living room with large marble fireplaces and an equally grand dining room.

'This is the more formal part of the house,' Ned explained.

He spoke with a justifiably proprietorial air. What must it be like to have this magnificence as your birthright? It was a far cry from her grandparents' two-bedroom terrace house in the shadow of the brewery where her grandfather had worked for most of his life.

'As a kid I thought it was all stuffy and boring,' he said. 'Now the house is mine, I like those rooms just the way they are.'

'Me too,' she said. Apart from the beauty of the work-manship, the rooms and their furnishings symbolised wealth, continuity, stability—all things she had never experienced.

Ned headed towards the end of the corridor. 'Here's where you'll find the rooms that have had a total make-over. Along here are the family room, the music room, my study, the room that was Mum's studio, and the new kitchen. Mum really went to town to give the house a completely new look for what she calls "the new era of Ned".' He rolled his eyes and Freya smiled.

'You didn't want someone other than your mother to work on the house?'

'She's my mother but she's also Jacqueline Travis, one of Melbourne's top interior designers who loves this house and who knows me very well. Why entrust the design to an outsider? I knew she would do a better job than anyone else.'

'There's that,' Freya said. He must have a good rela-tionship with his parents to be so confident. If so, she envied him. She'd scarcely known her mother, and her father not at all.

He laughed, a deep, full-bodied laugh as engaging as his smile. 'To tell you the truth, I've always been more interested in the outdoors. Refurbishing the stables? I'm your man. I have no interest whatsoever in fabric swatches and colour chips, and the proportions of table lamps. My only stipulation was hard-wearing, comfort-able furniture a man could throw himself into without fear of breaking anything.'

Ned was a big man, tall and well built. His shirt sleeves

were rolled up to reveal muscular, tanned forearms. His shirt did nothing to disguise a powerful chest. She refused to let her thoughts stray to the rest of his body.

He was a client.

'A wise idea,' she said, suddenly short of breath. Again she had to drag her attention away from him and towards the rooms she had been commissioned to photograph. He was hot, in an understated way that made him seem a degree hotter every time she looked at him. 'Please lead on, you've got me intrigued.'

The first room he showed her was a spacious informal living room. French doors led to the veranda, and a view to pear trees, resplendent in multi-hued autumn leaves. The interior design, while it paid homage to the history of the house, was fresh and contemporary and eminently liveable. Immediately Freya could see angles and details she wanted to capture through the lens of her camera.

Ned gestured to a large, high-backed easy chair covered in a deep blue linen fabric. 'My favourite chair,' he said.

Freya could just imagine him sprawling there, long limbs splayed out, the master of his house. 'It looks strong, yet good-looking too and I suspect it would be very comfortable.' *Like you.*

She bit her lip to stop the words from creeping out unbidden.

What was wrong with her?

Apart from him being a client, this guy was *so* not her type.

'It is,' he said. 'Not that I have an awful lot of time for relaxing. It's a particularly busy time of year with planting and preparations for winter.'

Freya was ignorant of country ways. But this property was vast, and Ned was in charge of it all. She doubted he got down and actually sheared sheep or mended fences. His role would surely be an administrative one. Wasn't a lot of farm routine governed by computers and machines these days?

As he showed her through the rest of the rooms, she checked them against the client's shoot list, getting more and more excited. 'I hope I can do the house justice with my photography.' She had shot some of the finest homes in Melbourne, but to her this was the most beautiful, the most inviting. It was a shame it was a million miles from nowhere.

'I'm sure you will,' he said. 'Hugh Tran wouldn't employ anyone who was anything short of exceptionally talented.'

'That's nice of you to say so.'

'He's a friend of my mother's. I've known your boss all my life.'

'I intend to repay his confidence in me,' she said. 'What about the upstairs? There aren't any bedrooms on the shoot list. Did your mother forget to—?'

'She hasn't touched upstairs.'

Did she not have time to work on those rooms before she got ill? Freya didn't like to ask. 'Really?' was all she said.

'None of those rooms have had a makeover yet.' He paused, shifted from foot to foot and, for the first time, looked slightly uncomfortable. 'My mother says it's up to my...my...future wife to have the bedrooms the way she wants them.'

'Oh,' Freya said, surprised at the flash of regret she felt. 'You're engaged?'

'No.' He paused. 'But I'll get married some day. Five and a Half Mile Creek needs an heir.'

His offhand comment might have been made as a joke,

but it shot her right back to horrible Henry and his talk of marriage as if it were a breeding programme.

'Of course,' she said a little stiffly.

'What about you?' he said.

'Me? Engaged?' She shook her head. 'Nowhere near it.' No need to tell him that she never wanted to get married or why. Or that she hadn't dated for six months. She was here as a photographer, not to swap life stories with the owner of the house.

'How long have you been working for Hugh?' he asked.

'He took me on as his assistant straight out of university. I was lucky to get the chance to work with someone as highly regarded as he is.'

He frowned. 'Surely more than just luck?'

She shook her head. 'Pure luck, really, that I encountered him. When I was a student I was waitressing at a café near his studio. He was a regular.'

She'd put herself through a creative arts degree and had had to scrape for every cent. But she didn't have to share that with Ned. Or further emphasise the differences in their social standing.

'His studio in Richmond?'

'Yes. I had no idea who he was but used to chat with him when I served him his coffee.'

'I bet he had a muffin every day.'

'You know that?'

'My mum and I lived with Hugh and his partner Gordon for a while when I was young and—' Ned stopped abruptly, as if he regretted the words.

'Really?' Freya said, intrigued.

'Long story,' he said, tight-lipped. If she knew Ned better, she might have tried to cajole the story out of him. But it wasn't her place to do so.

'Hugh and Gordon are generous and kind,' she said, her voice trailing away, inviting him to say more.

'Yes,' he said, refusing to be led. What *was* that long story about?

Fatherly wasn't quite the word to use about Hugh and the way he'd looked out for her from the get-go. But he was so much more than a boss.

At first she'd been wary of the photographer, as she had tended to be of older guys showing interest in much younger women. But Hugh had proved to be genuine.

'He knew I was a creative arts student—the campus was nearby,' she said. 'But it wasn't until I asked if I could photograph him for an assignment—he has such an interesting face—that I found out who he was and he discovered I was majoring in photography. He posed for me, and the shoot turned out so well I won a university prize for it.'

'Well done,' Ned said.

'Thank you,' she said. 'Hugh was as thrilled as I was.' Once she would have made some self-deprecating comment about her achievement. Now she had learned to own her talent and hard-earned skills.

'Then in my final semester, he let me do a student placement at his studio. When his assistant left I was beyond delighted when Hugh offered me the role. I've learned so much from him. I worked my way up to become a photographer on his team. I couldn't have had a better mentor.'

'He must have great confidence in you to have subbed you for this job. I look forward to seeing the results. Before I go back to work, I'll introduce you to our housekeeper, Marian. She can answer any further questions you might have, and give you lunch when you're ready.'

'No café on the next corner way out here, when you

need a coffee or a snack,' Freya said—and immediately regretted it. She intended her comment to be light-hearted but it came out, she feared, more like criticism. 'Not that I would expect there to be,' she added hastily. 'There are other wonderful things in the country besides…er… coffee.'

'Rest assured, we do have coffee in the house,' he said, rather coldly, she thought. 'Just ask Marian.'

'I…er…will, thank you,' she said.

'Can I help you with your equipment?' Yes, she hadn't imagined it. His tone was cooler, less friendly. It appeared she had unwittingly insulted him. She gave a mental shrug. He was the client. As long as he was polite, he could speak coolly to her. It made no difference.

'Yes. Please.' Not that she couldn't handle all her own gear. But his help getting it into the house would let her get started quicker.

Once her cameras and lenses, tripods, reflectors, diffusers and the laptop she used for work outside the studio were in place, Ned turned to her. 'My mother said for you to help yourself to any flowers from the garden.'

'I brought flowers in buckets from Melbourne for styling purposes. But fresh from the garden would be so much better.' She paused. 'I'd feel a bit nervous about hacking into the plants. I'm not a gardener.'

'Neither am I. But our head gardener is working in the rose garden today. Ask him for whatever you need.'

Gardener. Housekeeper. Freya could only imagine the number of staff required to keep this gracious house and its grounds looking immaculate. Her grandmother had cleaned houses for the wealthy. 'Thank you for your help,' she said.

He nodded, turned, and left her to it. Suddenly, the room felt very empty.

CHAPTER THREE

NED WAS IN his office in the administration block, which was housed in one of the original structures, built long before the homestead. It had been constructed from stone and timber from the land. His great-grandfather used to refer to it as the 'old house'. Every day, Ned was aware of how much smaller his ancestors must have been, as he had to duck his head to get through the doors.

Today he was preparing for a meeting with the senior members of the farm management team. At this time of year it was vital their efforts were coordinated. But he couldn't settle to his work. His thoughts kept returning to the photo shoot taking place up at the house.

More specifically, his thoughts kept returning to the photographer. Freya. She was smart. Lovely. Intriguing. And a city girl through and through. Scared of dogs. Perhaps equally nervous around horses. Very possibly fearful of lizards and snakes, which, while not often encountered, did share this land with the human occupants.

On his computer, he pulled up the notes from the last meeting, checked the points of action that had been decided. But they were just so many words on the screen. His mind was too occupied by thoughts of the intriguing girl who had appeared so unexpectedly in his life.

He couldn't escape the irony that the first woman he'd

found attractive in a long time didn't seem to meet even one of the criteria on his 'wife wish-list'.

Not that it should matter. He certainly wasn't thinking of her as a possible candidate. Their paths wouldn't cross again after the shoot was done. She was a temporary distraction.

But such a lovely distraction.

He glanced at his watch. Usually he would have his lunch delivered from the staff kitchen to his desk. Today he might head up to the house instead. Freya might need some help. Freya might have questions only he could answer. Freya might—

Hell, he just wanted to see Freya.

As Ned approached the kitchen he heard her laughter, and the rise and fall of chatter with his housekeeper, Marian. It was a heart-warming sound he didn't often hear these days. The large house had seemed very empty after his parents had moved away to their new life as 'citizens of Melbourne and the world', as his dad had put it.

Wil's wedding had brought the homestead back to life, packed to the rafters with celebrating family and friends. But a week ago the last guests had packed up and gone home. Now, in the evenings, the sound of his lone footsteps on the wooden floors echoed through the rooms. Some nights the only voice he heard was his own, talking to his faithful dog, Molly, who did her best to talk back. Not that he felt sorry for himself. He was used to his own company and, during the day, he interacted with the staff. It was his home that felt empty. Freya's laughter brought it to life.

He paused just outside the threshold to the kitchen. Freya sat at the table in the generous eat-in area that led off the cooking area. A steaming bowl of soup sat in front of her. Pumpkin and lentil by the smell of it, a favourite of his. She looked very comfortable, her face animated, as if she belonged there. But as he walked into the room, the chatter stopped abruptly.

Her eyes widened with dismay as she caught sight of him. 'Just having a quick lunch break,' she said, as if she'd been caught out neglecting her work. She pushed back her chair and made to get up.

Was he so formidable? His favourite cousin, Erin—she of the *'never a groom'* prediction at the wedding—had told him he needed to lighten up, that he had what she called a 'resting stern face'. He gestured for Freya to sit down. 'Don't get up. Please. Enjoy your lunch.' He reckoned a forced smile was perhaps worse than stern, so he didn't attempt one.

Freya sat back into her chair, picked up her spoon, then put it back down again. She pushed the bowl away from her. 'Actually, I must be getting back to work.'

Just when he'd joined her? Ned was surprised at how disappointed he felt. He frowned. 'Not right now, surely?' If that could be seen as pulling rank, he didn't care. Of course he had come up to the house just to see her; he couldn't deny that to himself any longer.

'I…er…do have a lot more to get done,' she said.

'Do you want lunch here, Ned?' Marian asked. 'Rather than in your office?' Marian ran the household efficiently and pleasantly. She'd proved to be a gem when his mother had fallen ill. Now she was invaluable to him in all matters household.

'Now that I'm here, lunch sounds like a good idea,' he said, as he pulled out the chair opposite Freya. Her hair with its cute purple stripe was pulled right back from her face, highlighting the slant of her cheekbones, her lush mouth. She'd ditched her scarf and shapeless long tunic for a black T-shirt that revealed subtle, yet pleasingly shapely, curves. 'How is your photography going?'

'Wonderful. Your house is a dream to shoot. When you've finished your lunch, why don't you come find me and I can show you some of the frames?'

She didn't meet his eye and he wondered why she seemed nervous when she certainly hadn't at their previous meeting.

'I'll do that,' he said.

'Ned, I...' She stopped.

'Yes?'

She leaned towards him, lowered her voice. 'I feel bad about my café remark earlier. You know, implying that you're too far from civilisation out here to have decent coffee. I didn't mean to offend but I fear I did.'

Too far from civilisation. Ned froze momentarily at her use of that phrase—so similar to his mother's words that had wreaked such havoc in his young life. But he quickly recovered. 'No offence taken,' he said gruffly.

'Thank you.' She smiled that appealing gap-toothed smile with obvious relief. 'First rule of commercial photography—never insult the client.'

'I wasn't insulted,' he said with a slow grin. 'It wasn't the first time I've heard a comment like that, believe me.' Not insulted, but disappointed when she had come out with the clichéd criticism.

'Just the same, it was wrong of me to pass judgement on a way of life that I know nothing about. And then of course I discover that Marian worked as a barista in Sydney and you have coffee here as good as any inner-city café. Fabulous food too. It's humble pie I should be eating, not soup.'

'Thank you, Freya, all compliments gratefully accepted,' Marian called over her shoulder from where she stood at the stove. Ned was surprised at the warmth in the usually reserved, middle-aged housekeeper's voice.

'We lead a very good life here,' he said. 'I would never swap country life for the city. Crowds and cars and endless rush are not for me. Not any more.' He wished he could show Freya the slow pleasures of rural life but he suspected she was on a city timetable where every moment counted in the rush to the next thing.

'Each to his own,' Freya said lightly. 'I'm a city person myself, bright lights and action, but I can appreciate the appeal of the country.'

She got up from her chair. 'I'm shooting in your study,' she said. 'Will I see you there?'

'Give me ten minutes,' he said.

When Ned got to the study, it was to find Freya intent on her work. She was bent from the waist, huddled low over her camera, which was set on a tripod with a twist of cables falling from it. The angle of her body was a perfect showcase for her pert behind and slender legs clad in skinny black jeans. Her T-shirt had ridden up to reveal an enticing glimpse of pale skin. He tried very hard not to stare.

'You're here,' she said, without looking back or taking her eye from the viewfinder. 'What a wonderful room. The gentleman's study updated.'

'It was my father's and my grandfather's before that. My father wanted the room kept the way his father had it, dark furniture, leather and smelling of old cigarette smoke.'

'It certainly doesn't look like that now,' she said.

His mother had completely transformed the room, ripping up the carpet, throwing out the velvet curtains, furnishing the room simply in neutral colours. His office in the administration block was for work; this was his private domain for his books, his personal computer, the horse paintings he had been given as gifts over the years. Now that it was more to his taste, he considered it a haven.

'I still haven't got used to this room being mine,' he said. 'I thought it would be many years before I took it over.'

'You're a lucky man to have grown up here,' she said briefly.

He couldn't debate that.

Her camera seemed to be trained on a disparate collection of items on a corner of his desk. There was an old book with a fraying fabric cover—an early history of Five and a Half Mile Creek; an expensive fountain pen he had been given for his twenty-first birthday but had never used; and a lucky horseshoe from Banjo, his first pony, propped against the book. Ned had nothing to hide, but he found it disconcerting that Freya had looked through the desk drawer and the bookshelves to find them—even though he had told her to help herself to anything she needed. He valued his privacy.

'The horseshoe,' he said. 'You've got it placed the wrong way.'

'Does it matter?' He could hear the frown in her voice.

'You're meant to have it open end up, so it collects good luck in the curve,' he said. 'If you have it the other way, the luck drains away.'

She glanced up at him. 'Do you seriously believe that? I wouldn't have taken you for the superstitious type.'

'I've had that horseshoe since I was a kid. It's always been displayed open end up,' he said stubbornly.

'Move it for me, then,' she said, returning to her viewfinder. 'But please be careful not to disturb anything else. I'm happy with this composition.'

Ned stepped in front of the camera and carefully turned the horseshoe around so it sat the correct way. He started at the sudden burst of the camera's motor drive and glared at her accusingly. 'Did you just photograph me?'

'Couldn't resist the image of your hand with the horseshoe,' she said without looking up. 'I think it could be cute.'

Cute? It wasn't a word that was ever used to describe him. 'Okay,' he said, bemused.

'Now hop out of the way, will you, please? I've been waiting for the sun to move out from behind a cloud to get the perfect light. Here it comes—' She paused. 'Darn. Not quick enough. You distracted me.'

Ned wasn't used to being ordered around by an attractive woman the same age as him. It was quite a novelty. Of course, he could remind her of who was the boss around here. But he admired her professionalism, her total focus on her work, her straightforwardness. He liked her honesty too. Honesty was important to him.

'We had to get that horseshoe right,' he said.

We. He hadn't meant to say *we.* This wasn't teamwork. She was here to do a job. He was here to facilitate her work. That was all.

'If you say so. I know nothing about horses or horseshoes.' She stilled. 'Wait. The light's perfect.' Again the sound of the motor drive.

'You got it?'

'Yep.' Freya stood up, flexing her back in a graceful, highly sensuous motion that fascinated him. Maybe she did yoga or dance. 'Do you want to look through the lens?' she asked.

He had to clear his throat. 'Why not?'

'You're the boss. If you're unhappy with the image, I'll try again.'

Freya stayed disconcertingly close as she showed him where to look on the camera. He was aware of her scent—something fresh and feminine, that brought to mind the flower garden he'd imagined she'd wafted in from. Right now, without her floaty scarf and dressed all in black, she seemed less ephemeral and very much more grounded and practical.

He looked through the lens—and was taken aback by her talent. This image was not a mere cataloguing of his mother's skills. It was a work of art. The book and horseshoe display on his desk was part of a broader image that expertly showcased the clever redesign of the room. The French doors opened to the garden, revealing a blur of autumn colour from the garden like a painted backdrop to the room. Somehow she'd included, on the nearest wall, the pen-and-wash painting of his favourite polo pony, Hero, that Wil had commissioned for him as a gift for being his best man.

He pulled away from the viewfinder and stood back up. 'How did you do that? Was it a special lens?'

'That would be giving away trade secrets,' she said archly, but looked pleased.

'It's brilliant,' he said. 'You've captured the design of the room but also the—'

'The heart,' she said. 'I could see you wondered why on earth I would choose to show the old book, the pen, the horseshoe.'

'How could you tell that?'

She laughed. 'You have an open face. Your feelings are no secret.'

How many times had he felt disconcerted in the short time he'd known her? 'Well, I—'

'I see your openness as a good thing. Better than the opposite, being cagey and closed off.' Her expression tightened momentarily and he wondered about her past. All he knew about her was her work history with Hugh, which, he reminded himself, was all he needed to know.

'Uh, that's good,' he said. So, did he have an open, revealing face or a 'resting stern face'? The way women put things sometimes baffled him.

'I try to bring the essence of the person into the room, hence the personal items,' she explained. 'In this case, the old book and the old-fashioned fountain pen represent the owner's heritage, the computer his modern-day reality. The horseshoe and the painting of the magnificent horse reveal something of his, er...your, interests.'

'Without giving away too much of the man,' he said thoughtfully.

'Would you like to see some of the morning's shoot?'

'I'd like that very much,' he said, suddenly very curious. What Freya mightn't realise was that her choice of objects and angles revealed something about herself too. Thoughtful, looking beyond the obvious, intuitive.

She picked up the laptop that sat on a low table nearby. 'Keep in mind these images are raw. I'll process and edit them when I get back to the studio. I bracket the shot, using different camera settings. But the folder I'll take you through has what I think might be the winners.'

Ned watched as she flashed through her morning's work on screen. Her style soon became apparent. There was something intimate in each image that brought a person's presence into the room and made it so much more than a cataloguing of furnishings and finishes. He had to laugh at her shot of his old work boots on the edge of the veranda. Who would have thought they would be worthy of artistic interpretation? 'I'm seeing the house where I grew up in quite a different way,' he marvelled.

'Of course you are. I'm seeing what is familiar to you for the very first time. Free of any memories. I'm hardly going to see it the same way you do.'

'But what you choose to emphasise, the angles you work with, are so unexpected.'

'Just my interpretation,' she said with that cute shrug.

'Your artist's eye?'

'If you like. Although these rooms are so wonderfully designed I reckon you could blindfold me, spin me around, let me randomly shoot and you'd still get a good picture.'

'I don't believe that for a moment. You're highly skilled. No wonder Hugh took you on straight from uni.' He narrowed his eyes as he looked again at the images on the screen. 'You've shown me possibilities I never thought about, made me question the familiar.'

'It's what I do,' she said simply. 'I suspect it's what all artists aim to achieve.'

'You've succeeded on every level.'

She flushed high on her cheekbones. 'Thank you. I love shooting interiors. Although I shoot food too. Some fashion and beauty. I'm an all-rounder.'

'Cat-food cans on Christmas trees?'

She laughed. 'That too. But interiors are my special interest, especially non-commercial. That's why Hugh thought I'd enjoy this assignment.'

Ned turned to look down at her. Her face was flushed and strands of her hair had escaped her hair tie and were wisping around her face. Some of them were purple. He resisted the urge to reach out and brush them back from her face. Her skin would be smooth and warm beneath his fingers. 'Are you enjoying it?'

She looked up at him, her brow pleated into a light frown. 'I am. Actually even more than I thought I would. There's something special about this place. I wasn't expecting...' Her voice trailed away.

There's something special about *you*. Again Ned had that sensation that Freya's presence here was meant to be. He found it deeply unsettling. Did that show on his supposedly easy-to-read face? He stepped right back from her. 'I'm glad to hear that.'

She closed the on-screen folder with the images he had been admiring. He noticed her hand wasn't quite steady.

'I even enjoyed the garden. I told you I'm not a gardener. And I know photographing the garden wasn't part of the brief.' She was speaking too quickly, avoiding his gaze.

Did she feel it too?

'But when your gardener was cutting me some roses, I took the opportunity to take a few shots.'

'I'd like to see them,' he said.

'Okay,' she said, opening another folder on her laptop. 'There's just a few, I only had ten minutes.' She scrolled through close-up images of roses, a black-and-white Australian magpie against autumn foliage, a bee burrowing into purple lavender flowers.

'These are magnificent. I reckon you've got a future in garden photography too.'

'Not all gardens are as spectacular as these,' she said.

'My mother will be thrilled. These are an unexpected bonus.'

Freya glanced down at her watch. 'She won't be thrilled if I don't get through her shoot list. I need to get on with it if I'm to finish before the light fades too much. I'll be done then and can head back to Melbourne this afternoon.'

'This afternoon?' He forced the shock from his voice. 'I thought you said you'd need two days to finish the shoot?'

'That was when I thought I'd be shooting bedrooms too. It turned out to be a smaller gig.'

She would be gone by the evening. He wouldn't see her again. Perhaps *ever*.

He couldn't let that happen.

'When you've finished and we still have light, why don't I take you up in my helicopter so you can see the rest of the property?'

Her eyes widened. 'I'd like that.'

He flew his own helicopter?

Ned continued to surprise Freya—not so much by his skills but by how much she enjoyed his company. She couldn't remember when she'd last chatted so easily with a good-looking man. His quiet steadiness made her feel at ease.

She liked him.

There were things she was curious about, like why this big, tough country guy was superstitious about horseshoes. And why he wasn't already married and filling this vast, empty house with 'heirs'. They tended to marry young in the country, didn't they? What else was there to do?

If Ned didn't live way out here at the back of beyond, and she in inner-city Melbourne, she might suggest they caught up for a drink some time. She could see herself being friends with him.

Just friends.

Okay, maybe more than friends. She couldn't deny she found him incredibly attractive. But that wasn't going to happen. There was a truckload of reasons why that couldn't happen. Still, she felt sad she would be saying goodbye to him in just a few hours.

Ned left her to go back to his work and she to hers. She watched him as he strode away, again admiring his back view and the confidence and strength that seemed innate in him. Again the room seemed preternaturally empty when he'd gone, as if he took the energy—the *essence*—of the space with him. She shook her head to clear her mind. It was weird to have these thoughts about a man she'd only known a few hours.

Excited at the prospect of a helicopter ride, she pushed through the rest of her work so the shoot list would be complete while the light was still good.

Freya had never ridden in a helicopter before and the experience was exhilarating. Ned sat in the pilot's seat in front and she beside him. They were strapped in by harness-style seat belts and wore large, noise-cancelling headphones to protect against the noise of the rotor blades and engine. They had to use microphones for communication. Any nervousness she'd felt dissipated as she saw how skilfully and confidently he controlled the helicopter. He was a man born to be in charge.

'We mainly use the helicopter to muster sheep,' Ned explained. 'Although I still prefer mustering on horseback the old-fashioned way. But it's a nice way to introduce you to the property.'

Freya was clueless about farming. But she was enthralled by the close three-hundred-and-sixty-degree views of the extensive lands belonging to Five and a Half Mile Creek. Below was a patchwork of extensive ploughed fields of rich, fertile soil, some a haze of luminous green with what Ned explained was newly planted winter crops of wheat and barley.

In the fading light of the afternoon, long shadows fell from the surrounding hills and gave the landscape a surreal quality. It was almost beyond her comprehension that one man could own so much land. And that they hadn't even reached its borders.

'This is a whole new world to me,' she said, snapping off some images on her smartphone through the clear windows. 'It's awe-inspiring.'

Vast tracts of fenced land were home to slow-moving mobs of sheep heading for stands of eucalypt trees, and dams. Throughout the property ran the snaking lines of the creek—a river to her eyes—that gave the property its name, with eucalypts growing along its banks. Ned swooped down to show her flocks of wild ducks on the surface of the water, so close the grass flattened and the water rippled.

He took her on an eagle's-eye-view tour of the homestead and gardens, then showed her what lay beyond the boundaries of the garden: the art-deco-style building that housed an indoor heated swimming pool; the blue rectangle of an outdoor pool; a full-sized tennis court. Ned explained he didn't swoop too low across the stable complex and training arenas because he didn't want to spook the horses grazing in the surrounding lush green paddocks. The staff accommodation seemed like a small village. Freya was stunned at the size and complexity of the place—it was impossible to imagine what it must be like to live here, to have grown up here, the sense of privilege and entitlement that must come with being born to such a place.

She didn't want the ride to end, but the light started to fade and Ned told her it was time to head for home. She felt a surprising level of disappointment as they dropped down to earth from her sojourn in the sky.

Once the rotor blades stilled and the engine noise abated, she took off her headphones and turned to Ned. 'Thank you for that, I'll never forget it.'

'I could tell how much you enjoyed the tour. I never take this place for granted but it was good to see the land afresh through your eyes, the same as you showed me a different aspect of my home through the lens of your camera.'

He told her one of the men would drive her back up to the house and he would see her before she left.

By the time she'd finished packing up her equipment, darkness had fallen and Freya felt overwhelmed by a nagging sense of melancholy. She didn't expect that Ned would come back to the house. Why should he? He'd taken time out from his work to give her the helicopter tour. He had already approved the early images on his mother's behalf. There was nothing further he needed to say to her. But she felt the need to say goodbye, to see him one more time.

She had thanked Marian for her help and was loading her gear into her van, saying a mental farewell to Five and a Half Mile Creek, when its boss was suddenly there, looming up next to her in the shadows. Her heart started a furious, irrational pounding.

'You're going?' he said.

'Yes,' she said, fighting to keep her voice even.

'I put the helicopter to bed but then got caught up in something else.'

'I didn't expect—'

'It's a long way to drive on your own.'

'I'll check into a motel on the way to break the journey.'

'How busy are you next week?' Was *he* going to suggest they catch up?

'Not too busy. It depends what Hugh has booked for me. Why?' She held her breath for his answer.

'I'd like you to come back and photograph the garden. Not for me. For my mother. As a surprise. For her birthday in June. Each milestone for her is precious and she would love—'

'Yes,' Freya said.

'Yes?'

She nodded. 'Yes. I'll do it.'

'Could you do Monday or Tuesday? The autumn garden is at its best now, the weather could turn at any time and—'

'I can do it either day.'

'You don't have to check your planner?'

'No. Those days are free.' If they weren't, she would make sure they were free. Even if she had to postpone jobs. Even if Hugh wasn't happy about it.

'You can stay here at the guest cottage.'

'That won't be necessary. I—'

'I insist.'

She shrugged, both defeated and elated at the same time. 'The cottage it is,' she said. 'How about I drive up Sunday so I can start Monday?'

'You might need to work Tuesday too. It's a big garden.'

'Agreed,' she said.

'You'll stay at the guest cottage Sunday and Monday nights.'

She hesitated, then put out her hand for him to shake. 'It's a deal,' she said.

He grasped her hand in his own much larger one in a firm, hard grip. Her hand seemed to tingle at his warmth and strength. Again came that curious feeling that it was more than sealing an agreement for a photographic shoot.

'A deal,' he said, in that gruff, deep voice.

She paused. 'June. That's pearl.'

His dark brows drew together in a quizzical expression. 'And that means…?'

'Pearl is your mother's birthstone, if her birthday is in June.'

He laughed. 'So now I know. It's taken me nearly thirty years, but now I know.'

She laughed too as she withdrew her hand, said goodbye, and drove away, still with a smile curving her mouth.

She felt irrationally pleased that she would be returning to Five and a Half Mile Creek. Also very aware that if she did so, she would have to confess to Ned that she knew Wil and that the story of her life would have to unravel along with that confession.

CHAPTER FOUR

FREYA'S RETURN TO Five and a Half Mile Creek five days later was very different from her first visit. Ned was there on the veranda waiting for her. Just Ned, with no scary dog in tow. Big, tall, gorgeous Ned who had been on her mind way too much back home in Melbourne. He waved, a broad sweep of his arm that said *welcome*. His smile was warm, genuine and aimed at her with what seemed like real pleasure. His hotness factor soared a few degrees higher. Even though he was still definitely not her type.

When she stepped out of her van it seemed natural for him to sweep her into a hug and for her to fall willingly into it. A *friendly* hug. She wasn't reading any more into it than that.

But it felt so good she had to close her eyes to try and gather her rioting senses. His chest was a wall of solid muscle, his arms firm and powerful around her. Held so close, she was intensely aware of Ned as a man. His warmth, his strength, his spicy male scent—with an undertone of what she suspected might be hay. Being in his arms was exciting. And something else—something unaccustomed—she couldn't quite put a name to. *Safe.* That was what it was. And feeling safe with a man scared the hell out of her.

She pulled away from the hug, made a play of patting

her hair into place and picking up her small overnight bag from the front seat.

'Let me take that,' Ned said, reaching for the bag. 'The cottage is ready for you.'

She hesitated. 'My gear. It needs to come in.'

'You can leave it in your van.'

'I never leave my stuff in the van.'

Ned laughed. 'You're not parked on a Melbourne street. Your equipment will be perfectly safe. You can even leave the van unlocked.'

She frowned. 'I guess there's no one nearby to steal anything.' Had she inadvertently insulted him again? On the long drive from Melbourne, she had been reminded of how very far away Five and a Half Mile Creek was from the city. When she'd been up in the helicopter with Ned they hadn't seen any other dwelling, his land stretched so far.

'Correct,' Ned said, not sounding in the least bit insulted.

'If you're sure,' she said, unable to stop the doubtful note from entering her voice. She lived in a densely populated urban area where no one left anything of value in their cars.

'I guarantee everything will still be there in the morning,' he said. 'But if it makes you happy, we can take it into the cottage.'

She took a deep breath. Put her hand up in a halt sign. 'No. I'll take your word for it. I… I trust you.' *Trust.* That wasn't something she was used to when it came to men.

'I'm glad to hear that,' he said with that slow smile she was beginning to find so appealing. 'You really can trust me, you know.' His gaze held hers for a long moment until she looked away, flustered. Did he mean something more than the obvious?

'I'll bring my cameras and lenses and of course my laptop.' She spoke too quickly. 'The rest can stay out here. But I will lock the van. And activate the alarm.'

'Whatever makes you feel secure,' he said.

Him.

Ned.

Freya had a from-out-of-nowhere feeling *he* could make her secure. Which was crazy considering their differences. And her fierce determination to maintain her independence. She didn't need to be looked after.

'Now give me that bag and we'll get you to the cottage. It's not far from the house, just down this pathway.'

Freya fell in step beside him. She was wearing flat boots and had to look a long way up to him. For every broad stride he took, she had to take two steps to keep up. 'I feel like I'm being meet-and-greeted at a posh country-house hotel,' she commented.

Uncanny how she felt immediately at ease with him again, as if there hadn't been nearly a week since she'd last seen him.

'The cottage is comfortable. But perhaps not posh hotel standard,' he said. She could hear the smile in his voice.

'Oh, but it is,' she exclaimed when Ned ushered her into the cottage. 'It's beautiful. Like a suite in the poshest of country-house retreats. But then what else would I expect in this place?'

Ned told her the guest cottage had been built some time in the nineteen seventies, to echo the Victorian style of the main house. But inside it had been completely updated—by his mother no doubt; Freya was beginning to recognise her signature style. The cottage was light and spacious with a roomy living area, two bedrooms, two bathrooms, a full-sized kitchen and a utility room.

It would contain her tiny apartment in the inner eastern Melbourne suburb of Richmond several times over.

If she had it in her to be envious, Freya would envy Ned the wonderful place he lived in, where even a guest cottage was worthy of a lifestyle shoot. There was also the enviable security of growing up in a happy family environment with a securely married mother and father. What seemed to her a dream childhood was worth even more than the obvious wealth he had been born into. Instead of envy she was happy for him, and more than happy the magic circle had been extended to include Wil.

Wil. She would have to bring up her connection to his brother sooner rather than later. Otherwise her omission would always be hanging over any interaction with Ned.

Ned carried her bag into the largest room. 'I think you'll be comfortable in here.'

'How could I not be comfortable in such a fabulous place?' she said.

Freya followed him in, which led them to both standing next to a large queen-sized bed. She and Ned so close to a *bed*.

It conjured up a sudden image of such overwhelming sensuality, of them together on that bed, that she could feel her cheeks begin to colour. She didn't dare look at the bed—or at Ned. Rather she turned away and admired the view from the French doors, which opened out into a private courtyard. A stream of nervous exclamations escaped her. There was a birdbath! And look at that lovely carved garden bench! Oh, and a climbing rose!

When her chatter petered out, she noticed Ned looked as awkward as she felt. He shifted from foot to foot. His gaze was averted from the bed too. 'I'll leave you to it,' he said. 'I hope you'll join me for dinner up at the house.'

'Thank you,' she managed to choke out.

Ned went to leave the room, hesitated, and then turned back. 'I look forward to seeing you later.' He dipped his head as he spoke and, to her astonishment, Freya realised this boldly confident man was shy. More to the point, shy around *her*.

She already liked Ned. This revelation only served to further endear him to her. 'I'm looking forward to seeing you too,' she said softly, looking up into his eyes. Still shocked by that erotic image of the two of them together on the bed, she fought the compulsion to reach up and kiss him on the cheek. Not a good idea. She was beginning to wonder what a simple touch might ignite.

But after he left, she sat hunched over on the edge of the bed and rested her face in her hands. What would Ned think of her when he discovered who she was? While she hadn't out-and-out lied to him, her silence when it came to the fact she had known his brother Wil would seem like a blatant act of dishonesty. And she had a very strong feeling Ned would not react well to that.

She wouldn't unpack her bag. There seemed little point as there was a real risk that when she confessed who she was, the truth about her background, Ned would react like everyone else in his social strata—with distaste at her humble origins. He could very well cancel the garden assignment and she'd be back on the road to Melbourne tonight. Lucky she'd left her photographic gear in the van.

But there was still the meal with him to face, so she had to shower and get ready. Would she be expected to dress for dinner? On the off chance, she'd packed a simple black jersey dress that fell to just above the knee and had three-quarter sleeves and a scoop neck. She could dress it up with her favourite lavender scarf around her shoulders against the cool of the April evening and her amethyst pendant, the only thing that she had from her beloved grandmother. She brushed her hair around her shoulders and applied more make-up than she usually wore. For some inexplicable reason, she couldn't escape the feeling she was going in to battle for something very important.

When Ned was on his own for dinner—which was more often than not the case these days—he ate in the informal dining area that led off the kitchen, with Molly by his side. But that felt too casual, too domestic, for a dinner with the boss of Five and a Half Mile Creek and the visiting photographer.

Instead, he'd elected to have dinner in the formal dining room. He thought Freya might appreciate the beautiful, nineteenth-century mahogany furniture imported from England so long ago by his ancestors, the priceless Persian carpets, the ornate chandeliers. The table sat twelve, and at one end places for two had been set with polished silver, gold-edged china and crystal stemware. Roses from the garden sent a heady scent through the room.

Marian had prepared the food, to be served by one of the young household staff. A simple meal, served spectacularly, his housekeeper had said.

Ned stood up to greet Freya as Marian ushered her into the dining room. *'Wow,'* she said, looking around her. 'When you said dinner, you really meant dinner party. This is fabulous. I feel I should be wearing a ball gown.'

Wow, Ned thought about Freya, who looked every bit as elegant as if she were in formal dress. She wore her purple wings—uh, gauzy scarf—which she slipped off to drape across the back of her chair. Her black dress, while not provocatively sexy, clung enticingly to her curves. The neckline revealed a tantalising hint of cleavage. Her pale hair tumbled below her shoulders and her mouth was slicked with glossy pink lipstick.

'You look very nice the way you are,' he said.

Nice was a safe, unloaded word she couldn't read anything more into. He swallowed a curse word when he remembered his reaction to being alone with her in the cottage.

Him. Her. A bedroom.

He'd had to curl his hands into fists to stop himself from reaching out for her and kissing her, from fantasising about sweeping her into his arms and carrying her to the bed. His wildly erotic thoughts were inappropriate, unwarranted, completely out of order as she was, if not an employee, a contractor. But he couldn't deny it. She was gorgeous.

And he wanted her.

Even if he couldn't do anything about it.

He offered her a flute of vintage champagne he'd brought up from the cellar. 'To celebrate a photographic shoot well done—my mother was delighted with the results,' he said.

'I wish all my clients celebrated in such style,' she said, raising the flute to her lips, looking over the rim up at him.

'You delivered superlative work,' he said.

'Thank you. I hope to do as well for you with the garden shoot.'

'I don't doubt for a minute that you will,' he said.

She looked around her, fixing her gaze on a portrait of his great-great-great-grandfather. 'Does this very grand room get used often?'

'Surprisingly, yes. My mother used to say there was no point in having all this if we didn't enjoy it. We often had family meals here and entertained too. Dad reckoned it was a good way for me to learn table manners and how to behave in company. I learned the correct knife and fork to use but some of those long dinners could be interminably boring to a young boy. I can still remember looking out of the window and aching to be outside.'

'It all looks very…civilised,' she said. A smile hovered at the corners of her mouth.

'So you concede a further touch of civilisation to this place?'

'I have no other choice,' she said. 'This room and all that's in it must have been the height of culture in its time.'

'Absolutely. The house wasn't built just for the family's comfort but also as a display of wealth and prosperity. In the old days, visitors from the city or other far-flung properties would stay a few days. Prime ministers and other notables dined here and stayed the night on tours of the district.'

'It's so different from the way I live, I find that difficult to relate to. It's like a parallel universe.'

'It's my world,' he said. 'But that's not to say I haven't enjoyed my times in the city too. My family has a house in Toorak and a few years back I bought an apartment not far from them. It's rarely used now though.'

'That's a shame,' she said.

Ned shrugged. 'It's there for when I need it.' He certainly wasn't going to share the Leanne fiasco with Freya. He'd spent so much time with her there he found it difficult to revisit—not because he missed her but because he didn't want to be reminded about what a fool he'd been to be taken in by her.

'Melbourne is such a great place to live,' she said.

'Tell me why you love it so much,' he said.

She smiled. 'Do we have all night?'

'How about your top five reasons?'

'Only five? Let me think.' She paused, put her hand under her chin in exaggerated thinking mode. 'Do you really want to hear this?'

'Yes,' he said.

'I guess the general buzz of the city, people everywhere, life, action, the river, there's always something to do. Melbourne is cultural, hip. I love the laneway cafés, the bars, the restaurants, the markets, the buskers. Last week there was a girl sitting on a milk crate on the footpath with an old-fashioned typewriter and she wrote me a poem; in return I took an arty photo of her in black and white and emailed it to her. It's fun to take high tea in one of the posh hotels. The shops, of course, the fabulous shops.' She smiled. 'I should stop now, but there's more.'

'Keep going,' he said.

'Okay. Then there are the museums, the art galleries, the concerts, the art-house movies, even the graffiti. Oh, and the exhibitions. The world comes to Melbourne with exhibitions from archaeological to pop culture to the costumes worn in the greatest movies.' Her face was animated, her cheeks flushed, eyes shining. 'I go to see them all.'

'I used to like the music, pub bands, concerts, jazz clubs, the buskers and sidewalk theatre,' he said.

'Those too,' she said.

'I busked myself once, down by Flinders Street Railway Station, when I was a uni student. I was embarrassed when people actually threw money in my violin case.' He'd tipped his earnings into the hat of a fellow busker who'd looked as if he needed the money.

'Seriously? You must be very good.'

'Out of practice now,' he said dismissively. He'd

blocked from his mind how much, at one time, he'd enjoyed life in Melbourne. But he'd been needed at home.

She laughed. 'I've gone way over the five-reason limit on why I love city life, haven't I?'

'I'm sure there are more,' he said.

'Actually…' She drew the word out and laughed. 'I'll spare you my further reasons. But, seriously, you have a place in Melbourne and never use it?'

'I do if I need to visit the city. Otherwise my brother Wil stays there when he's in Melbourne on business so it's not totally neglected.'

'Th-that's good,' she said.

Freya suddenly quietened. All that animation and vivacity switched off. Ned racked his brains to think if he had said anything untoward but he didn't get a chance to follow it up as their first course arrived—a salad of figs and pecans, both grown in their orchard, with leaves from the kitchen garden.

He wondered why Freya suddenly seemed to find it so difficult to relax. Was the setting for dinner too formal for her? By the time the Italian-style chicken dish was served, conversation between them had dwindled.

The only time Freya seemed really engaged was when they discussed the garden shoot for the following day. She wasn't eating much, pushing her food around her plate with her fork. The white wine in her glass remained untouched.

Ned found the stilted conversation increasingly uncomfortable. 'Are you okay?' he said finally. 'Are you concerned about the shoot?'

Freya put her fork down and looked him straight in the eye. She took a deep breath, which caused a delightful swelling of her breasts above her neckline, then took another as if she was girding herself.

'Ned,' she said. 'I can't put it off any longer. I… I have to tell you something. Something about myself.'

'Okay,' he said slowly, taken aback.

'I… I haven't been completely honest with you…'

There was something about her expression that made him believe he wasn't going to like what she said. She was married. She was engaged. She wasn't interested in men. Those were his main concerns. Oddly, if she confessed to having a criminal record he mightn't care so much. Her single status was more important. Which was insane, when she didn't check one box on his wife wish-list.

'Really?' he said, his voice thick with dread of what he might hear.

'I… I…' She groaned. 'I don't know where to start.'

'Is it that complex?'

'Yes, it is.' Her face contorted with anxiety and what might be poorly masked fear.

Fear of him?

Perhaps it was his 'resting stern face'. Ned forced himself to look calm, receptive, even though his thoughts were churning. 'Why don't you start with the most important thing you think I need to know?'

She chewed at her bottom lip, pulled at her lock of purple hair without, he thought, seeming to realise it. Then took another deep breath, exhaled it on a sigh. 'Ned… I… I'm not who I say I am. At least I wasn't when—'

'What do you mean?'

Her mouth turned down. 'My name is Freya, but I… I went by another name when I knew your brother Wil.'

'You know Wil?' The words exploded from him.

'Yes.'

A sickening disappointment churned through him. Wil was a very handsome guy who effortlessly attracted women. Ned loved him, was incredibly grateful he had him as a brother, but it wouldn't be the first time some girl had wheedled her way into friendship with him in an effort to get to his charismatic younger brother.

'You're one of his ex-girlfriends? He's married now. You need to leave him alone.'

His words were purposefully harsh. Wil was happy with Georgia; he deserved that happiness. Ned couldn't condone an obsessed former girlfriend showing up here at Five and a Half Mile Creek misrepresenting herself and trying to cause trouble. To think he'd found himself fantasising about Freya. One of his brother's cast-offs. The thought brought a nasty taste to his mouth.

He'd got her so wrong.

Freya shook her head. 'No! Ned. It's not like that at all. I'm not an ex-girlfriend. I'm so glad Wil has found a wonderful wife. You can't imagine how happy that makes me feel. I—'

He was not inclined to believe her. 'Then who are you?'

She sighed a sigh of profound sadness. 'It's a long story...'

'Better start at the beginning,' he said wearily. 'That is, if I really need to know the details of your past with my brother.'

'It really isn't what you think,' she said, her voice not quite steady.

She pushed herself up from the table, paced the distance between the sideboard and the windows, put her hand on her forehead in a gesture that should have seemed overly dramatic but somehow made him sympathise with her.

He didn't get up. 'The beginning,' he prompted, leaning back in his chair. Resting stern face felt entirely appropriate.

'I met Wil when I was thirteen. He was my friend.'

Ned sat forward again. He frowned. 'But Wil was in foster care then.'

Freya didn't meet his gaze, rather looked down somewhere towards her sexy purple suede shoes that tied around her ankles. 'So was I,' she said.

'You were in foster care?' He couldn't keep the shock from his voice. 'Not that there is anything to be…er… ashamed of.'

He knew from Wil, when his brother had finally opened up to him, that there were both good and bad foster homes. Wil's experiences, after being orphaned at five years old, had not been good. His tales from the dark side of state care had only made Ned care all the more for his adopted brother, to feel fiercely protective towards him.

Finally Freya looked towards him. 'I was the girl he defended against our predatory foster father. Wil warned me against him. Protected me. When the horrible guy tried to…to…attack me, Wil pulled him away from me, fought him and broke his nose. Wil got in terrible trouble for doing that—he got sent away. Thankfully for me, a case worker believed Wil when he said I was in danger, and I was taken away from that house. The next foster family was still horrible but I was safer. I… I never saw Wil again after that. But I've always been so grateful to him.'

Ned pushed back his chair, stood up, kept his distance from her, not sure if he could believe her. 'But that girl's name wasn't Freya, it was Tegan.'

Freya looked at him incredulously. 'You know of her? I mean *me*?'

'You're Tegan?' Ned's head was reeling.

'My real name is Freya. That foster mother didn't like it. She insisted on calling me Tegan. Punished me if I didn't answer to it.'

Slowly, Ned shook his head. 'Wil told us about Tegan.'

Her eyes widened. 'Really?'

Ned nodded. 'He tells it just like you do. By protecting Tegan, he got himself into big trouble. The man didn't press charges for assault. But Wil says it was an unforgivable crime for a child to attack a foster parent. He was never placed in foster care again. Instead he was sent to an institution, which he hated. By his account, he was angry and bitter at the way he'd been treated when all he'd done was protect a vulnerable young girl from abuse.'

'That girl is still so grateful to him. Always will be. So...so how did Wil end up in your family? I've often wondered what happened to him.'

'No one told you?'

'Not a word.' Her mouth turned down. 'They told me it was my fault a decent man had his reputation smeared.' She looked up at Ned. 'He was *not* a decent man.'

'So Wil told me.'

Freya looked slight and vulnerable now. He could only imagine how she had been as a terrified thirteen-year-old. Anger flooded through him. He would have broken the man's nose too.

'I can't believe Wil told you about me, that he remembered.'

'Over the years he tried to find you, to see if you were okay. I guess if he was searching for Tegan, that might have been why he had no luck.'

'If only I'd known.' She paused. 'There was nothing between us, you know. Nothing...romantic. We were friends. Both trying to survive in a horrid situation.'

'I believe Wil thought of Tegan as a sister. It would have meant something for him to know you were okay. And there you were, right under our noses, working for my mother's friend.'

'I was helping Hugh to edit Wil's wedding photos when I recognised him. A different surname from when I'd known him, but it was definitely Wil. I didn't tell Hugh. But when he asked me to come out here and do the house shoot, curiosity got the better of me. I wanted to see where Wil had landed so safely.'

'But you must have known he wouldn't be here.'

'Of course, I knew he'd be on his honeymoon. I didn't—don't—want to see him. I can't imagine his wife would welcome someone like me showing up, claiming a shared past. I'm just happy to know everything turned out so well with him. Is Georgia as nice as she seems in her photos?'

'Even nicer. She's a wonderful woman. The best possible wife for him. They're very happy.'

'I'm so glad. My life might have been very different if it wasn't for Wil. It wasn't just that he saved me from that predator, he taught me to be on full alert for any that followed. I was sad to lose him as a friend.'

Ned paused. 'He got sent to an awful residential group home, which is where my parents found him.'

'How did that come about?'

'My parents wanted a big family. But they only had me. They had a lot of love to give. One year they decided to take part in a programme that took needy kids out of residential care and took them home for Christmas. Something about Wil caught their eye. The manager tried to dissuade them, said Wil was a troublemaker. My parents insisted if they couldn't take him, they wouldn't take anyone.'

'How did you feel about that? A strange kid in your home?'

'I'd always wanted a brother. He was hostile at first. But I liked him straight away. I was patient and by the end of those holidays we were firm friends. I was over the moon when we adopted him.'

'He was the troublemaker. You were the peacemaker.'

'If you put it like that, yes.'

'His good deed helping me was rewarded.'

'As a family, we thought it was us who were rewarded.' Life after Wil had been different. Better. He had a brother; his mother became more content with country life once she had another child to lavish love and care on. 'Wil is an extraordinary man.'

'So is his brother,' Freya said, nodding thoughtfully.

Her words unexpectedly warmed him. 'What makes you say that?' he said gruffly.

'Your love for your brother shines through. You never refer to him as your adopted brother.' Her eyes narrowed shrewdly. 'You stepped up when your mother got ill when I suspect you might not have felt ready. You've been very kind to me tonight.'

'But that's just the way I operate.'

'Exactly. Perhaps you don't realise how extraordinary that is. Thank you for believing me.'

He frowned. 'Why would I disbelieve you? Your recollections and Wil's tally perfectly.'

'Not everyone would believe I had no agenda. Your family is very wealthy, for one thing. You might have thought I was after something. I wasn't going to tell you about my connection to Wil. It's not something I've shared with anyone. Even Hugh. But when you asked me to come back and photograph the garden, I knew I had to be honest with you.'

'I appreciate that you did.' He paused. 'But, Freya, there's so much more you're not telling me. About you. Your story. Why you were in state care.'

Freya tugged on that piece of hair again. Gently he reached out and disengaged her fingers. He held onto her hand, small and cool in his much larger hand. Felt an overwhelming urge to protect her. She seemed so strong, but he sensed a deep vulnerability under that smart front.

'It…it's not a particularly pretty story. I'm not sure you want to hear it.'

'I'm very sure that I do,' he said.

Freya had fascinated him from the get-go. He had taken it at face value she had a successful career in a highly competitive business. Hugh and his partner were sophisticated guys and she was close to them. Somehow, he had assumed she'd had a conventional upbringing. He led her by the hand. 'Come on back to the table. Try to eat something. Then share your story with me. Please.'

She shook her head. 'I really would rather not,' she said as she released her hand from his.

Freya had quickly realised that Ned was a kind man. Nurturing too, she suspected. And so good-looking— tonight he was looking especially handsome in a turtle-neck cashmere sweater in midnight blue that brought out the blue of his eyes. No wonder she'd had that moment of erotic fantasy over him back in the bedroom of the cottage. Again she wondered why such a man was still single. She could envision him with a bunch of kids. But he was also a son of the squattocracy.

After her first visit she had searched online and discovered there were politicians and entrepreneurs and high-ranking civil servants in his family tree. And wealth, lots of wealth. No wonder prime ministers came to visit.

Her history was so very different she wondered if they could ever connect, even as friends. Henry and his family had certainly thought she was not worthy of being his girlfriend. Not because of her talent or her brains or her personality, but because of her birth and the way she'd been raised. His rejection of her had left a scar, a scar slashed upon the scars of other, older hurts.

She'd met Ned on equal terms. He was the boss of Five and a Half Mile Creek, wealthy beyond her wildest aspirations, and she was in his employ, if only temporarily. But she was highly skilled and provided a creative service he valued—hence her second visit. That put them on an equal footing. Her nanna had cleaned houses for people like his family—how differently might he treat her if he knew that?

She managed to finish half her main course before she pushed her plate away, indicating with a shake of her head that she'd had enough. 'Don't you feel better now for having had something to eat?' he said in a jocular tone that made her smile, in spite of her nervousness.

'Yes,' she said. And she did. She was an erratic eater at the best of times. Hunger made her edgy. She had stopped at a roadhouse for a snack on the way but the offerings had been less than appealing and she'd only managed half of an indifferent burger.

Now with a proper meal inside her she felt stronger. Strong enough to resist the temptation to spill her story to Ned. She did not want his pity. Any semblance of equality between them would be shot if he learned where she came from. She would like to be friends with him. Especially now the truth about her and Wil was out. But friends needed to meet each other at least halfway on a platform of equality. That platform would be totally shot if he found out where she came from. She couldn't bear to see him turn away from her the way Henry had.

'Can we talk about something else, please?' she said. 'Perhaps tomorrow's garden shoot? The past is not a place I want to step back into too often. I prefer to keep it buried.'

'That's understandable,' he said. But his perceptive blue eyes narrowed. She had a feeling he had further questions to ask. She had no intention of answering them. She pushed back into her chair in an attempt to put more distance between her and Ned.

When the maid brought in the dessert of chocolate-and-raspberry brownies with a bowl of fresh raspberries and cream, and cheese on a marble platter, she welcomed the diversion. And kept the conversation purely on an impersonal level.

CHAPTER FIVE

VERY EARLY THE next morning, Ned stood at a distance, unobserved, watching Freya in his mother's prized rose garden. It was one of the different garden 'rooms'—differentiated, hedged spaces—that led into each other, ending at the boundaries of the orchards that adjoined the entire garden.

The morning was very still and new, the scent from the roses sweet and heady, sharpened by that of the lavender from the borders. Magpies carolled somewhere nearby and a flock of tiny finches were fluttering through one of the larger rose bushes. Freya's presence made the perfect scene appear even more perfect.

She was using a handheld camera to take, he assumed, a close-up of a half-unfurled yellow rose. Again, she wore black jeans, this time with a purple knit sweater against the chill of the morning. Even with sturdy, laced-up boots, she still looked every bit the city girl. Yet she fit. She was meant to be surrounded by flowers, he thought, in one of those odd observations that had come to him from their first moment of meeting.

He was still reeling from her revelations of the night before. The surprising connection with Wil. His shock that she'd been in foster care and in danger. His admiration for his brother shot even higher at the knowledge of his care for that little girl. Wil should be told about the discovery of Tegan. But not by him. It would be up to Freya to decide when to make contact. It was her story, her secret. He knew there was more to her past but she had clammed up when he had tried to find out more about how she'd ended up in state care.

Quite rightly. Her past was really none of his concern. Yet home was so important to him he found it unbearable to think of her shifting from foster placement to foster placement, just a little girl. He admired what she had made of herself after a start like that.

He didn't want to disturb her, so waited until Freya had stepped back from the rose bush and lowered her camera. He took a step forward, his boots crunching on some dried, fallen leaves. Freya whirled immediately around, staring with wide, panicked eyes, then flushed. 'Oh. It's you. I was worried…'

'Worried?'

'Your gardener warned me to keep an eye out for snakes.'

He laughed. 'The gardener was having you on. He picked you for a city slicker and couldn't resist teasing you.'

'He sounded pretty serious to me.' She put her camera down on the large metallic case nearby that held a number of other camera bodies and lenses.

Ned would have a word with the gardener later. There were people you teased about snakes and spiders and there were those you didn't. He wanted Freya to feel comfortable here, not frightened.

'There are snakes in the bush and on our land—it's their home—but we've taken precautions so we don't get them near the house. The lawn is kept short, the bushes trimmed so they don't overhang, no piles of debris allowed to accumulate. There's fine-gauge chicken wire under all the fences around the garden to keep out rabbits and other unwelcome visitors. And see all the gravel pathways? Gravel is sharp. Slithery things don't like it. Besides, they're actually as scared of us as we are of them.'

'Slithery things!' She shuddered. 'I'm hyperventilating at the thought. There are reasons I'm happy being a "city slicker" and snakes are one of them. They terrify me.'

'Most people are frightened of them. My mother is phobic, hence all the precautions. But if you live in a rural area you have to use common sense.'

He wanted to give her a hug, reassure her he was there to protect her from any scary thing that came her way. But after sharing her connection with Wil last night she'd put a barrier up against any overtures of friendship. Their 'goodnights' to each other had been stiffly formal, as appropriate between an employer and contractor. He had no idea if she would welcome a hug from him or push him away.

'Like run a mile if I see one?'

'I promise you won't encounter one in this garden. Just keep stamping your feet when you walk if that makes you feel any better. They don't like vibrations.'

Freya stamped her feet, though even in boots they weren't large or heavy enough to make much of an impact. She laughed. 'I don't think that would scare away so much as a worm.'

'You'd be surprised,' he said, smiling. He liked her resilience, the fact she could laugh at her fears. 'But I'm actually here to warn you about something else—the weather.'

She looked up at the sky. 'The weather app on my phone is playing up. The advance forecast was good but I haven't been able to check it since. Something doesn't feel quite right today.' Ned was surprised at how concerned she seemed.

'It's not looking good for this afternoon. We check against detailed meteorological information. Storms have been forecast.'

Again a frown that didn't seem to be warranted by a conversation about the weather. 'I'd better get a move on, then,' she said. 'This garden is so big. Every time I turn a corner there's more—and then the countryside beyond. It's so beautiful, isn't it? In Melbourne there are parks and open spaces, I love the Botanical Gardens, but it's not like *this*.' She encompassed her surroundings with a wave. 'I'm getting a real fix of nature.'

'You'll have to come back another time,' he said casually, offhand, no pressure. The connection with Wil was reason enough for her to return. But he wanted to have Freya as *his* friend. For her to come back to *him*, not his brother.

'To see the garden in another season, you mean?'

'That's a point. It's glorious in spring. The wisteria walkway is quite famous. And the daffodils. Plus even more roses. My mother used to open the garden for charity in spring and autumn.'

'Will you carry on the tradition?'

'I've got more than enough on my plate without adding that to it,' he said. Traditionally, the gardens of Five and a Half Mile Creek were the woman's domain.

'Waiting for that wife to come along and take over all that "lady of the manor" stuff?' she asked in a teasing tone, as if she had read his thoughts.

He swallowed hard. 'Is that a trick question?' It veered a bit close to his wife wish-list. Carrying on with those kinds of traditions was exactly what a good country wife would be expected to do.

'No,' she said. 'I'm just interested.'

He shrugged. 'If she wanted to. It would be up to her.'

'Or you could hire an event planner.'

'That's a thought,' he said.

'It seems so surreal to someone like me. Organising charity fundraisers is completely out of my experience.'

'I guess it might be,' he said. One of his mother's favourite charities helped children in need as both Freya and Wil had been—but he didn't want to mention it. 'Surreal indeed.'

She looked up at the sky again, squinting a little against the early morning sun. Her hair glinted pale gold and the tiny jewel in her eyebrow stud glittered. 'I'd better take advantage of the good weather while I've got it. I hope the storm will blow over and we'll have a good day tomorrow.'

'I hope so too. I'll leave you to it.'

He was just about to invite her to lunch at the house when she spoke. 'Do you think I could make a sandwich to bring out here for lunch? I don't want to waste a minute before the weather changes.'

So he wouldn't get to share lunch with her. He fought his disappointment. 'I'll ask Marian to organise it. She makes excellent sandwiches.'

'I'm sure she does, if the other meals I've had here are anything to go by. That would be wonderful, thank you.'

'I'll bring them out to you myself.'

'Oh, that would be wonderful too. But don't you have work to do? The boss of this huge place? I don't want to hold you up.'

'Even the boss has to stop for lunch.' Any excuse to spend time with her. He could catch up after she'd gone and he would have untold hours to himself.

'I guess,' she said.

'I'll see you at midday,' he said, starting to turn away.

'Wait,' she said. 'You're so thoughtful. I appreciate it.' She smiled that gap-toothed smile he found so enchanting.

'No problem,' he said. She seemed to take common courtesy as something out of the ordinary.

'Before you go.' She put up her hand to stop him again, then paused. 'While you're taking orders, no pickles, please.'

Ned smiled and turned to go, happier than he should be that he would be seeing her again at lunchtime. He would have to reschedule the work he had planned for that time. And think about how he could get Freya out here for a third visit after the garden assignment was done.

Freya liked Ned more each time she saw him. Watching him as he walked away, she could not help but admire—again—that stupendous back view. But it wasn't just about how hot she found him. It was about the person he was proving himself to be. She'd dreaded telling him about her connection with Wil, feared his reaction to her revelation she'd been in foster care. Horrible Henry's reaction had been an ill-disguised disgust.

Last night at dinner, she *had* seen disgust on Ned's face. But that had been when he'd thought she had some kind of ulterior motive in revealing her past with Wil. It had been followed by kindness and understanding. She had meant it when she had told Ned his face was open and easy to read. Easy for someone like her, anyway, who had had to learn from a tender age who she could trust, who she had to be wary of.

Last night she had seen Ned look at her with dismay as a duplicitous potential blackmailer, destroyer of his brother's marriage, possible gold-digger. There had been something else too. Something that she hadn't been able to place until later.

Disappointment.

Ned had been unable to mask his disappointment that she seemed to be interested—perhaps even obsessed with—his brother, which would cut Ned right out of the picture with her. It was so not true. Wil was movie-star handsome, had been stunningly good-looking and very manly, even at thirteen. But she had never been attracted to heartthrob Wil. It was conservative, kind, gorgeous Ned who had her heartbeat accelerating when he was nearby and her mind indulging in wild sensual fantasies when he was not.

Ned brought her a sandwich—no pickles—for lunch, along with a thoughtful selection of drinks and some fruit. He also brought lunch for himself and they enjoyed a quick, impromptu picnic under the shade of a glorious camellia studded with exquisite pale pink blooms. In the brief time they had for conversation, he filled her in on some of the history of the farm and his Scottish ancestors who'd originally settled the place.

During the conversation she'd had to force herself not to wonder how Ned would look in a kilt. Tall, brawny, reddish glints in his hair—he fitted the part. She could not, would not, allow her thoughts to stray to whether or not he would go commando under the kilt. *Friends* did not let their thoughts stray in that direction.

Then she got back to her work and he to his.

Now the afternoon light was fading, the threatened storm had rumbled, spat down some rain, and held off. The air felt still, heavily charged, uncertain. It worried her; she and storms did not do well together. She had shot as much of the autumn garden as she could, anticipating it might not be good conditions the next day. It was such a thoughtful gift for Ned to arrange for his mother, she wanted to do not just a good job but an excellent one.

She was struck by a pang of longing for Nanna, whose memory faded with each year Freya moved away from being twelve. She dreaded the day she couldn't remember her at all; she only had a few photos left, which she'd managed to hang onto through her years in care.

But one of her strongest memories of the woman who had mothered her was of her grandmother in her tiny scrap of a front yard, tending the red rose she had trained along the cast-iron lacework of the narrow front veranda of the single-level terrace.

Nanna had nurtured that rose, the old lemon tree, and the bed of white daisies that had made up her garden. Once she'd lost her leg to diabetes she couldn't work in it any more, hadn't wanted to. And Freya hadn't known what to do to help her. One of the reasons she'd returned to the area to live was that for a long time the old house had remained the same, and the climbing rose had lived on. Its tenacity had given her some comfort, some continuity. But gentrification had finally struck. Last time she'd driven past the house it had been gutted, modernised and the rose ripped out.

Ned would understand if she shared that memory with him, she realised. Might even give her one of his wonderful hugs. No matter how many times she told herself he wasn't her type, she found herself more and more attracted to him. Now she knew the feeling didn't run one way. That look of disappointment when he'd thought she was a former girlfriend of Wil's had confirmed it.

But Ned had said he wanted to get married, have kids; he had 'family man' stamped all over him. While she was a no-strings type of girl who never wanted to marry or have children. He wasn't the kind of guy to have a fling with—especially as there was a good chance she might have further meetings with him and his family. She wanted to see Wil, meet Georgia and baby Nina. It had been heart-warming and, somehow, healing to know that Wil had remembered Tegan.

She couldn't allow herself to get closer to Ned. Much as she was aching to do just that. It would have been sensible to say 'no' to his invitation to another dinner with him at the house this evening. The kitchen in the cottage was stocked with a few basics—she wouldn't go hungry if she said she was tired after a long day and stayed there. But, yet...she couldn't get her 'yes' out quickly enough.

CHAPTER SIX

THE RAIN HAD started in earnest as Freya had finished packing up her equipment. By the time she was dressed and ready for dinner with Ned at the house, it was coming down in torrents. Fortunately, the cottage was well supplied with all creature comforts—including a selection of folding umbrellas.

But the flimsy umbrella she chose was no match for the wind that gusted the slanting rain right at her the second she stepped out of the door. As she fought it along the pathway to the house, she questioned the wisdom of having worn her favourite purple suede shoes instead of boots thanks to an impulse to look her best for Ned. He probably wouldn't even notice.

The rain was coming down so hard it had driven channels into the gravel, forming small gushing streams. The path was well lit, but it was getting more difficult to avoid the streams and save her shoes and she found herself jumping from side to side as if in a game of aquatic hopscotch. She cursed out loud when the umbrella suddenly turned completely inside out. She was left with only a light jacket over her dress for protection against the elements.

Then Ned was there. 'Seems like you could do with some help,' he said. He was sensibly encased in a long oilskin raincoat and held aloft an enormous black umbrella.

'This darn umbrella is useless,' she spluttered and threw it on the ground.

'Don't tell me—you chose it because it was purple.'

'It was the first one I saw,' she fibbed. Of course she'd been attracted to the pattern of purple iris. The possible sturdiness of the umbrella hadn't been a consideration.

'Come here,' he said. 'You don't want to ruin those sexy shoes.'

Had he said '*sexy*' shoes?

In the split second she took to consider his choice of words, Ned had pulled her to him and under the shelter of his umbrella. Suddenly the stinging onslaught of the rain on her face stopped, but she was far too distracted by Ned's closeness to care. She was dry. She was warm.

He was hot.

'It's great to get rain. We need it. Trouble is when it all comes down like this at once, so much of it runs off.'

'Hopefully it will ease off,' she said.

His chest was a wall of solid muscle. As he led her towards the house, steering her through the channels, she leaned in closer. Just, of course, to make sure she was completely under the shelter of his umbrella.

'We're almost there or I'd pick you up and carry you,' he said.

'*What?*'

'You're a little thing. Nowhere as heavy as a full-grown sheep to sling over my shoulder.'

Before she had a chance to reply, they reached the house. In one fluid movement, Ned ditched his umbrella, put his hands under her armpits, lifted her off the ground and up the steps, depositing her on the veranda. Freya was back on her feet, out of the rain, before she had time to protest.

'Did you just compare me to a sheep?' she said, mock

glaring up at him, a smile twitching at the corners of her mouth. His hair was dark with damp and fat drops of water sat on his cheeks. He grinned. Her heart gave that curious lurch of recognition—she didn't know where it came from.

'A ewe, if I'm to be precise,' he said.

'I'm glad you at least amended that to be a lady sheep.' She couldn't resist his grin and responded with one of her own. 'Do you really lift and haul sheep around the place?' If so, no wonder the man was made of muscle.

'If needs be,' he said. 'I grew up learning to do everything that needed to be done with sheep. Rescue them, shear them, sometimes birth them. So, yeah, I've had to haul around the odd sheep or two over the years. No special treatment for the boss.'

He sounded so laconic, so laid-back, so *manly* she leaned up on tiptoe and kissed him on the cheek. 'Thank you, for rescuing me like a stray sheep caught in the rain.' She froze.

Why did she do that?

Her lips tingled from the connection to his skin, cool with raindrops. For a crazy moment she'd wanted to taste them, taste *him*. Her gaze connected with his for a long, still moment. The rain drummed on the roof of the veranda, splashed out of the overflowing guttering onto the garden beds below that bordered it. It released a green, earthy scent she was never aware of in the city.

'It was truly my pleasure,' he said slowly. He reached down and, with a touch that was very tender for such a big man, swiped under her eyes with his thumb, first one and then the other. 'Your make-up is smeared.'

She shivered with awareness of his touch, hoped he wouldn't notice, or he would blame it on the chill of the rain and her damp jacket.

'I… I must look like a drowned rat. Or…or sheep.'

'You look like a beautiful woman who has been caught in the rain,' he said in that deep, resonant voice.

'I… I should do something about it, get tissues or something.' She looked up into his eyes. They seemed to darken a further shade of blue as he looked back down at her.

'Yeah,' he said.

Still she didn't move. Neither did Ned.

Her gaze dropped from his eyes to his mouth. Such a beautiful mouth for a man: firm, sculpted, generous.

How would it feel on hers?

She felt herself swaying towards him, her lips parting in anticipation.

Not a good move.

A kiss on the mouth was a very different matter from a kiss on the cheek. A kiss on the mouth would take her across a line where she shouldn't go. Friendship with Ned was something she could handle. Anything else was a no-go zone. Especially when they were so very, very different.

Ned stepped closer. She ached to raise her face for his kiss. But it would be wrong.

This could go nowhere.

Freya felt suddenly seized by panic that she could so easily be overwhelmed by the desire to be close to this man. She forced herself to step back, broke the gaze, extinguished that dancing spark of awareness that had hovered between them from the get-go.

She wrapped her arms around her torso, blocking him out. 'I'm feeling chilled—'

He didn't hesitate. 'We need to get you inside to dry off.'

He took a few long strides to the door, flung it open,

ushered her inside. Without a steering arm on her elbow. Without touching.

Hands off.

She should feel relieved instead of bereft.

The grand house felt immediately warm and welcoming, with lamps glowing on tables, a hint of the scent of wood-smoke. 'There are towels and a hairdryer in the powder room,' he said. 'When you're ready, come down to the kitchen. You know the way.'

'Thank you,' she said. She looked up at him. 'Ned?'

'Yes?'

'You were right. I did choose that useless umbrella because it had purple flowers on it.'

'I knew it,' he said, with another of those grins that warmed her as much as the central heating in the house. 'Soon you'll have no secrets from me.' A smile stayed on his face as he turned away to stride down that magnificent hallway.

Freya's smile slipped. There were secrets she would never share. Her family history for one. Dark times she had struggled to get through. How could a man like Ned, who came from such privilege, ever understand?

As she looked in the bathroom mirror to check for signs of damage, she wiped away a raindrop sliding down her cheek and was horrified to realise it was a teardrop. Ned had come into her life totally unexpectedly. She liked him more with each minute. But she couldn't have him. He wasn't what she wanted. She certainly wasn't what he needed.

Friends, Freya. Think friends. That's all it can be.

Ned now knew that Freya didn't like pickles. But he didn't know any more of her dietary likes and dislikes. It wasn't the kind of thing he'd thought to ask. There were more important things he wanted to know about her. Like, was there a boyfriend in Melbourne? She'd said she wasn't married or engaged. But that didn't mean he didn't have competition.

Competition for what?

Ned pulled himself up short. He shouldn't be thinking of anything that even hinted at a relationship with Freya. She didn't check one box on his wife wish-list. As well, she thought his home was 'too far from civilisation'—the busy, frantic city she loved and he had come to loathe. But in spite of that, since that day the previous week that she'd flitted into his life, his days were filled with thoughts of her. He intended to enjoy her company while he could.

It was his staff's night off so it was to be an informal meal tonight. He hoped Freya would like the fillet of beef Marian had prepared. His housekeeper had put it in the oven just before he'd set off to see if Freya was okay coming up from the cottage in the rain. Some nagging thought had told him she might need help.

Freya had looked both forlorn and cranky with that silly umbrella, and his protective instincts had been aroused. Feelings of an altogether different kind had been aroused by holding her close and from that sweet, simple kiss on the cheek. An insignificant gesture to have had such an effect on him.

He'd ached to follow it up with a proper kiss but had been held back by the instinct that he had to take it easy with Freya. She was like an injured wild animal he knew took patience to tame. Not that she was injured—not physically anyway—or indeed wild, although there was an appealing feistiness to her. But she might be emotionally damaged as Wil had been by his past. She needed careful handling, a cautious approach. Even if a friendship was all that would evolve from their unexpected meeting as they were two total opposites.

He took the beef out of the oven to rest before serving it. 'That smells so good,' Freya said as she came into the kitchen. 'Did you prepare all this?'

She indicated the dishes on the countertop, then lifted the lid from a pan of mushrooms in a garlic-and-cream sauce. For a moment he was tempted to say 'yes' to impress her, but he would soon be caught out.

'Can't claim credit for any of it, although I did choose the wine. I can cook basic stuff but this is all Marian's work. She's made a brilliant creamy mash with truffle oil and a selection of vegetables from the garden. All we have to do is heat it up.' Ned had studiously ignored his housekeeper's blatant comments about what a lovely girl Freya was and how she hoped they'd see her more often at Five and a Half Mile Creek. As if he needed reminding.

'Sounds as good as any restaurant in Melbourne. Will Marian join us for dinner?'

He shook his head. For one thing, he didn't fraternise with staff—something he needed to remind himself of sooner or later. 'She lives with her husband in their apartment in the staff accommodation.'

'So it's just us?' she said.

'You okay with that?'

'Sure,' she said. But there was an edge to her voice he wasn't sure how to interpret. Had she been as unsettled as he had been by their moment on the veranda? Holding her close had been mind-blowing. It had taken all his willpower not to pull her into his arms and kiss her thoroughly. But he would wait for his cue from her. Once started, kissing wouldn't be enough.

She was enchanting, this quirky city girl. He found

it difficult to keep his eyes off her, to stop them from roaming her body to take in every detail. Her lovely face—all water damage now repaired, though she'd looked very cute in drowned-rat mode—her hair dry and sleek again and falling below her shoulders. Her curves, hugged by a dark purple dress, the colour of blackberries, and those sexy, sexy shoes tied with suede ribbons around her ankles.

'I don't know about you, but getting caught in the rain has made me hungry,' he said.

'I suspect a big guy like you might always be hungry,' she said. 'Carrying all those sheep around must help build up an appetite.'

He laughed. 'You might be right.'

Freya carried the platter with the beef on it over to the table in the dining area. Ned followed with more dishes. She stopped, platter still in hand, and called back to him over her shoulder. 'The…the dog is in here.' Her voice rose on the last words.

Ned muttered a curse. 'Molly. Sorry. I forgot to put her out.'

He followed Freya's anxious gaze to where his black-and-white dog lay stretched out full-length on her rug in front of the very smart wood-burning heater that had been installed as part of the renovation. He liked real flames as well as central heating. At the sound of her name, Molly opened one eye—the unclouded one—thumped her tail a few times, heaved a doggy sigh, and settled back down.

'She's pretending to be asleep,' Ned said. 'Hoping I'll leave her there toasting in front of the fire.'

'Is she really that smart?' He noticed Freya had moved from referring to his dog as 'it' to 'she'. A step in the right direction.

'Border collies are very smart dogs, and she's a very smart border collie. She's also very old and frightened of storms.'

'Frightened of storms?'

'Thunder in particular.'

Freya looked down at Molly, her expression again difficult to read. 'I'm frightened of storms myself.'

'You're also terrified of dogs. Don't worry, I'll take her out.'

'Outside? In the wet? In the cold?' she said.

'She does have a big kennel on the veranda.'

'It would be horrible out there for her.'

'Which is why I'll lock her in the utility room.'

'No! Don't do that.' Freya looked nervously across at Molly. 'She's not doing anything scary. Just lying there.'

Molly let out a convincing doggy snore. 'Fast asleep, in fact,' Ned said. Clever Molly.

'She's ignoring me, as if I wasn't in the room.'

'Just obeying orders. I told her to stay away from you.'

'Perhaps…perhaps you should leave her there.'

'If you're sure you're okay with it?'

'I think I'm pretty safe over here. And she…she's safe from the storm.'

'Thank you on my dog's behalf,' he said. 'She'd thank you herself but she's not quite *that* smart.'

Freya put the platter on the table. 'But I remain on this side of the room and the dog remains on the other.'

'Agreed,' he said. 'And now to get down to the serious business of eating.'

He would reward Molly with a slice of roast beef later. And he might concede to Freya a scrap of his 'must love animals' wife requirement. Because even though she was frightened of Molly, she'd shown empathy towards his dog. Surely that counted? Or was he clutch-ing at straws because he wanted Freya to fit in here? For them to have even the tiniest patch of common ground on which to meet?

CHAPTER SEVEN

FREYA DIDN'T MAKE friends easily. Her friends were often more akin to acquaintances, with Freya unwilling—subconsciously or not—to make the emotional commitment to trust somebody that true friendship required. She suspected this was a hangover from her years in state care. To get too close to another kid in foster care or a residential home usually ended with a move for one of them, sometimes without the opportunity to say goodbye. That was how it had been with Wil.

As a result, she had just a few good friends. They included a girl she'd met at uni, now a graphic designer living not far from her in Melbourne; another girl who'd been a receptionist at Hugh's studio when Freya had started as his assistant, now an account manager in one of the big advertising agencies; and of course Hugh and his partner, Gordon, who she sometimes felt were as close to family as she had in her life.

So she marvelled at how at ease she felt with Ned, as if they were friends of long-standing duration. In fact, she had friends she had never felt this level of connection with. One thing in particular stood out—she didn't need to consider her words before she spoke in her conversations with Ned. Overthinking before she opened her mouth was another habit she'd got into while in care, for self-preservation purposes.

With some of the foster families she'd been with, you never knew what the consequences of the 'wrong' answer might be—like admitting she was frightened of storms. Apparently that was something exceedingly immature, which had to be 'worked through', in the words of one cruel foster mother. It wasn't so much the rain, it was the thunder, the lightning, the utter out-of-control violence of a storm that scared her. You'd think an adult would have understood that and been kind to a terrified thirteen-year-old who'd just been sent—again—to live with strangers.

Ned was so darn kind he even considered the feelings of his dog. No way could Freya have allowed him to boot the poor animal out into the cold. If she'd insisted he would have done so, but how would he have felt about her as a consequence?

Their dinner conversation centred again around the history of Five and a Half Mile Creek. She heard how it had once been even bigger, but over the years land had been hived off and new homesteads built to accommodate second and third sons; how electricity and telephone connections had come early to the property, thanks to past Hudson members of parliament. Again, she marvelled at the long history and connection Ned had to this land. Such an enviable legacy of security and certainty.

But she heard nothing that led her closer to personal knowledge of this man who, despite her best resolutions to stamp down on her attraction, continued to intrigue her. He wanted to know *her* secrets, what about *his*? Why wasn't a super-eligible guy like Ned married, or in a permanent relationship? A friend could ask those kinds of personal questions, couldn't she? Especially if she was emboldened by the very good red wine he had served with the beef.

She decided on a roundabout way of questioning him. 'You'd make a good father, Ned,' she said as she nibbled on the flaky apple pastry his housekeeper had made for dessert.

Ned nearly choked on his pastry. He had to pick up his glass of water and gulp some down before he could speak. 'What makes you say that?' he spluttered.

'The way you are with Molly, for one thing.'

He laughed. 'She's a working dog, not a child substitute.'

'Not all working dogs get to loll in front of a fire and be fed roast beef when their master is pretending to stoke the fire.'

'You noticed?' She found his caught-out expression endearing.

'I pretended not to. It was too cute the way you were both being so sneaky.'

'When I was a kid it was a strict rule not to feed dogs at the table. I thought I'd learned to be surreptitious about breaking that particular edict. Because break it I did, many times over the years. My dogs were my best friends.' He glanced over at Molly as if enlisting her support. Freya found that endearing too. As a matter of fact, there was a lot she found endearing about Ned Hudson.

She rather liked the idea of being on his side. 'Where you fed her wasn't strictly the table, was it? It was her rug. And don't you get to make your own rules around here now, boss-man?'

He smiled. 'I like the way you're complicit with my rule breaking and setting.'

'I'm all for it,' she said. 'I'm sure Molly would agree.'

His voice softened. 'She's a good dog. An excellent companion.'

Freya hesitated. Decided to go ahead. Took another sip of red wine to fuel her bravado. 'But a dog isn't the same as a person.'

'True. But if you remember, until I was fourteen and Wil came along, I was an only child. There was a lack of companions my own age and the adults were usually too busy to give me much time. When I wasn't away at boarding school, my dog and my horses were my friends.'

Her heart turned over at the thought of the sweet young boy Ned must have been with his animal friends. It made a poignant image. Perhaps his life hadn't been as story-book perfect as she'd imagined.

'Even with Molly for company, you must get lonely in this big house.'

'Most of the time I'm too busy to be lonely.' He paused. 'But, yeah, I am on my own a lot. Not how I planned it, but how it's turned out.'

Freya knew she should probably leave it at that, but she wanted to know more. 'What's your story, Ned? How come you're on your own when you're pushing thirty?'

He picked up his wine, looked at her over the rim of the glass. 'I could ask the same of you.'

'You could, but I asked you first.'

'Fair enough.' He took a sip from his wine, put it back down. 'Timing, probably. Right person at the wrong time. Or just the wrong person.'

'Was it just timing? I'm surprised you're by yourself. You…you seem the marrying kind to me.'

Ned's laugh was more of a snort of incredulity than anything humorous. 'What do you mean by that?'

Freya clenched her hand around the stem of her glass.

Why had she thought this was a good line of conversation to initiate? 'I can't really put it into words. But I meant it in a good way. I can imagine you with a…a devoted wife and a brood of kids.' She stumbled on the 'devoted wife' bit, as she knew it was something she could never be to a man, no matter how much she wanted him.

'Why is that?'

'For a start, you're kind, caring, family orientated.' She could add 'solid, reliable, grounded in good values' but decided she'd gone far enough already. Besides, she didn't know that of him for sure.

Ned sat back in his chair. 'Hey. That all makes me sound kinda boring. How about adventurous? Fearless? A risk-taker?' He beat on his chest with his fists in a Tarzan-like display of strength. Under his light navy-blue sweater, his muscles rippled.

She laughed. 'All those too.'

'You could be right, though,' he said thoughtfully. 'In fact, I wanted to get married when I was eighteen.'

'*Eighteen?* Who gets married at eighteen?'

'An infatuated teenager?'

'That sounds about right.'

'It seemed very real at the time. She felt the same. Although, looking back, I can see the relationship would have been a disaster.'

'I'm intrigued, please tell all.' She was intrigued, but she was also more than a touch disconcerted at how distasteful she found the thought of Ned with another woman. Even when he was eighteen years old. This pretending to be 'just friends' with a man you were desperately attracted to wasn't as easy as she had anticipated. 'You must still have been at school.'

'Boarding school in Melbourne, my final year.' He named the most prestigious private boys' school in the state. 'Teresita was at our "sister" girls' school. Not that we saw much of the girls, except when it was deemed socially advantageous for us to get together.'

'I bet they fought to keep you apart,' she said. 'It seems so old-fashioned to have single-sex schools.'

To be fair, though, she'd liked the segregated, all-girls residential institution in which she'd spent her final years in care because she'd felt safer there. At her co-ed high school, she'd tried to avoid the boys. Even to the point of starving herself to minimise the curves that brought unwanted attention. There had been no high-school boy-friends for her. She'd met her first, older boyfriend at uni-versity. Hadn't discovered until it was all over that he'd been notorious for preying on 'freshers'.

'I don't know that I'd send any kid of mine to a single-sex school,' Ned said.

Freya nearly said *me neither*—but she had no inten-tion of ever having kids.

'So how did you meet your girlfriend?' she said in-stead. 'Your first girlfriend, right?'

'The schools had a joint orchestra. I met Teresita at rehearsals. She was a really talented musician. We hit if off immediately. Then we…we…'

'Fell in love?' she prompted. It was an effort to make her voice impartial when she thought of Ned falling cra-zily in love.

'Yes, we snuck out to meet whenever we could.'

'You're a musician? Those instruments in the music room are yours?'

'The grand piano is a family heirloom. I learned to play on it. But the violin was my instrument. If you saw Wil's wedding video you'd have seen me playing fiddle in the bush band.'

'I haven't seen it.' She made a mental memo to get hold of the video when she got back to Melbourne.

'I particularly enjoy playing the Celtic fiddle—foot-tapping, hand-clapping. But classical was what we played in the school orchestra.'

'You're a man of many talents. I'm impressed.'

The more she knew of Ned, the more impressed she became. There'd been no opportunity for her to learn to play a musical instrument. Music lessons were optional, expensive extras at the various schools she had attended. And the cost of an instrument—even the hire of one—prohibitive.

'Her diplomat parents were not impressed with me. When they found out that Teresita and I were together, they put an end to it. They made communication between us impossible. Then when our final exams were over, they whisked her home to the Philippines.'

'Did you see her again?'

'Never.' A note of bitterness sharpened his voice. Freya didn't blame him for it. He and his girlfriend had been old enough to be in love and plan a life together and had been treated like naughty children. The same way she had had to submit to the authority of people who hadn't always had her best interests at heart.

'I'm sorry. That must have been heartbreaking.'

'Not that a guy that age would easily admit to it, but yeah. I tried to contact her. Her phone was disconnected. The email address I had for her bounced.'

He looked down at the table, hiding his expression.

'I'm sorry,' she said, feeling the words were inadequate.

He looked up again. 'In hindsight, her parents were probably right. We were young and naïve. Didn't have anything much in common except music. We both had family obligations that governed our futures.'

'It would have been good if you'd been allowed to figure that out for yourself.'

'Yes, it would've. My parents didn't like me getting so serious so young either, but they didn't intervene. However, as I still had university to get through, I suspect they heaved a sigh of relief when Teresita flew home.'

Freya was glad of the opportunity to segue to a less fraught topic. 'What did you study at uni?'

'Agri-business at Melbourne. The degree equipped me for the role I knew was to come. From when I was a kid I wanted to be a vet, but that went by the board.'

'I could see you as a vet, you love animals so much. So why didn't that happen?'

'To study veterinary science was at least six years at uni. That meant a lot of time away from home and little opportunity to actually practise if I qualified, except on our own animals. Wil wasn't interested in farming. Dad needed me here.'

'Did you want to be here?' She thought she detected a trace of disappointment at having to give up his dream.

He raised his brows. 'I never resented the choice I made. I liked what I studied and it helped me modernise the way things are run here. It was a good path to take.'

Freya took another sip of her wine. It was all very well to hear about his qualifications. But she was becoming obsessed with his dating history. This might be the only chance she got to find out.

'What about at uni? You must have broken a few hearts there.'

He shook his head. 'I didn't break any hearts.' He said it so seriously, so sincerely, like the gentleman he was. 'Not that I was aware of, anyway. I had a girlfriend I met in second year. She came from up Moree way, in central New South Wales. Her family grew cotton on a big scale.'

Jealousy—ridiculous, unwarranted, irrational—speared Freya. That girlfriend was the right kind of woman for man-of-the-land Ned. The type he would marry to get that doting wife and brood of kids. His own kind. He wasn't her type, either, she had to remind herself yet again. They came from different worlds—she could no more imagine Ned living in inner-city Melbourne than she could imagine herself living here, in spite of his story of busking in the city.

'What happened?'

'We both went back to our respective properties at vacation time. Had to start over again back at uni.'

'She was a term-time girlfriend?'

'Pretty much. After we graduated, it just fizzled out. We kept in touch. She's married now.'

Good. 'And after her was—?' Surely he had a more up-to-date girlfriend story to share?

'This is quite the interrogation,' he said with that slow smile, his way of looking into her eyes, that felt as intimate as a touch. 'I hope you're going to be as forthcoming when I turn the tables on you.'

She flushed. 'Er...of course. Not much to tell from my side. I'm a dating disaster zone. I... I don't have what it takes to make relationships work. Not for long anyway.'

'I find that difficult to believe.' He narrowed his eyes and she was intensely aware of his scrutiny, that he liked what he saw. 'Perhaps you haven't met the right man?'

Because she always went for the wrong ones.

She'd tried with Henry but he'd turned out to be as much a dud as the self-centred musician, or the lying fellow photography student at uni. Besides, what was the point? She didn't want to get married or even live with a guy. Her independence and emotional equilibrium were too important. The good part of her life had only started when she had been able to take control of them. She had no intention of relinquishing her heart.

'Let's get back to you,' she said. 'You're far more interesting.'

'As long as I get equal time to question you,' he said. 'In fact, I'll trade question for question. Do you have a boyfriend in Melbourne?'

For a moment she was thrown. 'No,' she said. 'I haven't dated for six months.'

'Six months? What's wrong with the men in Melbourne?'

She had to smile at that. Almost replied, *They're not like you.* Realised that would sound provocative. 'Maybe they're not worth bothering about,' she said, too glibly. 'I've been working long hours, sometimes away on location, no time for dating.' She deflected him with another question. 'What about you?'

He shrugged. 'Living out here it's not easy to meet women. I've dated off and on. There was one woman I liked a lot. I met her at a trade show in Melbourne. We seemed to have a lot in common. Had a lot of fun on my visits to the city. But she turned out to be not the person I thought she was.'

His mouth tightened to a bitter line. This was the one, Freya thought, the one who had broken his heart and had him hiding way out here at the back of nowhere.

'Was it because she didn't want to live out here so far from—?'

'Civilisation?' he finished for her with a weary note to his voice.

'Actually, I meant so far away from Melbourne.'

'That was part of it. I had to make a choice between

her and Five and a Half Mile Creek. Her behaviour made that choice easy.'

'Did she—?'

'I don't wish to discuss it further.' His tone made it very clear the conversation was closed.

'I understand,' she said. 'And I'm sorry about another *too far from civilisation* gaffe from me.'

'It was also a saying of my mother's, so it's a bit like the screech of chalk on a blackboard to me.'

'But from what you said, she had a wonderful life with her garden and her fundraising parties and living in this beautiful house.' She waved her arm to encompass the room and the rooms beyond it.

'It wasn't quite like that.'

That wasn't the reply she'd expected. Freya realised Ned's mouth had set in a grim line and he had abandoned all attempt at finishing his dessert. So had she. She had fought her curves for so long, merely tasting a dessert to be polite had become a habit.

'What do you mean?' she said tentatively.

'All that wasn't enough for my mother. I don't know the ins and outs of my parents' marriage, but apparently the novelty of living out here wore off pretty quickly.'

'But you said your parents were madly in love.'

Freya struggled to assimilate this new information, so discordant with the picture she'd built up of Ned's life at Five and a Half Mile Creek. She didn't want to be disillusioned. She loved to hear about happy endings, there'd been so few in her life.

'I think they were very happy for the first few years. But farming isn't a nine-to-five job. My father wasn't around much. My mother had given up a very successful career. Once she'd completely redesigned every room she could get her hands on here, she got bored. Before long she'd started accepting commissions in Melbourne and spending weeks at a time away from here.'

'What happened to you when your mother went to Melbourne for work?'

'When I was little she took me with her and her parents looked after me. As I got older I wanted to stay here. I hated going to Melbourne. When I started school in Hilltop, she couldn't pull me out of class on a whim.'

Freya shook her head slowly from side to side. 'Ned, I don't know what to say. I'd pictured a perfect, idyllic childhood for you here.'

'It was all that, while my mother was around.' His eyes darkened with what she thought was remembered sadness. 'She called us every night, but I was miserable those times Mum went to Melbourne for weeks on end. I couldn't understand why she wanted to leave me and Dad on our own. And Dad, desperately unhappy himself, couldn't ease up on the work just because I was there. He hired nannies to care for me but no one could replace my mother.'

'Of course you would have been miserable.' Freya remembered how devastated she had been when Nanna had to go into hospital and she had had to first live with strangers. 'Wait.' She put up her hand in a halt sign. 'Didn't you say you lived with Hugh and Gordon for a while?'

'When I was nine my parents separated. Mum went back to Melbourne for good. I had to go with Mum as I was so young.'

'I'm sorry, Ned.' Again she felt her words were inadequate.

He locked his hands together on the table so his knuckles showed pale. 'You know last night you said you didn't like to revisit the past? I'm the same. I don't remember a lot of that time, just how much I hated it. I don't *want* to remember it. I was wrenched away from everything I loved. Had to change schools and live in Brunswick—' he spat out the name of the lively, inner-city Melbourne suburb as if it were something loathsome '—when I was used to the run of Five and a Half Mile Creek. I missed my dog, my horse, my home. Melbourne was so far away, I only got a visit from my dad every two weeks.'

Freya wished she could hug that homesick little boy. Heck, she wished she could hug the twenty-nine-year-old man. She wondered if that enforced separation had scored deep scars of pain and loss. Could that be the real reason the family man was still single? But with every word of his story, her spirits were sinking lower. He was even more of a country boy than she had thought. And she was a rural misfit.

'That's so sad,' she said, instead of the hug. 'But your parents seem well and truly together now.'

He unclenched his hands, she was relieved to see. 'For six months I lived with Mum in Melbourne. But, the story goes, she was as miserable as I was. She missed Dad and she realised she missed a lot about Five and a Half Mile Creek. Dad says he got his act together and delegated more of the running of the property to managers. He spent more time with my mother. There's always been a garden near the house. But that was when Mum went all out to expand and create new areas. She brought in top horticulturalists to help her make it the award-winning garden it is today. Dad worked alongside her. He once told me they'd never stopped loving each other. When she came home, it was for good.'

'And it was for you too.'

He paused. 'Do you remember the lucky horseshoe in my study?'

'With ends right way up to catch the good luck?'

'I kept that horseshoe by my bedside the entire time I was away, to remind me of Five and a Half Mile Creek. It went to boarding school and university with me too.'

'Seems like it worked. The good luck, I mean.'

'I don't like to think of myself as superstitious. But during that time in exile in Melbourne, I remember wishing so hard for what seemed like the impossible—a brother or a sister.'

Freya had to clear her throat against a sudden lump of emotion. 'Your wish came true.'

'Big time. Everything got better when Wil came into our lives. I finally got a brother. My mother got another son to focus her maternal energies on. Wil needed a lot of love and attention and my parents were the right people to give them to him. I remember the hours my dad and I spent teaching him to ride a horse, teaching him about trust.'

'You had a lot of love to give too.' Wil had hit the brother jackpot with Ned. Seemed Ned thought the same about Wil.

'He's the best brother any guy could have,' he said. 'Now I also have a wonderful sister-in-law and a cute little niece.'

Ned had a lot of love to give a woman. Freya appreciated that now. To the right kind of woman who could make a life here with him. Not someone like her, terrified of the isolation, the slithery things, the boredom of country life. Ned must think she was such a wimp, afraid of so much, even his old dog.

She had really tried to overcome those fears, had gone to therapy once she could afford it. But what she was most frightened of was tying her life to someone else's. Not only because she didn't want anyone to control her, but also because she had lost the only people she loved and trusted. Love meant loss, so it was better not to love. No amount of therapy had helped her with that. Yet somewhere deep in her barricaded heart, she had longed for love and an intimate connection with a man. She had cautiously let some of those barriers down for the rock musician but he had abused her trust and trashed her vulnerable heart. Never again.

There was something strong and compelling there between her and Ned. She had felt it from the get-go and was sure he had too. She couldn't put a name to it—it was more than sexual, although it was most certainly that too. But, nameless or not, it was an attraction she fought with the same strength she fought a rogue current at the beach that tried to drag her out to sea. For one inexplicably painful moment she wished she could be that fortunate woman, wrapped in the love of this good man. But it couldn't be. For with that kind of love came expectations she could never see herself fulfilling and compromises she couldn't make.

Ned got up from the table, picked up his plate of unfinished dessert. Freya did the same. He turned to head towards the kitchen and then turned back to face her. His expression was very serious, stern even.

'I don't know if there is such a thing as a "marrying kind",' he said. 'I've gone for steady girlfriends, relationships rather than casual encounters. I always thought I'd get married some day—most people do. But I'll be thirty in September—"some day" is sneaking up on me. Wil's marriage put it all into focus. I want the kind of loving relationship Wil has with Georgia. Holding Wil's little daughter Nina made me realise how much I want children of my own.' He paused. 'So I guess you could call me the marrying kind.'

'Heading for thirty does make you think,' she said, trying to keep her face inscrutable, her voice neutral. 'Although I've got a couple of years to go.'

'My parents' marriage taught me one thing. When I do get married, it will have to be to a woman who loves life in the country as much as I do. I wouldn't put myself through what my father went through when my mother left. And I wouldn't put any child of mine through what I went through.'

Freya had the feeling there was a deeper level to the conversation. That perhaps, without his putting anything on a personal basis, a position had been stated and a reply was required.

'I understand where you're coming from. I didn't have a home of my own for a long time. I've found my place in the city—it's where I live and where I work and...and it validates me.'

He forced a laugh; it was almost painful for her to hear. 'We're entirely at cross purposes.'

She choked out the words. 'Looks like it.'

CHAPTER EIGHT

LATER THAT NIGHT, Ned awoke to a clap of thunder so loud he felt the house shake. From her dog bed in the corner of his bedroom, Molly whimpered. Forks of lightning illuminated the room as if it were midday. Rain drummed down on the roof and gushed along the gutters and down the drainpipes outside his upstairs window.

Ned switched on his bedside lamp and swung out of bed. 'It's all right, girl,' he said to his dog, leaning down to pat her. 'You're safe here.'

Molly had been frightened of storms since she was a pup. Ned felt exhilarated by them. He loved the display of nature's power. And, as a farmer in a country where the threat of drought was constant, he relished the sound of the rain filling his property's dams and the collection tanks that provided household water.

Freya had surprised him when she had confessed to a fear of storms. He understood the fear of dogs, certainly the fear of snakes, which was shared by nearly every person he knew. But storms? She seemed somehow fiercer than that.

Freya.

Ned realised it wasn't just the thunder that had woken him, or Molly's whimper. Rather it was a strong impulse that Freya needed him.

Perhaps it was a remnant from a dream, or his concern for her alone in the cottage. He had suggested she stay in the house for the night but she had—unsurprisingly—insisted on her independence in the cottage. He had escorted her to her accommodation then gone back to his immaculate hotel-style bedroom.

Lying by himself in the king-sized bed, as he'd struggled to get to sleep, he'd felt lonelier than he could ever remember feeling. He was disconcerted by Freya's insistence he was the 'marrying kind', who wasn't married. It was nearly as bad as cousin Erin's 'never a groom' remarks. He was even more disconcerted by the fact Freya didn't meet one of his bride criteria but checked so many other boxes in terms of appeal, including being beautiful, sexy, smart, and damn good company. He couldn't get her out of his mind.

He checked the illuminated clock on his nightstand. Past midnight. He needed to see if she was okay. Ned was a practical, down-to-earth kind of guy. Yet somehow he thought he could hear her calling him, although common sense told him her voice was only in his head.

Hastily, he pulled on jeans and a sweater over his pyjamas, then his boots. He reassured Molly he wouldn't be long. As he turned towards the door, the room was pitched into sudden darkness. No lamp. No glow from the clock. Just the eerie sound of electric appliances whirring down after their power source had been cut off.

Blackout.

Power failures were nothing unusual out here. A tree could have come down over power lines. Ned grabbed his phone and put it on torch mode. He needed to get downstairs and slam down the lever that would turn on the emergency, diesel-driven generator. Power would be restored to the house within minutes.

But not to the guest cottage.

Ned ran down the stairs as fast as it was safe to do so in the darkness. He reached the emergency-power lever and activated it. Located the powerful, emergency torch. From the coat room he grabbed both his own long oil-skin wet-weather coat, and his mother's much smaller one. By the time he was out of the door, the power was back on at the house.

He hoped Freya was sleeping through it all. But that persistent, inner voice told him that might not be the case. She was frightened of storms and she was in the pitch black of a clouded night with no illumination from the moon and none of the street lighting she was used to in the city. The motion-detector lights on the outside of the house came on to light his way as he splashed down the gravel path towards the cottage.

As expected, the cottage was in complete darkness. He called her name once, twice, three times with increasing levels of urgency.

'Freya!' He banged on the door. 'Are you okay?'

He strained to hear any response from her. Nothing. If she was asleep, she might not thank him if he barged in uninvited.

Thunder struck again and the night sky lit up with forked lightning. This time he thought he heard a muted scream from inside. Without hesitating, he pulled out the key from his pocket and opened the door.

With the wide beam of the torch, he scanned the rooms. 'Freya!'

The living area and kitchen were empty. The bed in the master bedroom had been slept in, the quilt and sheets thrown back. The other bedroom was untouched. No one in either bathroom.

Where was she?

Had she tried to get up to the house and got lost in the dark?

A flash of lightning illuminated the entire area. The utility-room door was open; a dark shape lay huddled on the tiled floor near the washing machine. Ned's heart hammered and his mouth went dry.

He aimed the beam of the torch on the dark shape. Freya. She was curled into a ball, cocooned in the knitted grey throw rug from the bed, only the purple stripe in her hair visible, a set of headphones blocking her ears. Her breath was coming in shuddering gasps, but he could tell she was trying to mumble something.

He propped the torch so it cast a pool of soft light on her, and left his hands free. 'Freya?' He gently pulled the headphones off her head. She startled into a defensive position, threw her head back, stared at him mutely with huge unfocused eyes. 'Freya, it's Ned.'

Her eyes gradually focused in the dim light. 'Ned,' she croaked.

'Come here,' he said. He shucked off his wet coat. Freya hauled herself up as he reached down to scoop her up into his arms, throw rug and all. She was wearing only a T-shirt and light cotton pyjama pants and she was trembling. He held her close, his arms wrapped tightly around her. There was another loud clap of thunder and she moaned as she burrowed closer into his chest. He held her like that for what seemed like a long time, as her trembling subsided.

'Thank you,' she mumbled against his sweater. 'S… sorry. I… I usually do better than this in a storm these days.'

'No need to apologise. I'm glad to be here.'

She gave a great, heaving sigh, still with her face

pressed to his chest. 'The thunder woke me. I didn't know where I was. I… I panicked.'

Her voice wasn't steady, as if she had to fuel it with frequent small breaths. 'I've always been frightened of storms at night. When I was little, my nanna used to take me into bed with her and calm me.'

He thought about those years when she'd likely had nobody to comfort her. 'What about when you were in care?'

'There were always other kids in the room with me who were sympathetic; they were frightened themselves more often than not. Until…until the foster home where I was placed after the incident where Wil got involved. That foster mother had me down as a troublemaker. Warned me to steer clear of her husband with my "seductive ways".'

'What? How can these people get away with that?'

'It's their word against the children's.'

Ned stifled a curse. Again, he silently thanked Wil for protecting Freya all those years ago.

Freya snuffled as she talked to him in the dark, her voice edged with raw emotion. 'There was a storm. I cried out in the night. The woman came to the room I shared with her daughter. She said I was too old to be frightened of storms at age thirteen and that I was disturbing others in the house. She dragged me out of bed and locked me in the utility room. Told me not to be such a scaredy-cat and left me there all night. Every time it stormed, I'd be put back there.'

Ned growled. Unable to find words to express his disgust and anger at such cruelty. 'So why are you in this utility room?'

'Because there wasn't enough floor space in the closet.'

The thought of her cowering in a closet as a storm raged was heart-wrenching. 'I see,' was all he could manage to choke out, while holding her even closer.

'It's the thunder and lightning that scares me, not the rain. The fear is called astraphobia, and apparently it's quite common.'

'A phobia that the cruel woman who threw you in the laundry room only made worse.'

'Quite likely,' she said. 'I… I've seen a therapist who helped me with coping strategies. Wrap up tight in something warm, and cover my head. Use noise-cancelling headphones to block the sound of the thunder—I play music through mine—then chant a mantra to make less room for fear in my mind.'

'Please come up to the house. I hate the idea of you being down here by yourself. The power has gone off and I don't know when it'll be back on. There's an emergency generator for the house and you'll have light up there at least.' Otherwise, he'd stay here with her. He would insist on it.

There was another massive thunder clap. Freya shuddered in his arms but didn't make so much as a whimper.

'I… I can't go outside in that. Please. Let me stay inside. But don't go. I… I feel better…safer with you here.' As if he would leave her.

Ned picked up the torch, led Freya out of the utility room to the living room, where he lowered her to the sofa and sat next to her, propping the torch on the coffee table. He wrapped the rug around her again and drew her close. When she got her breathing back to a more normal rhythm, he spoke. 'How did you get to be in the care of such unfeeling—some downright dangerous—people, without anyone on your side?'

With only the light of the torch he couldn't see her

face to gauge her reaction to his words. She didn't reply. How could he help her if he didn't know what had caused her fears?

She opened her mouth to speak, then she sighed, as if she was too weary to keep up the blockade on her past life. 'My mother had me when she was seventeen. She'd run away from home to be with her older, drug-dealer boyfriend—my father, as it turned out. When she fell pregnant he booted her back home to my grandparents. To their tiny two-bedroom terraced cottage.'

'They took her in?' he said cautiously.

'As they'd done many times before. She was their only child. Only this time they did it on the proviso that she looked after herself while she was pregnant. That meant staying off the drugs. She complied. Nanna told me Mum wanted the baby. Wanted it to be healthy. The boyfriend stayed away. Nanna and Pop really thought she'd turned the corner. That maybe the pregnancy, though unplanned, might be the making of her.'

'But that wasn't the case?'

Her voice was gaining in strength. 'Unfortunately not. Once she'd had the baby—me—and got her figure back, the boyfriend crooked his little finger and she went running back.'

'Did she take you with her?'

'Apparently she tried to care for me. But a baby cramped his style. That's according to my grandparents. I remember Nanna telling me she worried herself sick for my safety every night I spent with my parents. One day, when I was only a few months old, my mother brought me home, said she couldn't look after me and asked my grandparents to look after me.'

Ned was horrified; her parents had had a duty to care for her. But he fought to keep his voice neutral, not judgemental. He didn't want her to clam up. 'That was probably a good thing.'

'Yes, it was. Pop could be a bit grumpy at times, but he was very caring. Nanna was wonderful in every way. A big woman with a big heart. She loved me and I loved her. For a long time, I thought she was my mother.'

'And your real mother?'

'She flitted in and out of my life. I don't really remember her. I… I don't think she ever gave me much thought. I remember overhearing my nanna saying that all that mattered to my mother was to get her drugs and be with the man who obsessed her. Of course I didn't know what that meant at the time. She was only in her early twenties when…when she and my father were both found dead of an overdose. I was five years old.' She stumbled over the words.

'Freya, I'm so sorry.' What else could he say?

'Looking back, I see how tragic it was, the…the sordid nature of both their short lives and their deaths. Back then it didn't really affect me. Nanna and Pop became my legal guardians. They were older than other kids' parents but that was okay. I grew up not knowing anything different. Abbotsford wasn't as gentrified then as it is now. I wasn't the only one in an unconventional family.'

'That must have made it easier.' He was struggling to find the right words to respond to her; he just wanted to hold her, to make amends for something he could not.

'I went to the very good local school, had friends. There wasn't a lot of money but enough. Pop worked at the brewery and Nanna cleaned houses, work that fitted with school hours so she could be there for me when I came home. I was happy, didn't question anything. Why would I?'

'So what changed?'

She paused, drew a deep breath and exhaled it. He could feel the rise and fall of her chest against his. 'You realise how difficult talking to you like this is for me? I've shared this with very few people. I prefer to put it all behind me. It was only seeing Wil in those photos that brought my past back.'

'I understand,' he said. He was straining hard against a rush of anger towards her selfish parents. But they hadn't been much more than kids themselves.

'"What changed," you say? Everything changed.'

'Everything?'

'My happy, secure little world fell apart. My grand-father died in an industrial accident. Nanna adored him, she took it hard, especially following the loss of her only daughter. On top of that, she had developed diabetes. Looking back, I don't think she really understood how to manage her condition. When I was ten, she had to have her leg amputated.'

Ned didn't try to disguise his shock. 'I'm sorry, how dreadful. How did that affect you?'

'There was no family to help. Social services stepped in. While Nanna was in hospital and rehab—not that I really understood what all that meant, just that she wasn't there—I was placed in care.'

'A foster home?'

'Kind people, actually. Then when Nanna got out of hospital, I was allowed home. But her health deteriorated. She was in and out of hospital, and I was in and out of care. Then she had to go into a nursing home, where she didn't last long. She died when I was twelve.'

'And you went into care for good?'

'Until I was eighteen. They kick you out on your own then.'

'You were still a kid. With no support.'

'Yep. Sink or swim. But you learn to toughen up.'

'And you swam. You must have to get where you are today. Talk about overcoming disadvantage.'

Ned tried not to think how strange this was, to be having this kind of conversation in the dark. But perhaps Freya would not be opening up to him like this if the situation were in any way usual.

'To be fair, it wasn't a one hundred per cent gloomy story.'

'Tell me the sunny part of the story,' he said. 'Please.' He needed to hear that her childhood had not been unmitigated misery—not that he would have been able to do anything about it. Although his brother had. Wil had helped her. Somehow that eased some of Ned's rage against the unfairness of Freya's early life.

The storm was still raging overhead and the room was illuminated by a flash of lightning. In the second it lit the space, Ned saw her flinch, but she continued. 'In spite of all the disruptions, I did okay at school. And I suspect I was mature for my age. When I was fifteen, my "potential for further study" was recognised and I was given a place in a girls-only residential home. It was run by an enlightened charity. They encouraged me to complete high school. I graduated with a decent university entrance score.'

'Impressive, after such a bumpy start. How did you manage to put yourself through uni? That must have been tough.'

'There was some government assistance and my work at the café paid the rest.'

'Then you met Hugh.'

'And my luck changed, thank heaven.' Her voice was hollow. The mask of fun, quirky Freya had slipped, and he realised it was only because she was too emotionally drained to keep it up. He was hearing her unvarnished truth. 'You know the rest,' she said.

Of course, Ned didn't know the rest, Freya thought, not all of it by a long shot. There were secrets in her past she would never reveal to anyone. She was already regretting letting down her guard and revealing so much. How had she allowed it to happen when she was usually so careful to curate the story of her life? Blame it on the storm. And Ned being there to help her in her storm panic with kindness and understanding.

She prided herself on her independence but she had never been more pleased than when she'd opened her eyes from her cocoon on the floor to see Ned. Big, strong Ned sweeping her up into his arms as if she were thistledown, holding her close, wrapping her in warmth and security. He'd murmured a litany of soothing, calming words as he held her, until the panic that had stricken her started to recede. She could not remember when she had felt so safe and cared for.

It was irrational, her fear of thunder and lightning. She had tried to desensitise herself by researching the scientific explanations of why and how they occurred, had thought she was getting on top of her fear. But this storm was especially violent and she'd been alone in unfamiliar surroundings. Now here was Ned. And she felt so much better for his presence. If it were possible for a person to physically fight thunderbolts and deflect lightning strikes to protect her, she felt Ned could do it.

'Thank you for being here,' she choked out, staying near to him on the sofa.

Pressed close to his reassuring strength, she felt she could stay like that for ever. Through the thin fabric of her T-shirt she was intensely aware of his body, of the hard muscles under the soft wool of his sweater, his thighs braced next to hers. His scent was already familiar and arousing. Desire, fierce and urgent, took hold of her. She eased back from her closeness to him just enough so she could look up at his face—his handsome face that could be stern but always kind. Her eyes were getting accustomed to the dim light of his torch and she could see concern and, thrillingly, an answering desire in his eyes. They had been moving towards this since the moment they'd met.

As she raised her face to his, he lowered his head to her. Then his mouth was on hers, firm and warm and utterly wonderful—as somehow she had known in her heart that it would be. With a little murmur of pleasure and delight she kissed him back, parting her lips to receive his tongue, meeting it with hers, tasting, exploring, possessing.

The throw rug she had grabbed from the bed fell away from her. She didn't need it, not when she had the warmth and security of Ned's arms around her. She reached up and wound her arms around his neck to bring him closer.

It was their first kiss, but somehow they seemed perfectly in sync, as if they already knew each other's wants and needs. As they kissed, the storm raged around the cottage but she was scarcely aware of it. Kissing Ned was so much more effective at distracting her than any mantra or headphones could ever be.

Their kiss grew deeper, more urgent, her breathing ragged in echo of his. 'Freya,' he moaned against her mouth.

His hands slid down her body, skimmed the side of her breasts, rested on her waist, then slid down to cup her bottom. She shuddered with pleasure at the intimacy of the touch, his hands warm and firm through the fine fabric of her pyjamas.

More.

She wanted so much more. Was this overwhelming desire a reaction to danger averted? If so, she wasn't going to fight it.

'I think I should take you up to the house, where there's light and warmth,' he said, his voice husky.

'Please. I... I've had enough of the dark.'

He lifted her up from the sofa so she stood next to him. She felt immediately bereft, so reached up to claim another kiss. He raised her up so she could wrap her legs around his waist, her face now on a level with his, their kiss deep and hungry and demanding.

Finally she came up for breath, murmured her pleasure as he kissed a pathway down her neck to the hollows of her throat. Her nipples tightened and tingled and she ached for him to touch her there.

Still holding her tight, her legs wrapped around his waist, he turned them both around. He hardly seemed aware of her weight and Freya delighted in how strong he was.

While making sure she was secure, he picked up his torch. He snagged a coat, which hadn't been there before, from where it was draped across the back of a chair.

He kissed her again, swiftly and thoroughly. 'I don't want to put you down, you feel so good right where you are.' His breathing was ragged. 'But it's still raining and you need this coat.'

Reluctantly, she unhooked her legs and slid to the ground. Solicitously, he helped her into the raincoat. It was a bit big for her, but obviously a woman's coat. Did it belong to a former girlfriend? If so, how did she feel about wearing it?

'The coat is my mother's,' he said, answering her un-asked question. 'I'll grab mine from the utility room where I left it when I found you. But I'll need the torch.' His fingers brushed her cheek. 'Will you be okay here without the light? It will only be for a few seconds.'

'Yes,' she said through gritted teeth, refusing to admit that the thought terrified her.

But somehow it was okay as she could hear him moving around and, true to his word, he was back before she had time to miss him. He shrugged himself into his coat, then put the hood of hers over her head. 'You look very cute,' he said, kissing her.

She returned the favour, reaching up and putting his hood over his head. 'You look cute too.'

'I'm not sure about the cute bit, but thank you.' He planted another kiss on her mouth as her reward.

'My shoes,' she said, taking a step towards the bed-room.

'You won't need them. I'll carry you to the house. Are you ready?'

He swept her up into his arms and cradled her close. She held onto his shoulders. 'You're so...chivalrous,' she murmured. Excitement thrummed through her.

'Any time,' he said in that deep, manly voice.

He pulled open the door and they were met with a blast of wind and rain that made Freya cringe. Outside in the storm, she was exposed and vulnerable to her worst fears. If there was a clap of thunder, she would die of ter-ror. But somehow she felt as though Ned was her shield against her fear and that it would be impossible to come to harm while she was with him.

'I'll make a run for it,' he said. 'I promise not to drop you.'

Could he really run with her in his arms? Turned out

he could. She laughed with exhilaration. He laughed too. Then they were both laughing as he ran with her along the gravel path, the torchlight wavering ahead of them. She was snug in the raincoat and Ned's arms. Not for a moment did she worry he'd drop her.

As he neared the building, sensor lights switched on to guide them to the beautiful house that lay ahead as a place of refuge from the terrors of the storm. And she was safe in the arms of this man she had known for so little time, yet wanted beyond all reason.

They were both breathless and laughing as he carried her through the door and deposited her in the welcoming warmth of the hallway. 'We made it,' he said.

'Your arms must be aching,' she said.

'Not at all,' he said. 'You—'

'Don't tell me, I'm lighter than a sheep.' But she laughed as she said it.

She shrugged off her damp coat and he hung it on a coat hook, then did the same with his own coat. Freya stood there in just her light pyjamas and T-shirt. She wore no underwear, was aware that the fine fabric clung to the curves of her hips and bottom, that the shape of her breasts and her peaked nipples must be clearly visible. He noticed and his eyes narrowed in appreciation. His gaze was like a caress and she ached for him to touch her.

He cupped her breasts in his hands, as he pulled her to him again in a swift, passionate kiss. It felt so good her knees weakened and she sagged against him. She wanted more kisses, more caresses, more Ned, but while she knew they were the only people in the house, she felt self-conscious in a way she hadn't in the darkened cottage. 'Here's not the place,' he said, picking up on her feelings as only he seemed to have the ability to do.

He took her hand and led her towards the grand staircase.

'Where are we going?' she said.

'Upstairs,' he said.

She hadn't been upstairs yet. But his answer excited her. Because right now, a bedroom seemed like a very good idea.

CHAPTER NINE

FREYA PRIDED HERSELF on her independence, yet she revelled in the way Ned swooped her up in his arms to carry her up the stairs. There was absolutely no need for him to do so; she could easily get up the stairs under her own steam—her bare feet were hardly going to be injured by contact with the dense, luxurious carpet—but she thrilled to it. It wasn't so much the heroic, he-man display of strength, but the way Ned made her feel—cherished, protected, of value. It was a total turn-on. 'I could get used to this,' she murmured.

'It's my pleasure,' he said.

He slipped his hand under her T-shirt, touching her bare back. His hand was callused from hard manual work, and its roughness against the smoothness of her skin sent shivers of delight coursing through her. Freya ached to feel his skin against hers but there were too many layers of his clothing between them. She would have to remedy that.

He gently placed her on the floor of the landing. 'My bedroom or the guest bedroom?' he said. 'Before you reply I should warn you, Molly is in my bedroom.'

Freya felt some degree of empathy with the dog over their shared fear of storms, but she did not want to share a room with her, much as the idea of being in Ned's bedroom appealed. 'The guest room, please.'

'I asked Marian to get one of them ready for you in case the cottage didn't appeal,' he said.

He took her hand and led her up the hallway. 'This is the room,' he said, and opened the door. Freya got an initial impression of six-star hotel luxury—an enormous bed, a door opening to an en-suite bathroom, muted tones of grey and blue, the storm outside muted by heavy curtains. But her focus was on Ned.

'I'm at a distinct disadvantage in these skimpy clothes, while you're fully dressed,' she murmured. 'Let's even the score.'

'Gladly,' he said hoarsely as he kicked off his boots.

She pushed his navy knit sweater up from his waist and helped him pull it over his head. It revealed a loose blue-and-white-striped shirt that wasn't exactly sartorially splendid but who cared? It wouldn't be on him for long. She fumbled with his belt and then the button fastening of his jeans. He helped her slide them down over his hips. Matching striped boxers? No. Longer pants than that.

'You've got stripy pyjamas on,' she said, bemused. Old-fashioned, long-sleeved dad pyjamas. Not that she had ever known her dad.

'Yeah. I threw my clothes on over them. Not for the first time. It's quick when I have to get up for an emergency.'

'Was I an emergency?' she asked flirtatiously.

'Yes,' he said simply. 'I was worried about you.'

Her heart seemed to flip over at the concern in his eyes. She wasn't used to that kind of thoughtfulness.

What was she doing letting things go this far when she knew there couldn't be a future with him?

She switched that inner voice off. She wanted Ned. He wanted her. That was all that was important. They were adults who knew what they were doing.

This was about tonight.

'I like your pyjamas,' she said stoutly, rising on tiptoe to kiss him, forgiving herself the fib.

'They're the kind I used to wear at boarding school. When it comes to clothes I just order replacements, the same again. Jeans, checked shirts, T-shirts. It saves time.'

'Why not?' she said. 'If you have your own look, stick to it.'

Again, he endeared himself to her. What you saw was what you got with Ned. He was straightforward and didn't pretend to be anyone other than he was. It was refreshing. She could even call it...lovable.

Slowly, she walked her fingers up his chest and started to undo the top button of his pyjama top. She narrowed her eyes. 'I think I'd prefer you in no pyjamas at all though.'

Ned was beyond thinking of anything but how much he wanted Freya. How alluring she was. How having her in his arms made his heart pound. How the prospect of having her in his bed was intoxicating. But through his excitement, an insistent thought pushed its way forward: Freya had to know what she was unleashing, and be sure it was what she wanted.

He put his hand over hers to still her unbuttoning of his shirt. 'Those pyjamas go off, you know what will happen.' His breathing was ragged and uneven.

'Yes,' she said. Her eyes gleamed with passion and anticipation.

Her answer aroused him even more; he wanted to stop talking and kiss her again. But Ned couldn't forget how vulnerable Freya was, how he'd felt when he'd seen her lying on that floor, a quivering mass of fear. He had to be responsible, even when all he wanted to do was divest her of her clothes and carry her to that bed.

'You're sure this is what you want?' he said.

'Very sure. I want *you*, Ned.' There was an edge of impatience to her voice.

He wouldn't hold back. 'I want you, too,' he said. More than she might imagine.

'Let's see if we can strip each other's pyjamas off at the same time,' she said with a mischievous laugh. She was *so* sexy. Her nipples were thrusting against her T-shirt. He ached to see her naked.

'Synchronised stripping?'

'Yes,' she said, laughing.

He lifted his hand from hers and she undid his top button. Her fingers were trembling, which told him she wasn't quite as assured as she wanted him to believe. He slid his hands under her T-shirt and went to pull it up and over her head.

'Uh, uh,' she said playfully. 'Let me get all your buttons undone first, so we're on an even playing field.'

Her teasing sent his excitement levels rocketing. He gritted his teeth and tried to sell himself on the virtues of delayed gratification.

Freya undid the buttons, one by one, her fingers tickling his chest, then pushed his shirt away. 'Oh, my. Ned, you have an amazing body,' she breathed. 'It's a crime to cover it up. Especially with those pyjamas.'

Ned didn't know why she found his pyjamas so unappealing—they were practical, did the job. But if she wanted to take them off, he had no problem with that. She splayed her hands across his chest, then ran them down to his waist. He gulped at the effect her touch had on his already aroused body.

'Your abs. Your pecs. You must work out, as well as

haul sheep around, to get muscle like this.' Her voice was even huskier than usual as she stroked across his chest, exploring. When she looked up at him, her eyes were glazed, the pupils huge. 'You really are the most gorgeous man.'

'Nice of you to say so,' he managed to choke out through the waves of arousal fogging his brain.

But he'd had more than enough of talking. He slid his hands up under her T-shirt to cup her breasts. No bra. She moaned when he rolled her nipples between fingers and thumb. As he shrugged his shirt off his shoulders, he—at last—pulled her T-shirt over her head. Her breasts were small, high and round, with pink, peaked nipples. 'Perfect,' he breathed. '*You* are perfect. Beautiful Freya.'

She went to say something self-deprecating but he smothered her words with a kiss that started on her mouth, travelled down her throat, and finished on one, then the other, of her lovely breasts.

Freya wanted Ned so much she could make love with him then and there on the carpet. Or up against the wall. But she was glad when he steered her towards the bed.

He placed her down on the quilt as if she were something precious. She wouldn't have cared if he'd thrown her down.

She just wanted him.

She lay next to him on the bed, facing him on her side, as they kissed and caressed each other until kissing was no longer enough, and their remaining garments were getting in the way. Impatiently, she tugged at his pyjama pants, untied them and pushed them off him. He was well built *everywhere*.

He made the act of removing her pyjama pants into an extended caress, stroking and kissing along the length of her legs as he slid them off her. Then there were no barriers to intimate exploration, and she murmured and sighed with pleasure at his caresses from his skilled fingers. He seemed to know exactly what would please her and her arousal mounted. Within minutes, she was overwhelmed by an orgasm so powerful she screamed out his name.

When, dazed, she came back to earth, it was to see him looking into her face, a sensuous half-smile playing around his lips. 'Did you like that?' he murmured.

'I don't think you need to ask,' she said, still gasping as her heart rate returned to somewhere near normal.

Kind. Considerate. Gentlemanly. They were all qualities she'd attributed to Ned. If she had at any time earlier at the cottage assumed this would be gentle comfort sex, those thoughts had been thoroughly dispelled. Ned was outrageously virile. And she loved it.

'Now your turn,' she said, caressing him.

He moved her hand. 'No, I want to be with you.'

'Even better,' she whispered.

'Stay lying on your side,' he murmured. 'I'm so much bigger than you, I want you to be comfortable.'

'Sounds good to me,' she said, wiggling into the best position to receive him.

He moved to meet her so he was intimately close. Then stopped. Cursed low and fluently. 'Protection. I don't have—'

'I'm on the pill,' she said breathlessly.

'I've tested clean,' he said.

'So have I.' She thrust her hips urgently towards him. 'Please, Ned,' she begged. 'I'm desperate for you. Don't make me wait any longer.'

He didn't, and she gladly welcomed him into her body. Immediately, he found her rhythm and she matched his, in perfect trust and harmony with each other's needs, so the act of making love seemed more profound than she had ever imagined it could be. She somehow felt complete, as if she had found something that had always evaded her. They came together, her cries of ecstasy mingling with his and the incessant storm that continued to rage outside the windows.

Afterwards, she drowsed in his arms and tried not to think about what came next. Because nothing had changed. They might be awesome in bed together but their lives were still at cross purposes. She couldn't be the woman he needed to live the life that had been mapped out for him. Forcing herself into a mould that didn't fit, just to please him, would only lead to disaster for both of them.

CHAPTER TEN

Freya woke the next morning to the joyous comfort of Ned's strong, warm body spooning her from behind, his arms tight around her. They'd fallen asleep like that after they'd woken at dawn and made love again. She felt deliciously content and boneless with sexual satisfaction. And happy. *So* happy. But it was a happiness she knew could only be momentary.

The rain was drumming relentlessly on the roof. Some found it a pleasant sound, but not her, as she always feared thunder and lightning might accompany it. Still, she was able to relax, as the security of Ned's embrace took the edge off her anxiety.

The noise that had awoken her came again—a scratching on the closed door accompanied by a piteous whining. This time Ned heard it too and he sat up, planting a quick kiss on her mouth as he did so.

'Molly needs to be taken outside for a bathroom stop. Trust me, at her advanced age, I don't ignore the requests, much as I would like to stay here with you.'

He swung himself out of bed and headed towards his discarded clothes. Freya caught her breath at the sight of him naked. Broad shoulders tapered to his superb butt, and long, powerfully muscled legs. Could a man look more wonderful? Desire rippled through her again.

Through sleepy eyes she watched as he pulled on the pyjama pants, then his sweater, not bothering with his boots. Every movement was a play of muscle on muscle. She could watch him for ever.

No. She could not have such thoughts about Ned. This level of intimacy was frightening. She could never entertain the words *for ever.*

Ned opened the door to his dog. 'C'mon, girl. Let's get you downstairs.' He turned back to face Freya. 'Don't go anywhere. I'll be back.'

As if she could go anywhere in a hurry.

As if she wanted to.

Not yet. The weather had put paid to any further photography in the garden. In theory, she should pack up her van and head back to Melbourne. But she wanted to spin this time out with Ned for a few more hours at least.

Freya yawned, stretched out her arms and snuggled back under the sheets, which smelled deliciously of *them.* Then pulled his pillow to her side of the bed and buried her face in it, breathing in his scent. She didn't know for how long she drowsed before Ned came back. He sat on the edge of the bed beside her and put his hand on her bare shoulder. 'Hey, are you awake?'

'Sort of.' She sat up, tugging the sheet in place to cover her breasts. Crazy really, when he'd seen every inch of her last night. And vice versa. This morning his face was shadowed with morning stubble, darker than his hair, and he looked sexy as hell.

He smoothed her hair, dishevelled from a night of lovemaking, back from her face. It was a tender gesture. 'Much as I'd like to climb back into bed with you, it's past nine and Marian is downstairs. I don't particularly want any gossip about you—about *us*—starting.'

Us? There could be no *us.*

'Me neither,' she said,

She was aware of a subtle shift in the dynamics between them, an awkwardness, a falling back from the joyous spontaneity of their passion the previous night.

He leaned towards her. 'Marian knows you moved up to this room from the guest cottage after it lost power. As far as she's concerned, I spent the night in my room. Not that I have to explain myself to the staff. But I would prefer to be discreet.'

'Me too,' she said.

His gaze was intent. 'Not that I'm ashamed of what happened between us. Far from it. But it's private and special.'

Her eyelashes flickered; she found it difficult to meet his gaze. 'For me too,' she said, her voice breaking.

'Special' was way too lacklustre a word to encompass the awesomeness of their lovemaking. Not just a joining of bodies but something so much more profound. She felt like weeping when she thought about how unlikely it was that she would ever again make love with Ned.

'Freya, this is bad timing, but I have to meet with my managers. There's some significant storm damage and the rain is playing havoc with the autumn planting.'

'I understand,' she said. 'The weather has played havoc with my photography of the garden too. Luckily I got a lot done yesterday, because I won't be able to shoot today. However, I think you—and your mum—will be happy with the results.'

He smiled that fabulous slow smile that warmed his eyes. 'I don't doubt that for a moment.'

'Thank you,' she said. 'I really enjoyed the shoot. But…what I'm trying to say is that I should head back to Melbourne.'

He sat back from her. 'About that. The creek has

flooded, broken its banks in places. It's not too bad for us but further downstream the causeway is covered.'

'What do you mean?'

'There's water across the road that leads from here to the highway. It's way too dangerous for cars to cross. So you actually can't drive to Melbourne. And the weather is too wild to take the helicopter up.'

'You mean I'm trapped here?' She could endure a couple of days in the country—but no more.

Immediately, she regretted the words as Ned's face fell. She'd hurt him. Just the first of a long line of hurts she would inflict on him and on herself if she…

If she let herself fall in love with him.

That was what the danger had been all along. *Love.* That trap was something she could not fall into. She couldn't start something she knew could not continue. There could only be that one night between them. One night she knew she would never forget.

'*Trapped?*' He scowled. 'Is that how you'd think of it?' She realised he was talking about more than a delay to her departure today. 'Would it be so terrible to have to stay here for a while longer? To stay with me?'

She met his gaze unflinchingly, although a cauldron of emotion was churning inside her. 'To stay today would be lovely. But…but after that, I have to get back to work. Things haven't changed, Ned. My life is in Melbourne.'

His jaw tightened. She read his reactions as they flicked across his face. Loss. Regret. Anger. 'Of course it is,' he said, tight-lipped. He got up from the bed, frowned. 'Did last night…did it mean anything to you?' He paused, shook his head. 'Don't answer that.' He turned on his heel.

Freya jumped up from the bed, dragging the sheet with her for modesty. 'Ned. No. Don't go.' He turned back to face her. 'It meant so much. I've never… It…*you*…were amazing. You are so wonderful…in every way.'

His face gentled. 'One night wasn't enough for me, Freya. Not with you. There are ways around every problem. You live in Melbourne. We don't inhabit different planets.'

But they might as well do. It wasn't just the physical distance from Five and a Half Mile Creek to Melbourne. It was the difference in their life goals. Differences that were insurmountable, as far as she could see.

'True,' she said. 'We…uh…we need to talk it through.'

'Being *trapped* here might be a good time to do so,' he said. 'I'll get back up to the house as soon as I can.'

'Good idea,' she said, trying to keep the rising panic from her voice. She hated confrontation.

He took a step towards her. 'I can't tell you how sexy you look in that sheet.'

'Er…thank you,' she murmured, clutching it close.

He kissed her, a short, sweet claiming of her mouth she was unable to resist returning with a little gasp of pleasure.

But already it felt like a kiss between strangers.

Ned was later back to the house than he had anticipated. Thankfully the rain had ceased but there was extensive storm damage. Trees and fences were down, and the men were out on motorbikes checking for further damage. They might not know for days about the furthest reaches of the property. That would mean having to take up the helicopter now the weather had started to clear, this time to survey what had been destroyed rather than to do a scenic tour. Nothing was as usual. The roof had come off a feed shed. The horses were spooked. As Freya had been last night.

It turned out she spooked easily.

He wasn't thinking about her reaction to the storm though. It was her reaction to him this morning that had his gut churning. He had a horrible suspicion she intended to bolt and that would be the last he ever saw of her. She'd told him she wasn't one for long-term relationships. That could translate to *no* relationships. He should have listened to her. But would that have stopped him last night from carrying her up the stairs to the bedroom? The answer was a resounding *no*.

Her purple van parked in the driveway confirmed his suspicion. Freya was loading her equipment through the open back doors. She was dressed in the black jeans and black tunic she'd been wearing the first time he'd seen her. There was no floating scarf—but that didn't mean she wasn't flying away from him.

'Ned,' she said as he approached. 'You've been a while. Marian has saved your lunch for you.'

He shouldn't have given her time to think. But he had to lead his team inspecting the property. As always, Five and a Half Mile Creek came first.

But at what cost?

Was that the real reason he'd been 'never a groom'?

'The damage is bad, but nothing that can't be mended.'

'That's good to hear.'

He looked pointedly at her van. 'Packing up?'

'It…er…seemed a good idea to get my things from the cottage while there's a break in the rain.'

'It looks like you're packing up to go,' he said.

'It…it doesn't hurt to be prepared for when the road is open again.'

'True.'

An uncomfortable silence fell between them. Freya

was the first to break it. 'Ned, about that talk. Should we have it now? Somewhere private?'

He was going to suggest the guest cottage, but then thought she would probably want to spend as little time as possible there after her traumatic experience. 'How about my study?'

'Okay.' She bit on her lower lip. Not a good sign.

Ned sat in the leather office chair in his study and swivelled it around to face her. She was sitting in his favourite easy chair. He would rather he was the one in that big chair and that he was pulling her down onto his knee. But the vibe she was giving off let him know that wasn't going to happen. She sat on the edge of the chair, her legs primly together. It felt uncomfortably like an interview—one where he had the distinct feeling he wasn't going to get the job.

'I love this room,' she said, looking around her.

'Me too,' he said. 'But then we both know that.'

'No idle chit-chat, then?' she said with a hint of her lovely smile.

'There are more important things to talk about. Like how we can continue to see each other. I… I don't want to let you go, Freya.'

Damn. He didn't want to stumble over these words, they were too important. He also didn't want to make too big a deal of it. He wasn't talking binding vows here, just making it clear he wanted to see her again. To take her to bed again.

Her eyes were very wide in her pale face. 'I don't want to let you go either, Ned.' Unfortunately the way she said it made him know her words would be followed by a *but*. 'But it can't work between us.'

'The distance is not insurmountable.'

'So you visit me in Melbourne, I visit you here,' she said. 'We date long distance.'

'Sounds like a plan.'

'And then what?'

'You tell me.'

'We hit a brick wall when it comes to a future together.' She leaned forward in her chair, grasped both hands together. 'We've had this conversation before. Cross purposes, remember? Completely different lives. Different plans for the future.'

'That was before last night.'

'Yes,' she said, her voice sad, her eyes not meeting his. 'That…that makes it so much more difficult.'

'More difficult for you to end things between us before they've even started?'

She nodded.

'Why?' He got up from his chair. Paced the distance of his desk and back. 'How can you just walk away? Last night…was something extraordinary.'

She got up to face him, a stubborn tilt to her chin. 'Because it's better I do so now rather than further down the track when it would hurt a whole lot more. Hurt both of us.'

'Don't I have some say in that?'

'You already have had a say,' she said. 'You've stated what you want in a woman—and it isn't me. I can't be the woman you *need* for your life here. The sooner I'm out of your life, the sooner you can forget me and move on.'

'I don't want to forget you.'

'It's best that you do. We're great in bed—'

He groaned. 'At last she says something I can agree with.'

'But that won't be enough. Not if we're incompatible out of the bedroom.' She drew a deep breath. 'You're the marrying kind, remember? I'm not. I don't want to get married or live with a man. I don't want to cede any part of my life into another person's control. For too many years I had people making decision about how I lived my life that weren't always in my best interest.'

'Doesn't it depend on the man? There has to be an element of trust, surely.'

'I don't trust easily,' she said, her mouth set in a stubborn line.

'Because you've encountered too many untrustworthy men.'

'Starting with my father. Followed by some truly scary foster fathers. Then there are the controlling types. It's amazing how many of *them* want to be foster parents. Even Pop, who I loved, kept Nanna under his thumb. When he said "jump", you asked how high on the way up. Nanna was too busy looking after him—and then me—to look after herself.'

'You're lumping all men into the one category. There are plenty of good men around.'

Her face softened. She reached out just long enough to touch his cheek before she dropped her hand again. 'Including you. You're one of the good guys. Someone I could perhaps learn to trust over time. If circumstances were different.'

'Yet you don't intend to give me the chance.'

'You've also told me you want kids, right?'

'Yes. More than one. I didn't like being an only child.'

'You should know that I have never wanted to have children. I don't know that I could be a good mother, not after the upbringing I had without one of my own. Not only that, I saw too many unwanted children in my time in state care. I couldn't bear the thought of a child of mine ever ending up one of them.'

'The father might have something to say about that,' he said gruffly.

'There's something else.' Her mouth twisted. She looked up. 'It isn't just that I don't *want* to have children. I might not be *able* to have them.'

'What do you mean?'

She took a deep breath. 'I have a condition called polycystic ovarian syndrome. It's a hormonal imbalance. I take the pill to help alleviate the symptoms. My doctor tells me I might need fertility treatment if I wanted to get pregnant.'

'But you *could* get pregnant?'

'Possibly.'

'That wouldn't bother me,' he said. 'The trying, I mean.'

'It would. If you really want a family. In the future, I mean. You…you need to put me in the too-hard basket, Ned,' she said, her voice wobbling.

'You realise we're talking about the roadblocks to a future together?' he said with a puzzled frown. 'When we hardly know each other. It's…bewildering.'

'I know,' she said. 'It's kind of bizarre. I… I felt some kind of connection from the word go.'

'Me too.' He pulled her into his arms and she didn't resist. He held her close. 'I hear everything you're saying. You're right. Of course you're right. We have nothing in common.' Not one match on his wife wish-list. Yet last night, with her naked and passionate in his arms, that had seemed irrelevant. 'But I still don't want to let you go.'

She pulled away from him, and looked up at him, still within the circle of his arms. 'Would you leave Five and a Half Mile Creek for me?' She put up her hand in a halt sign. 'Don't answer that question. It's purely theoretical.'

'Freya,' he said brokenly. 'I—'

Did it always come down to that? He could have Five

and a Half Mile Creek, or he could have love? Not that he was talking *love* with Freya.

'We would only end up resenting each other,' she said. 'So let me climb into that too-hard basket where I belong, and let me drive back to Melbourne.'

'You'll go no matter what I say, won't you?'

She nodded. 'It's how it has to be. For both our sakes.'

Ned held her close again and for a long moment they stood silent. He wanted to protect her, but she didn't want to be protected. He wanted to make love to her again; she had no such interest. For her, last night had been a one-night stand. He'd be wise to think about it as that too.

'The causeway is clear, the road open,' he said. He'd known that for a couple of hours; he'd been checking the emergency services for news of further flooding, hadn't wanted to tell her, so as to spin out her time here.

'I know. I've been checking the traffic app.'

'The weather could still be dangerous.'

'Sunshine on its way, according to the radio.'

Not for him, he thought. Not without Freya in his life.

'This is unendurable,' he said.

'For now.' Her voice was muffled as her face was pressed against his chest and, he thought, from the effort of pushing back against tears. He was enduring the same struggle himself. 'When…when you're settled with your country-loving wife and a brood of kids you won't even give me a thought.'

His wife wish-list had been a stupid idea. He saw that now. Because it didn't take into account the possibility of falling for a woman who was wildly unsuitable and yet who had, last night, made him happier than he could ever have imagined he would feel. He would have to re-think everything.

He cleared his throat. 'And when you're back enjoying the buzz of the city, you'll look back and shudder at the thought of the…the slithery things.'

He'd been going to say *the country guy who wasn't exciting enough for you* but that sounded maudlin and self-pitying and probably not true. It was circumstances rather than the people they were which made this—*them*—impossible. Because he did want kids. Badly. The feelings when he'd held baby Nina at her father's wedding had been powerful and from the heart. And giving up Five and a Half Mile Creek would be like giving up part of his soul.

She pulled away from him. Swiped at her eyes with the backs of her hands. 'I should leave sooner rather than later.'

'Yeah. Best to make a clean break. I'll head on back down to…to check on the horses.' And to gain comfort from the unconditional affection of his equine friends. Animals were so much more reliable than people.

'When you get back, I'll be gone,' she said.

His heart sank to the level of his boots at the thought of her absence. No more purple in his life. 'And after that?'

Her eyes flickered nervously. 'Perhaps, given time, we…we could salvage a friendship from this. If your mother likes the garden shoot, perhaps I could come back in spring.'

'Yeah. Perhaps.' He knew his words sounded hollow, but then so did hers.

That wouldn't happen. He wouldn't hire her again. How could he be 'just friends' with her after what they'd shared?

It was only sex, he told himself.

But he knew what had passed between them was so much more than that.

He could not endure watching her little purple van carry on down the driveway, taking her out of his life. 'Take care,' he said as he turned on his heel and walked away without looking back.

CHAPTER ELEVEN

Two months later

NED HAD HEARD from Freya three times in the last eight weeks. The first time had been three days after she'd left, when she'd sent the images from the garden shoot via an app capable of transmitting high-resolution images. Every photo had, of course, been a work of art. The file had been accompanied by a brief, impersonal email saying she hoped he would be pleased with the shoot. He had replied in kind, aching to say how much he missed her, knowing it would be inappropriate.

Her next communication had been two days after that. She'd sent an e-card, produced by her. It had been designed around the image of his hand putting his lucky horseshoe to rights, taken on the day of her first shoot in this very room, and included the words *Thank you, Ned*.

It was, as she'd said at the time, a 'cute' image and she'd turned it into a clever design. She was a very talented artist.

Freya had sent the card on a Sunday evening, perhaps when she was alone, possibly having regrets. He'd hoped so, anyway. He'd been alone too and, foolish guy, had immediately replied. He'd suggested they catch up in Melbourne, some time soon. She had tortured him by taking a day to reply, only to dash his hopes with a note saying it was too soon, she wasn't ready. Since then, nothing.

He missed her. Even though she'd only spent a few days here in total, she had made such an impact on his life. Every day, thoughts of her had drifted into his mind. He worked all hours, galloped his horses, pounded out reps in his home gym, swam laps in the enclosed heated pool. But nothing stopped those images of her from taunting him. Freya had inveigled her way into his thoughts along with a truckload of *what ifs* and *if onlys* that he wasn't used to entertaining.

Recently those thoughts had been of the same disturbing kind he'd felt on the night he'd rescued her from the cottage during the storm. That she needed him, that she was calling for him.

Wishful thinking, mate.

He was just looking for an excuse to see her.

Still, the idea wouldn't let go that she needed him. Though in reality it was more likely he needed her.

He scrolled down to the emails he'd sent last Friday— not to Freya, but to his family friend Hugh Tran, her boss.

Hi Hugh
I'll be in Melbourne next week. Would like to discuss enlarging and printing some images of the garden shoot Freya did for Mum. Will you be around on the Wednesday?
Ned

Hi Ned
Yes to Wednesday, it would be great to see you. It's Freya you will need to see re the garden pics. I'll make sure she'll be at the studio on Wednesday morning.
Hugh

Hi Hugh
Excellent. See you Wednesday morning around ten.
Ned

Ned shut down his computer. It was Monday night.
There was too much to do here to waste the time it would
take to drive to Melbourne. He'd fly the helicopter down
tomorrow, land it at the helipad in the family home in
Toorak, then spend the night in his penthouse apartment
nearby. On Wednesday he'd make his way to Hugh's
Richmond studio in the car he kept at the apartment for
his and Wil's use. He had no other appointments. There
was only one reason for a trip to Melbourne.
To see Freya.

Traffic coming into Richmond on this wintry morning
had been hell and Ned was glad he'd left Toorak in plenty
of time to get to Hugh's studio.

He'd actually been early, and spent ten minutes finding
the café he thought might be the one Freya had worked
in, and where she'd first met Hugh. As he sat in his car
and drank his takeaway coffee he marvelled, not for the
first time, at how incredible it was that Freya, who Wil
had known as Tegan, had been so close to the family for
all that time, and at the coincidence that had brought her
to Five and a Half Mile Creek—and him.

The studio was a low, squat building painted in bright
multicoloured blocks, and shared the narrow street with
other converted warehouses, auto workshops and a scat-
tering of terrace houses in varying stages of renovation.
There was an abundance of graffiti on fences and walls.
Ned couldn't understand how anyone could find such
vandalism exciting—let alone call it art. He wasn't happy
about leaving his new-model, luxury sports car parked

on these mean streets. Then he smiled to himself, the thought reminding him how reluctant Freya had been to leave her equipment in her van parked on his driveway. This was her territory.

Ned had to concede there was an energy and excitement to the place. He'd forgotten—or made himself forget—how much he'd once enjoyed that aspect of city living. He wasn't yet thirty, yet he viewed city life like some rigid, over-critical middle-aged man. How had he let that happen? Why had he allowed his world to shrink to the perimeters of his own land?

The interior of Hugh's premises was spartan, with a number of studios ranging from the cavernous to the small that only came to life when they were dressed for a shoot. The small reception area was decorated simply with a series of blow-up photographs in black and white. Ned wondered if any of them were Freya's.

Hugh greeted him effusively. Ned towered over Vietnamese-Australian Hugh, but the older man's hug was strong and as affectionate as ever. Ned had always liked him; as a child he'd called him 'Uncle Hugh'.

'I didn't tell Freya you were coming,' Hugh said, when the hugs and extended greetings were over.

Ned wondered why. Because she would be elsewhere if she was aware of his visit? How much did Hugh know—or guess—about what had happened between his protégée and his old friend's son at Five and a Half Mile Creek?

'Okay,' Ned said, fighting a battle with himself to appear unperturbed. 'I guess she doesn't need notice and can readily access the photos I want to discuss with her.' Which could as easily be done over the Internet, as Hugh would well know.

'Sure she can,' Hugh said. 'She's in Studio Two.'

'I remember where that is,' Ned said. He couldn't wait a minute longer to see Freya. Eight weeks was a long time—would she have forgotten him?

He headed in the direction of the studio but Hugh stopped him with a restraining hand on his arm. 'Do you remember when you were living in Brunswick with us, and you found that injured magpie?'

'Vaguely, yes.' It had been a long time ago and Ned had helped many injured birds and animals since. 'I got it flying again.'

'You did. Just keep in mind how good you are at helping birds with broken wings.'

Ned wondered what on earth Hugh could mean. But he understood as soon as he saw Freya.

The studio door was open and she didn't appear to hear him coming in. Dressed in her usual black, she was sitting at a desk, working simultaneously on three computer screens, head down, fingers flying, intent on her work.

'Freya,' he said as he got closer.

She froze. Swivelled around on her chair. Stood up. One hand clutched at the back of the chair, the other at her heart. *'Ned.'*

The colour drained from her face, her eyes widened, then started to roll upwards as she seemed to fold in on herself.

Ned caught her before she fell, eyes closed, against him. He held her tight. Terror gripped him with icy claws. 'Freya. *Freya.*'

She was breathing, but he picked her up and laid her on the floor on her side in the recovery position. He opened her mouth to check for any obstruction, didn't find anything. He had his phone out ready to call for an ambulance when she opened her eyes. Gradually they came into focus. 'Ned?'

Thank heaven.

'I'm here, Freya.'

'Wh…what happened?'

'You collapsed. I think you fainted. I'm calling an ambulance.' He started to stab in the emergency number on his phone.

'*No.* Don't do that.' She struggled to get up and he helped her first into a sitting position on the floor and then back into her chair.

'But you're ill. I'm worried—'

'I'm not ill, Ned. I… I'm pregnant.'

What was Ned doing here?

One part of Freya rejoiced as she scanned his well-remembered features; the other cringed from the severity of his frown.

'*Pregnant?*'

'I'm sorry I didn't tell you.'

'You mean—?'

She nodded. 'The baby is yours.'

Even through her feelings of shock, lingering nausea and guilt, Freya was stunned by the expressions that flitted across Ned's face. Initial disbelief, suspicion and astonishment were replaced by a dawning wonder.

'But how?'

'The…er…usual way. Um…three times that night, if you recall.' She felt herself blush, which was crazy after all they'd bared to each other during their time together.

'But you told me you couldn't get pregnant.'

She shook her head. 'I said I'd been told I could have trouble falling pregnant. Significant difference.'

'And you were on the pill.'

'I'm on a very low-dose pill and I have to confess I...er...forgot to take it that...that last morning. I didn't worry when I realised I'd skipped it, as I was convinced I couldn't ever get pregnant. The chances were so low for me to conceive.'

He seemed to be reeling at her news. 'You don't look pregnant.'

'I'm only eight weeks, not showing yet.' She patted her still-flat tummy.

'So...it's somewhat of a miracle?'

'In a way, yes. I got the shock of my life when the doctor told me I was pregnant. I thought I had a gastric flu. That was actually the first time I fainted. You know I never wanted to have children. But then...then I was overwhelmed by this...this joy bubbling through me, sudden and totally unexpected. It's knocked my life off course, but I really want this baby.'

'Why didn't you tell me? Did you *ever* intend to tell me?'

She couldn't meet his gaze. 'I... I was scared to tell you.'

'*Scared?*' The word exploded from him. 'Scared of *me*?'

She felt at a disadvantage sitting down but as she stood up she felt a little dizzy. Ned was there like a shot to support her. *Ned.* She couldn't believe he was here.

She shook her head. 'No. Never scared of you.'

'Well, you did faint at the sight of me,' he said wryly.

'It was a shock to turn around and see you there. Why didn't you warn me you were coming?'

'Would you have been here if you'd known?'

'Yes. No. I don't know. What I mean is I was scared of your reaction. That you might think I... I'd got pregnant on purpose.'

'As you made it very clear you didn't want to have children, I doubt I would have jumped to that conclusion.'

'But I could have been scamming you. I couldn't bear it if you thought that.'

'As if I'd think you were out to scam me,' he scoffed.

'You did think it. You're very wealthy. That night at dinner, when I told you who I was, I saw the look on your face when you thought I might have come to Five and a Half Mile Creek to stake some claim on Wil. Your disgust when you suspected I was a…a gold-digger. Maybe even a blackmailer. I was terrified to tell you I was pregnant in case…in case you thought I would make demands on you.'

'Were you?' For the first time she saw that wonderful Ned smile. Her heart had felt frozen since she'd left him. Now his smile made it start to thaw.

'Yes.'

'Of course I expect you to make demands on me,' he said.

She stilled. 'Wh…what do you mean, demands? I can support myself and the baby. I won't ask—'

'I expect you to demand that I marry you,' he said, his smile splitting into a big grin.

Freya was so shocked that for a long moment she couldn't find her voice but she couldn't help a shaky smile in return. Why did just being near Ned make her feel so much better? 'That's lovely of you, Ned, but I'm not asking you to marry me.'

'So I'll ask you to marry me,' he said immediately. 'Shall I go down on bended knee? Or will a standing proposal work?'

'Neither. I don't expect you to marry me, although I do appreciate the gesture.'

His frown banished every trace of his smile. 'You

don't get it, Freya. This isn't a *gesture*. I'm not just doing the gentlemanly thing here. I want you to marry me. You're pregnant with our baby.'

'And you want to do the "right thing".'

'The right thing, yes. For you, for me, for the baby. Hudson children are not born outside...outside wedlock.' He stumbled on the old-fashioned word.

'But we hardly know each other.'

'We know enough.' He had a stubborn set to his jaw.

'All those barriers that stopped us from dating, let alone getting married, are still there.'

'Except one—that you didn't plan to have children and I did. I'm over the moon about this, Freya. I haven't stopped thinking about you since you left. I've missed you. There's something there between us, something... almost inexplicable. Can you deny it?'

Slowly, she shook her head. 'No. I can't deny it. I felt it. And... I missed you too.' The night she'd sent that e-card she'd thought she would die of the yearning for him. 'But all those other reasons for keeping us apart are still there.'

There was a loud knock on the door, followed by Hugh.

Her boss looked from Ned to her and back to Ned. 'So she's told you?'

'Yes,' said Ned, not taking his eyes off her. 'I'm shocked, but delighted I'm going to be a dad.'

'But has she told you the rest?'

Freya glared at Hugh, willing him to stay quiet.

'What do you mean "the rest"?' Ned asked.

'That her doctor has told her she needs to take it easy for the first few months of her pregnancy. That she shouldn't be working. Certainly not hauling around heavy equipment or travelling around on shoots. I've put her on light duties.' He indicated the desk where she was working on editing images and designing brochures for a client. 'But what I really want to do is sign her off on leave.'

'She should come to Five and a Half Mile Creek where she can relax and I can take care of her,' Ned said immediately.

'Those are exactly my thoughts, too,' said Hugh, beaming.

'And what about *my* thoughts?' Freya asked.

'I suspect you'll want to do what you think is best for the baby,' said Ned. 'Sometimes you have to accept a helping hand when it's offered, Freya. Will you come back to Five and a Half Mile Creek with me?'

'You know I don't need rescuing, right?'

'I'm aware of that.'

'Okay,' she said. 'I'll do it.' Hugh smiled and nodded in approval before quietly slipping out of the door. Another burst of joy had shimmered through her as soon as she'd agreed. It must be hormones; there was no other explanation. 'On the condition we don't tell anyone I'm pregnant, it's early days yet.'

'Good. I accept that condition. But I have one of my own.'

'Yes?' she said.

'I don't intend to stop asking you to marry me.'

'And I won't stop saying no,' she said.

'Game on,' he said.

That brought a hysterical laugh from her. In no way was this a *game*.

Ned waited for Freya in the living room of her tiny, one-bedroomed apartment above a small Korean supermarket, just a few streets away from Hugh's studio. She was in the bedroom packing what she needed for her trip back to Five and a Half Mile Creek with him. Her photography equipment was already stashed in his car. She didn't go anywhere without that, she'd said.

The apartment was what he might have expected from creative Freya—warm and vibrant, decorated in an eclectic manner. Silk scarves in a myriad jewel colours were draped over worn leather chairs; exotic wall hangings caught the eye; Moroccan lamps, fat scented candles, an orchid in full bloom, all were artfully placed to make the best of the small space, highlighted of course with splashes of purple. Shabby but chic oriental carpets softened the dark floorboards. It could have looked chaotic but it didn't. The room was intensely personal, yet immediately welcoming.

Through an open window that faced the street wafted spicy scents, the sound of a blues guitar from the bistro next door, and bursts of laughter from a group of students waiting at a bus stop. She would never feel alone here, he thought. Or hungry—he'd counted six restaurants and cafés with cuisines from around the world on her block alone. As well as several of the coffee shops she liked so much.

He thought he remembered going to see bands at the big pub on the next corner. One of his friends at uni had lived somewhere nearby in a slovenly student flat, with a shifting population, that had been quite a shock to the boy from a Toorak mansion and the splendours of Five and a Half Mile Creek. And he'd loved it.

Freya came out of the bedroom carrying a suitcase that he immediately took from her. Over her shoulder he could see her bedroom was decorated in the same eclectic style, an old brass bed piled with colourful cushions.

'I like your apartment,' he said.

'I love it,' she said. 'Small space, big mortgage, but

it brings me joy. The one thing I wanted above all when I got out of care was my own home that no one could kick me out of. I started to save for a deposit the day I started working.'

Ned had grown up with two luxurious homes and the security of knowing he belonged there. Freya had had no such assurance. He admired her for making her own, secure home through her own efforts.

'Well done,' he said.

He looked around him. Charming as it was, it was a single person's space. Not much room for a baby. He knew Nina came with a whole lot of paraphernalia deemed essential by her parents.

'There's an enclosed sunroom off my bedroom, which will be the nursery, in case you're wondering,' Freya said as she headed towards the door.

As she led Ned down the stairs to the street Freya remembered her orchid. She didn't know for how long she'd be away but it would be at least a week, she imagined. The plant might die in that time. 'I need to pop in to my neighbours in the supermarket and ask them to water my potted plant while I'm away,' she said.

He raised his eyebrows. 'You trust them with a key?'

'Of course,' she said. 'All the people living nearby have each other's keys in case of emergencies.'

'Yet you wanted to lock your car in the country?'

'That's different—that's protection from strangers. These are my neighbours. We're quite the little community here and look out for each other. We know the people in the other shops and restaurants as well. I feel really safe. It's another reason I like living here.'

'I see,' he said. As she followed him to where he was parked, she wondered if he actually did. And yet it struck her how at home he seemed on these city streets in black jeans and an edgy deep charcoal coat. More than a few women's heads turned in his direction—something she found disconcerting.

She hadn't quite got her head around the situation she'd found herself in—agreeing to go back to his home with the father of her baby. But she was still feeling vaguely nauseous and light-headed and didn't want to get into heavy discussions about expectations—and certainly not about marriage.

Nevertheless, she tried to keep up some kind of conversation with Ned as she sat beside him in his car—a fabulously expensive European model he'd mentioned he kept garaged in Melbourne to be used when he was in town. What was that saying? *The rich are different.* Every moment with Ned made her aware of the truth of it. He didn't even seem aware that ordinary mortals couldn't dream of such an extravagance.

A fifteen-minute drive from Richmond took them into a completely different world—affluent, elite Toorak, one of the most expensive suburbs in Australia. Its gracious streets were home to socialites, celebrities, and the seriously wealthy. Toorak hosted consulates from major-player countries like Britain, the USA and China. And the Hudson family from Five and a Half Mile Creek.

Ned explained he needed to pick up his stuff from his apartment where he had spent the previous night. Then he would drive to the nearby family mansion to access the helipad near the tennis court and swimming pool. They would leave from there via helicopter, the same one Ned had taken her up in on her first visit to his home.

Ned's city home was the penthouse of an elegant Georgian-inspired apartment block. An elevator whisked them straight up from the underground garage to the entrance hallway of his apartment.

'You call this an apartment?' she said, looking around her. 'It's the size of a large house.'

'I'm used to wide open spaces,' he said. She wasn't sure if he was joking or not.

'You must have felt very cramped in my little space.'

He would have felt as if he was slumming it. Again, she felt slammed by the differences in their social standing—although she told herself she was his equal in every other way.

'For a big guy like me it's a touch on the small side. But it's warm and welcoming and it expresses your personality perfectly. Your apartment must be a really fun place to live. If we'd had time I would have liked to follow the strains of that jazz guitar down to the bistro and settle us in to listen with a coffee and a baguette. It reminded me of the time when I used to have a lot of fun in Melbourne before—'

'Before what?'

'Before I had to step up to my responsibilities,' he said shortly, not inviting further discussion.

The house-sized apartment was splendid, decorated in tones of grey and silver with ebony woodwork. Opulent but masculine. Veering on the sterile, Freya thought, but of course didn't say. It seemed a lonely place. Although the heating was on, she shivered.

'Did your mother design the interiors?' Her voice actually echoed in the emptiness.

'Of course. I got her to refurbish it a few years ago.'

'But it must have been quite new then. Why—?'

'Because I wanted to eradicate all trace of that woman I told you about. She spent a lot of time here.'

'She really hurt you,' Freya said slowly.

'I got over it,' he said curtly.

'But what—?'

'I was spending way too much time with her here in Melbourne, neglecting my duties at Five and a Half Mile Creek. When my mother was diagnosed with cancer, my father had to beg me to come back. Beg his own son, the heir to the property. My girlfriend didn't care enough about me or my family to even consider coming back with me. That's it. I don't want to discuss it any further.'

'I see,' said Freya. It explained a lot about why Mr Eligible was still single, why he buried himself out there at the property with little chance of connecting with anyone.

'Do you want something to eat while we're here?' he said. 'The kitchen is stocked. I have a housekeeper I notify when Wil or I are coming to Melbourne.'

Freya put her hand to her throat. 'No, thank you. I don't trust myself not to feel nauseous on the helicopter ride.' She patted her handbag. 'I've got some dry crackers here.'

'If you're sure, then we'll get moving. I'll get my bag from my bedroom.'

She followed him down the hallway, curious to see more of his home away from home. His bedroom was palatial, dominated by an enormous, super-king-sized bed. His monogrammed leather overnight bag was already packed.

As he picked it up Freya tried not to look at the bed. He turned and his gaze connected with hers. He was also trying not to look at the bed. Tension hummed between them. Her nipples hardened.

She still wanted him.

He was the father of her baby. But to give into the

urge to put her arms around his neck, kiss him and tumble together onto the bed would be foolish beyond belief.

She was pregnant, but nothing else had changed between them. The contrasts between the way they each lived in Melbourne only reinforced their innate incompatibility.

CHAPTER TWELVE

DESPITE HIS STATEMENT of intent, once back at Five and a Half Mile Creek, Ned did not bombard Freya with proposals of marriage, for which she was profoundly grateful. To marry Ned because she was pregnant—when marriage had otherwise been so completely off the cards—was a monumental decision. To choose not to marry and somehow share the custody and upbringing of their child was equally monumental.

Whatever her decision, her life had been turned completely upside down by her unplanned pregnancy. Because, despite her long-held opinion that she never wanted to have children, she was happy at a deep, soul level at the prospect of being a mother. Already she felt a fierce love for her baby.

Ned had done everything he could to make her enforced rest comfortable. Not in the cottage—she couldn't bear to go back there—but in the luxurious guest room they had shared. He'd made no demands on her, rather behaved like a considerate friend. The attraction between them still hummed along, but it was as if they had—by mutual consent—put it on hold until she felt better.

She'd been shocked—and more than a little scared—of how exhausted she'd been and how much sleep she'd needed. Even now, after five days here, she was only halfway back to her old energy levels. During her days of bed rest, she'd thought a lot about what Ned had said about needing 'to accept a helping hand'. Was to accept help in the form of a marriage proposal the right thing to do?

She'd spent the last ten years fiercely defending her independence and found it difficult to cede even a scrap of it for fear of losing control of her life. Now she was responsible for another life growing inside her. She still couldn't quite get her head around the idea. Perhaps she wouldn't until her baby was born and they met face to face. But her baby would grow into a child, then a teenager, then an adult. The decisions she made now would affect his or her entire life. It was up to her to make the right choices to the best of her ability.

After breakfast, she headed down to the horse yards. During her explorations of the property, beyond the bounds of the house and garden, she always took her camera with her and had found a new delight in photographing Ned's horses.

Today she'd asked Ned if she could take photos of him on horseback and he'd agreed. He waved a greeting as he led Hero, his black thoroughbred gelding, out of his stable and towards the competition-sized sand arena. Freya had to turn a gasp of admiration into a pretend cough. The gasp wasn't for Hero—though he was a superb-looking horse—it was for Ned. He wore perfectly fitted riding breeches that outlined every muscle, a tight-fitting polo shirt that emphasised his broad shoulders and powerful torso, and high black boots that were quite the sexiest thing she'd ever seen him wear. She felt quite light-headed, not with low blood pressure but with a heady mix of admiration and desire.

She watched him mount his horse and take Hero through a series of warm-up exercises. On horseback

Ned was magnificent. A highly skilled athlete. This was Ned in his true environment. He'd fitted in in Toorak too, but no wonder he preferred it here.

He was training Hero for polocrosse, a game Freya had never heard of, but which he'd explained was a combination of polo and lacrosse, and sometimes referred to as rugby on horseback. He took Hero through a series of quick changes of direction.

Freya marvelled at the rapport and respect between rider and horse—each a superb specimen of their species. No use of cruel whips or spurs for Ned, just commands transmitted through his hands and legs, he'd explained. Love too. He obviously loved his horse as he loved his dog.

As he would love his child.

She pushed that thought quickly to the back of her mind, although she knew it wouldn't stay there for long. And certainly didn't entertain the thought of what it might be like if Ned loved *her*.

She set up her camera on a high tripod. On his advice, she stayed outside the railings that surrounded the arena. He'd explained that, while his horses were very well trained, and bred for temperament as well as skill, horses were flighty creatures and he wanted her safe at all times.

She signalled to Ned that she was about to start shooting. He cantered Hero towards her, in a tightly controlled pattern of turns. In her heart, she knew her shots of him would be good. Better than good. The combination of man and horse was awesome. She was loving this.

No one could be more ignorant about horses than her. It had taken her by surprise at how fascinated she had become by them, since she'd been back at Five and a Half Mile Creek. How she'd found a new interest in photographing horses. She was even growing to appreciate the scent of a clean, healthy horse.

Ned dismounted and swung himself over the fence. Freya hadn't fainted since that day in Hugh's studio when Ned had come to find her, but the sight of him, muscles defined, a slight sheen of sweat, his smile of intense satisfaction with his ride, almost made her swoon.

Her feelings towards him were all over the place, rocketing from elation in his company, plummeting to despair when she believed he was only interested in her because she was carrying his child. It was safer to keep her distance, to suppress that desire. There were enough hormones surging though her already, disrupting what should be a rational process of decision-making.

He fitted in here like the person he was—someone born to this level of wealth and prestige. Whereas she felt she would never fit. They might as well live on different planets. Yet her child would be born to this as Ned had been. How could she deny her child their birthright?

Back in Melbourne at his palatial penthouse, she had been aware that Ned wasn't just from the country, he belonged in the city too. But she and he came from two very different Melbournes. She had never been more aware of the differences in status and background between them. Much as she fought those feelings of insecurity, they continued to creep through, not a good combination with those fluctuating hormones.

Now, she resisted the urge to throw her arms around his neck and press her body to his; rather she kept her distance. 'Brilliant,' she said. 'I'm in awe of both you and Hero.'

Ned patted his horse on its sweat-flicked neck. 'He's a well-mannered, honest horse and a joy to ride.' Freya risked a cautious pat too. Ned handed the reins to the sta-

blehand to take Hero back to the state-of-the-art stables
and wash him down after his workout.

I'd like to wash Ned down after his ride.

Freya flushed as she fought the image of gorgeous Ned
naked in the shower and her soaping all over his body.

Darn hormones.

'I brought a snack from the house,' she said.

Although it was brilliantly sunny with a bright blue
sky, it was a chilly winter's day. When Ned pulled on
a thick padded jacket, she was glad he'd covered up all
that temptation. As she walked beside him she was careful not to brush against him or have any contact whatsoever. Just in case she acted on erotic impulse instead
of reasoned decision.

They headed towards a table and chairs that had been
set up for people who might want to watch the action on
the arena. It was a beautiful setting with graceful eucalypts planted in stands around the perimeter of the arena,
apple trees where the observers sat.

She'd brought some cookies and a flask of coffee from
the house for Ned. There was fizzy mineral water for her.
She could no longer stomach coffee, which she usually
enjoyed—another change caused by pregnancy.

Freya realised it was the first time she had been completely alone with Ned since she'd arrived here. She took
the nearest chair. He solicitously tucked a woollen rug
around her knees, although she was warmly dressed. He
flung himself down on the next chair and poured himself a mug of coffee. 'You're spending quite a bit of time
with the horses,' he said. 'When are you going to show
me some photos?'

'When I get some that really do the subjects justice,'
she said. 'It's quite a learning curve for me.'

'And you're a perfectionist. I have every confidence

you'll be brilliant at equine photography. There could be a business in it, you know. Look how you took to garden photography. I've told you how much my mother loved your shoot. Best birthday present I've ever given her, she told me.'

'I'm so pleased to hear that,' she said. She'd put her heart and soul into those photos. To please Ned, she realised, more than his mother.

'By the way, you might be interested to know my father gave her pearl earrings. He's obviously in the know about her birthstone.'

Freya laughed. 'That's cute. Did you see your mum for her birthday?'

'Of course. My parents are still in Italy but I flew out for a quick visit to surprise her. They'll be back in a few weeks.' He paused, put his mug back down on the table. 'You know, they'll be over the moon at the news of another grandchild.'

'You haven't told them, have you?' she said on a surge of panic. They'd agreed to keep the news secret even from his family, until they'd come to terms with what it meant to them both as parents.

'Not yet. But they'll have to know.'

'I realise that.' She sighed. 'This property, the history, your family, they're part of our baby's heritage, aren't they?' All this wealth and privilege and the security and certainty that came with that.

Ned went quiet and Freya realised it was the first time she had said *our* baby.

'Yes, they are,' Ned said, wondering if Freya realised the significance of what she'd just said. Up until now it had been *her* baby. 'And it's a wonderful heritage. Perhaps our child will be riding a pony on this very arena in a few years' time.'

'How old were you when you first got on a horse?'

'I'm told I begged to get up on horseback as soon as I could walk. By eighteen months I was being led on a miniature pony. I could ride her by myself when I was four. Strictly supervised, of course.'

'Do you think you're *born* a horse person?'

'I think *I* was born that way, but you can come to it at any age. Why do you ask?' He held his breath for her answer.

'I've never had anything to do with horses. But I'm fascinated by yours. They're so beautiful and I… I find myself wanting to be around them.'

Just the answer he wanted to hear.

Common ground at last.

'Do you think you'd ever want to ride one?'

She nodded. 'I actually think I would. A small, gentle one, that is. I watch you and think it must be an incredible feeling, to be in a partnership with the horse you're riding.'

'I could teach you,' he said. 'After the—'

'Baby is born,' she finished for him. 'Maybe.'

She wasn't going to commit to anything. He paused, cautious about where he wanted to take the conversation. 'Why do you dislike the country so much?'

She paused. 'You know, I've started to wonder that myself? I think it's because I've never actually spent time in the country. It's the unknown and…and I'm frightened of the unknown.'

Ned remembered how when Wil had first come here, he hadn't been able to sleep because it was so quiet and dark and he'd found the sounds of animals scary. Wil's aim had been to hitch a ride on a truck and run far away to live life on his own at age thirteen. He'd been a bird with broken wings too. Until Five and a Half Mile Creek and the love of his adoptive family had worked their magic on him. Ned wanted that magic for Freya too.

'Could it be that you fear the unknown because you were thrust into unknown territory every time you were placed with a new home? That must have been very scary for a child.'

'It was. So when I finally took charge of my life, I clung to the familiar. You know Richmond is next door to Abbotsford, where I lived with my grandparents? I haven't strayed far. Any time I want to, I can go there and see the house I lived in when they were alive and I had a family. The house is different now, of course, but it's still standing.'

'Could be a kind of security, not necessarily a bad thing. Like a little kid has a blankie. Wil's little Nina has one.'

Freya laughed. 'I'm too old for a blankie.'

But not for kindness and security. Everyone needed those, no matter how old they were. And he ached to give them to her.

'What about you?' she said. 'Why did you hate the city so much?'

'I think it goes back to my childhood.' Though now he realised the disaster of his relationship with Leanne had a lot to do with it too.

'You said you felt like you were in exile when you had to live in Brunswick, which, by the way, is a very cool place.'

He snorted. 'I certainly didn't think so. I felt like a caged animal. I was utterly miserable away from here. I... I think, deep down, I saw being sent to the city as a punishment.'

She frowned. 'Why is that?'

'Even when I was little, I was aware of the tensions between my parents and I'd do my best to try and make it better.'

'The peacemaker, even then.'

He shrugged. 'It didn't work though, did it? I failed. It was my fault Mum and Dad didn't want to stay together. Or that's how it seemed from my childish perspective. I was punished for my failure by being sent to the city. And yet, as my parents saw it, they were passionate people who just needed to sort out their differences—oblivious to the effect it was having on me. I must have been very difficult. I remember poor Hugh and Gordon trying to take me to fun things in town and I wouldn't have a bar of it.'

'You were stubborn even then.'

'Am I stubborn now?'

'Yes. Very.' She paused. 'I think we both are. Neither of us has budged on the barriers we think make a relationship between us impossible.'

'Except for the no-kids thing.'

'By accident, not design,' she reminded him.

'A happy accident.'

She smiled at that but then sobered again. 'We haven't considered any compromise. But, the way I see it, that compromise would be one-sided. You won't budge from your country life, I'd have to be the one to move here.'

'I've been thinking about that.'

Her brows rose. 'Really?'

'That surprises you?'

'Frankly, it does. That condition seemed non-negotiable.'

He turned in his chair so he faced her directly. 'You said something, that last visit, about how you were worried you wouldn't make a good mother because you had been neglected by your own mother.'

'I remember. Since then I've thought about that a lot. Now that I'm actually going to be a mother myself, I realise I did have a mother's love. Only it was from my grandmother. Also, I'm a very different person from my mother. I'm twenty-eight, not seventeen. I've got a career. Savings. And—'

'And, don't forget, the baby has a fantastic father who wants to be part of its life.'

'I was coming to that.' She smiled, her eyes sparkling. 'Our baby does indeed have a fantastic father.' She had been studiously avoiding his touch, but when he took her hand, encased now in a fine-knitted purple wool glove, she held it tight as if she didn't want to let him go.

'And a fantastic mother. I have no doubt about that.'

She looked down to her lap, didn't meet his gaze. 'I'm sorry about…about the way I handled the pregnancy. I should have told you as soon as I knew. It was just such a shock. Then I got so ill. And we'd parted so finally and I thought—'

'I know what you thought and we've sorted that now. But there's something I still have to sort. Let me get back to what I started to say. You were worried about the influence on you of your rather tragic young mother. Now think about my parents.'

She looked up. 'Well, I don't actually know them so I can't—'

'Why didn't I see it before? A creative young woman with a successful career comes out here to work her design magic on the house. Falls for the farmer who owns the place. She gives up her life in the city to move out to a place she thinks is—'

'Too far from civilisation,' Freya said.

'See the parallels?'

'I'm beginning to,' she said slowly.

'The wife is miserable. Her husband is out on the land all day. She misses her career, the stimulus of the city. They don't get the big family she'd hoped for, just one little boy. But her husband refuses to spend more time than he absolutely has to in Melbourne. Even though they own a mansion in Toorak and he's wealthy enough to employ a manager. He finally makes a compromise but not before he nearly loses his wife and son.'

'Replace *interior designer* with *photographer*. History repeats itself.'

He shook his head slowly to emphasise his point. 'Only you didn't let it. You called it quits and went back. The city girl with the purple hair saw sense, while the practical, steady farmer stayed blind to it.'

'True. But the irony is, the more I'm here, the more I love it. I'm beginning to think I could be happy living in the country. Not all the time, but some of the time.'

'Are you serious?'

'Surprisingly, yes. Your cousin Erin called in yesterday afternoon. From the sound of it, people out here have quite an active social life. I had no idea.'

'They do. We have to make our own fun but country life can be very social. Being able to ride a horse helps.'

'So Erin said. I liked her a lot, by the way. We're already friends.'

'Why didn't you tell me she was here?'

'She asked me not to.'

He frowned. 'And why would that be? I love her, but my cousin has a habit of putting her oar in where it's not wanted.'

'Well...'

'What did she say?'

'She told me to put you out of your misery and marry you.'

'What?'

'There's more. She said you obviously adore me and you'll be the world's best father.'

'How did she—? Did you tell her—?'

'She told me she breeds horses and she can always tell when a mare is in foal. And that she was clearly looking at a woman in the early stages of pregnancy.'

Ned fumed. Erin had better not have said anything to Freya about him having been *five times a groomsman and never a groom*. 'I'll have words with her.'

'Actually it was quite funny. She compared me to a brood mare—she actually used that term—you compared me to a sheep. What is it with you country folk?'

'We're well meaning,' he said. 'But maybe we need to get to the city more.'

'It might help,' she said with a laugh.

'Freya, I say that in jest but I mean it. Why do we have to be city girl and country boy? Why can't we each be both city and country?'

Freya stared at him. Her heart started to pound so loudly she was sure Ned must hear it. 'I'm not sure what you mean.'

He pushed his chair back but kept his gaze on her. 'I didn't expect to inherit Five and a Half Mile Creek for quite a few years more. Perhaps because I've come to the management of the property sooner rather than later, I've felt I had to prove myself. I've put it ahead of anything else, certainly ahead of my personal life.'

'Understandable,' she said. 'It's an immense responsibility.'

What was he trying to say?

'Then you tootled up the driveway in that little purple van, like something out of a story book, and—*wham*—turned my life upside down.'

'Did I?' she said.

He smiled. 'You know you did.' He reached out and brushed his fingers through her hair, sending shivers of awareness through her.

The first time he'd touched her since she'd been back.

'By the way, what's happened to your purple stripe? It's fading.'

'I'm being really careful what I eat and what I put in my body, and that includes hair-dye chemicals.'

'Pity. I like it. Promise you'll dye it again after the baby is born?'

'I… I promise.' She would do it for herself, not because it pleased him, she told herself. Heck, she'd do it for him if he found it pleasing. 'So you were saying about the city and country thing?'

'I'm not genetically completely country,' he said. 'As I've told you, there are things I like about city life too. Music in particular—jazz, classical concerts, rock concerts. Seeing your great little apartment made me remember how much fun I'd had there.' He frowned with concentration as he worked his way through his thoughts.

She leaned closer. 'What exactly are you trying to say, Ned?'

'That my life doesn't have to be strictly in the country. Neither does yours.'

'You mean it could be both?'

'We could live between here and the Toorak apartment. You liked it, didn't you?'

'It's fabulous. Although I would like to see it more warm and welcoming—a home, not a showcase.'

'You could keep up your career.'

'Your mother going off to Melbourne didn't work for your parents.'

He shook his head. 'I'm not talking about that kind of arrangement where you go back to the city by yourself for weeks on end. We'd go together. No separations.'

'But your work?'

'A lot of my work is behind a desk anyway and could be done as well in Toorak as it is here. My managers already do most of the hands-on work so I don't really need to do as much as I do.'

'But you do it because you like it. Wouldn't you miss it?'

'I'd miss you more,' he said slowly.

She squeezed his hand tightly, almost too overcome to speak. 'Th...thank you.'

'We could cut down on the travelling time by flying. You've seen how easy it is to fly by helicopter. We have a light plane too. You could get your pilot's licence if you wanted.'

Her, a pilot? Why not? 'You've really thought about this.'

His mouth twisted. 'I've had a lot of time on my own to think.'

Ned.

She hated to think of him being on his own. She put the hand he wasn't holding on his cheek and, for a long, still moment, looked into his eyes. What she saw there made her heart turn over.

She let her hand drop. 'It makes sense,' she said, excitement starting to fizz and spark.

'One more thing. I didn't like boarding school. As I suspect we're both family folk at heart, our child might not like it either.'

She shuddered at her ever-present memories of her disrupted childhood. 'You could be right about that.' No way would her child ever be treated as she had been.

'Our schedules might be determined by term time as well as by seasonal farming events. Elementary school at our nearest town, Hilltop—'

'You'd send your child to a state school?' That surprised her.

'I went there—my parents thought it important. It's where you form friendships that are important out here where families are far-flung. But there isn't a high school, so that would be a private school in Melbourne. What do you think?'

'It sounds rather wonderful, a perfect compromise, in fact. But I—'

He put up his hand again. 'You don't have to say anything. I've dumped a lot on you. I just want you to think that the compromise doesn't have to be one-sided. And that I really want to be a good father to our child.'

Freya was so tightly wrapped in the rug, that she struggled to get out of her chair. Ned laughed and pulled her to her feet. Then she was in his arms, and they were kissing as if it hadn't been more than two months since their last kiss. How she'd missed his kisses, his hugs, *him*.

She felt instantly aroused and wondered if the hay stacked in the barn would make a good spot to make love. But no, that would be too scandalous. Later, perhaps, when there was no one else around, it could be fun though.

'Ned, you're right. We do need to think about this. But the way my thoughts are going, I… I suggest you ask me again to marry you fairly soon.'

'Or you could ask me.'

'I find myself feeling surprisingly traditional about this. It has to be you doing the proposing.'

'I'll come up with something special,' he said with his endearing grin.

'In the meantime, I have a complaint about the guest room.'

'I'll get onto Marian, I—'

She put her finger across his lips. 'It's not something Marian can fix. You see, the bed is too big and too lonely without you...'

He placed his hand on her tummy for the first time, and she thrilled to the protective gesture. 'Is it okay to, uh...you know...when you're pregnant?'

'Please don't tell me what the situation is with brood mares. But my doctor says it's perfectly okay to make love. I say, the sooner the better.'

'You don't hear me complaining,' he said as he put his arm around her and walked her towards the house.

CHAPTER THIRTEEN

NEXT MORNING, WORKING on her laptop, Freya scrolled through the photos of Ned riding Hero she had taken the day before. They were good, really good. She had captured the speed, agility and power of the man on horseback but also the intensity of the communication between man and animal.

That both Ned and his very valuable horse were extremely good-looking did help. But it was the spirit of the images that made her catch her breath. She loved her work as a commercial photographer but had always wanted to work artistically too, perhaps towards an exhibition. Maybe this change in her life marked more exciting new directions than she had imagined.

She lingered on one image where Ned was looking straight at the camera and grinning at her. It wasn't the most artistic of the shots but she loved it.

She loved him.

She had fought hard against falling in love with Ned, but it had been a losing battle. In another parallel with his parents' story, she had fallen for the boss of Five and a Half Mile Creek. She wouldn't go so far as to say love at first sight, although she couldn't actually pinpoint the moment. Ned with his kindness and strength and—yes—hotness had breached the barriers around her heart.

Today, Ned was going to propose again, and this time she would accept without hesitation. There was no reason not to. She loved him and she was pregnant with his baby. A baby who she would make sure had a much better childhood than she'd had. Not in terms of material wealth, although there appeared to be that in spades. But to be born to happily married parents was a great gift. Parents who loved each other.

Ned hadn't actually said he loved her but then she hadn't told him how she felt either. Not with words, anyway. Yesterday, she'd been surprised when he hadn't responded when she'd told him his cousin Erin had said he adored her—either to confirm or deny it. But she didn't doubt that she loved him and she would let him know that in both words and actions.

She was working in the room that had originally been Ned's mother's design studio. As soon as he'd brought her here last week, Ned had allocated it to her as her personal space. His study was next door. She loved this room as much as she loved his study. The light was perfect, and it opened out onto one of her favourite parts of the garden.

The winter garden had its own stark beauty. Although many of the shrubs and trees had lost their leaves, there were big, fat red rosehips on most of the roses. Pansies and hellebores gave patches of subtle colour in mauves and pinks and purples. She would like to document every season in this garden. Perhaps she could even get interested in gardening. Possibly it was something she could bond over with her future mother-in-law.

Last night, after Ned had gone to sleep—the joy of knowing she would sleep in his arms every night of their lives!—she had thought about the wider implications of marrying Ned. She would gain a new family. Her baby would be born into a family of loving parents, grandparents, numerous cousins and an uncle and aunt. When she finally reunited with Wil and met Georgia it would be as their sister-in-law. How wonderfully that had turned out.

Before she settled back to her screen, she patted Molly on the head where she lay at her feet. It had been unnerving—and at first a little frightening—the way Ned's dog had attached herself to Freya on her return to Five and a Half Mile Creek.

Ned said Molly had appointed herself as Freya's protector. Maybe the old dog instinctively knew she carried her beloved master's child. After all, she'd had pups of her own. At first, Freya had shooed her away but Molly had been persistent. Once Freya had lost her fear, she had come to welcome the sweet animal's company. And Molly was very cooperative about having her photo taken.

Freya bent her head again to culling the images of yesterday's shoot. So many to pick from. She paused at one where Ned's head was angled as if he was listening to what Hero had to say to him about the manoeuvre they were making. Ned would love it. In fact it was such a good shot she decided to print it out to show him. It could actually be worthy of framing.

There was a printer in Ned's office. She'd already used it so the link was in her laptop. No need to disturb Ned down at the admin building. Besides, she wanted it to be a surprise.

She went next door into Ned's office, accompanied by Molly, her claws clicking companionably on the wooden floor.

Ned's computer stood quietly on his desk. As she hunted for photographic paper, she accidentally knocked his mouse and his screen brightened into life.

She would never snoop. But she couldn't escape the image on the screen. It was a personal page on one of the big dating sites.

Ned's page.

Her mouth dried. What was this doing open? There was a nice enough photo of Ned, though she could do a lot better—he looked a bit self-conscious. And there… there was his profile with a list of requirements for his ideal wife.

Freya felt the blood drain from her face and she had to hang onto the edge of his desk for support as she read the particulars of Ned's ideal wife.

1. Genuine enjoyment of country life essential.
2. Management experience to help run the business would be advantageous. Accountant or lawyer ideal.
3. Love of animals, particularly horses. A vet or vet nurse would be very welcome.
4. An interest in gardening.
5. A good cook.
6. Conservative, country-focused values.

What a pompous list. Nausea rose in her throat. She didn't meet one of his requirements. Not one. The gardening was only a new possibility. No wonder he wanted to encourage her interest in horses. Freya cursed a long string of the impressive curse words she had learned during her time in care. Molly whimpered, aware of her distress.

Ned hadn't out-and-out asked for a woman with childbearing hips but that requirement was implicit in the rest of his requirements. She was ahead of the game there, she thought cynically.

She was bearing his child, the heir to Five and a Half Mile Creek and a fortune. That heir would need to be legitimate. He'd actually told her that Hudson children were not born out of 'wedlock'. Of course he wanted to get married to legitimise his offspring—no matter how unsuitable the mother was as a wife. And then what for her? Find herself discarded and facing a custody battle she'd never be able to afford to fight?

How could she have got him so wrong?

Her first instinct was to run away, back to her apartment in Melbourne. But Ned had driven her here and she had no means of escape. Her van was parked back at the studio.

Again, she was trapped. Only this time she didn't feel horror at being trapped, rather an intense wave of sadness, because she had been beginning to think of Five and a Half Mile Creek as home. And Ned as the man for her.

Freya dragged her feet out into the hallway and back to the studio. There was an elegant, comfortable armchair that faced the view of the garden. She had already pinpointed it as a perfect chair to sit in while breastfeeding her baby.

Now she flopped into it, exhausted, shaken, *betrayed*. Molly gave a huge doggy sigh, circled, lay down and rested her head on Freya's feet. Freya closed her eyes against her frantic, anguished thoughts and tried to make sense of her future.

Because it couldn't be here.

It wasn't every day a guy got to propose to the woman he loved. Ned was on such a high, he was whistling the tune of Mendelssohn's *Wedding March* as he strode along the corridor to his study. For some sentimental reason, he

wanted to be holding his lucky horseshoe when he asked
Freya to be his wife.

He headed to where the horseshoe was propped, ends
up as it should be, and stopped suddenly. Odd that his
computer monitor should be on; even odder that Freya's
laptop was on his desk. He went to move her laptop, accidentally nudged his keyboard, and his screen lit up.

Hell.

Stricken, he stared at the screen. That stupid list on
that stupid dating site.

Freya had seen it.

Who knew what conclusions she might have drawn?
He cursed long and loud.

Ned picked up his horseshoe—he really had need of it
now—put it in his pocket, and headed into Freya's studio.

She was lying back in the armchair, with Molly
stretched out by her feet. For a moment, he watched her.
Freya's eyes were closed but Ned wasn't convinced she
was asleep. Her breathing pattern didn't seem authen-
tic. Molly looked up at him, thumped her tail in greeting. He liked how his dog was so protective of Freya and
was relieved Molly didn't growl at him for hurting her
new mistress.

Because Freya must be hurt. Really hurt. And who
could blame her? No wonder she didn't want to open
her eyes.

Ned squatted down on his haunches next to the chair,
where he could look directly into her face. 'Freya? Are you
awake?' A suspicious flickering of her eyelashes, but no
reply. 'Blink once if you hate me.' A definite blink. As to
be expected. 'So you're not talking to me?' Another blink.

'I won't even ask if you think I'm the stupidest guy
on earth. Because you'll wear your eyelids out blinking
your agreement.' No blink.

'The dating site. I never used it. Not once. But the sub-scription came up for renewal and I had the page open to cancel it. I forgot to close it down.' Inwardly he groaned. 'That list.' Her mouth tightened. 'I wrote it after Wil and Georgia's wedding. I was so happy for them but it made me realise how lonely I was. How much I wanted a wife and family of my own. Your new friend, my cousin Erin, wouldn't stop teasing me about my single status. But it's impossible to meet anyone out here you haven't known all your life. A dating site seemed a reasonable option.'

He paused. 'Are you listening? I don't want to be giv-ing this speech for Molly's benefit. Two blinks if you're listening to me.' Two blinks.

'Okay. I'll continue my spiel, which, by the way, I'm finding quite humiliating.' Was that a slight upward curve of her mouth? 'I hadn't had a lot of luck with love, right back to schooldays and Teresita. Then there was the di-saster with Leanne. The list was more a defensive thing, really. I didn't dare put down into writing that I'd de-cided…that…that love hurt too much for me to pursue. I could do without it. Still listening?' Blink.

'Then along you came. And with you came something I had never imagined. I was enchanted with you from the second I met you.' He paused. 'Can you please open your eyes? Maybe talk to me. I'm really sorry you saw that list. Gutted in fact. But it means nothing.'

Slowly Freya's eyes opened. They were wary and tear-stained. The sight wrenched at his heart. He hated to see her hurt, to know that *he* had hurt her. Slowly, she sat up straight and swivelled to face him. Now it seemed he was kneeling in supplication before her—which seemed entirely appropriate.

'I don't meet one criterion on your list.' Her voice broke. 'Not one.'

'They were stupid criteria for a wife.'

'They read more like an ad for a housekeeping manager.'

Ned winced.

'I expect she would have come wielding a stock whip,' Freya said.

'I'm impressed you know what a stock whip is. You're really turning into a country girl.'

'Ned,' she said warningly. 'Don't push it. You're lucky I'm even hearing you out.'

'I know. And I've got a new wife wish-list.'

She frowned. 'I don't know what you mean.'

'It's much shorter than the old one. Do you want to hear it?'

She blinked.

He grinned. And held on tight to his lucky horseshoe.

'I haven't written the list down, but I'll pretend I'm reading it out. Try not to interrupt me.'

'Okay,' she said.

He thought on his feet—or rather on his knees. 'One. Must make me laugh and help me not to take myself so seriously. Two. Must love the colour purple. Three. Must accept that she is loved from the depths of his heart by her husband-to-be. Four. Must be named Freya Delaney.'

He was suddenly too choked up to think of any more.

Freya leaned towards him, her eyes glistening. 'I think I might fit those criteria.'

Ned got to his feet and pulled her up from her chair to look at him. He cupped her face in his hands—her lovely face that had become so utterly precious to him. 'Does that mean you'll do me the honour of becoming my wife?'

'Do you want me to blink or say *yes*?'

He laughed. 'Please say *yes*.'

'Yes,' she said immediately. Then blinked as well. 'Nothing would make me happier than to be your wife.'

He kissed her, long and sweet and tenderly. 'I love you, Freya.'

'I love you, too, Ned. From…from the depths of my heart.'

He took her left hand in his, and held it up. 'I haven't got you a ring.'

'I don't expect…'

'There's a safe in the next room containing a collection of family jewellery. Wil gave Georgia our grandmother's emerald ring. I can have my choice of ring for my bride. But I would rather you designed your own engagement ring, unique to you. I thought…amethyst and diamonds.'

Her smile wobbled at the edges. 'Of course I would prefer that, Ned. You know me so well already.'

'I felt I knew you as soon as I met you.'

'I had the same feeling,' she said. 'As if…as if we were meant to be.'

'Your ring will have nothing to do with the past, just our present.'

'And our future, Ned,' she said, rising on tiptoe to kiss him. 'Our wonderful, wonderful future.'

EPILOGUE

Six weeks later

BECAUSE FREYA HAD never intended to marry, she'd never thought much about weddings. But her wonderful Ned loved weddings and all that went with them.

Ned had been a groomsman five times and was—by her own definition—the marrying kind. As soon as they'd got engaged, he'd been full of plans for a traditional wedding in the country town church where generations of his family had wed. Because she loved him, and in the spirit of compromise they intended to follow in their life together, Freya had agreed to a church wedding.

But she'd cringed at the idea of a formal ceremony, held in a church packed with guests she didn't know and who didn't know her. Ned, however, wanted to celebrate their marriage in the company of his family, his many friends, and all the Five and a Half Mile Creek employees, in the Hudson family tradition.

Again she and Ned had compromised and agreed to an intimate, family-only wedding in the church, followed the next day by a big party for everyone at Five and a Half Mile Creek. There, Ned could proudly introduce Freya as his wife to the greater community.

So now Freya stood in the vestibule of the flower-bedecked church, ready to make her walk down the aisle towards Ned, where he waited for her with his best man, Wil, and his father. His parents, Jackie and Dave, had flown back from Italy for the wedding and Freya and Ned had wanted them to be part of the ceremony.

First down the aisle was tiny Nina, Wil and Georgia's toddler daughter, determined to show off her new-found walking skills, looking adorable in a flouncy white dress with a huge bow at the back and cute little satin shoes. Freya couldn't help but wonder if she might have a little girl, or a little boy like Ned. Her heart swelled at the thought. Either would be loved.

Halfway down the aisle, Nina tired and sat down on her bottom. Amid fond laughter from everyone else, the littlest attendant was then swept up in the arms of her mother, dark-haired Georgia, who, holding her daughter, continued down the aisle. She was followed by Ned's cousin, red-haired Erin. Both bridesmaids wore simple long gowns in different shades of lavender and carried purple iris. Jackie was next, in an elegant purple silk suit she'd bought in Italy for the wedding. Freya had warmed to her future mother-in-law the minute she'd met her, and they were already close. Ned's father had welcomed her with a big hug and had taken it upon himself to school her in all things country and the history of the Hudson family.

Once all the attendants reached the altar, the organist—Ned had insisted on an organist—struck up the wedding march processional and Freya prepared to walk down the aisle. She'd thought she'd be nervous, but she wasn't. She was exhilarated and excited about taking her place next to Ned.

'Ready?' asked Hugh.

'Looking forward to it,' she said.

Both Hugh and burly, bearded Gordon were accompanying her down the aisle. Not to 'give her away'—she didn't agree with that part of the ceremony—but to represent her family. The two men weren't family by blood, but they were family of the heart to not only her but also Ned.

Family.

She had longed for it since she'd lost her nanna and now she had found her place with Ned and his family. A week ago, she'd reunited with Wil to find the bond of friendship still strong after all those intervening years. She'd made another friend in his wife. Georgia had sobbed with joy that her husband had met again the girl who'd been one of his very few friends in a dark childhood, and who was now marrying his beloved brother.

'Let's go,' Freya said to her escorts, as she looked ahead to where Ned waited for her. He looked very handsome in a morning suit. She had to force herself to step sedately as she made her way up the aisle, when what she wanted to do was lift up the skirts of her long gown and run to him.

As Ned stood at the altar with his brother and father by his side, he realised Freya had been absolutely right to keep their wedding ceremony simple and limited to the people who were closest to them. The warmth of his inclusive family—who had embraced her with love and welcome—had already worked magic on his beautiful Freya, who was learning to trust and love in return. And their baby would be born into that caring circle.

Now he watched, with hammering heart and dry mouth, the exquisite vision floating her way up the aisle towards him. She was wearing an elegant, full-skirted white dress with long, tight sleeves—flattering on her newly rounded figure. A voluminous white veil trailed behind her.

More wings to bring her to him.

Purple and white flowers were twisted through her hair and in her bouquet.

'She's lovely, Ned, in every way,' Wil said to him, in a low voice. 'I can't tell you how happy I am that you and Freya are getting married. When we were kids, I wanted Tegan for a sister. Now she finally will be.'

'I've thanked you in my head, so many times, for rescuing her from that dangerous situation.' Ned spoke to Wil but he couldn't keep his eyes off Freya.

'Now she has you to look out for her,' said Wil. 'Things couldn't have worked out better, could they? It's as if it was fated to be.'

'You could say that,' Ned said, watching as his bride moved nearer. That first day he'd thought Freya had floated in from the rose garden on fairy wings. She'd proved to be only too earthy and real and he loved her all the more for it.

As Freya and her escorts moved closer, Ned noticed another one of the curiously smug glances between Hugh and his mother. Earlier, he'd even caught them in a self-congratulatory fist-bump. Something about that exchange made him wonder why the house had needed photographing at all, when his mother was retired.

Then all he could think about was Freya, as Hugh handed her to him and he took her hand in his to draw her close. 'Hello, soon-to-be-wife,' he murmured.

'Hello, soon-to-be-husband,' she whispered, with the lovely, gap-toothed smile that had entranced him from the beginning, her eyes luminous with love. 'Do you have your lucky horseshoe in your pocket?'

'All ready to catch our good luck.'

As they stood facing each other in front of the priest, their family members stood close by, as if they, too, were making vows—pledging to help support the young couple on their journey into marriage and parenthood and a lifetime of love.

His beloved Freya, who'd said she would never marry but was marrying him; who never wanted to have children but was carrying his baby; repeated her vows in in a clear, steady voice that rang with sincerity and commitment. He was so overcome with emotion that he choked out the words, although he hoped with equal sincerity. But he didn't stumble as he slipped the simple platinum wedding band next to the amethyst-and-diamond ring already on the third finger of her left hand, then held his hand steady as Freya slipped a matching band onto his ring finger.

'I now pronounce you man and wife,' proclaimed the priest.

Ned had never heard such wonderful words.

'I love you, wife,' he said.

'I love you, dearest husband,' she murmured back. 'For ever and for always.'

Ned didn't wait for anyone to give him permission to kiss his bride, but pulled her to him and claimed her mouth with his. She wound her arms around his neck and kissed him back and they kissed and kissed to the accompaniment of cheering and clapping. They only pulled away, laughing and joyous, to accept heartfelt congratulations and well wishes for their new life together.

* * * * *

THE TEXAN
TRIES AGAIN

STELLA BAGWELL

To my beloved editor, Gail Chasan.
This one is for you!

Chapter One

"If I hear anyone mention that damned bridal bouquet one more time I'm going to scream," Emily-Ann Broadmoor muttered. "Catching the flowers at *your* wedding is not going to get *me* a husband. The whole idea is a silly old wives' tale. So why do you keep harping on the subject?"

Unaffected by her friend's annoyed outburst, Camille Waggoner chuckled and used her toe to push the wooden glider into a rocking motion.

From their comfortable seat beneath a large, old cottonwood, Emily-Ann could see a portion of the Hollister family, along with many friends and ranch hands, beginning to gather beneath the roof that covered the wide patio behind the Three Rivers Ranch house. Tonight, Maureen Hollister, the matriarch of the family, was throwing a barbecue for two reasons. For the first time in more than two years, Camille, the prodigal daughter, was back for a short visit. And second, the massive ranch was welcoming a new foreman.

"I'm not harping," Camille said, "and you don't think the folklore is nonsense. That's why you're afraid. That's why you don't want me, or anyone else, suggesting that your time as a single woman is coming to an end."

Emily-Ann stared at her best friend since elementary school, until the absurdity of Camille's prediction caused her to burst out laughing.

"Camille, pregnancy has done something to your brain. You're losing touch with reality."

Smiling smugly, Camille pressed her left hand to her growing belly and Emily-Ann didn't miss the diamond wedding ring sparkling on her finger. Camille Hollister had become Matthew Waggoner's wife nearly four months ago in a beautiful little Christmas ceremony down on Red Bluff, the Hollisters' second Arizona ranch.

Since then, Emily-Ann had never seen her friend so happy. And why not? After being the foreman at Three Rivers Ranch for many years, Matthew was now manager of Red Bluff, along with being one of the sexiest men to ever step foot in Yavapai County and beyond. Plus, he was madly in love with Camille. How could any woman be so lucky?

Certainly not herself, Emily-Ann thought drearily. She considered herself fortunate if she got a wink from the old man behind the meat counter at Wendell's Groceries.

"My thinking has never been clearer," Camille spoke concisely, then reached over and gave Emily-Ann's hand an affectionate pat. "I'm so glad you could make the party tonight. The two of us haven't had a chance to spend time together. Not since my wedding and that was such a hectic occasion with so many people around us that we hardly had a chance to talk."

"We've talked on the phone several times since your wedding."

Camille frowned. "Not the same. When we have a conversation I want to see you."

"You should've told me," Emily-Ann said dryly. "The next time I call we'll do FaceTime."

Camille chuckled. "That's not the same, either. So what have you been doing with yourself since the wedding? Other than running Conchita's?"

Conchita's was a little coffee and pastry shop located on a quiet street in Wickenburg. Since Emily-Ann was the only employee, other than the owner who prepared the pastries, the job kept her very busy six days a week. The salary she made was never going to do more than pay her rent and other living expenses, but she loved the job.

"I don't have time to do much," Emily-Ann reasoned.

"You're still doing online college classes, aren't you?"

Emily-Ann shrugged. "Yes. Just a few more hours and I'll get my degree. But sometimes I wonder why I chose such a field to get into. I'll probably make a miserable nurse. Taking care of a sick cat isn't like tending an ailing human."

"I happen to think you'll make a wonderful nurse. When your mother's health started to fail, you were always so good with her."

"I had to do what I could. We couldn't afford a real nurse to take care of Mom," Emily-Ann replied, not wanting to think about that especially hard time in her life.

"Well, there's always a demand for nurses." Camille smiled encouragingly. "You should be able to get a job right in Wickenburg."

"Making coffee for my friends would be far less stressful," Emily-Ann said frankly. "But Mom had a dream for me and I don't want to disappoint her."

Camille slanted her a meaningful glance. "Just like I didn't want to disappoint Dad about getting a college degree. Now your mom and my dad are both gone. But let's not dwell on that sad stuff tonight. It's party time." With a cheerful smile, Camille reached over and hooked her arm through Emily-Ann's. "And it looks like Jazelle has just arrived with a cart to restock the bar. Let's go get something to drink."

The two women walked across the backyard to join the group of people mingling on the patio. There were far more guests than Emily-Ann had expected and she was glad she'd taken extra care with her appearance this evening. Even though her mustard-colored blouse and dark green skirt weren't anything fancy they flattered her curvy figure and she'd taken the time to braid a top portion of her hair and pin it to one side. She'd never be beautiful like Camille or her sister, Vivian, but for tonight she felt as though she looked decent.

"Emily-Ann! I didn't know you had arrived!"

At the sound of the female voice, Emily-Ann turned to see Maureen Hollister hurrying toward her. The lovely woman in her midsixties gathered her up in a tight hug.

"I'm so glad you could come tonight and be with Camille," she said happily. "My two little gingers. It's just like old times seeing you girls together."

"Except that now we don't have our matching bangs and Groovy Girls dolls," Emily-Ann joked.

Maureen laughed. "Too bad you grew out of those days. But I have the dolls packed away in a trunk of toys. Someday you two might want to give them to your daughters."

"Uh—in about three months or so, if Camille has

a girl, she'll need hers," Emily-Ann told her. "But you might as well keep mine packed away in mothballs."

Maureen wagged a finger at her. "You're forgetting, honey. You caught Camille's wedding bouquet. Your time is coming!"

Laughing, Camille rolled her eyes toward Emily-Ann. "Don't scream."

Confused by her daughter's remark, Maureen frowned. "Scream? Why would she want to do something like that?"

"Nothing important," Emily-Ann answered, then quickly steered the conversation in a different direction. "Thank you for inviting me tonight, Maureen. I can't wait to eat some of Reeva's barbecue. Is there anything I can do to help in the kitchen?"

"Not a thing. I want you and Camille to stay out of the kitchen. Katherine and Vivian are helping with the food and Isabelle and Roslyn, bless their hearts, have volunteered to keep all the little ones upstairs and occupied. So everything is under control, I think." She looked at Camille. "I need to get back to the kitchen. Be sure and introduce Emily-Ann to the folks she hasn't met."

Maureen hurried away just as a group of men sauntered over to the bar, where Jazelle, the Hollisters' housekeeper, was mixing drinks. Spotting them, Camille grabbed Emily-Ann's arm and tugged her in the direction of the men.

"Come on, I want you to say hi to my brothers."

Emily-Ann had never been a bashful person and she loved meeting people, which was the main reason she loved her job at the coffee shop. But for some reason tonight, she felt hesitant about joining the group of men to say hello.

"I honestly don't think they want to waste their time with me, Camille," Emily-Ann suggested. "Let's just get a drink and go back to the glider."

Camille frowned at her. "Since when have you turned into a wallflower? Now quit being ridiculous and come on."

Camille tugged her forward and Emily-Ann had no choice but to follow her friend over to the group of men, all of whom were dressed casually in jeans and boots and various shades and styles of cowboy hats.

"Hi, guys," Camille greeted. "I thought you all might want to say hello to Emily-Ann."

Holt, the middle sibling of the Hollister clan, stepped forward with a wide grin. "I want to do more than say hi. I want a hug from Little Red."

Laughing at the nickname Holt had given her years ago, Emily-Ann hugged the tall, good-looking cowboy, who'd often been considered the wild playboy of the bunch. Now the horseman was settled down with a wife and new baby son.

"Hello, Holt." Stepping back from his affectionate hug, she smiled at him. "How does it feel to be a new father?"

The twinkle in his eyes was the same sort of joy Emily-Ann saw on Camille's face. Yes, the Hollister siblings were all happily married with children and babies now. The reality left Emily-Ann feeling as though she was standing on the porch in the cold rain, while everyone inside the house was cheery and warm and together.

"Having a son is just incredible," Holt responded to her question. "Even if I have to get up in the night to change diapers."

"Hah!" Blake, the eldest of the Hollister brothers and manager of Three Rivers Ranch, reacted with a short laugh. "I think I'll ask Isabelle just how many diapers you've changed in the wee hours of the morning."

"Not nearly as many as me," Chandler, the veterinarian of the group, boasted.

Chuckling, Joseph, the deputy and youngest Hollister, gouged an elbow in Chandler's ribs. "That's what you think, brother. Blake has us all beat. He has twins."

"Thank you, Joe," Blake said with an appreciative grin.

Camille pulled a playful face at her brothers. "I didn't bring Emily-Ann over here to listen to you four boast about your diaper changing. You're supposed to be saying hello to her."

"Hello, Emily-Ann!" they all said in loud unison.

Emily-Ann could feel a blush stinging her cheeks.

It was true she'd known the wealthy Hollister family for years, but since Camille had moved away, she'd not been here to the ranch for any reason and she felt a little awkward about showing up tonight. In spite of Camille being a dear friend, that didn't put Emily-Ann on their social calendar.

Just as that self-deprecating thought went through her mind, Blake stepped forward and gathered her up in a hug. "I see you at Conchita's fairly often, but it's nice to have you here on the ranch. Jazelle is mixing drinks. Tell me what you'd like and I'll get it."

"Not yet," Camille told him, her gaze searching the ever-growing crowd. "I thought Matthew and Tag might be over here with you guys. Where—oh, I see them coming now."

Grabbing her by the upper arm, Camille tugged her forward and Emily-Ann followed, albeit reluctantly. She was fairly acquainted with Matthew, Camille's husband, but the tall cowboy with him was a total stranger to her. A wide-brimmed cowboy hat, the color of dark coffee, shaded a tanned face with roughly honed features. His eyes were hooded beneath a pair of dark brows, while his chin jutted forward just enough to give him a dash of arrogance. Or it could be the way he was looking at her, as though she was a geek, or worse, that made him seem arrogant. Either way, Emily-Ann would've been happy to avoid the man entirely. But she couldn't escape the tight hold Camille had on her arm. Not without making a scene.

"So you two finally made it to the party?" Camille teased, directing the question mostly to her husband.

Matthew's grin was a bit guilty. "Sorry, honey, I've been showing Tag some of the more important things down at the ranch yard."

"Uh-huh," she said with a perceptive smile, "like the saddles and tack and training arena and cow barn and—"

Matthew stopped her with a laugh. "We didn't get that far," he said, then inclined his head toward Emily-Ann. "Nice to see you again, Emily-Ann. Glad you could make it to the party."

"Thank you, Matthew," Emily-Ann replied, while trying not to pay extra notice to the tall, hard-looking cowboy standing next to him. From this distance, she could see his eyes were warm brown and his hair a mixture of rust and chocolate. "It's wonderful having you and Camille back at Three Rivers. Even if it's just for a short while."

She felt Camille's hand urging her to take a step toward the foreman, and though she wanted to glower at her friend, Emily-Ann purposely kept a smile fixed upon her face.

"Tag, I'd like for you to meet Emily-Ann Broadmoor, my best friend since childhood," Camille introduced. "And Emily-Ann, this is Taggart O'Brien. He's going to be Three Rivers's new foreman."

The man's lips curved into a semblance of a polite smile and Emily-Ann found her gaze transfixed on his mouth. The lower lip was full and plush, while the top was thin and tilted upward just enough to show a glimpse of white teeth.

Extending his hand to her, he said, "Hello, Ms. Broadmoor. It's a pleasure to meet you."

A strange roaring in her ears very nearly drowned out the sound of his voice and, in spite of feeling as though she'd suddenly fallen into some sort of trance, she managed to place her hand in his.

"Thank you," she told him, while her swirling senses recognized the hard-calloused skin of his palm and the warmth of his fingers curling around hers. "Nice meeting you, too, Mr. O'Brien."

With an impatient roll of her eyes, Camille interjected, "Oh, this just won't do at all. Surely you two can use your first names. We're all family around here."

"I'm fine with it," Taggart said. "If Ms. Broadmoor doesn't mind."

"First of all, Emily-Ann is a Miss, not a Ms.," Camille corrected him, then turned a clever smile on Emily-Ann. "And she doesn't mind. Do you?"

For the life of her, she couldn't figure out why Camille was making such a big to-do out of this introduction. It wasn't like she'd be seeing the man after tonight. And from the stoic look on his face, he was totally bored by this whole meeting anyway.

Well, that was okay with her, Emily-Ann decided. She wasn't exactly thrilled about exchanging hellos with this hard-looking cowboy, either. With that thought in mind, she pulled her shoulders back and tried to forget she'd always been the poor little girl who lived on the shabby side of town.

"I don't mind," she answered, then forced her gaze back to Taggart O'Brien. "Everyone calls me Emily-Ann."

The faint smile on his lips twisted to a wider slant. "Well, everyone calls me Tag, or a few other things I shouldn't repeat."

He released her hand and Emily-Ann resisted the urge to wipe her sizzling palm against the side of her skirt.

"Tag is from West Texas," Matthew informed her. "This is his first trip to Arizona and definitely his last. The Hollisters will see to that. He's going to be a permanent fixture around here."

"Welcome to Arizona, Tag," Emily-Ann said with genuine sincerity. "I hope you like it here—in spite of the heat."

His brown eyes were roaming her face as though she had two noses or something equally strange. The sensation was definitely unsettling, she thought, almost as much as the unadorned ring finger on his left hand. Surely this sexy-looking rancher was married. From the looks of him he had to be somewhere in his thirties. Plenty old enough to have a wife and kids stashed away somewhere.

He said, "I'm used to hot weather. And from everything I've seen since I arrived, I think I'm going to like it here just fine. The Hollisters are great and the area is beautiful."

"Yes, the Hollisters are the best," Emily-Ann murmured, then purposely turned her gaze on Camille. "Uh—don't you think it's time we go get that drink?"

"Sure! I can't have anything alcoholic, but Jazelle will mix up something tasty for me." She looped her arm through Emily-Ann's, then cast a pointed look at her husband. "Would you men care to join us? It shouldn't be long before they start bringing out the food."

Smiling just for her, Matthew wrapped his hand around his wife's free arm. "I don't know about Tag, but I'd love to."

Taggart hated parties, even when they were being held partly in his honor, such as this one. He'd never been good at mixing and mingling with people and being single made everything more awkward when he was introduced to the unwed women in the group. He didn't have a wife to help him escape unwanted company, or to give him a reason to excuse himself.

Yet in this case, he wasn't looking around for an escape route. Emily-Ann Broadmoor didn't appear to be one of those boring cookie-cutter young women who spent hours trying to improve their appearance and five minutes or less educating themselves on things that actually mattered.

She wasn't batting her long lashes at him or slanting him a coy look. She wasn't grabbing his arm and hanging on as though she'd suddenly lost the strength to stand on her own two feet. No, this woman was refreshingly different, he thought. She might even be one he'd like to get to know as a friend. There couldn't be any harm in that, he assured himself.

"I'm more than ready for a drink and dinner." Purposely stepping up to the pretty redhead's side, he offered her his arm. "What about you, Emily-Ann?"

For a moment he thought she was going to ignore him or simply walk away, but then she smiled and wrapped an arm through his.

"Thank you, Tag."

The four of them moved slowly through the crowd toward the bar area where the four Hollister brothers were sipping cocktails and chatting with a few of the ranch hands. It was a sight that Taggart would've never seen on the Flying W back in Texas. Once the Armstrong family had taken over, the hands were never invited to mix with the employers, unless it was to take orders.

Hoping to shake away the unpleasant thoughts, he glanced down at Emily-Ann. She wasn't exactly a beautiful woman, but she was very pretty in a unique sort of way. Her square face had a wide plush mouth, high cheekbones and a sprinkling of pale freckles across the bridge of her upturned nose. Long brown lashes shaded eyes that were emerald green. Or, at least, that had been his first impression of their color. Until she'd turned her head and the light had hit them from a different angle. Then her eyes had taken on the color of a spring leaf that hadn't yet ripened in the sun.

"Do you come out here to the ranch often?" he asked her as they followed Matthew and Camille through a group of milling guests.

"When Camille lived here I visited the ranch quite often. Now I don't have much reason to drive out here. Most of the family stops by the coffee shop where I work, so I see them regularly."

Ahead of them, Matthew and Camille paused to acknowledge a small group of old acquaintances. While Taggart and Emily-Ann stood waiting, he turned his gaze back to the redhead. And suddenly he wished the gentleman in him had never offered his arm to this woman. The casual touch of her hand was causing hot sparks to shoot all the way up to his shoulder, making it difficult to concentrate.

Doing his damnedest to ignore the unexpected reaction, he tried to focus on her last remarks. "You work as a waitress?" he asked.

"I guess you could call me a waitress," she told him. "The coffee shop is small and I run it by myself. The owner does the pastry baking, then leaves everything else up to me."

"I'd never be able to do your job," he told her. "I'd end up eating all the profits."

The smile on her face drew him like a warm fire on a frigid night and he silently cursed himself for being so responsive to her. He was in no position to be feeling such things toward any woman.

A week had hardly passed since he'd arrived here on the ranch. Boxes of his belongings were still stacked in the modest house where Matthew had lived during his tenure as the ranch's foreman. What with getting to know the Hollister family and learning his way around the ranch, he'd hardly had a chance to draw a good breath, much less unpack. He didn't have time for a woman. And even if he did, he wasn't in the market for marriage or even a serious affair. Furthermore, he never would be.

Her rich voice suddenly broke into his dire thoughts. "Once you have one of Conchita's pastries you're hooked. I try not to eat them, but it's a fight. Now Holt's wife, Isabelle, is a different matter. She comes in and eats a pile of brownies or whatever she wants and never gains an ounce. It isn't fair. Little Carter hasn't turned a month old yet and Isabelle already looks great. Must be all that horseback riding she does."

Taggart could've told Emily-Ann, she had no cause to worry about her figure. It was nice. Hell, it was more than nice, he thought. She was curvy in all the right places and he had no doubt she'd feel soft in his arms. Just the way a woman ought to feel.

The unsettling thought forced him to clear his throat. "Do you ride horses?" he asked.

She nodded. "When Camille and I were much younger we rode all over the ranch," she answered, then went on in a pensive voice, "Because she was my friend I got the chance to do things that I couldn't have done otherwise. But now, working and taking classes doesn't leave me much leisure time. And with Camille living at Red Bluff things have changed. But then you already know that. I mean, you're here because Matthew runs Red Bluff ranch now."

"Yes, that's why I'm here. To try to fill his boots," he said wryly. "It's not going to be an easy job."

She smiled at him. "If Blake and Maureen believe you can do the job, then I'm positive you can."

He was thinking how the confidence in her voice made him feel just a bit taller when Matthew and Camille turned back to them.

"Sorry about that," Matthew said. "Everyone wants to talk. You'd think I'd been gone for five years instead of five months."

Camille slanted a loving glance at her husband. "Shows how well you're thought of around here."

The first time Taggart had met Matthew and Camille, he'd not missed the affection that naturally flowed back and forth between the newlyweds. It was obvious they were deeply in love and though he was happy for them, seeing them together was a constant reminder of all that he'd lost. All that he'd never have.

"My wife is trying her best to give me the big head," Matthew said with a chuckle, then gently nudged Camille onward.

The four of them moseyed on through the crowd until they reached the long bar constructed of native rock and topped with rough cedar boards. Behind the rustic counter, Jazelle, a young blond-haired woman was pouring a hefty amount of tequila into a tall pitcher of margarita mix.

"Oh, I'll take one of those, Jazelle," Emily-Ann spoke up.

"Same for me," Taggart added his request.

Jazelle poured the concoction over two iced glasses and handed them over, while Camille continued to study the large assortment of refreshments lined up on the counter.

"I can't make up my mind," she said after a moment.

After giving his wife an indulgent smile, Matthew said to Jazelle, "I know what I want. Just give me plain ole coffee."

Camille groaned. "That's too hot. I want something sweet and cold."

"We know Camille can't have alcohol so just give her tomato juice," Emily-Ann joked. "Or water."

Pulling a face at Emily-Ann, Camille said, "Don't listen to her, Jazelle. She doesn't know about cravings. She's never been pregnant."

"No. I haven't been pregnant," Emily-Ann replied. "And I'm beginning to think I'll never be."

"Oh, come on, Emily-Ann," Jazelle teased, "I wouldn't be saying anything like that. You caught Camille's wedding bouquet. You know what that means."

Somewhat puzzled by the whole exchange between the women, Taggart watched a dark blush steal across Emily-Ann's cheeks. The added color made her face even prettier, he decided.

"All right, that does it!" Emily-Ann muttered. "As soon as I down this margarita, I'm going home and tearing that damned bouquet into shreds and throwing it in the trash can."

Instead of getting angry at her friend's ominous threat, Camille burst out laughing. "Sorry, Emily-Ann, but you're not going anywhere—except to the dinner with your friends. Tag, just grab her arm if she tries to leave."

Taggart had no way of knowing what exactly the women were arguing about, other than it had something to do with a wedding bouquet. The word had seemed to set off a mild explosion in Emily-Ann. And why had she said that about never being pregnant? Was there a reason she couldn't have, or didn't want, children? Maybe she was one of those women who decided motherhood is not for her. But Taggart seriously doubted that. Her body moved with a sensuality that said she was made to make love to a man.

"I'm not sure I should try that," Taggart said. "She's a redhead. She might slap me."

Camille laughed again, while Emily-Ann gazed over the rim of her frosted glass at him.

"I'm sorry, Tag," she said, then smiled impishly. "I'm not really bad-tempered. Until I get around my old friend."

He was about to tell her that he wasn't thinking she was bad-tempered when Blake suddenly appeared at his side and clamped a friendly hand on his shoulder.

"Sorry to interrupt, Tag, but there's a group of men from the cattlemen's association who are anxious to meet you."

"Sure," he said, but as he walked away with the ranch manager, he wondered if he'd get a chance to talk with Emily-Ann again before the night was over. And wondered, too, why he'd want to.

Chapter Two

Damn it all, Taggart O'Brien had already ruined her evening, Emily-Ann silently cursed. She'd been looking forward to seeing the Hollisters and spending time with Camille. Now she couldn't focus on anything, except the tall Texan with warm brown eyes and slow, melting smile.

Absently pushing a pile of brisket and potato salad around her plate, she lowered her lashes and glanced at the object of her thoughts. He was sitting across the portable table and three chairs down from hers. Since everyone had sat down to eat, Matthew and the Hollister brothers had consumed Taggart's attention, but that hadn't lessened the impact of his presence.

Before the party had started this evening, Camille had told Emily-Ann how the whole family had nothing but praise for the man. At the time, Emily-Ann hadn't taken much note of her friend's chatter about the newly hired foreman. After all, she'd never be crossing paths with the man. But now that she'd stood close to him, looked into his brown eyes and felt the hard warmth of his arm beneath her hand, her thoughts were spinning with questions about him.

Her reaction to him was worse than foolhardy, Emily-Ann thought ruefully. All she had to do was glance at him to know he could have his pick of women. And for all she knew, he might have a special one tucked away somewhere. Most likely back in Texas where he'd migrated from. Yet those assumptions did little to stop the race of her pulse when she looked in his direction. Nor did they stop her from wondering if she might have the opportunity to speak with him again before the party ended and she headed home to Wickenburg.

"Are you angry with me?"

Camille's question had Emily-Ann turning a look of surprise on her friend. "Why, no," she said. "Why would you think that?"

"You've not said more than ten words since we sat down. And instead of eating, you've been using your food to build a dam across your plate."

Shaking her head, Emily-Ann said, "There's nothing wrong. I guess the margarita ruined my appetite."

Camille hardly looked convinced. "Look, I'm sorry I teased you so about the bouquet. As far as I'm concerned, you can toss it in the garbage. I won't say another word about it."

Feeling more than a little ashamed of herself, Emily-Ann smiled at her. "Don't be silly. I'm not angry at you. And I'm not about to throw the bouquet away. Why should I? It's probably the closest thing I'll ever have to bridal flowers."

"Well, if I hurt your feelings—"

Emily-Ann let out a good-natured groan. "You're being ridiculous now. You could never hurt my feelings. So tease all you want."

"So if it's not me, then what is it?" Camille persisted. "In all our years as friends I've never seen you this quiet."

Emily-Ann shrugged. "Sorry. I guess I've been thinking a lot tonight. Seeing your family and how much things have changed in the past few years. In some ways it makes me a little melancholy."

Camille reached over and squeezed Emily-Ann's hand. "But we're all so happy now," she said. "Even Mother is really smiling again."

Yes, Emily-Ann had noticed how cheerful Maureen seemed tonight. She'd also observed how Gil Hollister, brother to Maureen's late husband, Joel, was never very far from the woman's side. Emily-Ann had met the man a long time ago, during one of his brief visits to the ranch, but over the past years, she'd not seen or heard much about him. Other than the fact that he worked as a detective on the Phoenix police force. Then a few months ago, at Camille's wedding, word began to spread that after thirty years of service, the man had retired and was moving back to Yavapai County.

"I am glad about that," Emily-Ann said. "There for a while it was like the real Maureen had gone into hiding."

Camille nodded and Emily-Ann watched her friend's eyes travel down the table to where Maureen and Gil were sitting side by side. In many ways, the man in his sixties reminded Emily-Ann of Joel, Camille's late father. Although Gil's hair was graying somewhat, the dark sections that remained were the same color that Joel's had been and he also possessed the same strong, stocky build as his brother.

"I think Uncle Gil is making a big difference in her life," Camille said thoughtfully.

Emily-Ann searched her friend's face. "Are you and your brothers okay with that? I mean, I know how much you all adored your father. Maybe you're thinking your uncle is trying to move in and take his place."

Camille released a heartfelt sigh. "Daddy was ten feet tall to all of us. No one could ever replace him. But as far as I'm concerned I don't want Mother pining her life away for someone who can never come back. I can't say for sure how each of my brothers feel, but I do know they want Mother's life to be full and happy."

Several years ago, Joel's body had been discovered out on the range not far from the ranch yard. His boot was still hung in the stirrup and he'd obviously been dragged for miles before the horse he'd been riding had finally come to a halt. The family and anyone who'd ever known Joel Hollister had been devastated by his untimely death.

Emily-Ann had hurt for the loss her friend had endured. Even so, she knew that Camille had been blessed for having a father for nineteen years. Emily-Ann had never had one. Not a real father, anyway.

"Yes, I'm sure your brothers feel that way," Emily-Ann said thoughtfully. "And your uncle seems like a genuine kind of guy."

"I think so, too," Camille replied, then smiling she pointed to the food on Emily-Ann's plate. "Eat. Before you turn that stuff into a pile of hash."

It wasn't until hours later, after most of the guests had gone, that Taggart slipped away from the handful of people left on the patio and walked around to the side of the house where a view of the ranch yard could be seen in the distance.

Leaning his shoulder against the large trunk of a cottonwood tree, he gazed out at the numerous barns and sheds and endless maze of connecting corrals. Before he'd ever thought about leaving West Texas and the Flying W behind, he'd heard of Three Rivers Ranch. It had a reputation for prestigious horses and crossbred cattle that could thrive under the harshest conditions. Taggart had expected the livestock to be top-notch. What he hadn't expected was the sheer vastness of the property. Even by Texas standards it was massive and rough and beautiful.

"Did you decide you needed a little peace and quiet?"

The female voice startled him and he glanced around to see Emily-Ann stepping out of the deep shadows. He'd not known anyone was around and he wondered if she'd been watching him. The idea sent a shaft of heat slithering down his backbone.

"Something like that," he answered, then asked, "What about you?"

She joined him beneath the tree. "I've been up-stairs to see the kids and the babies. Billy, Chandler's baby, is teething now and yelling up a storm. He makes that coyote out there in the hills sound wimpy."

Taggart chuckled. "Doc will be proud to hear his new son has stronger vocal cords than a coyote."

She didn't make a reply and Taggart glanced over to see she was gazing thoughtfully out at the ranch yard. In many ways, she seemed at home here on Three Rivers, but in other ways, he sensed that she felt apart from the Hollisters and their friends. Although, he couldn't imagine why that would be. They all treated her like a family member.

Because she was my friend I got the chance to do things that I couldn't have done otherwise.

Her remark about Camille had struck Taggart and left him wondering what she'd meant by it exactly. That the Hollisters being rich made them different from her? Well, that was hardly a surprise. The Hollisters' wealth superseded most everyone in the area, including him.

"Is this place anything like the ranch where you worked before?" she asked.

Her question brought him out of his reverie and as he continued to rest his weight against the tree trunk, he allowed his gaze to linger on her face and hair. At the moment, it was splotched with moonlight and he couldn't help but wonder what it would be like to kiss the silvery spots upon her skin.

"The Flying W was big, but not this big. There weren't any mountains on it, but there were lots of what we Texans call cuts and breaks. It's where the years of rain and wind create deep gorges and cut banks into the ground."

"What about trees? Did you have many of those?"

"Some blue cedar and cottonwood. But they were few and far between and the wind usually kept most of the leaves stripped off the cottonwoods. That's the way it is up near the panhandle. But there was plenty of cholla cactus and it's real pretty when it blooms."

"Sounds desolate," she commented.

"I suppose it is—in a way. But it was home to me."

He could feel those green eyes of hers studying his face and though they were partially covered by shadows, he knew they were full of questions. Many of which he didn't feel comfortable answering. Not now. Maybe after this place began to feel like home to him, he'd want to talk about his life back in Texas.

He said, "Now you're thinking if I felt that way, why did I ever leave. Right?"

"It did cross my mind," she admitted. "But you don't have to tell me. That's your business. Not mine."

She was exactly right. And he should feel glad that she respected his privacy. Yet a part of him was disappointed that she wasn't interested enough to pry at him. Had moving to Arizona turned him into a wishy-washy fool, he suddenly wondered? Or was this sexy redhead the reason his thought process had gone haywire?

"The Williamsons, the people who owned the Flying W, were great to work for. I started as a day hand there when I was twenty-two. Three years later I'd worked my way up to foreman."

"Sounds like Matthew. He was very young when he first started working here on Three Rivers."

"Matthew has been blessed and he knows it. The Hollisters will always be here. They'll always hold the reins. He's never had to worry that a syndicate or some other owner would come in and start changing the way the ranch should be run."

"And that's what happened at the Flying W?" she asked.

Nodding, he tried not to feel bitter. His old job was behind him now and the problems there would continue to go on without him.

"The Williamsons built the ranch years ago and owned it, up until a year ago," he explained. "But then Mr. Williamson, who's in his mideighties, suffered a mild stroke. He recovered nicely, but his daughter didn't waste time in persuading him to sell the property. She convinced him that the ranch was the reason for his stroke."

"Was it?" Emily-Ann asked.

The choked sound he made was intended to be a laugh, but it held no humor. "That was a joke. She was the reason the old man carried around a load of stress. She'd been married and divorced twice and the cost of her mistakes had pretty much bankrupted her parents. So he sold to a family from Georgia. The Armstrongs know nothing about the West or raising cattle. Nor do they want to learn. So you can pretty much figure out the problems that caused for me and all the hands."

"Were you the only one who left the ranch's employment? Or did the other hands feel like you and leave, too?"

"All the original crew of men who worked the Flying W have left and gone on to different jobs now. I was one of the last holdouts. I guess I was foolishly hoping that something would change. That Mr. Williamson would find a way to buy the ranch back. But it never happened."

She looked at him. "I'm going to assume that the daughter was an only child. There were no other children to help with the ranch or the finances?"

Taggart shook his head. He'd been the closest thing to a son to Walt Williamson. But Emily-Ann didn't need to know that. Nor did she need to know that the daughter had always been bad-mouthing Taggart because he refused to warm up to her sexual propositions.

"Unfortunately, Joanna was the only child the couple had. Things might have been different if there'd been another grown son or daughter or around the ranch."

She moved a step closer and Taggart caught the gentle scent of flowers and desert wind on her hair. The fragrance was alluring and unique, just like her.

"Well, I don't know about the other men you worked with on the Flying W and whether they've moved on to better things. But you certainly have. You're going to love working for the Hollisters. They're fair and honest and they care for their cattle and horses the same way their forefathers did a hundred and fifty years ago."

The sight of her upturned face grabbed something inside of him and to save himself from doing or saying something idiotic, he forced his gaze back on the ranch yard.

"Yes. I've learned this place has a long, colorful history," he said. "I feel honored to be a part of it now."

She smiled. "I'm guessing your family probably wasn't keen on you moving away to another state."

As always when he thought of his parents, a part of him shuttered down. It had been so long since all of his family had been together and even then, his father had never really put his wife and children before himself. His mother had worked hard to put meals on the table and made sure that Taggart and his little sister were clean and cared for. She'd been the rock that had held them all together.

"My mother has been dead for a long time and my father, such as he is, only comes around when he wants something. I do have a younger sister, Tallulah. We're close."

"Does she live in Texas?"

"Yes, in a little town close to the New Mexico line." He looked back at her. "What about you? Do your parents or siblings live around here?"

She looked away from him and for a moment Taggart thought she was going to totally ignore his question and then she finally spoke in a small voice.

"My mother passed away a few years ago," she said. "And my father was—never in my life. I don't have any siblings. I wish I did. I think things would've been a lot better if I'd had a brother or sister. But it didn't turn out that way."

It was easy to tell from the strained sound of her voice that it was difficult for her to talk about her family, or lack of one. Taggart could have told her that he understood, that he, too, had come from a broken home. But he'd already told this woman much more than he should have. In fact, he couldn't believe he'd told her all those things about the Flying W or his parents. It wasn't like him to divulge such personal things about himself to anyone.

Down toward the ranch yard, he could hear a few penned calves bawling and farther on a stallion called to his mares. The familiar sounds were comforting to Taggart, but apparently Emily-Ann hadn't taken notice of them. She was focusing on the lonesome wail of a coyote far off on a ridge of mountains west of the ranch house.

"When I was a young girl I used to be afraid when I heard a coyote," she said wryly. "I was a town girl and didn't know much about the outdoors. Camille told me that coyotes are very family oriented and that when they mate it's for life. I never did really believe her. She's such a romantic I figured she made it up. Because the whole thing sounded so dreamy and tender."

He grunted while wishing a part of him could still feel loving and tender. But there were no soft spots left in his heart, no room for a romantic dream to dwell and grow.

"I can assure you that Camille told you right. Coyotes do mate for life. So do mourning doves—until one of the pair dies."

Until one dies. Yes, Taggart had mated for life, he thought. Only that life hadn't lasted long.

"Oh," she said, then laughed softly, "I've learned something tonight. Mainly that I should believe Camille when she tells me something."

He pushed away from the tree trunk. This wasn't good, he thought. Standing out here in the shadows with a voluptuous redhead that smelled like an angel and looked like a seductress.

"I should get back to the patio," he said. "Most of the guests are leaving and the Hollisters are probably wondering where I've gotten off to."

"Time I was going, too. The drive back to my house takes about thirty minutes and I have to open Conchita's early in the morning." Smiling at him, she offered him her hand. "I've enjoyed talking with you, Tag. And I wish you the best with your new job. Maybe one of these days you'll get the urge for a pastry and some coffee and drop by Conchita's. It's open every day but Sunday."

His fingers tightened around hers and before he knew what he was doing he was tugging her forward until the front of her body was very nearly touching his.

She looked up at him and Taggart's gaze took in her wide green eyes and parted lips. She was clearly surprised by his action, but not nearly as stunned as he was feeling.

"Tag, what—"

"I couldn't let you walk off," he said. "Not until I told you how much I've enjoyed these few minutes with you."

Her breasts rose and fell as she drew in a deep breath, then quickly exhaled. "If you really got to know me, you wouldn't be saying that."

Her hand felt so soft and warm that all he could think of was pulling her closer, letting his hands roam her back and his lips explore hers.

"Why?"

He watched her teeth bite into her bottom lip. "Because I'm not your kind of woman."

That was far from what he was expecting her to say. "I wonder how you came to that conclusion. You don't know me—yet."

Her nostrils flared and he could see a vein at the base of her throat throbbing at a rapid pace. It was obvious he was making her nervous, but she was doing a hell of a lot more to him than that. Just holding her hand, feeling the heat of her body radiating toward his was enough to stir a flame deep inside him.

Her lips twisted with wry resignation. "Let's just

say I know my limitations. And you're on the other side of the boundary. But it would be nice to be your friend, Tag. I'd like that."

Maybe she'd like things that way, Taggart thought, but he wouldn't. At some point from the moment he'd met her a few hours ago, until now, his mind had tossed away the idea of wanting to be her friend and changed to wanting to get to know every inch of her. The idea was shocking and scary, but it was there in his head anyway and he couldn't get it out.

"That's not the way I see things, Emily-Ann. I'm seeing you in my arms—like this."

Confusion flashed in her eyes, then she opened her mouth to speak, but he didn't wait to hear her reply. Instead, he bent his head and placed his lips over hers.

Soft, sweet and velvety smooth. Her lips were all that and more. And for a long, long moment Taggart lost himself in the pleasure of kissing her.

It wasn't until his arms slipped around her waist and he felt her hands fluttering helplessly against his chest that he realized he had to end the contact. Otherwise his senses were going to forget where he was, and why a kiss was all he dare take from this woman.

Forcing his head up, he drew in a ragged breath and watched her eyelids flutter open. He saw surprise flickering in the green depths and something else he couldn't quite identify. Was that longing, or regret, or a mixture of the two?

It doesn't matter, Tag. You can't get caught up in what this woman is thinking or feeling!

The voice in his head made him want to curse out loud. Instead, he did his best to smile and act as though her kiss hadn't shaken him all the way to the soles of his boots.

"You go around locking lips with women you've only known a few hours?" she asked.

The husky note in her voice was such a sexy sound it made him want to pull her back into his arms and kiss her all over again.

"Uh—no. I don't normally—kiss any woman." His throat felt raspy and he tried to swallow the sensation away as he lifted his hat from his head and swiped a hand through his hair. "Must be something about the moonlight."

An incredulous look appeared in her eyes and then she let out a cynical snort. "Aww, shucks ma'am, I just couldn't help myself," she said in an exaggerated drawl. "Am I going to hear that next?"

"No. And you're way off on the accent. I'm not from South Texas. I'm from West Texas."

Her nostrils flared. "There's a difference?"

"A huge one."

Something flashed in her eyes and then her gaze dropped to the middle of his chest. "Sorry. I shouldn't have been so flippant," she mumbled. "But you have the wrong idea about me."

Long brown lashes were veiling her eyes, yet he could see enough of her lips to know they were trembling. Damn it, he'd never intended to insult her.

"No. I got the wrong idea about myself," he said flatly. "I'm sorry. And you're right. I shouldn't have been kissing you. Instead, I should've been asking you to be my friend."

Her gaze lifted to his and Taggart felt punched by the mistrust he spotted in her eyes. What kind of man did she think he was? One that held little regard for women? Oh Lord, he'd made a mess of things.

"If you truly mean that," she said, "then I'd like to be your friend, Tag."

Friend. Yes, he definitely needed friends in this new life he was making for himself here in Arizona. But did he need a friend like Emily-Ann? She made his stomach flutter and his mind turn to dreams he'd given up long ago. If he wasn't careful she could play havoc with his peace of mind.

But for the past ten years he'd managed to keep his heart tucked safely behind an impenetrable wall. There was no reason for him to think Emily-Ann could ever breach it.

"I do truly mean it," he told her, then smiled and reached for her hand. "Let me walk you to the patio, my new friend."

She smiled back at him and as they strolled side by side through the shadows, she didn't pull her hand away from his. And Taggart couldn't summon the inner strength to let go of her.

Chapter Three

Human anatomy. Learning the subject was far more difficult than Emily-Ann had expected and she wondered for the umpteenth time why she'd ever believed she could acquire a nursing degree. A person needed a high intelligence and laser focus to make it through chemistry, physiology, microbiology and all the other terrifying classes that ended in *y*. Emily-Ann possessed neither of those attributes. Especially the focus part.

Ever since she'd gone to the Hollister party a little over a week ago, she'd been going around in a goofy daze and trying, without much success, to shake Taggart O'Brien from her mind. She still couldn't figure

out why the man had taken the time to have a conversation with her, much less kiss her.

When she'd walked upon him in the darkness,
she'd not intended to strike up a conversation with
the man, much less get tangled up in his arms. She'd
simply planned to acknowledge his presence with a
few words, then move on. But that plan had quickly
gone awry and now, days later, her mind was jammed
with thoughts and questions about the man.

*Forget the long, tall Texan, Emily-Ann. He's more
than trouble. He's a walking heartache. That phony
explanation of why he'd kissed you was pathetic.
You know exactly what that little embrace had been
about. He was just testing the waters, trying to see
if you'd be willing to go to bed with him. That's all
any man wants from you, sweetie. A tumble between
the sheets and a goodbye kiss.*

The taunting voice in her head caused her to close
the textbook with a loud snap and a long sigh. She
was wasting time trying to concentrate on her stud-
ies, she decided. And anyway, the clock on the wall
said it was a quarter to three. It was time to start
shutting the coffee shop up for the evening.

Sliding off one of the wooden chairs provided
for the customers, she walked behind the tall glass
display case that served as a counter and stuffed the
textbook into a duffel bag she'd stored on a shelf
against the wall.

Up until an hour ago, she'd seen a steady stream

of customers all day. Now there were only a few pastries left on the red plastic trays inside the display case. Conchita would definitely be pleased with the sales, she thought, as she began to load the leftovers into white paper sacks.

She was halfway through the task when the bells fastened over the door facing jingled, announcing that someone had entered the shop. It never failed, she thought, as she finished placing a baked donut covered with nuts into a sack. The minute she started to put everything away, someone wanted to come in for coffee or pastries, or both.

Glancing through the front glass of the display case, she could see the customer was a man wearing blue jeans and worn brown boots covered with dust. Other than the Hollisters, she didn't get too many cowboys in the place, especially at this time of day.

"I'm closing, but you're welcome to get a take-out order." She pulled her head from the case and raised up to find herself looking straight into Taggart O'Brien's face.

A slow smile creased his cheeks. "Hello, Emily-Ann. Looks like I picked a bad time to come in."

Anytime would be a bad time for her peace of mind, she thought. Especially when just looking at him set her heart thumping like a rocket about to shoot into space.

She nervously swiped the tip of her tongue over her lips. "No problem. I'm just dealing with the pastries that were left over from this morning. Whatever doesn't sell I drop off at the local nursing homes. The residents love getting them."

"That's a nice gesture," he said.

She shrugged one shoulder while wondering why he'd showed up today. For a day or two after the Hollister party, she'd thought, even hoped, that he'd come by to say hello. But after more than a week passed, she'd given up and decided he'd forgotten all about her.

"I like seeing the smiles on the old people's faces whenever I walk in," she told him.

"I'm smiling. I hope you're liking mine," he said in a teasing voice.

As he walked up to the glass counter, Emily-Ann's gaze traveled over his face and she realized his image was even more striking than the one she remembered at the party. Seeing him in the light of day, his complexion was a much darker brown and so was his hair. The arrogant chin was more like a concrete abutment, but that feature was definitely softened by the faint dimples bracketing his lips.

Had she actually kissed that mouth? The mere idea caused a shiver to slide down her spine.

"It's nice to see you again, Tag," she said, while hoping her voice sounded casual to his ear. "You're a long distance from Three Rivers. What brings you to town?"

"I got a hankering for pastries."

It felt like his gaze was swarming all over her and she wondered what he was thinking. That she looked rather plain in her brown shirt and faded blue jeans?

As her fingers fiddled with the long red braid lying across her shoulder, she assured herself that it didn't matter if her makeup had disappeared hours ago. She didn't want to impress this man. She wanted to forget him. Well, sort of.

"I don't know about the bunkhouse cook, but I know that Reeva, the Hollisters' cook, keeps all kinds of sweets made for the family. I'm sure she'd be happy to serve you some of them—whenever you get a hankering."

He chuckled. "Well, I did have to make a trip to the saddle shop. So I'm treating myself now. That is, if I'm not too late to get something."

Emily-Ann couldn't help it. She was so happy to see him, she couldn't act cool if she tried.

Smiling, she said, "It's not too late at all. What would you like?"

He gazed at the baked goods that were left in the display cabinet. "Hmm. I'm partial to chocolate so give me a brownie and what is that round thing that's covered in chocolate?" he asked. "It looks good, too."

"That's a Bismarck. It's like a donut covered in chocolate icing and the center is filled with custard."

"I'll take that, too. But if you've already drained the coffeepot, I'll just drink water."

"No problem. I can make a single cup for you.

Want to have a seat?" She gestured to the little square table where she'd been sitting only minutes before he'd arrived. "Or you might like to sit outside. The weather has been beautiful today."

"I'd rather eat outside—if you can join me," he said.

"I'd love to," she told him. "Like I said, I was closing up anyway."

While she gathered the pastries he wanted and made the coffee, he meandered around the small room, studying the old local memorabilia that adorned the walls, particularly photos of Wickenburg in its early, gold rush days.

"This is interesting," he said. "I like history. It makes us who we are, don't you think?"

"Yes," she agreed. "In more ways than most people imagine."

With the coffee done, she carried the cup and a small tray holding the pastries out to him.

"If you want anything in your coffee, it's all over there." She pointed to a small table containing all sorts of creamers, milk, sugar and sweeteners.

"No thanks. I like it black." He took the goodies from her, then asked, "Aren't you going to have something with me? At least some coffee. I hate to eat without you having something, too."

She groaned, while thinking the temptation of spending time with him was far stronger than the call of her sweet tooth. "Well, since I didn't eat lunch I suppose I could have a brownie," she said. "Just give me a minute and I'll make another cup of coffee."

Once she had her food and drink, the two of them walked outside to where a group of three small wrought iron tables and chairs were grouped beneath the lacy shade of two mesquite trees.

At a table nearest to the stone walkway leading up to the building, he pulled out one of the chairs and helped her into it. Once he was comfortably seated across from her, she asked, "So how has your new job been going?"

One corner of his lips curved upward. "It's been going well, I think. I've not had any complaints from Blake and Maureen yet. They have far more confidence in me than I do in myself. And they seem to understand I need time to learn the ranch—and the men."

She thoughtfully sipped her coffee. "Have the guys all accepted you as their new boss?"

"That's my biggest concern. Because if I don't have their respect I'm going to have problems. And since they all thought Matthew could walk on water that makes him a tough act to follow. But I'm trying. And so far they've all seemed fairly receptive of me. I don't know for sure, but I expect that's because Blake probably laid down the law to them before I ever arrived."

She pinched off a bite of brownie. "You're selling yourself short, Tag. The Hollisters don't have stupid men working for them. They can see you know your business."

The full-fledged smile he shot her caused her breath to momentarily hang in her throat. How could a man who looked like this still be single? It didn't seem possible.

He's single, you ninny, because he wants to be that way. He's thirty-two. He's had plenty of time to marry if he'd wanted to.

Mentally shaking herself, she sipped more coffee, while across from her, he ate the brownie in four bites then started on the Bismarck.

"Can you see that I know my business?" he asked with a soft chuckle.

Her cheeks suddenly felt hot. "Uh—well, I've not seen you in action. And I don't exactly know the things that a ranch foreman does, but you look like you'd be very comfortable on a horse—with a rope in your hand. This town is full of cowboys and after a while it's easy to tell which ones are genuine and who's trying to play the part."

Amusement crinkled the corners of his eyes. "I'm relieved to hear I look genuine."

As Emily-Ann nibbled her way through the chocolate dessert, she couldn't help but wonder if he'd thought about their kiss. Probably not the way she'd thought about it. Not the way she'd obsessed over the taste of his lips, the scent of his hair and skin, and the hardness of his body. Hopefully in a few more days the memories would dim. But for now they were as fresh as though it had just happened.

"The other night at the party, did I hear you mention that you were taking some sort of classes?"

Surprised that he'd remembered, she said, "Yes. I'm taking online classes to become an RN."

"A nurse. That's an ambitious choice. So I guess that means you don't always plan to work here at the coffee shop."

She glanced over her shoulder at the small square building with slab pine siding and a tiny covered porch, then turned her gaze back to him. "I love working here. But it pays just enough for me to get by. And my mother had a dream for me to be a nurse."

"What about your own dreams?"

She'd not expected that kind of question from him. In fact, Camille and Maureen were the only two people who'd ever asked her about her private wants and wishes.

"A minute ago you mentioned ambition, but I've never really had much of that, Tag. If it wasn't for me making a promise to my mother before she died, I doubt I'd be pushing myself to get a nursing degree. I'd probably be content to just sell coffee and donuts and keep living in the same little house that I grew up in."

"Nothing wrong with that if you're happy. Money, and the things it can buy, doesn't necessarily equal happiness. I know. I saw it firsthand with the Armstrong family. Cold and bitter. The whole bunch of them."

"Well, I don't want to become a nurse just to make a better salary. And deep down, I'm not doing it just to follow my mother's dream. I've thought about it long and hard and even though I'm not exactly ambitious, I'm drawn to the idea of helping people. You see, Mom was in bad health for a couple of years before she passed away. I saw how much it meant for her to have the right care."

"If it means anything I think you have the nature for nursing, Emily-Ann. And since you're studying to be a nurse, do you have any suggestions to treat a horse bite?"

She frowned. "You've been bitten by a horse?"

He put down his coffee cup and pushed up the sleeve of his pale blue shirt. As Emily-Ann caught a glimpse of the wounds on his forearm, she took hold of his hand and pulled it across the table toward her.

"This is serious, Tag." She studied the crescent-shaped tears that appeared to go deep into the flesh of his forearm. The gashes were an angry red with dried blood crusted around the edges. "You need a tetanus shot and possibly some stitches. How did that happen?"

"I was playing with one of Holt's young stallions and made the mistake of turning my back on him. He nabbed me on the arm to let me know he wanted the game to keep going. I'm going to stop by Doc's animal clinic on the way home. He'll take care of it."

She rolled her eyes. "We do have regular doctors here in town. No need for you to go to a veterinarian."

Chuckling, he pulled his hand back and refastened the cuff at his wrist. "I'll feel more comfortable with Doc treating me. Regular doctors make me nervous."

"What about nurses?" she asked pointedly.

One corner of his mouth cocked upward. "Nurses unsettle me, too. Especially when she has a syringe and needle in her hand."

She showed him her empty palms. "I can't give you a tetanus shot. But I could clean those wounds for you," she offered. "I keep antiseptic and things like that in the coffee shop. Just in case I cut or burn myself."

"Thanks for the offer, but I'd rather just sit here and drink my coffee." He gazed around the shaded dining area, then across the street to where a fat saguaro shaded a small building that housed an insurance agency. "This is quiet. No bawling cows or nickering horses. Not that I don't like those sounds, but sometimes a man wants to just listen to the wind. And a woman's voice."

She cleared her throat and his gaze swung back to her. Emily-Ann was surprised to see the humor had disappeared from his face. In fact, if she didn't know better, he looked lonely, almost lost. Which hardly made sense. This man had everything going for him. He'd just landed a prestigious job as foreman of Three Rivers Ranch. Why should he be feeling anything but ecstatic? Unless he was missing some woman back in Texas, she thought.

"You forgot the coyotes," she said in an attempt to lighten the moment. "None of those howling around here. Although, they do show up in town once in a while."

He smiled and she was relieved to see his good humor returning. The other night at the party she'd been drawn to his easy, laid-back nature. It was a nice change from the guys she'd dated in the past who'd been so busy trying to play the cool, tough man that they'd rarely smiled. And even when they had, it had looked so phony she'd had to bite her tongue to keep from laughing.

"No. Can't forget them." He took the last bite of Bismarck, then wadded up the empty wax paper.

As Emily-Ann watched him tilt the foam cup to his lips, she realized she didn't want him to leave. Spending time with him made her feel different, almost special. She realized that was foolish. Especially since she'd believed her past mistakes with men had taught her some valuable lessons.

"So has anything exciting been going on at Three Rivers since the party?" she asked, then before he could answer, added, "I guess everything about the place must feel exciting and new to you."

"It does," he agreed. "Matthew has been trying to show me the different sections of the ranch and how they're used throughout the year. The majority of the land has to be explored on horseback. So we've been spending lots of time in the saddle."

"Camille implied that she and Matthew would be staying for a few more weeks. Maybe until the end of the month. I hope they do. Once they go back to Red Bluff I'll only get to see her occasionally."

"Matthew tells me that Camille owns and operates a little diner down there. I think he said the town was called Dragoon. Is that right?"

Emily-Ann nodded. "Yes. It's a tiny desert town. Not much is there, but the diner is located on the edge of a main highway that runs from Wilcox to Benson. So she has lots of travelers who stop in to eat."

"Hmm. Just between me and you, I'm surprised that Camille runs a diner." He shrugged. "Not that anything is wrong with running a diner. It's just that she's a Hollister. There's no need for her to work at such a strenuous job."

"You're right about no need. But her being a Hollister explains everything. In spite of their wealth, or maybe because of it, they all have a fierce ambition. Camille couldn't sit around and twiddle her thumbs any more than her brothers or sister, Vivian, could. Besides, she loves to cook and she's darned good at it. If you ever make a trip down to Red Bluff, you'll see what I mean."

"I plan to go for a visit later on in the year," he said. "Just to see how Matthew is putting that Hollister property to use."

"You know, Camille was a bone of contention for a while with her family. When she moved down to Red Bluff and refused to come back here, her brothers threw a fit, so to speak. And Maureen wasn't happy about it either," Emily-Ann told him. "But that's all been smoothed over now that she and Matthew have married and are going to have a baby soon. Funny how things can look so bleak for a while and then everything suddenly turns to sunshine again. Sort of gives a person hope. You know what I mean?"

Smiling faintly, he put down his cup and leaned back in the chair. "I know exactly what you mean. And everybody needs hope."

He was right. Everybody needed hope. But no one had ever clung to it as much as Emily-Ann's mother. She'd always looked forward and believed that the men in her life were actually going to come through with all their promises. In the end, Emily-Ann had ended up having no contact with her biological father and her stepfather had been little more than a stranger who'd come and gone as he pleased.

"Well, I need to be going," he said after a moment. "Doc is expecting me and I promised Matthew I'd be back to the ranch in time to go with him to check on some calves."

All sorts of words she wanted to say rushed to

her tongue. But none of them were appropriate or proper. Besides, she didn't want him to get the idea that she was gushing over him.

She gestured to his injured arm. "Promise me that you'll have Doc treat that bite wound. It could become seriously infected if you don't take care of it."

"I promise as soon as I leave here, I'm going straight to his clinic," he told her.

"Well, I'm glad you came by, Tag. Now that you know where the coffee shop is you might get a hankering to drop by for another pastry—sometime."

He looked across the table at her. "I expect I will. But before I go I have something else on my mind—to ask you."

That serious look had returned to his face and she wasn't sure what to make of him. Nor did she understand what had caused her heart to suddenly leap into a ridiculous tap dance. "Oh. What's that?"

"Would you be willing to have dinner with me? I can't tonight. But I think I'll be free tomorrow night—if you are."

Free? He couldn't possibly know just how long ago a man of any caliber had looked in her direction, much less asked her on a date.

"Uh—I'm not busy, if that's what you mean. But I—"

"But what?"

She frowned, unwilling to believe that this cowboy wanted to spend time with her. "Are you—would this be like a date?"

"I guess you could call it that. Why?"

She felt her jaw drop and she realized she was probably staring at him like she'd lost her senses.

"Well, you—uh, you said we were going to be friends."

"That's right. Friends can eat dinner together, can't they?"

She was growing more flustered by the second. "Yes. But friends don't go on dates."

A slow smile spread his lips and she found herself staring at his white teeth. What would it feel like to push her tongue past their rough edges? To taste his inner mouth and press her body so close to his that not even a hair could be wedged between them?

Oh Lord, she was already losing control, she thought desperately, and they'd not gone any farther than the front yard of the coffee shop.

He reached across the table and clasped his hand around hers. The contact caused her heart to thump even harder.

He said, "After we go on a date we might decide we want to be more than friends."

"No!"

His brows arched in question and before he could make any sort of reply, she tried to explain, "I mean—you don't know who I am, Tag."

"Why don't I? Your name is Emily-Ann Broadmoor. You work at this little coffee shop and you're studying to be a nurse. You've always lived in Wickenburg and you're not married or attached. Right?"

The sigh she released was rough and shaky. "Yes. But you don't understand. I'm not a girl that someone like you would want to date."

He appeared unaffected by her admission. "Why not?"

Annoyed with herself and with him, she pressed her lips together and shook her head. "Look, Tag, I know you're a smart guy, so don't insult my intelligence by playing dumb. There are social ladders, you know. And I'm on the bottom rung. Got it now?"

"No. I don't have it. You can't be a friend of the Hollisters and be on the bottom rung. That just isn't possible."

"The Hollisters see everyone as equal. And when two little girls become friends in elementary school—they don't care about such things. They just want to be together. And because of Camille, the Hollisters have always included me. It's not that way with everyone around here. And please don't ask me why. It's something I don't want to get into. Not now."

She rose from her chair and gathered the remnants of her snack from the tabletop. "I need to go back in and finish closing up," she told him.

He rose and, with his trash in hand, followed her into the building. After the door had shut behind them, he asked, "Would you like to know what I'm really thinking?"

Walking behind the counter, she began to sack up the last of the pastries. "Sure. Go ahead," she told him.

He tossed his trash into a nearby basket, then pulled out his wallet and placed several bills on the glass countertop.

"I think you're talking a lot of nonsense. If you're afraid to go out with me just come out and say it. That would be much better than you giving me all this double-talk about you not being good enough— or whatever it is you're trying to say."

She closed the doors on the back of the case and placed the last of the sacked pastries on a cabinet top that ran along the back wall of the room. Behind her, she could hear Taggart's boots shuffle restlessly against the tiled floor.

He was obviously waiting on her reply. But what could she say without lying? She was afraid to go out with him. Afraid she'd do something foolish like fall head over heels for him.

Turning, she walked over to where he was standing. "Okay. You're right. I am a little afraid to go out with you, Tag. I—you see, I haven't wanted to date anyone for a long time. It never turns out good for me. And to be honest, I like you too much to ruin things between us."

He shook his head. "Having dinner together isn't going to ruin anything."

Before she could stop it, a cynical laugh rushed past her lips. "That's what you think."

He grinned a charming little grin at her. "I promise I'll be a perfect gentleman."

She laughed again, only this time it was a sound of amusement. "I believe you."

"So does that mean you'll go?"

It was stupid for her to keep hesitating, she thought, when every cell in her body was screaming at her to accept his invitation.

"Yes, I'll go. I just don't understand why you're asking me. If you'll look around town you'll see there are all sorts of women who are much prettier than me."

"Maybe I want more than pretty," he said, then smiling smugly, he tapped a finger on the bills he'd placed on the countertop. "Here's the money for my things. I'll see you tomorrow night. About seven. Is that time okay with you?"

"Sure."

She scratched down her address on an order pad and handed the small square to him. "That's where I live. And I put my cell number below. Just in case you change your mind and need to call me."

He slipped the paper into the pocket on his Western shirt. "No chance I'll change my mind," he said, then tipping the brim of his hat at her, he left the shop.

After the door had closed, Emily-Ann let out a long breath and sank weakly onto the wooden stool sitting next to the cabinets.

This morning as she'd driven to work, she'd pretty much convinced herself that Taggart had put her out of his mind. Now she was going on a date with him. It was a bit unbelievable to Emily-Ann. And what was Camille going to think about it?

She wasn't going to tell her, Emily-Ann thought. Not yet. If she did, her friend would immediately start harping about that damned bridal bouquet again. No, she'd wait until the date was over and Taggart came up with a reason not to see her again. Then she'd have proof that she needed more than a bridal bouquet to find a man to love her.

Chapter Four

Taggart hadn't realized just how many things he'd accumulated until he started unpacking the boxes he'd brought with him from Texas. Dishes, bedding and bath linens, clothing, boots and toiletries. Each evening before he'd gone to bed, he'd tried to unpack at least one box and put the items where they belonged.

This evening Matthew had insisted they wrap up work early so he could finish getting his house in order. Now, as he stacked coffee cups and cereal bowls in one of the kitchen cabinets, he was interrupted by a knock on the front door.

Forgetting the task for the moment, he went out to the living room to answer the door.

"Blake, come in," he said, surprised to find the ranch manager standing on the wide wooden porch.

"I can just stay a minute. Mom and I are about to leave for Prescott to a cattle buyer's convention."

Taggart pushed the door wide and gestured for Blake to enter the house. "I was in the kitchen trying to put away the last of the dishes. This moving thing is a pain."

"I'd be happy to send Jazelle over here to help you. That is, if Katherine and Roslyn can make do without her. These days she's turned into more of a nanny than a housekeeper," he added with a chuckle. "Poor girl. Mom has decided she needs to hire someone to help her and I agree."

"Thanks for the offer, but I have most of the necessary things put where they belong. Come on back to the kitchen," Taggart told him. "We can talk while I finish with the dishes."

"Fine. This won't take long," Blake said, while following him through the living room. "Actually, I stopped by because I have something to give you."

Inside the kitchen, Taggart gestured toward a long white farm table with matching chairs. "Pull up a chair. I have a bit of coffee left in the carafe if you'd like a cup."

"Thanks. But I'm fine." He reached inside his

Western-cut jacket and pulled out a long envelope, then handed it to Taggart.

"What is this?" Taggart asked curiously.

"A check."

Taggart paused and looked in stunned fascination at the ranch manager. "What for? Are you terminating my job already?"

The question produced a long, loud laugh from Blake. "Not hardly. We couldn't be happier that we have you here. The check is a little bonus. Just to show how much we appreciate you. We understand it's been costly for you to move out here. Especially with you bringing horses and tack, besides your household goods and personal things. We want to help cover the expense."

"I don't expect that, Blake. And it's totally unnecessary." He opened the envelope and the amount of the check he pulled out very nearly floored him. "No! No way can I accept this. I didn't spend a fraction of this on moving cost."

Blake laughed again. "Don't argue. Just trust me. You'll earn it all back before the first month is out."

Shaking his head, Taggart said, "I don't know what to say. This is far beyond generous, Blake."

The ranch manager swatted a dismissive hand through the air. "No need for you to say anything about the check. But I would like to know how you're settling in. Not with the house, I can see things here are taking shape. I'm talking about the ranch and the men. You and Matthew have been so busy, I've not had a chance to talk with either one of you."

Taggart studied the eldest Hollister brother, while thinking how differently he was being treated here at Three Rivers compared to the last year he'd spent on the Flying W. No matter how hard he'd worked, the Armstrongs had never been satisfied. They'd demanded more from him and all the hands, all the while insisting they had to cut their wages or go under. Which the whole crew had known was utter nonsense. It had been a hellish situation and one that Taggart was glad to have behind him. "Everything is going good, Blake. Thank you for asking."

Blake gave his shoulder an affectionate slap. "That's what we want. But if you do have any problems of any kind I want you to feel comfortable about coming to me. Or Mom. She stays in the thick of things and knows more about this ranch than I'll ever learn in my lifetime. But you've probably already figured that out for yourself."

"Matthew told me what an incredible woman his mother-in-law is and I'm beginning to see he wasn't exaggerating. Today Maureen helped drag calves to the branding fire and I'm being honest, she outworked most of the men," Taggart replied.

"That's Mom," Blake said with a grin, then turned to go. "And speaking of Mom, she's probably waiting on me. I'll see you tomorrow."

"Uh, Blake, if you have another minute I would like to ask you something."

At the back door of the kitchen, Blake paused to look at him. "Okay. Shoot."

Feeling a bit foolish, he cleared his throat, then asked, "How well do you know Emily-Ann?"

If the question surprised Blake he didn't show it. In fact, he chuckled. "I thought you were going to ask me something about roundup."

"I'm not worried about roundup," Taggart told him.

Blake looked even more amused. "But Emily-Ann does worry you?"

"Not exactly worries me," Taggart tried to explain. "More like she confuses the heck out of me."

"I didn't realize you were interested in her."

Taggart could feel his cheeks growing warm. He never discussed women with anyone. Since he'd lost Becca, he'd never really thought that much about any particular female. But since he'd met Emily-Ann something had happened to him. He couldn't seem to get his mind off the curvy redhead or that kiss they shared the night of the party.

"I'm taking her out to dinner tonight," Taggart admitted, then with a helpless shake of his head, added, "To be honest, Blake, she came damned close to turning down my invitation. Which is her right, of course. I hardly expect just any and every woman to go out with me. But she—well, it's like she mistrusts me or something."

Blake grinned. "You must've done something right. She's agreed to go out with you. But as far as giving you advice about women, I'm not the right man for that job. You need to talk to Holt. He's the charmer of the family."

Taggart swiped a hand through his dark rumpled hair. "Go ahead and laugh, Blake. I realize I sound like I'm twenty years old instead of thirty-two. It's just that she puzzles me. She seems to have a low opinion of herself and I can't figure why. I thought you might clue me in about her."

Blake's grin quickly vanished. "I don't know that much about Emily-Ann's personal life, Tag. Except that it hasn't always been easy. She's had to deal with plenty of heartaches and hardships. But she's a good person and very hardworking. We all love her."

"Hmm. It's odd that you say that. She has the notion that you Hollisters just tolerate her because she's Camille's friend."

Blake muttered a curse. "That's not true at all," he said, then after a thoughtful moment added, "but I can see where she might see things that way. Feeling accepted doesn't always come easy for some people. Especially when they've been raised up hard. I figure Emily-Ann needs to move on from the stigma of her past. But that's a hard thing to do, too."

Taggart frowned. "What about her past?"

Blake shook his head. "That's something she'll have to tell you."

Blake let himself out and as the door shut behind him, Taggart thoughtfully picked up the check from the countertop.

The bonus was nearly half of the year's salary he'd made on the Flying W. The Hollisters' generosity was hard to believe, much less accept. He wasn't worth this kind of money.

Let's just say I know my limitations. And you're on the other side of the boundary.

Emily-Ann's words suddenly pushed their way into Taggart's thoughts and he wondered if her lack of money made her think there was a wall separating them. Or did her reluctance have something to do with a man? One that she'd loved and lost?

Taggart intended to find the answers to his questions.

With a critical eye, Emily-Ann studied herself in the dresser mirror. Throughout the day, she'd promised herself she wasn't going to fret over her appearance tonight. She'd told herself she wasn't going to agonize over what to wear or how to do her hair. Glamming herself up for Taggart would be foolish and futile. She couldn't turn a dandelion into a lovely rose.

Yet, in spite of all the self-lecturing, she'd taken pains to pick out a dress that flattered her complexion. And she'd done her hair three different times to get it to drape perfectly against her temple.

And why not, she asked herself. Futile or not, any normal girl would want to look her best when she went on a date with a man. Especially a man like Taggart.

Turning away from the mirror, she reached for the thin yellow cardigan lying across the foot of the bed. Even though it was April, and the days were hot, the nights cooled enough for a jacket. And since Taggart hadn't given her any hint as to where they might be eating, she had no idea if she'd be spending any time outdoors.

With the sweater thrown over one arm and her handbag in tow, she left the bedroom and walked out to the living room to wait for Taggart to arrive. As she took a seat on the couch, she wondered what he would think about her house.

What can he think, Emily-Ann? It's the same little bungalow your mother lived in when you were born. You've never gotten beyond its walls. Except for a few little road trips, you've never ventured outside Wickenburg. You have a small, modest life. Before the night is over he's going to see all of that for himself.

Emily-Ann was fighting against the disheartening voice in her head when she heard the sound of a vehicle pull up in the short driveway in front of the house.

She was struck with the urge to jump up and go meet him on the front porch, but she quickly told herself that she needed to behave in a dignified manner. He didn't need to see that she was chomping at the bit to welcome him. Besides, he needed to get a good look at the inside of her house. Just so he'd see the huge gap in their living conditions.

After a short moment, a knock sounded on the door and Emily-Ann tried to gather her composure as she went to answer it. But as soon as she pulled back the door and saw him standing across the threshold, everything inside her began to tremble.

"Hi, Emily-Ann."

"Good evening, Tag. Please come in." She pushed the door wider, then waited while he stepped past her and into the house before she shut it behind them.

"I don't suppose you had trouble finding the place," she said as he came to a stop in the middle of the small room. "Wickenburg isn't very large."

"No problem," he told her. "GPS wasn't going to let me make a wrong turn."

"Would you like to sit for a minute?" she asked gesturing toward an armchair. "Or are you ready to go?"

"Since we have plenty of time I'll sit a minute," he said.

Emily-Ann watched him sink into the armchair, then remove his Stetson and place it on his knee. She'd expected him to want to leave. Most men did once they saw her house. Not that it was cluttered or nasty. But the old furniture had seen better days and the flooring needed to be replaced.

"If you'd like something to drink I can make coffee," she offered. "Or I have soda."

"Thanks," he said, "but I'm fine."

Feeling more nervous than she could ever remember being, she sat down on the couch directly opposite of where he was sitting. As she smoothed her skirt over her knees, she could feel his gaze sliding over her and to know he was looking at her was enough to light a fire in her cheeks.

"So how—"

"I thought—"

They both spoke at the same time and then laughed.

"Sorry," Taggart told her. "You go first."

"I was only going to ask you how things are going on the ranch," she said, while thinking how terribly sexy he looked tonight. He was wearing a deep blue shirt with black diamond-shaped snaps down the front and on the cuffs. A bolo tie with a slide fashioned from black onyx hung loosely below the collar of his shirt. He looked dressed up without being too fancy. In fact, he looked exactly right.

"They're going great. Better every day, in fact."

"That's nice. I'm glad for you. And the Hollisters," she added. "Before you came, Blake and Maureen were very concerned about losing Matthew."

"Well, they haven't exactly lost him. He's just working a different property now."

"Yes. But this ranch in Yavapai County is the biggest one," she reasoned.

"I'm reminded of that every day I pull up in the ranch yard and see all the hands coming out of the bunkhouse. Back on the Flying W I maybe had to deal with a third of the amount of men that I do here. For the first day or two after I arrived, I felt daunted by the sheer size of everything."

"But now you're growing accustomed to it, I'm guessing."

"More and more every day," he replied, then glanced around the small room. "You have a homey little place here, Emily-Ann. I like it."

"You're being overly nice, Tag. And it isn't necessary. I'm sure you see plenty of things that need repairing or replaced. I do what I can, whenever I can."

He frowned at her. "I'm not being overly nice. This room feels lived-in and I'm sure the rest of the house does, too. And that's a nice feeling. It's something you can't fake."

"Well, the house is very old. I think it was built in the 1940s and had several different owners until my mother moved into it in 1990. I was born a few months later. Some of my friends often tell me I should move into an apartment building. That it would be more modern and I wouldn't have to worry about the upkeep. Which is true. But I wouldn't feel comfortable. Here I have a little yard and my neighbors aren't right on top of me."

He smiled. "I think you should tell your friends to mind their own business."

She let out a long breath. Maybe Taggart truly was different, she thought. Maybe he didn't care that her closet wasn't full of fancy clothes or her house needed repairs. Maybe he actually wanted to be with her just because she was Emily-Ann and no other reason.

Laughing softly, she said, "That's not a bad idea. Do you have everything moved into your house now?"

He chuckled. "Everything is inside the house, but that's about all I can say. I still have things piled here and there in boxes. But I'm a typical bachelor, Emily-Ann, I don't care if my bed is made or I have to dig my clothes out of a box. I have more important things to think about. But I like the house. It even has a little fireplace and a small patio out back."

"That's nice. Actually, I've never been inside the house," she admitted. "Camille and I used to ride horses by the place. But, of course, that was years before she and Matthew got together so we never stopped or anything. In fact, right after he went to work for Three Rivers Ranch, he was married to someone else. But his wife was—I'll just come out and say it—she was awful. You see, she was hollow on the inside. No substance at all. When she flew the coop I don't think anyone was surprised. Not even him."

By the time she stopped speaking she realized he was eyeing her closely. Embarrassed heat suddenly poured into her cheeks. "Oh my, I'm sorry, Tag. I'm running off at the mouth and sounding like the town gossip. But I—didn't mean it that way. It's just that I wanted you to know that—well, I think I should just shut up before I make myself look even worse."

Shaking his head, he smiled faintly. "You don't sound like a gossip—you were just telling me about the past. And actually I'm thinking how fortunate Matthew was to have a second chance at happiness."

Relieved that he understood, she nodded. "Yes, if only everyone could be that fortunate."

Suddenly restless, she rose to her feet and draped the light sweater over her bare shoulders. "If you're ready to go, I am," she told him.

"Sure." He rose from the chair and levered the hat back onto his head. "I've not said anything yet, but you look extra beautiful tonight, Emily-Ann."

Beautiful. The only time she ever heard that word and her name coupled together was when her mother spoke them. To hear Taggart call her beautiful filled her with pleasure. It also made her very wary.

She'd made the mistake of believing a man's pretty words before. She couldn't make those same missteps with Taggart. And yet with all of her heart she wanted to believe he was sincere.

"Thank you. Since you didn't say where we'd be going I hope my dress is suitable."

He stepped closer as he eyed the off-the-shoulder dress made of red calico printed with tiny yellow flowers. A matching belt cinched in the waist, while the tiered hem fluttered against her calves.

"The dress is perfect," he murmured. "I like it."

Oh my. His voice reminded her of cool water trickling over rough stones. And he smelled like a real man. One with strong hands, broad strong shoulders and a constitution to match.

"I'm glad," she said huskily, then clearing her throat, she purposely stepped away from him and retrieved her purse from an end table. "I'm ready."

As soon as the last words came out of her mouth, she very nearly laughed. She was far from ready to deal with the feelings that Taggart was creating inside her. But she wasn't going to shy away from him. For once in her life, she was going to believe, if just for one night, that she was good enough to have this man's respect.

Jose's, the restaurant Taggart had chosen, was located on the edge of town, where the empty desert stretched toward a far range of jagged mountains. The building was a rambling, hacienda type with stucco walls painted a pale turquoise and a red tiled roof. A deep porch ran the width of the front and was shaded with a roof supported by arched columns. Potted plants hung from the center of each arch, while an enormous bougainvillea covered with yellow-gold blossoms grew far past the roof. At the opposite end of the porch, a single saguaro with three arms stood against the darkening sky.

As Taggart and Emily-Ann walked across the graveled parking area to the building, he said, "I'm sure you've probably eaten here dozens of times. But Doc tells me the place has great food."

"To be honest, Tag, I'm rarely ever out this way. I usually just fix myself something at home. Or if I do decide to treat myself, I grab something close in town. This is very nice. And it's lovely here, don't you think?"

He looked down at her, while thinking nothing could look as lovely as she did at this moment with the twilight falling on her soft features and the smile on her face directed solely at him. He'd never known a woman as guileless as Emily-Ann and when he was with her, he forgot most everything. Even his vow to never let himself care for another woman.

"If the food is as good as the outside looks, then I think we're in for a treat," he told her.

Inside the restaurant, a hostess ushered them to a table covered with an orange-and-white checked tablecloth. In the center a fat brown candle flickered in the faint breeze wafting down from the blades of a ceiling fan. Beyond the small table, a long window exposed a view of the desert, while the sounds of a Spanish guitar played softly in the background.

Taggart helped Emily-Ann into one of the cushioned chairs, then took a seat for himself. All the while it struck him that he could've driven for miles and not found a more romantic spot than this. He'd not exactly planned this type of dinner, but now that they were here, and he saw the enchanted expression on Emily-Ann's face, he was glad.

As soon as the waiter arrived, Taggart ordered wine for each of them, then picked up the menu and began to study the long list of dishes offered.

"I should've asked if you like Mexican food," he said. "But I see they serve typical American food, also."

"Oh, I love Mexican food," she exclaimed. "It's my favorite. What about you?"

"Well, where I come from we had what you call Tex-Mex food. It's a little different from the Mexican food served here in Arizona, but it's just as good. I like it all," he admitted.

"Do you eat in the bunkhouse with the men?" she asked. "Or do you cook for yourself?"

"I do both. Depending on what I have planned in the mornings or if I'm tied up late with work in the evenings. The cook in the bunkhouse is a gruff old guy. But he makes fairly good biscuits and beans and steak. Blake eats in the bunkhouse, too, on certain days. I think he enjoys being a regular cowboy."

Emily-Ann nodded. "Blake went to college to get a degree in ranch management thinking one day when his dad grew old and retired he'd take over the job of manager. No one could've dreamed that Joel was going to die so young and that Blake would have to step into his father's position. Katherine, his wife, says that the job weighs on him at times, but he'll do whatever he has to do to keep the ranch thriving."

The waiter arrived with their drinks and after they'd given him their choices from the menu, Taggart took a long sip of the dry, fruity wine.

"Do you know Katherine well?" he asked, picking up on their conversation where they'd left off.

She nodded. "Yes. She comes by the coffee shop on the days that she's working at the school. She's secretary for Penny—the school principal."

"She and Blake seem like the perfect match."

"Perfect," she agreed. "Their twins are adorable. And their older son Nick is such a nice kid. Blake was the second of the Hollister men to get married. Joe, the deputy, was the first. I know you met him at the party."

Taggart had especially liked the youngest Hollister brother. "Yes, I did. He seemed like a quiet guy, but when his mother started talking about ranching, he really opened up. I got the impression that he does quite a bit of ranch work when he's off duty. By the way, he introduced me to Sam, foreman of the Bar X."

Emily-Ann gave him a huge smile. "Ahh, Sam. He's adorable."

"I've heard that women find him charming." He slanted her a wry smile. "I see that includes you, too."

Laughing softly, she drew the wineglass to her lips. "What can I say? His face looks like a piece of cracked and crinkled leather. He's as thin as a rail and his legs are just a little bowed. But there's something about that old man that—I don't know what it is. But women feel drawn to him. I think it's mostly that soft look in his blue eyes when he looks at us. Like he cherishes all females."

"Well, he's certainly snagged a nice one. Isabelle's mother rarely left Sam's side the night of the party. I hear they're going to get married."

Emily-Ann sighed and Taggart could see the starry expression in her eyes. She was clearly a romantic. But he'd come to that conclusion the first time he'd met her. So why had he brought her to dinner? Why was he here drinking wine with her and watching candlelight flicker golden fingers upon her bare shoulders?

Because you've lost your mind, Taggart. You've forgotten how it felt when you watched Becca being lowered into the ground. Because you can't remember what it was like to have every dream and hope you've ever carried in your heart crushed into bits of ashes.

No, damn it! He silently cursed at himself as he fought to block out the voice in his head. He hadn't forgotten anything. But he was determined not to allow the past to haunt him tonight. He was tired of remembering. Tired of living in the past and trying to hold on to a memory that only brought him pain.

"Honestly, I was shocked when I heard the news about Gabby and Sam," Emily-Ann replied. "I mean, yes, Sam is a charmer. And I have no doubt he'd treat a wife like a queen. But Gabby is so opposite from him. Besides the fact that she's probably twenty years younger and very attractive, she's a city person—an artist. Sam spends his days on the back of a horse."

Amused, he grunted. "What do you think I do?"

"The same thing. But I figure you're—" pausing, she made a palms-up gesture "—more of a well-rounded man than Sam."

"Hah! Don't kid yourself. I got the impression that Sam has already forgotten more than I'll ever know about anything. And sometimes it's that stark difference in people that make them attracted to each other." He leveled a smile at her. "But that's enough about those folks. What about you, Emily-Ann? How many hearts around here have you broken?"

Above the rim of the wineglass, her eyes made a slow study of his face. "Seriously? You have the idea that I've broken a heart?" Laughing cynically, she lowered the glass back to the table, but her fingers continued to grip the stem. "That's funny, Tag."

"Why?"

Frustration tightened her features. "Because—I'm not a girl who men fall in love with. That's why."

He frowned at her. "That's nonsense."

"I'm sorry," she said. "But it's true."

"You'll never convince me."

As he watched her lips curve into a wan smile he tried to imagine another man kissing her mouth, feeling her warm breath on his face, tasting the smooth skin of her cheek. But the image refused to form in his mind. Not because she was undesirable; everything about her was alluring. No, it was impossible to imagine her with another man because he was already thinking of her in possessive terms. As his and his alone.

The faint smile on her face suddenly vanished and she let out a short, mocking laugh before turning her gaze to the window. "Oh yes, you'll be convinced. You'll soon learn that I talk too much, that I'm irritating and sometimes even ditzy. I'm a bit plump for most men's taste and my mouth is too wide. My eyes are too big and I couldn't grow a long fingernail if I tried."

He could see she was deadly serious, but Taggart couldn't help himself, he had to laugh. "Oh, Emily-Ann, do you realize how ridiculous all of that sounds?"

Her gaze returned to his face and the cynicism

Taggart spotted in her green eyes took him by surprise.

"Yes, I can admit that most of it is trivial stuff," she said sullenly. "But that doesn't change the fact that I'm Emily-Ann Broadmoor. Everyone knows my father was the real estate tycoon's son. The one who believed he was too high-class to marry the poor girl he'd gotten pregnant. Too important to be a father to the child she bore, or to ever acknowledge he had a daughter. And I'm no different than my mother, Tag. I'm the girl the guys want to take to bed, but never fall in love with!"

By the time she spoke the last few words her voice was wobbling and her face had turned to the color of paste. The dark pain in her eyes was like a knife in his chest and he desperately wanted to round the table and take her into his arms. He wanted to tell her in so many ways how very precious she was to him. But that would be the same as saying he was falling for her. He wasn't ready for that. And from the sound of things, she wasn't either.

"Emily-Ann, I—"

His words were suddenly interrupted as she jumped to her feet and blinked at the tears filling her eyes. "I'm sorry, Tag. I—you'll have to excuse me."

She hurried away from the table and for a moment Taggart thought she might run from the restaurant completely. Relief rushed through him when he saw her turn in the direction of an alcove where the restrooms were located. Clearly, she was seeking a private space to collect herself. He could only hope she wouldn't allow this little episode to ruin their evening.

Sighing heavily, he reached for his wineglass and emptied it with one long swallow. Her emotional revelation had shaken him. Not because they were in a public place. And certainly not because he'd learned she'd been born out of wedlock. Nowadays no one looked down on a woman for being a single mother. Most of the time it was because she'd chosen to parent the child alone rather than enter into a marriage that wouldn't work. No, the part about her lack of a father hadn't meant that much to Taggart. Hell, for the majority of Taggart's childhood his father had been absent and now that he'd grown into adulthood he saw the man even less.

No, the part of Emily-Ann's admission that had cut Taggart so deeply was the last part. The part about being used instead of loved. Is that how she viewed most men? Did she put him in that same category? The idea sickened him.

Where do you come off being so righteous, Taggart O'Brien? Isn't that exactly what you've been thinking about Emily-Ann? You don't want love or marriage. But when you look at her, you definitely imagine having sex with her. You're no better than the rest. If you had any gumption about you at all you'd take her home and never see her again. And maybe, eventually, she'll meet a real man who'll give her real love.

Sighing heavily, he wiped a hand over his face, then stared out the window at the darkening desert. He'd asked Emily-Ann to have dinner with him tonight because in spite of the great job he'd just landed at Three Rivers, and the money it was bringing to him, he wanted more than that. She made him feel alive again. She made him feel like a man.

He couldn't give her up now. But how did he think he could hold on to her when the very thing she wanted from a man he no longer had? His heart was buried back in Texas.

Chapter Five

By the time Emily-Ann returned to the table, she had pulled her emotions together, but that didn't stop her from feeling like a complete fool. And when Taggart rose to his feet and promptly reached for her hand, she wanted to burst into tears all over again.

"I'm so sorry, Tag," she said lowly. "I hope I didn't embarrass you."

He smiled at her and the warm light in his brown eyes was more comforting to her than he could possibly know.

"What's embarrassing about your date going to the ladies' room? Everything is fine. I've ordered more wine and the waiter said our food should be arriving any minute."

He pulled out her chair and helped her into it as though nothing had happened. Emily-Ann couldn't possibly guess what he was actually thinking, but he was certainly making it easy to face him after the emotional debacle she'd pulled.

After he'd settled back into his own chair, she looked across the table at him. "Thank you, Tag. And I promise there won't be any more hysterics tonight."

"Forget it." He leveled an empathetic look at her. "To be honest, I'm glad you told me everything that you did. I understand you a little better now. There for a while I thought you didn't like me all that much."

She laughed and her reaction put a happy smile on his face. *Thank God*, she thought. Before she returned to the table, she was afraid he'd probably clamp a hand around her arm and lead her straight outside to his truck. And she wouldn't have blamed him. No man wanted to deal with an overwrought woman on their first date.

"I like you, Tag—a whole lot. And that outburst I had, it had nothing to do with you," she said, then promptly shook her head. "Well, that's not true. It had everything to do with you. Because I kept thinking I was ashamed for you to know about my life—my family. I thought you wouldn't want to be with me."

He reached across the table and squeezed her fingers. "I'm sorry that you ever thought such a thing. None of it makes any difference, Emily-Ann. I mean, I hate that your mother had her problems. But you know what I see when I look at you?"

She tightened her fingers around his. "No. Tell me."

"I see that your mother did a good job of raising her daughter."

She felt a part of her heart melting and she blinked her eyes as more tears threatened to appear. "That's the nicest thing anyone has ever said to me, Tag," she murmured. "I'll never forget it."

He started to reply, but the waiter suddenly arrived with their dinner, putting an end to the intimate moment. Still, Emily-Ann didn't mind the timing of the interruption. The night had just begun and she'd already stored away a lot of memories with this special man.

When Emily-Ann and Taggart left Jose's, the night had cooled drastically and she draped the sweater she'd carried with her around her bare shoulders and buttoned the top button to hold it in place.

Taggart understood she needed protection from the cold, but throughout their meal, he'd loved the sight of her bare shoulders. She had that creamy complexion that most redheads possessed and the freckles that dotted the bridge of her nose and cheekbones also speckled her shoulders. Several times during dinner, he'd caught himself fantasizing about kissing all those tiny brown dots and wondering if they were on other parts of her body.

But the fantasy of making love to Emily-Ann was not something he could act upon. The last thing he wanted was for her to think that this time he was spending with her was a prelude to sex. Still, none of that stopped him from resting his hand against the small of her back as they walked slowly to his truck. And to his relief, she didn't move away.

"It's still early. Would you like to take a drive out on the desert?" he asked, as he helped her into the passenger seat.

"I'd love to," she answered. "There's some interesting scenery to the west. But you're the driver, you choose."

"West it is."

After he'd settled himself behind the steering wheel, Taggart drove away from the parking lot and turned onto a street that would eventually lead them to a main highway.

"I've not been in this direction yet," he said once the city of Wickenburg began to appear in the rearview mirror. "I've mostly just driven the highway between town and Three Rivers."

"It's pretty in any direction," she commented, then asked. "Have you ever been to Prescott or Phoenix?"

"No. But sooner or later, I'm sure I'll be going for one reason or another. Actually, Maureen and Blake were going to Prescott tonight for some sort of cattle buyer gathering."

"And they didn't ask you to go with them?"

He grinned. "No, thank goodness. I think they're taking pity on me because we've been so busy. And spring roundup is about to start. That keeps everyone tied down for a week or more."

"I'm glad you didn't have to go to the meeting."

He said, "I'm glad, too. But I feel a little guilty. The Hollisters gave me a huge bonus check today. It was a total surprise. To be honest, the amount of it blew me away."

"You don't think you deserved it?" she asked.

"Not yet." He grunted with wry disbelief. "Heck, I'm not worth that kind of money."

"I don't think you've quite yet absorbed the huge job you've taken on. But the Hollisters do and they clearly appreciate you and trust that you're going to do things right."

"Yeah, I suppose. But I felt very undeserving." He glanced over to see she was studying him with an earnest expression. The idea that she was interested in his job and that she cared enough to discuss it with him not only surprised him, it drew him to her in a way he'd not expected.

"That's the way I felt when you asked me out to dinner," she said. "Very humbled."

"Oh, Emily-Ann. I don't ever want you to feel that way. Not about me or anything else."

From the corner of his eye, he could see she was smiling at him.

"I don't ever want you to feel that way, either," she said. "So we're even."

After traveling several more miles westward on the lonely strip of asphalt, a large picnic area appeared on the right side of the highway. Three concrete tables and a trash receptacle were positioned among two tall saguaros and several Joshua trees. At the moment there didn't appear to be anyone around. In fact, there wasn't any kind of light suggesting civilization was anywhere nearby.

"Let's stop and stretch our legs," he suggested.

"Sounds nice."

He parked the truck to one side of the graveled area and helped Emily-Ann down from the truck. The night had grown even colder than when they'd left Jose's and she quickly pushed her arms into the sweater.

"If it's too chilly for you we can get back inside the truck," he suggested.

"Not at all. It feels good."

Anchoring a hand on the side of her waist, he guided her forward past the tables and over to one of the Joshua trees. To the north of them a ridge of mountains jutted upward toward the starlit sky.

"This is beautiful," he said.

She asked, "I know you said Three Rivers's property looks different than the Flying W where you used to work. But what about this area? Does it look anything like your old stomping ground in Texas?"

"No. The only thing similar is the vast openness."

"Did it snow there?"

"Yes. Sometimes we even had blizzards. That's when ranching is especially hard work."

She looked up at him. "It rarely ever snows here. But that's okay. I'm a terrible driver on slick roads."

Icy fear suddenly lodged in his throat and he outwardly shivered as he tried to swallow away the sensation.

"Tag? Are you okay?"

He wiped a hand over his face. "Yeah, sure. I was just thinking that you should always be careful when you're driving. I lost someone I cared about to a car accident. I don't want anything to happen to you."

"Oh."

As her gaze continued to slip over his face, he could see all sorts of questions in her eyes and Taggart prayed that she wouldn't quiz him. Someday he would tell her everything. But not tonight. Not when he was beginning to feel a change coming over him. A change that he desperately needed.

"Then I promise I'll be extra careful from now on," she said, then with a cheerful smile, changed the subject completely. "See that area to the north? Where the mountains are in the far, far distance?"

He followed the line of her pointed finger. "Yes."

"That's where lots of gold was found in the Congress Mine back in 1884. A town by the same name boomed there for many, many years. But hardly anything is there now. And Constellation, another nearby mining town, is more or less a ghost town. Maybe you'd like to see them sometime? That is, if you like that sort of history. To me it's fascinating to think of all that sudden wealth and how it affected people back in those days when there was very little law and not much civilization."

"I'm sure there were a few men who were murdered for their gold," he said thoughtfully, then glanced down at her. "I would like to see the area sometime if you'd be willing to show me around."

"I'd like that," she said, then laughed. "Actually, one of the women who works at Chandler's clinic lives at Congress. And in her spare times she likes to pan for nuggets. Maybe we could hike up one of the canyons and try it. A good-sized nugget nowadays would buy new flooring for my living room."

He laughed. "That's a practical thought. But only one nugget would be enough?"

"I'm not greedy. Acquiring wealth never really was that important to me. Except…"

When her words trailed away, he looked down to see she was gazing wistfully out at the dark desert.

"Except what?"

"Oh, there were many times when my mother was alive that I wished I could have given her things and made her life easier. I did what I could, but I wish I could've done more." She turned her gaze up to his face. "Do you ever feel like that about your mother?"

He tried not to let the emptiness inside him show on his face. His mother had been the only real anchor he'd ever had in his life. When he'd lost her, it was like he'd drifted out in a big rough ocean with no way to swim back to shore.

"I used to. Before she died." His sigh could barely slip past the achy lump in his throat. "When Blake gave me the bonus check today, I couldn't help but think about her. She would've been amazed and proud. I wanted to change things for the better in her life, too. But her heart gave out before I had the chance."

She reached for his hand and, as the warmth of her fingers tightened around his, a sweet sort of contentment poured through him. The sensation was like nothing he'd ever felt and he wondered if he would ever experience it again. Or was this night something out of the ordinary and tomorrow all the magical feelings would vanish with the light of day?

"At first I didn't think the two of us had much in common," she said softly. "But I'm beginning to see that isn't entirely true."

With his hand still entwined with hers, he turned so that he was facing her. "We do have things in common and the best one is that we like each other's company. Don't we?"

She let out a long breath as her fingers tightened ever so slightly on his. "Yes, we do."

His free hand lifted and he touched the hair that framed part of her forehead. "You're a special woman, Emily-Ann. I want you to always remember that. Promise me that you will."

Starlight illuminated her face enough for him to see her lashes flutter and then her gaze latched on to his. The contact caused his stomach to clench.

"I promise," she whispered.

He allowed his fingers to drop to her cheek and as the tips moved ever so slightly against her petal-soft skin, he knew the rest of her would feel just as incredibly smooth.

"Emily-Ann," he said softly, "would you mind if I kissed you?"

Her gaze continued to cling to his and what he saw there caused his heart to hammer. She wanted him. Maybe just as much as he wanted her.

"I'd be disappointed if you didn't."

He drew in a sharp breath and then before he could change his mind or analyze the wisdom of his actions, he bent his head and softly placed his lips over hers.

She tasted just as good as she had the night of the party, yet somehow he managed to keep his passion tempered throughout the short kiss. Not for anything did he want her to get the idea that he had sex and only sex on his mind.

"That was nice," he murmured as he nuzzled her cheek with the tip of his nose. "Very nice."

Her tongue came out to nervously moisten her bottom lip. "Yes, it was. But I think we—uh, should head home now. I have an early morning scheduled and I'm sure you do, too."

In other words she wasn't going to give him, or herself, a chance to let a second kiss carry them away.

Well, that was good, Taggart thought. That was exactly how it needed to be. Until he was sure that she trusted him. Moreover, that he could trust himself.

"You're right. We should be getting back to your place. I have to meet Matthew at the cattle barn at five thirty in the morning."

His hand still on hers, he gently turned her in the direction of the truck. As they walked slowly back to the vehicle, he was acutely aware of her hip brushing against the side of his leg and the flowery scent of her hair drifting up to his nostrils. Over the years, he'd forgotten all the little things that made a woman enticing. Having Emily-Ann so close was a reminder of all that he'd been missing as a man and he wondered how long he'd be able to keep his desire reined in and his common sense intact.

When Taggart entered the cattle barn early the next morning, Matthew hadn't yet arrived. But he found Chandler busy wrapping up a C-section on a young cow. Since the two ranch hands that were trying to assist him were inexperienced with the process, they were both relieved to see Taggart.

"Boy, are we glad to see you, Tag," Jerry, the taller of the two men told him. "Me and Flip are trying to take care of this little guy, but we've never done this before."

While Chandler continued to stitch the cow's uterus back together, Taggart squatted over the newborn calf that was lying on a special bed to keep it warm. The mucus had already been cleaned from his nose and the rest of his body dried of afterbirth.

"He isn't struggling to breathe and you have him dry and warm. Looks like you've done things right so far," he told the two men.

"Yeah, but Doc says we'll have to see that he gets his mama's milk in the next couple of hours. That ain't gonna be easy," Flip said.

"Easy or not, the calf needs his mother's colostrum," Taggart told the men. "If the mother doesn't want to nurse we'll have to change her mind."

He turned back to Chandler, who'd already moved on to stitching the incision in the cow's flank.

"How is she, Doc?" Taggart asked.

Not bothering to look up, Chandler continued to stitch. "She'll be fine. And the calf doesn't appear to be too stressed. Hopefully, he'll stand within the hour."

Taggart glanced over at the black calf. "He looks big."

"Hell yes, he's far too big for this girl to give birth the normal way. I've been telling Blake the bull he has on this bunch of heifers is too large. I hope you can convince him to do something about it."

"He wants big healthy calves," Jerry spoke up in Blake's defense.

Chandler frowned at the ranch hand. "What good is that going to do if the mamas die trying to give birth to them?"

"I'll talk to him about it," Taggart assured Chandler. "But I'm not sure I'm the right person to convince him."

Chandler muttered a curse as he tied off the suture and poured antiseptic over the incision. "You're the foreman, Tag. It's your job to give him advice about the cattle."

"I know, but Blake is—"

"Not some sort of ranching god," Chandler insisted. "He's just the manager. He doesn't know everything."

Taggart heard shuffling feet behind him and looked over his shoulder to see Jerry and Flip exchanging amused glances. They might think it funny to hear Chandler say Blake didn't know everything. But Taggart hardly found it amusing. He didn't want to get caught in a war of wills between the two brothers.

Taggart said, "I'll talk to him about the bull. If Blake is agreeable to the idea, we could exchange him with the one on the Buzzard Gap range. He's nicely built but a bit smaller."

"Good choice," Chandler said.

With his job finished, the vet gathered his tools and medications, then turned his attention to the calf. Taggart joined him and watched closely as Chandler checked the calf's vitals.

"Thank God his respiration is good." Hanging the stethoscope around his neck, he rose to his full height. "I wish TooTall was here. He's a wizard with calves like this."

"TooTall? Is he a ranch hand I haven't met?" Taggart asked.

"He's Matthew's foreman down on Red Bluff. They're also the best of friends. I don't know if it's because TooTall is Yavapai or what, but he understands livestock and instinctively knows how to care for them. As for this little guy, I'll have to leave him in your hands, Tag. I've got to get to the clinic, pick up Trey and be at the Rafter R Ranch by six thirty. And considering that place is twenty minutes west of Wickenburg, I'm going to be late."

Chandler started out of the barn in a long stride and Taggart called after him, "Don't worry. Doctors are never on time. And put the calf out of your mind. I'll see that he's taken care of."

* * *

It wasn't until the end of the day, after Taggart and Matthew had ridden back into the ranch yard, that Tag had a chance to stop by Blake's office.

Since he'd started working at Three Rivers, which had been about three weeks ago, he'd only been in the ranch manager's office a handful of times. He was already learning that his secretary, Flo, a redhead in her late sixties, had a louder bark than she did bite, and that Matthew and Holt were two of her pets.

Now, as Taggart stepped into the outer office where her desk was located at one end of the long room, the secretary peered over the tops of her bifocals at him.

"Hello, Tag. How's it going today?"

He took a moment to walk over to the woman's desk. So far he'd never seen the work space anywhere close to being tidy. Papers and envelopes, manila folders, and all types of pens and pencils were scattered across the desktop, along with several coffee mugs. Among the jumble was an up-to-date computer and monitor, but so far he had yet to see her using it.

"Busy. Very busy," he told her. "What about you?"

"It never lets up. And at this time of the year Holt gives me the task of filling out all the registration papers for the new foals." Tapping a pencil against the desktop, she regarded him with a thoughtful gaze. "Are you enjoying Three Rivers Ranch so far?"

"I am. The Hollisters are good people."

"You got that right," she said, then sighed. "I miss the heck out of Matthew, but he just had to go and get himself married. Good for him, but just terrible for my heart."

She laughed then and Taggart chuckled with her.

"I hope you're not thinking about getting married yet, Tag. I'm beginning to like you and I'd hate to see you go, too."

Him married? Before his mind could scoff away that idea, Emily-Ann was pushing her way into his thoughts. Not that she'd ever been that far away. All day long she'd been lurking at the edges of his mind, making it hard for him to focus.

"Rest easy, Flo. I don't have any kind of plans for matrimony. And even if I did, I wouldn't leave Three Rivers."

He was about to ask her if Blake was still in his office when a door leading into the man's private office opened and Blake stuck his head around the wooden panel.

"Flo, is—" He paused as he spotted Taggart standing in front of the secretary's desk. "Tag! I didn't know you were here. Did you stop by to see me or Flo?"

Taggart grinned at the secretary. "Well, Flo is much prettier than you. But I'm not sure she wants to talk about cows."

Flo batted a dismissive hand at the two men. "You two go talk about cows. I have work to do."

Blake motioned for Taggart to join him and he followed the ranch manager into his private office.

The room was furnished with plush leather furniture and decorated with all sorts of photos taken from different sections of the ranch. Some of them depicted huge herds of horses, while others were images of cattle grazing on desert mountain slopes and along the river's edge.

"Would you like some coffee? It's only two hours old," Blake said with a chuckle. "But I can have Jazelle bring us some fresh."

"Don't bother with that. I'm fine." He started toward one of the wooden chairs in front of Blake's desk, but detoured at the last moment when one particular photo on the wall caught his eye. It was a picture of a very old cabin shrouded by cottonwoods, pines and blooming sagebrush. "This is neat. I'm guessing it must be on the ranch somewhere."

"It's the original Three Rivers Ranch house. That's where my great great grandparents lived when they first arrived in Yavapai County."

Taggart was amazed. All along he'd assumed that the Hollisters had always had wealth. Obviously this photo proved that theory wrong.

"Are you saying the ranch started like this and grew into what it is today? That's incredible, Blake." He turned away from the photo to see Blake was sitting in the executive chair behind his desk. The wan smile on his tired face held a touch of pride.

"I agree. Sometimes I have to stop and remind myself that the ranch wasn't always like this." He shrugged one shoulder. "Actually, I think my great great grandfather came to Arizona planning to find a fortune in gold. But he didn't take to mining and soon figured out he could make money by raising beef to feed all the miners and people who'd flooded in to the area in search of wealth. And as it turned out, he figured right. The gold ran out, but the need for beef still remains."

Taggart sank into one of the chairs and propped his ankles out in front of him. He'd had a long day and it wasn't over yet. But when he listened to Blake talk about his ancestors and the beginning of the ranch, he realized that he'd become a part of something bigger than he could've ever imagined. It was a heady feeling for the little boy who'd once worn hand-me-down clothes and helped his mother stuff rags around the window facings to keep the dust and cold wind from blowing into their house.

"The man obviously had a vision," Taggart remarked.

"Yeah. And sometimes not following the crowd takes courage," Blake said, then lifted a brow in his direction. "But you didn't come by to talk about the history of the Hollisters and Three Rivers. What's on your mind?"

"Bulls. And calves," he said bluntly. "Chandler had to perform another C-section this morning. The fourth one out of that particular head of heifers. I understand that four is a mighty small number when you're dealing with thousands, but the way I see it, each cow and calf is important."

"Damn right each one is important." He swiped a hand over his face. "I haven't had a chance to talk to Chandler today. Is the cow/calf pair okay?"

Taggart nodded. "The cow is in fine shape. The calf is a little weak, but he's coming around. I have Flip and Jerry caring for him."

Blake's brows pulled together in a frown. "And that's two men you could use elsewhere."

"I'm not concerned about being shorthanded."

"Then you're worried that more C-sections are going to be needed." He rose from the chair and walked over to a small table holding a coffee maker and all the fixings. After he poured himself a cup of the black liquid, he carried it over to a long leather couch and sank onto the end cushion. "Last year I took a chance and put Rambler—that's the bull on Juniper Flats—on that particular herd of heifers. Every rancher wants big healthy calves and I was hoping there wouldn't be problems. Looks like I made the wrong choice."

"I wouldn't say you made the wrong choice," Taggart reasoned. "A man has to take chances if he ever expects to get what he wants."

Grimacing, Blake sipped the coffee. "True. But in this case it looks like I need to make another choice."

Taggart shifted uncomfortably on the chair. "I'd like to make a suggestion. That we move the bull that's presently on the Buzzard Gap range to the heifers' pasture. His size would be much more compatible. I think it would cut down on the number of difficult births."

Blake leveled a knowing look at him. "You've been talking to Chandler about this."

"Only this morning when he was finishing up the surgery. But if you're thinking I'm here to be Doc's voice, you're wrong. I'm speaking for the welfare of the heifers and babies."

"Well, I'll tell you, Tag, Mom and I hired you because of your experience and knowledge. We value and welcome your opinion."

While Blake leaned back against the couch and thoughtfully considered the situation, Taggart rubbed a hand against the stubble on his jaw. His face hadn't seen a razor since last night, before he'd picked up Emily-Ann. But he'd never liked shaving and avoided the task as long as he could. If he looked grungy now, he doubted the ranch manager cared.

"All right, Tag, I'm going to go along with your suggestion. Even though part of the breeding season has already taken place, it might save us problems on down the line."

More relieved than he cared to admit, Taggart

thanked him and the two men went on to discuss how and when to move the bulls. Once everything was decided, Taggart stood.

"I've taken up enough of your time," Taggart told him, then glanced at his watch. "You've probably missed dinner with your family."

Blake chuckled. "The twins are always waiting to join me, so their daddy never eats alone," he said. "And speaking of dinners, how did yours go with Emily-Ann last night?"

With everything Blake had to deal with, Taggart hadn't expected Blake to remember about the date with Emily-Ann, much less ask about it.

"It was good. I enjoyed it and I think she did, too."

Blake nodded with approval. "Glad to hear it. She deserves a nice guy like you."

She certainly deserved a nice guy, Taggart silently agreed. But he could hardly put himself in that category. Not when half of his thoughts about Emily-Ann were far from nice. In fact, they were downright naughty.

Clearing his throat, Taggart said, "Emily-Ann deserves the best. But I—I'm not really in the market for anything serious."

Crossing his arms across his chest, he studied Taggart for a long moment. "Dear God, don't tell me you're like Holt used to be."

"How's that?" Taggart asked.

Blake snorted. "Too many women and not enough

time. That was Holt's motto—until he met Isabelle. I didn't know a man could be that transformed until I saw it with my own eyes."

Taggart was as far from a womanizer as a man could get. And he sure couldn't picture himself as a husband or daddy. Not now. With a shake of his head, he said, "I don't think I need to be transformed. Not like Holt."

Laughing, Blake shooed him toward the door. "You must be tired. Get on out of here."

Taggart left the office and as he shut the door behind him, he saw Flo still working diligently over a ledger book. Did people still use those things? Apparently, she did.

Not bothering to glance up, Flo said, "I heard laughter. You must have said something really funny to make Blake laugh."

"Just a little something about my love life, Flo."

That brought her head up and as she stared at him with her mouth open, Taggart hurried out of the office.

Chapter Six

"Oh, look at that yellow-print dress! It's adorable!" Camille exclaimed as she and Emily-Ann paused on the sidewalk to peer in the plate glass window of Cactus and Candles Boutique. "You would look great in it!"

Emily-Ann groaned. "I don't have the waistline for that. But you do."

"Don't be silly. You have curves from here to yonder and the belt at the waistline will show them off. Now me, I have no waist at all right now."

"Well, not at the moment," Emily-Ann told her as she eyed Camille's very pregnant belly. "But you'll have one soon. Come on, let's go in and you buy the dress for yourself. It'll look great with a pair of cowboy boots."

Laughing, Camille grabbed her by the hand and the two women went into the little boutique.

An hour later, they came out with Emily-Ann carrying two sacks filled with dresses, shoes and fashion jewelry.

"You shouldn't have bought these things for me," Emily-Ann continued to argue as she loaded the items into the back seat of Camille's truck. "I thought we came out this afternoon to spend time together, not your money."

"Oh, pooh, I didn't spend that much. And if I can't buy my friend something once in a while, then what good is having money?" Camille said as she slipped behind the steering wheel. "Besides, do you know how often I go shopping for girly things?"

"I doubt very often," Emily-Ann said as she climbed into the passenger seat and fastened her seat belt. "From what you say, you're usually at the diner, or working on the baby's nursery. And what about that sweet little tot you're carrying? There's a children's store on the next block. It has all sorts of clothing and toys and baby furniture. Let's go in there and I'll pick out something for him."

"Whoa, did you say *him*?"

Emily-Ann grinned. "I did. A boy is what I think it's going to be. Why? Do you or Matthew want a girl?"

Smiling, Camille reversed the truck onto the street. "Well, I think a girl would be nice. After all, I have four brothers and only one sister. As for Matthew, it doesn't matter to him. I think he's already got it in his head that we're going to have a dozen babies."

"Uh, that might be kind of hard on you, don't you think?"

Camille laughed. "Well, twelve was kind of an exaggeration on my part. But I know he wants at least two or three children and so do I."

Emily-Ann looked over at her friend. "I can't imagine how you must feel, Camille. To have Matthew love you like he does and to know you're going to have his baby. You must feel like you're floating on a cloud or something."

Spotting the sign of the children's store hanging beneath the awning over the sidewalk, Emily-Ann pointed to an empty parking spot. "There's the store. Pull in here."

Camille parked the truck, but kept the motor and the air-conditioning running as she turned on the seat to look at Emily-Ann. "Before we go in I want to say something about your floating-on-a-cloud idea. Marriage isn't a big party where everything is fun and perfect."

Emily-Ann grimaced. "I might be scatterbrained at times, but I have sense enough to know that nothing in life is perfect. Including people and marriages.

God knows I had to watch Mom suffer through years of a worthless husband. But you're very happy, Camille. And you do have a man who loves you."

"You're right on both counts. But that doesn't mean every day is smooth sailing. I'm busy trying to keep the diner a profit, while planning for the baby. And Matthew is working long hours to build up Red Bluff. But," she added with a dreamy grin, "we're doing it all together. And that makes everything worthwhile."

Shaking her head, she said, "If you're trying to give me marriage advice, Camille, you're wasting your time. It's going to take more than your bridal bouquet to find me a good man. It'll take a miracle."

Camille reached over and pressed Emily-Ann's hand between both of hers. "This life I have with Matthew—that's what I want for you, Emmie. To have someone who loves you. Someone you can share the good and bad times with. I know it will happen for you if you just let it."

The image of Taggart's handsome face suddenly floated to the front of Emily-Ann's mind, yet to imagine a man such as him loving her, sharing his life with her seemed impossible.

Three days had passed since he'd taken her to Jose's for dinner and she'd not seen or heard from him even once. But that discouraging fact wasn't enough to get the man's kiss out of her mind. And he had kissed her. Oh yes. The memory of when they'd stood beneath the Joshua tree and he'd pulled her into his arms was still achingly fresh in her mind. But apparently it had been a forgettable moment for him. Otherwise, he would have surely contacted her by now.

Determined not to let Taggart O'Brien ruin this evening with her friend, she purposely put on a cheery face. Not for anything did she want Camille to guess that she was pining foolishly over something she couldn't have.

"I'll try to let it happen. And maybe one day it will. Right now I'm just thrilled for you," she said, then tugged on her hand. "Now come on. Let's go buy the kid something he can have fun with later on."

Camille laughed. "You're saying *he* again. I might as well give up and accept the fact that we're going to have a son. That's what TooTall has been saying all along anyway. And you can't argue with that guy's predictions."

"Oh yes. TooTall is the mystic Yavapai. The one who kept telling Matthew he was going to marry you." She thoughtfully tapped a finger against her chin. "Wonder what kind of prediction he'd make for me?"

"Hmm. Probably that once you become a nurse you're going to fall in love and marry a handsome doctor."

Emily-Ann burst out laughing. "I wouldn't take a doctor if you handed him to me on a silver platter. If he wasn't working, he'd always have his patients on his mind. Just give me a good ole Joe. Preferably, one with a heart."

Rolling her eyes, Camille cut the motor and reached for her handbag. "You know what's wrong with you, Emmie? When it comes to men you're just too picky."

Laughing again, Emily-Ann opened the truck door. "Come on. Let's see if we can find junior a pair of miniature chaps like his daddy wears."

By the time Taggart left Hollister Animal Clinic and pulled into Emily-Ann's driveway, it was nearing eight thirty. He doubted she would be in bed at such an early hour, but he also realized it was rather late to make an unexpected visit. But three days had passed since their date and he'd waffled about contacting her. If she slammed the door in his face, he couldn't blame her.

A short moment after he knocked on the door, he saw the flutter of a curtain at the window, then the rattle of the doorknob.

"Tag!" she exclaimed, as she pulled the door wide. "Is something wrong at the ranch?"

Bemused, he asked, "You think something has to be wrong for me to drop by and say hello?"

She hesitated for only a second. "Well—uh—no. I'm just surprised to see you, that's all. Please come in."

He stepped into the room and waited for her to

deal with the door before he spoke. "I apologize for coming by so late. I did try to call you a couple of times, but the signal on my phone kept failing. I had to bring a mare to Doc's clinic this evening and I just got away from there."

She stood with her hands folded in front of her, surveying him with uncertainty in her eyes. It was obvious she still didn't trust his motives and that frustrated the heck out of him. But maybe she had a right to be suspicious of him, Taggart thought. Especially when he didn't know himself just where his feelings for Emily-Ann were headed.

She said, "You and the Hollisters keep late hours."

"That's part of the job," he said, as he took in the pretty picture she made in a dark red skirt and white blouse. "Were you—er—busy? I don't want to interrupt."

"You're not interrupting. In fact, I was just about to make myself a sandwich. Would you care to join me? Or have you already eaten?"

Relieved that she was inviting him to stay, he took off his hat and raked fingers through his flattened hair. "A sandwich would be great. I haven't eaten since early this morning."

She motioned for him to follow her. "Come with me to the kitchen."

On the way out of the living room, he dropped his hat on an end table, then trailed her through a short hallway that led off in three different directions. A wide door directly in front of them was open and as she entered the brightly lit space, he could see it was an old-fashioned kitchen with knotty pine cabinets and a single white porcelain sink.

A stack of books was piled at one end of the farm table and she quickly began moving them to the far end of the cabinet counter.

"I've been studying for a test. Human anatomy. The last one I made a B, but I'm afraid this one is going to be much harder," she said, then gestured for him to take a seat. "Make yourself comfortable and I'll get the sandwich makings."

"I can help if you'll tell me what to do," he offered.

"Thanks, but I can manage."

She opened the refrigerator and bent down to the crisper. Taggart couldn't bring himself to look away from the rounded shape of her bottom and the way the fabric of the skirt clung to the tempting curves.

He drew in a deep breath and let it out. "Do you normally eat this late?"

"No," she answered, with her head still half- hidden in the refrigerator. "After I closed the shop this afternoon I went out with Camille on a little shopping venture and she insisted we go for milkshakes. So I'm just now getting a bit hungry."

After piling packages of lunchmeat and cheese onto the cabinet counter, she glanced over her shoulder at him. "What about you? You didn't have time to stop for supper?" she asked.

"No. Everyone on the ranch has been very busy. We're getting ready for spring roundup and that takes all hands and the cook."

"Yes, I've heard Camille talk about those days. She and Vivian used to go help." She gathered more items from the refrigerator and shut the door. As she washed a tomato and a head of lettuce at the sink, she said, "I haven't heard from you since we went to Jose's. I'd pretty much decided you probably didn't want to see me anymore."

"Why would I decide that?" he asked, while feeling like a heel. Not that he owed her any explanations. It wasn't like they were a couple or anything. But it was like Blake had implied, Emily-Ann deserved a nice guy. She deserved to be respected and he wasn't giving her that by ignoring her. Nor was he being a nice guy by leading her along to nowhere.

"Personal reasons," she said frankly. "What else?"

Taggart couldn't bear the distance between them. Not while she was talking as though there was nothing between them except a meal and a bit of conversation. Damn it, he'd kissed her. Had she already forgotten that? Or did she have the idea that a kiss meant nothing to him?

How could she possibly figure out what you're thinking? About kissing or anything else, Taggart? She doesn't know who you really are. You haven't told her about Becca or the baby, or any of the things that are still twisting your vision of the future.

Heaving out a heavy breath, he walked over to where she stood. "Well, I could say I've been working overtime and I wouldn't be lying. But that doesn't mean I couldn't have pulled out my phone and sent you a text."

Her gaze locked on the task of slicing the tomato onto a plate, she said, "That notion did cross my mind. But you've mentioned before that you don't like phones. And anyway, it's all okay, Tag. You don't owe me explanations or anything. It's not like we'd planned to see each other again."

Her casual attitude stung him. Which was really stupid. That's the way he wanted things to be with Emily-Ann. Simple and easy with no ties or promises. So why did he want to grab her and hold on? So he could be hurt all over again? And possibly hurt her, too?

Shoving away that dismal thought, he said, "I didn't call or send a message because I've been telling myself that the best thing I could ever do for you is to never see you again. I mean—as in a date."

She dropped the knife and turned to face him. "Why? Because you thought about all those things I told you—about my mother? About the irresponsible bastard who fathered me?"

Frowning, he gently placed his hands on her shoulders. "No! You're not even close. The doubts are inside of me, Emily-Ann. I think you ought to know that when it comes to women—well, several years ago some things happened in my life that changed everything for me. Now, I honestly don't think I could ever be a husband to any woman. And I don't believe I'm supposed to be a father. So you see, if we started dating and getting close…it…wouldn't be fair or right for you."

Her eyes darkened as she continued to stare at him. "Then why did you ask me out in the first place? Why in hell did you kiss me?"

His fingers tightened on her shoulders and it suddenly struck him that trying to be a nice guy was the toughest challenge he'd ever faced. "Because I like you. Because I was lonely and wanted company. Your company. And why do you think I kissed you? You're damned desirable, Emily-Ann. And I'm not made of steel."

"Here's a revelation for you. I'm not made of steel either," she muttered.

Groaning, he said, "Now you're angry with me."

A resigned look came over her face and then she turned away from him and walked to the end of the cabinets. As she pulled out plates and glasses, she said, "No. I'm not angry with you, Tag. In fact, I want to thank you for being honest and not leading me down a dead-end street. That's more than I've ever gotten from other men. It's just that the other night—when we were together—I honestly began to think you might be different. I was wrong. But that's okay, too. I've been a fool before. Many times."

She looked at him and smiled, but the expression didn't reach her eyes. Actually, everything about it said she was looking at the biggest disappointment she'd ever seen in the shape of a man. Until this moment Taggart didn't know it was possible to feel lower than a heel, but he did. He was now on the level of a snake.

"But that doesn't mean we can't still be friends," she told him, then held up a hand as he took a step toward her. "But no kissing. No romance. No ideas that we're going to be a couple. Ever."

He felt sick inside. He felt like he'd been hammered and nailed and tossed aside like a horseshoe that couldn't bend to a shape that would fit.

"That's—uh—fine with me, Emily-Ann. We can be friends and not hurt each other."

"Right. I'm good at being a friend. Not so good at being a lover."

Lover. His lover. Dear Lord, he had to be the biggest hypocrite walking the earth. He was standing here trying to pretend that he wasn't aching to take her to bed right this minute. But having sex with her wouldn't work. No. Not now or ever.

He tried to smile, but the best he could do was twist his lips to a lopsided slant. "Now that we have all that settled, let's have that sandwich. What do you say?"

She didn't smile back at him. Nor did she bother looking him in the eye. Instead, she quickly turned

back to the cabinet. "I say the sandwiches are coming right up. And I've changed my mind, you can
help by getting ice for the glasses and putting the
plates on the table."

Well, that was that, he thought. She knew where
he stood and he understood how she felt about it.
Problem solved. All he needed to do now was to
figure out how to get rid of the empty feeling in the
middle of his chest.

With a silent sigh, he rose to his feet and joined
her at the cabinet.

It was silly of her to feel deflated, Emily-Ann
thought, as she choked down the last bite of ham-
and-cheese sandwich. From the very first, she'd
known that she didn't have the slightest chance of
having any kind of meaningful relationship with Taggart. Even after their evening at Jose's and that kiss
on the desert, she'd continually told herself not to
set her dreams on the man. She wasn't his kind of
woman. And heaven knew he wasn't her kind of man.

And yet, her heart was heavy with disappointment. Maybe if Taggart had been the first man to
tell her he wasn't the marrying kind, she could shrug
the whole thing off. But now she had to add him to
a long list of guys who'd been too commitment shy
to give her a serious thought. It was something that
had happened to her over and over. And in spite of
Camille's optimism that Emily-Ann would find true

love someday, she was beginning to accept the fact it wasn't meant for her. Just as it hadn't been meant for her mother.

Rising from her seat at the table, she went over to the cabinet and began filling a coffee maker with grounds and water. "If I'd known you were going to drop by I could've had something better than sandwiches for you. But I do have a few fried apple pies—if you'd like one for dessert."

"No. I've already eaten two sandwiches and most of your potato chips. I don't want to eat up all your groceries," he said.

Shaking her head, she opened a flat plastic container and placed three of the small pies onto a paper plate. "I can't eat them all. Besides, you bought my dinner the other night. So we're even on the groceries. Sort of. You got the short end of the stick."

He smiled at her. "I don't think so."

Grabbing two mugs from the cabinet, she filled them with coffee and carried them and the plate of pies over to the table.

"Did you make these?" he asked as she placed one of the pies onto his plate.

She chuckled. "No. Don't worry. Conchita made these for the shop. Fried pies are something she doesn't do on a daily basis. Just whenever she gets the urge. I'm not that good of a cook. I can do simple things like spaghetti or pork chops and mashed potatoes. I do try brownies once in a while, but they usually turn out like rubber. Conchita tells me I'm cooking them too long. Easy for her to say. She's cooked for fifty years."

"Mmm. The pie is delicious," he said. "And so is the coffee."

She gave him a wry smile. "At least I'm good at that."

He consumed the pie and she motioned for him to take another. "They're small. And I don't want to be tempted. So please eat all of them."

While he continued to eat, she asked, "Was the mare you brought into the clinic injured or something? I hope she's going to be okay."

"She doesn't have any kind of injury. Holt wanted a few tests done on her that Doc could only perform at the clinic. She lost her first foal, so he wants to make sure everything is well with her before he breeds her again."

"It was nice of you to haul her to the clinic for him. I'm sure Holt wants to spend as much time as he can with Isabelle and baby Carter."

Taggart sipped his coffee. "I'm not so sure Holt was going straight home. He wanted to use the extra time to have a talk with Blake. I think the brothers are trying to figure out the situation with Gil and their mother."

Emily-Ann shrugged. "What's to figure out? Gil has moved back and he wants to spend time with Maureen. That's the way I see it."

"Yes, but he's moved into the ranch house with the rest of the family."

"Makes sense to me, too," Emily-Ann said. "The house is huge. Even with Blake and Chandler living there with their families, there's still plenty of room."

Nodding, he said, "On the surface it should be that simple. The way I see it, if Maureen wants to be close to her late husband's brother, then that's her business. Not Blake's or Holt's or anyone else's. But from what Doc has conveyed to me, the brothers are still trying to solve the mystery of Joel's death."

"Don't you mean murder?" she asked grimly, then shook her head. "I realize the family doesn't come out and say those words in front of just any and everybody. But Camille and I have discussed it. And Isabelle has also talked to me about the situation. She says Holt is haunted over the circumstances of his father's death. Camille says the same thing about Matthew."

Nodding soberly, he said, "Losing a loved one is bad all around. But I figure the not knowing makes it even harder for the Hollisters, Gil included. After all, the man lost his brother. Being a detective for thirty years makes Blake and his brothers wonder if he's really come back to Three Rivers to do some investigating of his own, or if he's only interested in their mother."

"Maybe he's interested in both," Emily-Ann reasoned. "I didn't talk to the man that much the night of the party, but he seems very sincere. I only wish—"

He arched an inquisitive brow at her. "What do you wish?"

She looked away from him and sighed. "Only that my mother could've had a man like him in her life."

"Did your mother ever marry?" he asked.

Glancing back at him, she nodded. "Yes, once. Gorman Smith was a salesman from California. Somehow he ended up here in Wickenburg—that was about the time I turned a year old. Back then I think he sold tires or cars. Later on, he turned to selling insurance policies. But never had much money to show for it."

"Where is he now?"

"I have no idea and I'll be happy to keep it that way. As a stepfather, he wasn't abusive or anything. He was just mostly absent, if you know what I mean. The neighbor next door was more of a father to me than Gorman ever was." She clutched her coffee cup and tried to keep her emotions in check. "Iris thought he could do no wrong and when he talked about all of his big dreams, she honestly believed he was going to achieve them. She was always telling me that someday Gorman was going to make our lives much better."

"Did your mother love the man?"

Emily-Ann stared into her coffee cup. "That's

the saddest part about it. She loved him with all her heart."

"I don't see that as sad, Emily-Ann. Loving the man must have made her happy, otherwise she would've kicked him out."

Lifting her gaze to his, she said, "Mom didn't know any better. She was gullible and softhearted and Gorman used that to his advantage. A week hadn't passed after her death when he packed up and lit out."

His eyes narrowed as he studied her face. "Were you grown then?"

"I was eighteen and had just graduated high school. So I suppose I qualified as an adult. I tell you one thing, I was better off with him gone than I would've been with him sitting around drinking beer and bragging about his next moneymaking scheme."

"I'm sorry, Emily-Ann," he said quietly. "I wish it had been different for you and your mother. But you're still very young. You can make your life what you want it to be."

No, Emily-Ann thought. It was impossible to make a man love her if he didn't want to. But then that kind of self-pitying attitude was not going to get her anywhere. In fact, she needed to be smart enough to see that she didn't need a man in her life to make her happy. She didn't need babies like the Hollister families were having right and left. After all, she was going to be a nurse. The profession would provide all the caring and nurturing she needed to feel fulfilled.

"You're so right. And I want to be a nurse. Anything else, I'll leave up to fate."

Rising from her seat, she began to clear the remains of their light supper from the tabletop.

Taggart rose, too, and carried his empty plate and cup over to the sink. "Fate isn't always kind, Emily-Ann."

"Neither are some people."

"I suppose you're talking about me now," he said.

She twisted open the hot water knob and dropped the stopper into the sink. As it filled, she glanced over to see a frown on his face. Both his expression and remark surprised her.

"Why no. I don't think you're unkind at all, Tag."

"Well, I feel very unkind and very phony." His frown was more like a look of anguish as he stepped toward her. "I'm a hypocrite, a liar and a coward to boot. A while ago when I told you I didn't want us to be anything more than friends I was lying. Hell, even as I was speaking the words, I wanted to make love to you."

Make love or have sex. She didn't know which one he meant and her mind was spinning at such a rapid speed she couldn't begin to absorb everything he'd just said. But she had managed to latch on to one key word. *Want.* He wanted her.

"If that's the way you honestly feel, then why did you lie to me?"

Groaning, he wrapped his hands over her shoulders. "I was trying to be a gentleman and do the right thing. Blake says you deserve a nice guy and he's right. You deserve a good man and everything he can give you. But I—" He paused and shook his head with defeat. "These past few minutes I've come to realize that I'm too selfish to give you up to some other man. I want to be the guy who holds you, kisses you—makes love to you."

By the time the last of his huskily spoken words had passed his lips, he was drawing her into the tight circle of his arms and Emily-Ann's heart began to thump so hard and fast she felt light-headed.

Her breathing turned to shallow sips as she dared to flatten her hands against his chest and slide them slowly and surely up to his shoulders. "I lied, too, Taggart. I don't want to be just your friend. I want to be everything to you."

Desire flashed in his brown eyes before his head dropped and his face hovered so close to hers that she could see the pores in his skin, the tiny lines marking his lips.

"Everything," he murmured. "Yes. That's what I want, too."

His soft breath caressed her cheeks and lips and she closed her eyes against the onslaught of sensations rippling over her skin.

She whispered his name but that was all she could manage to say before his lips settled perfectly over hers.

The contact was instant combustion and as his mouth created a firestorm upon her lips, flames spread throughout her body, scorching every spot, every cell it touched.

Beyond the incredible heat washing through her, she was aware of the hard band of his arms tightening around her, drawing her ever closer to the hard wall of his body. Yet it was his kiss that continued to monopolize her senses.

She wanted more. And as his tongue prodded at the opening between her teeth, she realized he felt the same. She opened her mouth to welcome him inside and he immediately began a slow search of the ribbed roof and sharp edges of her teeth. The erotic exploration was more than enough to set off an ache deep between her thighs and, with a needy groan, she wrapped her arms around him and allowed herself to become lost in the total domination of his kiss.

Somehow, her swirling senses managed to register the loud thump of her heartbeat, the humming of the refrigerator and the faint tick of the clock hanging on the wall near the table. Outside the window, the branches of an ash tree scraped against the glass. Strange that she could be aware of all these things and yet not know how much time had marched by since he'd taken her into his arms.

She didn't have a clue as to whether the embrace had gone on for short seconds or several long minutes. Nor did she recognize how the kiss had grown into something far deeper, until his hands latched on to the sides of her hips and pulled them tightly against his. The bulge of his erection straining against his jeans was evidence that he wanted her as much as she wanted him.

She was wrapping her arms around his neck and trying to press herself even closer when he suddenly tore his mouth from hers and stepped back. The unexpected break was so abrupt, Emily-Ann very nearly staggered backward and into the wall of cabinets.

Darting a confused glance at him, she could see he was breathing hard and staring at her with dark, narrowed eyes.

"Tag, what's wrong?" Fearing he was about to bolt from the kitchen, she latched a hand over his forearm. "If you try to tell me that you don't want me, I'll know you're lying. Because you do. Just as much as I want you."

A look of torment came over his face and then he rested his forehead against hers. Emily-Ann couldn't resist slipping her arms around his waist.

"I'm sorry, Emily-Ann. I realize I probably look like an ass to you—or something far worse. But this isn't how I want things for us. I want our time together to be right—special. Not acted out on a hurried whim."

Our time together. The words rolled around in her head, but she dared not take them to heart.

"And how are you going to feel tomorrow, or the next day?" she asked. "Are you going to change your mind again about me—us?"

As she waited for him to answer, she could only think how she didn't want to let him go. She wanted to lead him to her bedroom, shut the door and not let him out until the morning sun was shining through the window.

A wry smile touched his lips. "It wouldn't make any difference if I did. I can't stay away from you. Tonight proves it."

God only knew how very much she wanted to believe him, but so far he'd not done much to help her build any kind of trust.

The doubts circling her thoughts must have shown on her face because he frowned and shook his head.

"You don't believe me," he said.

A sudden feeling of hopelessness washed over her and it cooled the last remnants of the hot desire she'd felt only moments ago. "It's hard to trust you, Tag, when one minute you're hot and the next you're cold. You tell me you want to stay away from me and then you tell me you lied."

She slowly turned away from him and walked over to the table where the last of the leftovers of their meal remained. As she plucked up the bread and a basket of potato chips, he came up behind her and slipped his arms around her waist. His warm body lightly touched hers and she did her best to keep the traitorous stirring in her body far away from the region of her heart.

"Emily-Ann, I don't want to be like the other men who've let you down. I'm trying to be honest," he said, his voice muffled by her hair. "But we've not known each other all that long and it would be wrong of me to start making promises that I can't keep."

Some things happened in my life that changed everything for me.

What could have happened? If it was affecting him that much, why didn't he want to share it with her? She wanted to question him, to demand that he explain. But something told her that now was the wrong time to try to peel away the curtain where he'd hidden his past. Besides, if he ever did truly start to care for her, she wouldn't have to push him to share those things inside him. He'd tell her all on his own.

I know it will happen for you if you just let it.

Camille's advice joined Emily-Ann's tumbling thoughts and suddenly she realized what her dear friend had been trying to tell her. If she ever expected to find love, she was going to have to open her heart and take a chance.

Smiling softly, she turned and looked up at him. "I understand, Tag. Really."

Surprise widened his eyes. "You do?"

Nodding, she reached up and smoothed a finger over the day-old whiskers on his face. "I do. Because I—I'm a little mixed-up. Part of me wants you with a vengeance, while the other part wants to run until I put miles and miles between us."

His sigh was a sound of relief. "That sort of describes what's been going on with me." His hands wrapped gently over her shoulders. "We can figure this out, Emily-Ann. We just need time—together."

"I like the sound of that," she told him.

He bent his head and placed a soft, swift kiss on her lips. "It's not polite to eat and run. But it's getting late and I have a long drive back to Three Rivers." Lifting a hand, he traced fingertips along her cheekbone. "And if I continue to stay I might not be able to leave."

With a clever smile, she looped her arm through his. "And I might not let you leave. So I'll walk you to the door."

Out in the living room, he let himself out and Emily-Ann stood in the open doorway and watched as he crossed the small porch.

When he reached the bottom of the steps, he turned and lifted a hand in farewell. "I'll call you soon," he promised.

She laughed softly. "This from a man who dislikes phones?"

"If it gives me a chance to hear your voice I can

deal with it for a few minutes." He shot her a smile, then disappeared into the shadows shrouding the driveway. After a moment, his truck fired to life and then he was driving away.

Emily-Ann watched until she could no longer see his taillights in the distance, then walked thoughtfully through the house until she reached the kitchen. And as she finished cleaning up the remnants of their meal, she prayed that Taggart wasn't going to make a mess of her heart.

Chapter Seven

With his back propped against a desert willow, Taggart stared into the low flames of the campfire and listened to the distant sound of a ranch hand singing along to the rhythmic twangs of a guitar. The last calf had been turned loose at the branding fire two hours ago. The horses had been fed, watered and confined in a simple rope corral the cowboys had erected next to the wall of a rock bluff. The long day's work had finally ended.

The cowboy's song trailed away, but plenty of sounds remained to fill the silence of the night. A hoot owl joined the crackle of the flames, while in the far distance coyotes yipped and howled.

I've heard that coyotes mate for life.

Even when Emily-Ann had been talking about the wild animals, he'd caught a dreamy, romantic note in her voice. She wanted to think and believe that there was such a thing as true love that lasted forever. But he figured her past held her back from truly believing she'd ever be a part of such a union. Just like his past was throwing up a thick wall every time he tried to picture a long-term future with her.

There were some people that weren't ever meant to live a happily-ever-after, he decided, as he closed his eyes and rubbed fingertips against the weary lids. He didn't know if Emily-Ann was one of those misfortunate few, but he definitely figured he was. Why else would Becca and the baby have been taken away from him so cruelly and suddenly?

He'd been sitting there for several long minutes, his thoughts drifting, when a familiar voice sounded nearby.

"Tag, are you asleep?"

Roused by the question, Taggart opened his eyes to see Chandler standing a few feet away. Since the veterinarian hadn't worked roundup today, he was surprised that the man had driven several miles from the ranch house to join them here at camp tonight.

"I wasn't asleep. Just resting my eyes. I think the hot sun has burned holes in both of them." Taggart slowly pushed himself away from the tree. "What are you doing here? Blake told me you had a heavy day scheduled at the clinic."

"I had a hell of a whopper day at the clinic," he told him. "But it all went well. I came out tonight because Holt and Blake wanted to talk. While Mom isn't here," he added pointedly.

Since they'd started the roundup five days ago, this was the first and only night that Maureen hadn't remained in camp. This evening a couple of hours before dark, she'd ridden back to the ranch to deal with some paperwork that Flo couldn't put off any longer.

"Is anything wrong?" Taggart asked.

Chandler grimaced. "Nothing is wrong. We just rather her not know that her sons are putting their heads together—behind her back, that is."

"I'm sorry. I don't understand. I thought Maureen knew everything about the ranch."

"She does. But this isn't about the ranch. It's about Dad."

"Oh." Taggart reached for his hat lying near his thigh and levered it back onto his head. As he rose from his seat on the ground, he asked, "Is there something you need for me to do?"

"Yes, there is. We want you to join us. We all figure that you're a part of this family now and it wouldn't be good if you didn't know and understand what's going on."

Glancing around, Taggart noticed that sometime

during his drowsy musings, the last of the men had slipped away from the fire to hit their waiting bed-rolls.

"Damn, Doc, I'm just the foreman. I don't have any right to sit in on a family meeting."

Chandler frowned at him. "If you had known Dad you would've loved him and he would've felt the same about you. And don't ever let any of us hear you say you're *just* the foreman. That's not the way we are here on Three Rivers. We're family."

Seeing that Chandler was completely sincere, Taggart felt humbled. "All right. Since you put it that way, I'd be honored to sit in."

At the opposite end of the night camp, a chuck wagon and a large tent sat near a huge mesquite tree. A paint horse was tied to a nearby picket line and Taggart recognized it as the late Joel Hollister's personal horse. The one he'd been on when he'd met his death.

"That's Major Bob. How did he get here?" Taggart questioned him about the horse, while thinking Chandler had surely driven one of the four-wheel drive vehicles from the ranch yard.

"I rode him over. Major Bob loves spring roundup and since he's getting a bit of age on him, we don't want to use him hard every day. I'm going to leave him for Mom to ride tomorrow and I'll ride one of the extra mounts back to the ranch tonight. That will make her and Major Bob happy."

And one of the first things Taggart had learned since he'd arrived at Three Rivers Ranch was that one of the main priorities of the Hollister brothers was making their mother happy.

Chandler motioned for Taggart to follow him into the tent and once they were inside, he saw that Blake, Holt and Joseph were sitting in folding chairs along the east wall of the tent, while opposite from them, Gil had taken a seat on the edge of a sleeping cot.

"You guys look like you're getting ready for a poker game where gambling isn't allowed," Chandler attempted to joke as he handed Taggart a folding chair.

"I wish," Joseph said with a grunt, then glanced at Taggart. "Welcome, Tag, glad you're here."

While Taggart gave the youngest Hollister a grateful nod, Chandler said, "None of you need bother telling Tag to keep his mouth shut about this. He already understands Mom isn't to know."

"Good," Holt said, then shot a meaningful glance at his uncle. "Then we all agree that what's said here stays among us?"

The older man leaned forward and rested his elbows on his knees. Just from looking at him, Taggart doubted any man in this tent would want to tangle with him physically, or for that matter, try to match wits with the man. He had a tough, sharp image that reminded Taggart of a drill sergeant he used to know back in Texas.

"Maureen isn't going to hear anything from me that might cause her sadness or worry," Gil said. "You men can rest assured of that."

Holt nodded, then gestured to Joseph. "You're the head investigator, Joe, so you need to be the one to do the talking."

"Don't you think you should key Tag in on the main points?" Chandler spoke up. "He's walked into the middle of this thing without knowing much."

"Right," Joseph said, then glanced at Blake. "You fill him in on what we know and I'll get the evidence."

As soon as the word was spoken, Taggart saw Gil's brows shoot up with sudden interest, but he didn't interrupt with questions. Instead he waited patiently while Blake recounted all they knew about their father's death. Including the horrific way they'd found him hanging from the stirrup of the saddle.

Once Blake finished, Holt said, "You see, Tag, ever since Dad died, we brothers have searched and dug to find the truth of what happened. At first Mother was all for it. And then all of a sudden, she made a complete turn around and ordered us to leave it alone. She didn't want to hear about it or think about it. Basically, she wanted to put the tragedy behind her."

"She has her reasons for that," Gil spoke up.

All five men turned stunned looks on the retired detective.

Blake was the first to speak. "You know what those reasons are?"

"I do," Gil answered. "But I want to see this evidence you have before I say anything."

Taggart got the impression that Holt wanted to press the man for answers, but then he shrugged and said, "Show him, Joe."

The deputy reached behind his chair and retrieved a small cedar box. The sort that women used to store jewelry or other personal trinkets.

"It's not much, Uncle Gil. But it's more than nothing. We've all been thinking that since you've come home to Three Rivers, you'd be willing to help us find Dad's killer. You do think Dad was murdered, don't you?"

Grim-faced, the man said, "I've never thought anything else. None of it made sense. He was too good of a horseman to lose his seat in the saddle. And there was no sensible explanation as to why he rode off by himself that day. The ranch was extremely busy and the way I remember it, he was scheduled to meet with a cattle buyer that afternoon."

"That's right," Joseph agreed, then opened the box and handed it to Gil. "We found the spur rowel first. We know it belonged on Dad's spurs because it's unique and very expensive. Mom gave them to him as a special gift."

Gil placed the rusty rowel in the palm of his hand and studied it as though the piece of metal could give him the answers they all needed. After a moment he returned the rowel to the box and pulled out two tiny pieces of tattered fabric. Taggart could see that it had once been blue plaid, but sun and outdoor elements had faded it.

"That was the shirt Dad was wearing that day," Chandler said, his voice hoarse with emotion.

Joseph explained they'd found the items in two different arroyos on the far side of the ranch property, not far from water well pump number nine.

"But that's not all," Holt said, then turned a questioning look on Joseph. "I thought we agreed we were going to show him the rest?"

"We are," Blake muttered.

"Yeah, the rest." Grim-faced, Joseph fished a piece of paper from his shirt pocket. "I found this not long ago when I was going through Ray's private notes about Dad's case."

"Ray?" Gil questioned. "You mean the late Sheriff Maddox?"

Joseph nodded and Taggart quickly tried to remember where he'd heard that name. But before it could come to his mind, Blake provided the answer.

"In case you don't know, Tag, Ray Maddox was also an old family friend of ours, who happened to be the sheriff of Yavapai County for many years. He was also Tessa's father."

Taggart looked at Joseph, who was holding on

to the square of paper as though it was a snake that could strike any moment.

"So your father-in-law was the late Sheriff Maddox," Taggart said thoughtfully. "Did he inspire you to become a lawman?"

"Partly. He and Uncle Gil inspired me. And I actually worked under Ray for a short time before he became so sick he had to retire. He eventually passed away from a lung disease. That was before Tessa and I married. And before anyone knew he was actually Tessa's father. But that's a long story in itself."

"Yeah," Holt interjected. "Long and twisted. And we don't want to be here all night."

Joseph glanced once again at Taggart. "You can hear the sheriff's story later. But to explain this—" He tapped a finger against the paper in his hand. "Tessa and I live on the Bar X. The ranch was an inheritance from her father and we live in the same house where he always lived. Over time we've discovered lots of notes and papers he left behind. Many of them about Dad's case."

"And this one?" Gil asked. "I'm assuming it has some sort of clue."

Joseph said, "Ray seemed to think it important enough to put in his files. But it was something he never shared with our family before he died. We've concluded that he probably kept it to himself for Mother's sake. And we sure as hell don't want her finding out about it. Not unless it proves pertinent.

If that's the case, we won't have a choice. We'll have to tell her and our sisters."

He handed the paper to Gil and as the man quickly scanned the notes, Taggart noticed all four of the Hollister brothers were watching intently for his reaction.

Finally Gil looked up and Taggart could see something like wry acceptance on his face.

"This is—" He muttered a curse, then let out a chuckle that wasn't anything close to an expression of humor. "It's obviously going to come as a surprise to you guys, but Maureen already knows about the woman at the stockyards in Phoenix. She talked to me about it months ago."

Stunned silence followed the man's revelation and Taggart watched the four brothers exchange bewildered glances.

Blake was the first to speak. "Mother knows? How? None of us have breathed a word about it."

Gil said, "She was going through some of Joel's old business correspondence and happened to run into a small day planner with notes about meetings he had scheduled. Several entries were things like—see her during the sale. And—she'll be waiting outside. From the dates posted next to the notes, they're close to the time that Joel died."

Incredulous, all four brothers stared at him as they tried to digest this news.

Eventually, Blake said, "She hasn't said a word to us about it. Why?"

"Yeah, why?" Holt demanded. "Why did she tell you and not us?"

Instead of taking offense at Holt's accusing tone, Gil shook his head and quietly explained, "She didn't want any of her children to get the idea that their father might've been an adulterer. That's why she's been so preoccupied for the past months. She's been worried you guys might uncover the fact that Joel had been associating with a woman before he died. That's why she kept ordering you all to leave the whole matter alone."

"Oh my God," Joseph murmured.

Chandler looked sick as he pulled off his hat and raked a hand through his hair. "We've been stupid," he said flatly. "Mother is stronger than all of us put together. We should've known she could handle whatever we uncover. Now all this worrying and sneaking about has been wasted time."

"That's hardly the point now," Blake said, then leveled his attention on Gil. "The crux of the matter is does *she* think Dad was an adulterer? Furthermore, do you?"

Gil grimaced. "Do you really have to ask that question, Blake? Neither one of us could ever believe such a thing about Joel. Maureen was everything to him. No. There had to be some other reason for him to be associating with a woman."

His expression calculating, Joseph nodded in agreement. "I have a feeling this woman, whoever she was, might be the key to the whole mystery."

"Exactly, Joe," Gil said. "We need to try to identify and locate her."

"Does that mean you're going to help us?" Holt asked his uncle. "Joe's a damned good deputy, but I figure all of our heads put together is better than one."

Joseph shot Holt an appreciative grin. "Thanks, Holt, for the compliment. But you're right. We need to work together on this."

With that decided, the men began to offer suggestions on how to go about identifying the mystery woman. Taggart was content to sit back and take it all in. But as soon as there was a lull in the conversation he decided to speak up.

"I'm just a listener here," Taggart said. "But I do have a question. Are you going to let your sisters in on this information? And are you going to tell your mother that you guys have been aware of *the woman* for the past few months?"

"Those are good questions, Tag," Blake said, then looked to his brothers for answers. "What about it, guys? Should we tell our sisters?"

Joe was the first to answer. "I vote no. Not until we figure out whether any of this information is relevant."

"I agree," Chandler said. "Camille is pregnant

and running her diner. She doesn't need the extra worry. And Vivian already has enough stress with baby twins and a teenager, plus her job as a ranger. And we know how both of them adored Dad. They considered him a saint."

"He wasn't a saint, but close to it," Gil said. "And I think all of you are not giving your sisters enough credit. They would never consider the idea that Joel had a mistress or anything close to it."

"Probably not," Holt agreed. "But the whole issue about *the woman* would worry them. Just like it nags at us guys. Who was she? And why was Dad seeing her? I vote no. If we learn more, then we can let Viv and Camille in on it."

"I vote no, also," Blake said firmly, then glanced at his uncle. "What about Mother, do we tell her?"

"I think it might save some awkward feelings if I explain the situation to her," Gil said. "She thinks she's protecting all of you by trying to sweep the issue under the rug. She needs to understand that finding the truth will be better for the whole family."

Taggart wholly agreed with the man. Nothing good could ever come from hiding things. Ever since he'd left Emily-Ann's house, five nights ago, he'd begun to realize that more and more.

Until he explained about Becca and the baby, Emily-Ann would never be able to understand his reluctance to get involved in a serious relationship. If he ever expected to have a life that included her, he would have to find the courage to confess what losing them had done to him. Yet the scarred part of his heart kept asking why bother to pour out all those bad memories. Doing such a thing wouldn't take away his fear of loving and losing a second time.

Love. He'd seen the emotion here tonight with the Hollister men. Love was guiding the decisions they made concerning their family. Love caused them to put the feelings of others first, rather than their own. And as Taggart had listened to them, he'd begun to wonder if he'd ever truly loved anyone.

He'd believed Becca was his true love and when she'd told him that she was pregnant, he'd wanted the child just as much as he'd wanted her. At that time, he'd been twenty-two and considered himself old enough and man enough to deal with the responsibility of a family. But now as he looked back on their brief marriage, he wondered if he'd been more infatuated with the idea of proving to himself he was a better man than his father, rather than truly loving Becca.

So what were these feelings that were pushing him toward Emily-Ann? he wondered. He'd been trying to convince himself they were nothing but lust. He'd not made love to a woman in a long time. So long that he didn't even want to think about it. And yet, something told him that going to bed with Emily-Ann wasn't going to satisfy the hunger she'd built in him.

"Want to go have a cup of coffee, Tag? I think the pot is still hanging over the campfire."

Chandler's voice pulled Taggart out of his deep musings and he looked up to see Chandler standing in front of him. Directly behind him, the other men were filing out of the open flap of the tent.

Quickly rising from the chair, he said, "Sorry. I—was doing some thinking. I didn't realize the meeting had ended. I think I need that coffee in the worst kind of way."

Smiling, Chandler gave his shoulder a friendly pat. "I'm the one who should be apologizing. You just got started as foreman and you've had to jump straight into spring roundup. You have a lot on your mind and I've made matters worse by dragging you into this family issue about Dad."

"No. Don't apologize," Taggart told him. "I'm glad I was here and glad that I know what's going on with your father's investigation. I just wish I could help in some way. If Joe ever wants me to ride with him to look for more evidence, I'd be happy to."

"I'm sure he'll take you up on the offer," Chandler told him. "Now let's go have the last of the coffee before it turns to black mud."

Emily-Ann laughed as she watched the baby boy cuddled in Isabelle's arms take a tiny taste of sugary frosting from his mother's finger.

"Look at that puckered expression on his face," Emily-Ann exclaimed. "He thinks it's awful."

Laughing with her, Isabelle glanced down at her son. "Just give him a year or two and then he'll change his mind about the taste of sugar—unfortunately. I never knew a man who didn't have a sweet tooth. I'm sure little Carter will have one, too."

The two women and baby were sitting outside the coffee shop at one of the wrought iron tables. Late afternoon sun was flickering through the limbs of the mesquite tree, while a breeze helped to cool the flimsy shade. When Isabelle and the baby had shown up, Emily-Ann had been on the verge of closing shop, but she'd gladly put the task on pause in order to visit with her friend.

"I'm so glad you had a chance to come by," Emily-Ann told her.

Isabelle offered the baby his pacifier. "I know I'm keeping you from closing up, but I wanted to stop and chat with you for a few minutes."

"I'm glad you did. I rarely get to see you and Carter. He's growing so fast. And he looks just like Holt. But I'm sure you hear that all the time."

The pretty blonde grinned as she shifted the baby's weight against her arm. "All the time. But that's okay. His daddy is a handsome devil."

Both women laughed at that and then Emily-Ann sighed as she continued to study the baby's sweet face. "Gosh, it doesn't seem like it's been that long ago when you first met Holt. You came by here hopping mad because he wouldn't give you the time of day."

Chuckling, Isabelle rolled her eyes. "You kept telling me Holt was a dreamy hunk. I thought you were crazy. He was so infuriating I wanted to slap his face."

"Now look. You two are happily married and you have little Carter Edmond."

"I have to admit you were right, Emily-Ann. Holt has made me so happy."

Emily-Ann smiled gently at her friend. "You know, you're the first and only woman who's ever asked me to be their maid of honor. You can't imagine how special that made me feel."

Isabelle reached across the table and squeezed Emily-Ann's hand. "I moved here to Arizona not knowing a single soul and you were so kind to me. You were the first person to befriend me and I'll never forget that."

Emily-Ann waved a dismissive hand through the air. "Being your friend was and is my pleasure."

After a long sip of iced coffee, Isabelle asked, "Have you seen Camille lately?"

"Last week. With roundup going on, I think she was going to drive up to the reservation and spend a day with Vivian and the kids. Otherwise, I guess she's been hanging close to Three Rivers. Normally she would go out to camp and stay the night, but with the baby coming she says she needs a soft bed to sleep in."

"Amen to that," Isabelle agreed, then added, "Actually, Holt texted me earlier in the day and said that roundup was wrapping up and that everyone would be heading back to the ranch this evening. So our men will finally be home."

That meant Taggart would be home, too. Since roundup started six days ago, he'd actually sent her three text messages. All had been short and simple. More or less to let her know things were going well and that he was thinking of her. But did that mean he would be anxious to see her again? Several days had passed since he'd stopped by her house and they'd wound up having that heated kiss in the kitchen. Considering the fickle way his mind worked, she could only guess how Taggart might be feeling about her now.

Isabelle's expression took a shrewd turn. "I heard in a roundabout way that Tag took you out to dinner. How did that go?"

Emily-Ann felt her cheeks turn a hot pink. "How did you hear that? I haven't told anyone about our date. Not even Camille."

"Blake mentioned it to Holt. I think they were surprised, because the foreman is such a quiet kind of guy when he's around them. He never talks about going out or doing much socially. But you know how the old saying goes. It's those quiet ones that are real tigers underneath."

Emily-Ann was suddenly remembering their heated embrace. At that moment she wouldn't have hesitated to make love to him. And since then, she'd thought of little else. "I don't think he's actually the dating sort. He more or less told me that he asked me out because he was lonely."

"Aww. That's awful. Uh—not that he asked you for a date, but that he was lonely. It's terrible to feel that way. I remember how it felt after my divorce and I moved here to Yavapai County. I lived out there on Blue Stallion Ranch all alone, with no one to talk to but the horses and the wind. And then Ollie and Sol came. Those two old men were a lifesaver."

Not wanting to dwell on the idea of Taggart being lonely, Emily-Ann changed the subject. "How are Ollie and Sol, by the way? Remind me before you leave and I'll sack up some leftover pastries for them."

"Thanks. Both men are doing great. They'll love getting the pastries."

"And your mother? She didn't want to come to town with you today?"

Isabelle let out a wry laugh. "Are you joking? And be away from Sam for that long? Mom met him over at the Bar X early this morning and they've been out riding horses all day. She's going to be too stiff to walk tomorrow."

"So are they planning a wedding yet?"

The baby began to squirm and fuss. Isabelle placed him against her shoulder and gently patted his back. "Oh yes. At first they insisted they both wanted a quiet simple ceremony. But I think they're realizing that won't work. How do you do quiet and simple with all the Hollister family and Sam's countless friends? Not to mention Mother's longtime friends from San Diego. I told her they should elope to Vegas. Sam loves whiskey and cards. He ought to enjoy it."

Emily-Ann was laughing in agreement when she heard the cell phone in the pocket of her skirt announce an incoming message.

"Excuse me, Isabelle. I'd better check this," she said as she retrieved the phone. "I'm expecting to hear from Conchita. She wasn't feeling well this morning and I've been half-afraid she's going to have to miss cooking pastries for tomorrow."

Emily-Ann quickly opened her message box and then promptly felt her jaw drop.

Isabelle quickly questioned, "What is it? Is something wrong?"

"No. Uh—it's not Conchita. The message is from Tag. He wants to know if I want to come over for supper. He'll cook for me."

A wicked twinkle appeared in Isabelle's brown eyes. "That's a long drive out to Tag's place. Do you think it would be worth it?"

Emily-Ann's short laugh sounded like a breathless schoolgirl and she realized she was reacting idiotically. "Well—yes. But I—" Pausing, she released a long sigh. "To be honest, Isabelle, I don't know if seeing Tag will end up meaning anything."

Frowning, Isabelle asked, "Why? The whole Hollister family has been raving about him. He must be a good man. And if he's interested in you—that's a beginning. Or maybe you're not attracted to the man."

Emily-Ann groaned. "I might get a little daffy at times, but I'm not completely crazy. Have you looked at him?" she asked, then shook her head. "No. Probably not. Because the only man you see is Holt. But Tag is—a hot hunk. How do you think I could not be attracted to him?"

"By the hesitant tone I hear in your voice," Isabelle reasoned. "Something about the man worries you."

Biting down on her bottom lip, Emily-Ann turned her gaze to the nearby street. "I'm afraid he's going to end up being like all the rest, Isabelle. The kind that just can't do commitment."

Isabelle snorted. "Don't you think it's a bit too early to be pinning that sort of label on the man? Just think about all the concerns I had about Holt. Everyone in Yavapai County knew he was a womanizer—even me. But I took a chance that he could change and would change. It takes some courage, Emily-Ann, but you might find that Tag just might be worth the risk."

She thoughtfully studied her friend. "I can't imagine how brave you had to be to marry Holt Hollister."

Her smile full of love, Isabelle turned her head and pressed a soft kiss to baby Carter's cheek. "Right. And who knows, someday Tag might give you a little guy like this."

A baby? It wasn't difficult to see herself making love to Taggart. But after that, everything about her future went gray. The only thing she could see was how her mother must have felt when she'd been abandoned by her lover, and her family, because she was pregnant. It wasn't that Emily-Ann would ever be afraid to raise a child on her own. Anything her mother could do, she was positive she could do. But no way did she want a child to ever feel as shunned by its father as Emily-Ann had felt all these years.

"You're just like Camille," Emily-Ann said teasingly, "always trying to find me a husband."

"Well, you did catch Camille's bridal bouquet. That's definitely a sign of things to come."

Emily-Ann let out a loud groan. "Oh, not you, too."

Isabelle looked confused. "What's wrong? What did I say?"

"Nothing. I'll just say that the next time I touch a bridal bouquet, it'll have to be my own. Otherwise, I'm not going near it!"

A comical look on her face, Isabelle said, "Okay, if you say so. Right now I've got to get home. I've been training three young colts and two fillies. And I've not yet ridden the girls today. I need to get home and do that before daylight goes and Holt gets home."

Holding the baby in one arm, Isabelle started to gather up the trash on the table with her free hand, but Emily-Ann quickly brushed her aside.

"Forget that," she told her. "I'll clean up here."

"Thanks."

Isabelle shouldered her purse and Emily-Ann plucked up Carter's diaper bag and accompanied her friend to the truck she was driving.

After Isabelle and the baby were safely strapped in for the trip back to Blue Stallion Ranch, she stuck her head out the open window of the vehicle. "Call me in a few days and let know how supper with Tag goes."

Emily-Ann frowned at her. "I didn't say I was going."

Isabelle let out a calculating laugh. "Who are you trying to fool? You and I both know that you're going."

Her friend drove away and without giving it another thought, Emily-Ann pulled the phone from her pocket and tapped out a message to Taggart.

I'll be there by six thirty.

Before she walked back to the table where she

and Isabelle had been sitting, her phone dinged with his reply.

Great. I'll see you then.

Chapter Eight

After six days of riding through thorny chaparral, wrestling calves and spending his nights on the ground in a sleeping bag, Taggart should have felt too tired to do anything except collapse on the bed and stay there. But the idea of seeing Emily-Ann again was enough to energize him.

For the past two hours, he'd been rushing around the house straightening the rooms as best as he could, showering and changing into a respectable pair of jeans and shirt, then cooking what he thought would be a halfway presentable meal for Emily-Ann.

After chopping salad and baking potatoes, he was

about to throw steaks into an iron skillet when he heard her knock on the front door.

Setting the cuts of beef aside, he made his way through the house until he reached the front door. When he swung it wide, she was standing on the edge of the porch, petting one of Chandler's cur dogs.

"I see you've met King," Taggart said, while he took in the sight of her smooth red hair hanging to her waist and the pink-and-white flowered dress clinging to her curves. She looked luscious and as pretty as sunshine on a Sunday morning.

Smiling, she continued to stroke the dog's head. "He's beautiful. Is he yours?"

He stepped out of the doorway and walked over to her. "No. He's one of Doc's many dogs. King likes me, so when I left the ranch yard this evening, he decided to follow. Halfway here, I felt sorry for the guy and stopped and let him ride in the truck the rest of the way."

She straightened away from the dog and Taggart leaned forward to press a kiss on her cheek. Her skin was soft and smelled like a gentle rain on a meadow of wildflowers. It was all he could do not to gather her into his arms and taste her lips.

"Hello," he murmured as he forced his head to lift away from hers.

Her gaze darted shyly up to his and the warmth he saw in the green depths made everything about being with her feel good and right.

"Hello, Tag."

"I'm glad you're here," he said.

The corners of her lips lifted ever so slightly. "I'm glad I'm here, too."

She gestured to the dog. "I take it that Chandler doesn't mind King having a second home."

"Not at all. Doc knows I'll bring him back home in the morning." He pushed the door wide and gestured for her to come in. "After I sent the invitation for supper, I worried you might not want to make the long drive out here at night."

They entered the living room where she paused to take a slow survey of the leather furniture, dark green drapes and a large braided rug. To Taggart the room looked fine, but from a woman's perspective it probably looked stark.

She said, "It doesn't bother me to drive at night. I know the road well and there's hardly ever any traffic out this way. Especially after you turn onto Three Rivers' property."

"Hopefully, you'll think my cooking is worth it," he said with a smile. "But before we head to the kitchen, I should warn you not to expect much. With me being gone on roundup this past week, I've not had time to restock my cupboards."

"I can eat anything. Even soggy oatmeal."

"I promise it won't taste that bad. And I do have a nice surprise." He walked over and took her by the arm. "Come on and I'll show you."

"Your house is nice," she said as he guided her to the kitchen. "I like the arched doorways and the floors are real wood. Did you put the polished gleam on them?"

He laughed. "Are you kidding? If I sweep once a week that would be a miracle. This house isn't large by most standards, but it's the biggest one I've ever lived in. I'm about to decide I'm going to have to hire a cleaning lady to keep it looking livable."

"Hmm. That would be a big help. I suppose Jazelle doesn't have time to do it for you. She's already stretched pretty thin helping Reeva in the kitchen and Roslyn and Katherine with the babies. And then she has Raine, her own little boy to take care of whenever she goes home. He's about five now, I think."

"I saw Raine a few days ago. Nick, Blake's teenaged son, brought the boy down to the ranch yard to see the cows and horses. He's a cute little fellow. By the way, I've never asked anyone, but does Jazelle have a husband?"

"No. She's never been married." She cast him a sly look. "Jazelle is very pretty—you've obviously noticed."

He slanted her an impish grin. "She's pretty, but she's not you. And I was wondering because of the little boy. That day I saw him at the cattle barn I got the feeling he didn't have a daddy."

"That's very perceptive of you."

He tried not to grimace. "I'm experienced with the subject of missing fathers."

"Well, so am I," she said, then promptly changed the subject. "Now what is this surprise you have?"

They entered the kitchen and he led her over to the cabinet counter where the pie Reeva had given him was wrapped in aluminum foil.

"Bless her sweet heart, Reeva sent word for me to come to the big house—that she had something for me. She got the idea that I deserved a pie for wrapping up my first roundup here on Three Rivers. I told her I was going to share it with you."

"That was thoughtful." She sneaked a peek under the edge of the foil. "Oh, it's pecan!"

"One of my favorites," he said.

She chuckled. "One?"

"I have many."

She looked at him and in that moment, Taggart realized how much he'd missed her these past few days and how very much he wanted her now.

Wrapping his hands around her upper arms, he looked into her eyes and suddenly without warning, a soft, mushy feeling spread throughout his chest.

Damn. What was the matter with him? How could this woman make him feel happy and vulnerable at the same time? It didn't make sense. But he'd heard there was no logic to being in love. Could that be what was happening to him? Whatever the reason for this strange upheaval inside him, he didn't want to think it was love. That was for other people.

"Is something wrong?" she asked. "You're looking at me like I have a smudge on my nose or something."

He released the long breath he hadn't realize he'd been holding until now. "Sorry. I guess I've been staring. It's just that you look so beautiful tonight I—can't help myself."

An impish smile wrinkled her nose. "Are you feeding me cheese as an appetizer?"

"If I am it's not the fake processed kind. It's the real deal."

He tried to smile back at her and lighten the moment, but the emotions swirling through him wouldn't allow him to do anything other than place a kiss on her forehead.

When his lips continued to linger against her skin, both her hands reached out and anchored a hold on the front of his shirt.

"I probably shouldn't be so obvious, but I've missed you, Tag."

His insides began to quiver with longing and he drew in another deep breath and blew it out. "I'd like to kiss you and show you how much I've missed you. But I'm afraid if I did, we might never get to eat."

Laughing softly, she purposely stepped away from him and moved down the cabinets until she reached a large gas range with a built-in grill on top. "You're cooking steaks," she said, observing the two pieces of meat soaking in a bowl of dark-colored marinade.

"I'm guessing you would probably prefer chicken, but steak was the only thing left in the freezer."

"I love steak. But I do have a question. Why cook them in a skillet when you have this great indoor grill that most people would give their eye teeth for?"

Joining her at the stove, he switched on the blaze beneath the black skillet.

"Because the iron gives it a flavor I like," he explained. "But I can grill yours if you'd rather have it cooked that way."

"Oh, no. I'm anxious to taste the difference."

"Coming right up." He tossed a chunk of butter into the skillet and gathered up the bowl containing the cuts of meat.

Next to him, Emily-Ann asked, "Can I do something to help?"

The best thing she could do to help him, Taggart thought, would be to tell him to forget about the supper and make love to her. But his mind was taking rapid leaps into uncertain territory. Emily-Ann might be thinking about food and nothing more.

Jerking his thoughts back to the present, he gestured to a row of cabinets to the right of them. "You might start with setting the table and icing some glasses. Unless you want to drink wine or beer."

As she headed to the cabinets, she said, "I'll skip the spirits tonight. You never know when an antelope or deer might walk onto the road. And I did promise I'd drive carefully for you. Remember?"

Hell yes, he remembered. That night he'd come very, very close to telling her about Becca and the car crash that had taken her and the unborn baby, and ended the future he'd planned for their lives together. But just when he'd thought he could get the painful words out to Emily-Ann, a barrier of some sort had lodged in his throat and he'd done well to breathe, much less talk about the incident that continued to shadow the choices he made for himself.

"I do remember," he murmured. "And I'm glad you're being cautious—for my sake and yours."

More than an hour later, after Emily-Ann and Taggart had finished eating the meal and pieces of Reeva's pecan pie, she insisted on helping him put the kitchen back in neat order.

After the last dish was dried and put away, Taggart said, "There's a bit of coffee left. Might be nice to have a cup out on the front porch. Unless you'd prefer to stay inside."

Throughout the meal, Emily-Ann had tried to keep her gaze from constantly straying to Taggart, but she'd mostly failed at the effort. The days they'd been apart had felt like ages to her and everything about him, from his dark wavy hair, to the warm light in his brown eyes and the stubble on his chin, was mesmerizing her. While they'd worked side by side doing the dishes, her fascination for him had only increased and several times she'd had to catch herself from reaching over and touching him.

Sitting outside in the cool night air might be enough to put a brake on her runaway urges, she thought, but she doubted it.

"The porch sounds great," she agreed.

Taggart poured their coffee and with cups in hand, they walked back through the house and onto the front porch. At one end a wide, wooden swing hung from the rafters, while on the opposite end, a group of wicker furniture with tropical-printed cushions invited a person to relax.

"Where would you like to sit?" he asked.

"The wicker looks comfy, but I love to swing. Is that okay with you?"

"I've spent so many hours in the saddle this past week that a wooden swing will feel like I'm sitting on a cloud," he assured her.

With a hand resting against the small of her back, he guided her over to the swing. King, who'd been lying in the shadows, followed them across the porch and waited until they were seated before he flopped down on the floor near Taggart's feet.

"It's a lovely evening," Emily-Ann remarked.

His arm came around the back of her shoulders and a soft sigh slipped past her lips.

"If it's too cool for you I can go in the house and find a jacket," he offered.

Even if she'd been freezing, she wouldn't have wanted him to move. Snuggled next to his side, with the warmth of his thigh pressed against hers and the low, raspy sound of his voice in her ear, she wondered how something that felt so good could possibly last. It couldn't. Not for her. But she wasn't going to allow herself to worry about that tonight.

"I'm fine," she told him. "Besides, who can pay attention to the chill in the air with a view like this?"

Situated at the foot of a ridge of rocky hills, the house was shrouded by several mesquite trees, but the gnarled limbs didn't block the landscape directly in front of them. Beneath the starlit sky, she could see a shadowy vista of wide-open range peppered with tall century plants, Joshua trees and saguaro cactus. To the right, in the far distance, the lights illuminating the Three Rivers Ranch yard glowed like a beacon in the wilderness.

Normally Emily-Ann would have been hypnotized by the beauty, along with the pleasant sounds of the breeze whispering through the mesquites and the call of the night birds. But all those things were just a lovely backdrop to Taggart's presence.

"Blake told me this house was built back in the late 1950s by his grandfather. Back then, the foreman of Three Rivers had a big family and needed a place to live," Taggart explained. "All I can say is that the Hollisters didn't hold back, this house would've been expensive to build even back then."

While he was talking, his fingers had begun to trace abstract designs against her arm. The light, feathery touch against her skin was creating far more goose bumps than the cool night breeze and it was all she could do to focus on his words.

"When Camille and I were in elementary school, I remember the foreman who lived here was an older man with a wife and five kids. Then about the time we became teenagers, he retired and the family moved away. That's when Matthew took over." She glanced curiously over at him. "Did you have a house of your own when you worked on the Flying W?"

He shook his head. "No. I didn't live directly on the ranch. I had a place of my own not far from the nearest town, which was Canyon. The commute back and forth to the ranch wasn't all that bad. But this—" He paused and gestured to his surroundings. "It's like nothing I've ever dreamed. To be honest, when I sent my résumé to the Hollisters for this job, I didn't think I had a chance in hell of getting it. But I didn't see any harm in trying. Sometimes miracles do happen."

Like her sitting here with a man like him, she thought. She'd never dreamed a man of Taggart's caliber would ever ask her out for dinner, much less cook for her. To be fair, the men she'd dated in her past hadn't been losers. But most of them had still been floundering around, struggling to figure out what they wanted to do with their lives. Some of them hadn't had a clue how to better themselves, while others were working on plans.

Even so, they'd all had one thing in common, having a little fun with her, and then moving on. These past few weeks, she'd been telling herself that Taggart had to be different. He was responsible and settled. He was admired and successful. She just didn't yet know if he'd want to be in her life for the long haul.

She placed her cup on a small table situated close to the arm of the swing, then reached over and covered his hand with hers. "If you hadn't sent in your résumé, I would've probably never met you. Or do you believe in fate and that our paths would've crossed somewhere at some point in our lives?"

The gentle look on his face stirred her heart with feelings so tender they brought a rush of moisture to her eyes. Oh my, what was this man doing to her? She felt like a fallen leaf at the mercy of the desert wind. He was carrying her away, tumbling and swirling, and she could only hope she didn't end up landing at the bottom of a steep arroyo with no way of climbing out.

"I do believe in fate," he answered, his voice pensive. "Sometimes it's good, other times it's bad."

"Yes," she solemnly agreed. "And my mother's fate was mostly bad."

He turned his head and for long moments he studied her face as though he was weighing whether he could trust her. With what, she didn't know.

Finally he said, "You've probably noticed that I don't talk about my mother much. Not because I didn't love her—I loved her very much. But talking about her hurts. A lot. And I'm beginning to think you understand how that feels."

"It's never easy to talk about my mother," she murmured. "And even when I think about her, it puts an ache in my chest. She had a rough life, but I try to put that out of my mind and remember the good times we shared as mother and daughter. That helps."

Nodding, he glanced down at the yellow cur sleeping at his feet. "When I was twenty-three my mother, Carolyn, died of a heart attack. She'd never been in perfect health, but her death was totally out of the blue. Or that's the way it had felt at the time. But after I'd had time to think about everything, I realized it was a miracle she'd lived as long as she did."

This was the first time he'd ever really talked about his family and, as she studied his solemn profile, it was fairly obvious that his young life hadn't been easy. "Your mother had a chronic health problem?"

Her question elicited a cynical snort from him.

"No. Her husband—my father, Buck O'Brien was the chronic problem. To put it plainly, the man was a selfish bully. He did his best to keep her and us kids browbeaten. He made her life pure hell. And me and my sister—we just clung to Mom and tried to stay invisible."

This was the first time she'd ever heard such bitterness in his voice and, though it was an ugly sound, she could understand where it was coming from. She'd had plenty of experience dealing with the negative emotion and knew firsthand that once it took root inside a person, it was hard to push aside.

"Were your parents married when she passed away?" Emily-Ann ventured to ask.

His gaze left King to settle on her face. "Oh, yes. At that time he'd been scrounging around the area between Canyon and Hereford taking on little construction jobs wherever he could find them. He was working as a carpenter during that time, but that was only when he really wanted to work. Mom was the one who paid the bills and kept things afloat for them. Not him. She had a bookkeeping job at the same feeder lot where I worked tending cattle."

Emily-Ann shook her head. "Gorman, my stepfather, was mostly shiftless, too. But in most other ways he was very kind to Mother. So I can sort of understand why she loved him and remained married to him. But if your father was actually mean to your mother, why didn't she divorce him?"

Sighing, he gently trailed his forefinger over the back of her hand and down each of her fingers. "I can't answer that, Emily-Ann. Maybe because the choices she made were something only a woman could understand. Or maybe because I've never been in love like that—where a person is blinded to the other's faults. I often wanted to blame it on the fact that she was insecure. She didn't think she could survive without him. But in truth, she would've made it so much better on her own."

Losing her mother had knocked Emily-Ann flat and it had taken her a long time to pull herself together and move forward. She'd often heard that losing a mother was even harder for a man to deal with. Whether that was true or not, she could tell, just from the pain in his voice, that Taggart had suffered deep grief.

"Your mother didn't want to be on her own, Tag. Just like mine didn't want to be," she reasoned, then asked, "What happened with your father after Carolyn died? You mentioned that you don't see him often, but does he still live in that part of Texas?"

"He comes and goes. My sister and I never really know when he's going to leave or show up. Usually when we see him it's because he wants money."

She stared at him in disbelief. "The man asks his children for money? That would take some gall."

"He's got that in spades," Taggart said, his voice heaped with sarcasm.

She turned her hand over and wrapped her fingers tightly around his. "When I first met you, Tag, I would've never guessed that our lives were similar.

We both lost our mothers and we both suffered because of the choices they made in their lives."

"Yes. But there's more to mine, Emily-Ann. I—uh—"

When he faltered, then failed to say anything more, she prompted, "You what?"

His gaze continued to delve deep into hers until she thought he was going to ignore her question completely. And then a long breath rushed out of him and he said, "I've been married."

Stunned, she stared at him while questions darted wildly through her mind. "Married? I suppose that means you're divorced?"

Pressing the toe of his boot against the floor of the porch, he paused the gentle movement of the swing.

"No," he said. "It means I'm a widower."

Her gasp was so loud that King lifted his head and looked at her.

"A widower," she repeated blankly, then shook her head. "You were married and your wife died?"

"No, she didn't just die. She wrecked the car she was driving and it killed her and our unborn child."

His revelation struck her so hard that her stomach made a sickening roll. "Oh. Oh my, Tag. I—don't know what to say."

"You don't have to say anything," he said wryly. "I just—felt like it was time that I told you about Becca and the baby. I thought that—well, you ought to know why I've been shy about getting involved with you."

Several years ago some things happened in my life that changed everything for me.

The words he'd spoken to her that night when he'd come to her house were suddenly skipping through the forefront of her mind. His comment hadn't made complete sense to her then, but it was becoming clear now.

"I'm so sorry," she murmured. "I thought your reluctance was all about me—not meeting your standards."

"That was stupid thinking on your part, Emily-Ann. You meet all my standards and more. I think that's why—when I look at you—when I'm with you like this, I get so scared I can hardly breathe. I tell myself that I can't take another chance with a woman. But then when I'm away from you, I hurt to be back with you."

Agony was wrapped around his every word. It knotted his voice and twisted his rugged features. She wanted to take it all away. She wanted to slip her arms around him and assure him that tragedy wasn't likely to strike twice. But she couldn't move, or think beyond the notion that he'd been in love with another woman. So much so that he'd married her. That the two of them had been expecting a child together.

"I—how long ago did this happen?" she finally managed to ask.

"Ten years ago. I was twenty-one when I first met Becca and turned twenty-two when we got married. She was two months pregnant when we stood before the county judge and exchanged vows. She didn't want to get married then. She wanted to wait until the baby was born. She didn't want folks thinking I'd married her because I had to."

Emily-Ann couldn't stop herself from asking, "Did you?"

"No. I mean, yes, I did feel obligated when I'd learned she was pregnant, but no one was holding a gun to my back. I believed I loved her."

Emily-Ann's brows lifted as she watched his features twist even tighter. "You believed? You weren't sure?"

He groaned. "Back then I thought I was sure about my feelings for her—about getting married and everything that went with that decision. Looking back on it all, I don't know. We were so young. I did care for her deeply and the baby—I was a little scared at becoming responsible for a child, but I wanted it. Wanted it with all my heart. But four months after we married, they were both gone from my life."

Oh God, Emily-Ann thought sickly. How could she ever expect to compete with the ghost of his wife and unborn child? Ten years had passed and he was still tortured over losing them.

"Four months. You'd hardly begun your married

life together. You must have felt like your whole
world was turned upside down."

"To be honest, I was so numb everyone around me
was probably thinking I'd turned into a zombie. And
then just about the time I was beginning to wake up
and start living again, Mom was struck by the heart
attack. All of it together just about wiped me out."

The mere thought of the grief he'd gone through
squeezed her heart with pain. "I can only imagine,"
she murmured.

His eyes softened and then his fingers gently
smoothed the hair at her temple. "It was a bad, bad
time," he admitted. "But now—meeting you has
made everything different for me. You're the first
woman since Becca that I've ever really wanted—
or needed."

Wanted. Needed. But not loved.

Even as the thought zipped through her brain, she
realized it was wrong of her to think it. She and Taggart hadn't known each other that long. She couldn't
expect him to fall instantly in love with her. Actually,
she was crazy to think he would ever fall in love with
her. But tonight, as he'd talked about his grief and
shared things about his life that he probably never
shared with others, she'd felt closer to him than she'd
ever felt to any man.

"I understand that you're afraid to try again. But
you needn't feel alone, Tag. I'm just as afraid as you
are. But I—" Feeling more emboldened than she had

a right to be, she wrapped her hands over his fore-arms and pressed her fingers into his warm flesh. "I'm willing to take a chance that you're not pur-posely setting out to break my heart."

He groaned. "Oh, Emily-Ann, I—that would never be my intention." Reaching up, he gently touched a forefinger to the center of her lips. "You've already had too much pain and hurt in your life. And so have I."

The cold fear around her heart began to melt and spread warmth to every part of her body. And then with her gaze locked on his, she placed a soft but-terfly kiss upon his finger.

He whispered her name and then he was draw-ing her into his arms and lowering his mouth down to hers.

He'd kissed her before and each time the intimate contact had shaken her, but this time was different. This time she felt a connection that was boundless and far too strong to break.

By the time he eventually lifted his head and looked down at her, Emily-Ann was not only breath-less, she was totally on fire for him.

"I think it's time we—uh—went in. Don't you?"

Without hesitating, she nodded and he quickly rose to his feet and helped her up from the swing. Then with his hand wrapped tightly around hers, he led her into the house and down a dark hallway until they passed through a door on the left.

"Wait here and I'll turn on a lamp," he said as they stepped just inside the dark room.

Emily-Ann stood where she was and while she waited for him to cross the room and deal with the light, she could feel her heart beating hard and heavy in her chest. Not with the fear of what they were about to do, but the concern that he might find her terribly disappointing. If that happened, she'd most likely never see him again.

If sex is all he wants from you, Emily-Ann, then you don't need him.

A soft light suddenly glowed at the head of a queen-size bed and then Taggart turned and smiled at her. And that was all it took to send the taunting voice, along with every other doubt, flying out of her head.

"Don't look at all the boxes that still need to be unpacked," he said.

Emily-Ann didn't bother glancing around at the room. Her focus was zeroed on him as she walked over and slipped her arms around his waist.

"Who cares about boxes?" she asked, turning her lips up to his.

Growling with need, he bent his head and kissed her. "All I care about is you. And this."

While his lips feasted on hers, his hand reached to the back of her dress and tugged on the zipper until it reached the bottom. Emily-Ann dropped her arms and allowed the fabric to slide over her shoulders and onto the floor. Cool air wafted over her half-naked body, but before it had a chance to chill her skin, he was lifting her off her feet and placing her in the middle of the bed.

Once she was settled, he stepped back and with hungry eyes she watched him remove his clothing. By the time he got down to a pair of black boxers and climbed onto the bed to join her, Emily-Ann knew her fate for tonight was sealed. Even if a thousand horses suddenly stampeded through the bedroom, she couldn't have left his side to save herself.

Chapter Nine

His body already on fire for her, Taggart rolled Emily-Ann into his arms and buried his face in the side of her neck. She smelled sweet and mysterious and the scent acted on his senses as much as the feel of her soft skin beneath his lips.

Making love to Emily-Ann had been in the back of his mind almost from the very first time he'd met her. But he'd not thought it would actually happen tonight. He'd hoped, but not believed.

Now that she was in his arms, her bare skin sliding against his, her sighs whispering across his ear, he was half-afraid he was going to wake up from a beautiful dream and find he was still in a bedroll out on the range.

"Aren't you going to turn out the light?" she asked.

Lifting his head slightly away from hers, he looked down to see her lashes were partially lowered over drowsy green eyes, while her oh-so-soft lips were already swollen from his kisses. She looked utterly fascinating. Especially to a man who only a few weeks ago believed his libido had crawled away to die.

"In a bit. Right now I want to be able to see you—how beautiful you look lying on this old quilt with your red hair spilled everywhere." He slipped his fingers beneath the lacy white straps of her bra and slid them downward until they fell onto her arms and the fleshy mounds of her breasts spilled over the loosened cups of her bra. "And I have a feeling you're going to look even better without these pretty little pieces of lace."

Her breathless little laugh was self-mocking. "There's nothing little about me or my lingerie."

"Everything about you is perfect to me, Emily-Ann. From the freckles on your nose to your rounded bottom."

She chuckled. "You're crazy."

"If I am, then please don't try to fix me. I want to stay this way."

At the middle of her back, he unfastened her bra,

then tossed the whole thing aside. The pale pink nipples of her breasts beckoned to him and, cupping his hands around the soft fullness, he bent his head to taste the rosy centers.

In a matter of seconds, she was making mewing sounds deep in her throat, while her body arched up to his. Her wordless plea for relief didn't go unnoticed. He quickly peeled off her panties and tossed them atop her dress on the floor.

When his finger found the intimate folds between her thighs, it was hot and moist and waiting just for him. Watching her face, he slipped inside and reveled at the softness he was touching, the longing he saw gripping her features.

Slowly, he stroked her until her hips were writhing against his hand and his own body was on the verge of exploding.

"Tag, oh Tag. Don't make me wait to have you."

Moving away from her, he stood and pushed off his boxers. His manhood was throbbing to be inside her and yet a part of him was reluctant to make the ultimate connection. Once he entered her, it would be the beginning of the end, and he didn't want that to happen. Not when each second of being with her like this was awakening every cell in his body.

"Is something wrong?" she asked.

Shaking away his thoughts, he pulled open the drawer in the nightstand, then frowned. "No. It's just now dawned on me that I might not have any condoms. I—they're not something—I have much need for."

She must've heard the embarrassment in his voice, because suddenly she was sitting on the side of the bed, reaching for his hand.

"No need to worry. I take the pill. Everything should be fine. Unless you're worried about—other things."

He looked at her while wishing they didn't have to discuss such an awkward subject.

"If you're worried," he said. "I can tell you that I've not had unprotected sex since I was married."

"Well, you shouldn't worry about me. I've *never* had unprotected sex."

The impish smile on her face made all the clumsiness of the moment go away and with a wicked chuckle, he eased her back down on the bed.

"Then we don't have a thing to worry about—except making this our night," he said.

Her eyes sparkling like stars, she reached up and linked her hands at the back of his neck, then drew his mouth down to hers. Taggart kissed her softly over and over until the need to deepen the kiss was as strong as the need to join his body to hers.

As soon as her mouth opened to accept his tongue, his knee parted her thighs and he entered her with one smooth thrust.

A moan vibrated deep in her throat and her hands

tightened on his shoulders, but other than that, she went stock-still beneath him.

The reaction caused him to lift his head and he was stunned to see tears slipping from the corners of her eyes and roll into the edge of her hair.

Uncertain, he whispered, "Emily-Ann, do you want to end this now?"

Her hands reached up and gently cradled his face and all he could see in her eyes was a longing so deep and tender that it caused a wave of emotion to flood the center of his chest.

"Oh, Tag, I never want this to end," she murmured. "I want you so much. So much."

He struggled to push his words past the tight cords in his throat, but when they did finally release, relief poured out with them. "And I want you, sweet Emily-Ann. More than you could know."

Lowering his head, he kissed the tears away from each corner of her eyes, then moved his mouth to hers.

The moment their lips connected, she arched her hips up to his, drawing him deeper inside her. Sensations such as he had never experienced shot at him from all directions and wiped his mind of everything but her. Having her, loving her.

Her legs wrapped around his and she instantly began to match his rhythmic thrusts. After that, his mind became a blur as his senses tried to absorb everything at once. The hot smoothness of her skin against his, the womanly scent that swirled around him, the sweetness of her lips and the yielding of her body as she gave everything up to him.

Time became nonexistent for Taggart. All he knew was that he didn't want the euphoria to end. He couldn't allow it to end. But she thwarted his plans when she began to writhe in abandon and her fingers raced frantically across his back, then down to his hips.

When she urged him to quicken the pace, it was more than his brain could stand and the rest of his body had no choice but to surrender. Suddenly and totally, he was blinded by a shower of shooting stars and then he was clutching her tightly to him, crying her name and letting the undulating waves of passion overtake him.

This wasn't the way it was supposed to be, Taggart thought a few minutes later, as he drew Emily-Ann's warm limp body next to his. He wasn't supposed to be feeling all mushy and enchanted just because he'd had sex with a woman.

Sex. Who was he trying to fool? The union they'd just shared had been far more than physical. It had touched him somewhere deep inside and now all he wanted to do was gather her close and let his heart sing with joyous wonder.

He was in trouble. Deep, deep trouble.

That dire thought was suddenly interrupted as

she stirred and nuzzled her nose against the side of his neck. He slipped his arm around her waist and snugged her next to his damp body.

"You never did turn off the lamp."

After the wild, stormy ride the two of them had just taken together, her observation caused him to chuckle.

Resting his cheek against the crown of her head, he said, "I didn't have the time. Besides, I like being able to see you."

Her fingertips created tiny circles across his chest and he wondered why her hands felt so magical whenever and wherever she touched him.

Her voice drowsy, she said, "I dreaded for you to see me without my clothes. But you know what, after a bit I didn't care."

"I think somewhere in that remark you were giving me a compliment."

"I am," she said. "You made me forget my imperfections."

He caught her hand and lifted her fingers to his lips. After he'd kissed each one, he said, "I don't know how you see yourself, Emily-Ann. But I see you as lovely and womanly and everything a man could want."

"I wasn't fishing for compliments. But—" she tilted her head in order to plant a kiss on his jaw "—I'll take them and wrap them up with a bow and put them away in my dresser. I might need them later when I'm looking in the mirror."

Smiling, he rubbed his cheek against the side of her head. "Oh, Emily-Ann, you're so—"

"Silly?"

"No. I was thinking more like precious." He turned her face to his and as he looked into her eyes, fear suddenly niggled the back of his mind.

He was feeling too much, he told himself, and thinking things that he had no business thinking. Getting this close to Emily-Ann was like asking for trouble. But he wasn't going to dwell on the danger now, not when everything about her made him feel so good.

"Tag, you don't have to say all these nice things to me," she said. "I don't expect that from you."

He inwardly winced. "I never thought you did. But I need to say them. And maybe someday you'll realize I actually mean them."

Doubt shrouded her green eyes and he was amazed at how much he wanted to take the dark shadows away. And stunned even more to realize how much he wanted her to believe in him.

A vulnerable quiver touched her bottom lip. "I want to believe them, Tag. I want to believe everything about this night."

He pushed his fingers into the hair at her temple and stroked the silky strands away from her face.

"I'm glad," he whispered. "Because it's far from over."

The tremble to her lips stopped as the corners tilted upward. "Just so I get to work at Conchita's by six thirty in the morning."

He gave her a wicked grin. "I'll give you enough time to make the drive."

Her provocative laugh had him laughing along with her and with a hand on her waist, he rolled the both of them over, until he was lying on his back and her warm body was draped over his.

And when she lowered her head and covered his mouth with hers, Taggart realized he wanted to believe everything about this night, too.

Two days later, Emily-Ann had closed up the coffee shop and was climbing into her car to drive home when Camille's truck pulled up behind her.

Sticking her head out the window, her friend called out to her, "Not so fast! I just got here!"

Giving her a cheery wave, Emily-Ann left the side of the car and walked over to greet Camille.

"What are you doing in town so late in the evening?" she asked, as Camille climbed down from the truck cab.

"Mother sent me after a few personal items she needed from the drugstore. Personally, I think she sent me on this mission to give me a chance to see you."

"Oh, she thought you needed someone other than relatives for company?"

"Something like that." She glanced over Emily-Ann's shoulder to see she'd already hung the closed sign on the door of the coffee shop. "Were you on your way home? Or were you going somewhere?"

"Home. I have another test to do tomorrow and it deals with chemistry. I've been studying between customers, but I need some uninterrupted time to study if I ever expect to pass." Plus, it was damned hard to keep her mind on chemical equations when all she really wanted to think about was Taggart and how the night at his house had changed everything.

Camille groaned with disappointment. "Don't you have time to go to the Broken Spur for a milkshake?"

Emily-Ann frowned. "No more milkshakes for me—I'm cutting back. And why do you want to go to that old café on the outskirts of town? There's a fast-food place a couple of streets over from here where you can get a milkshake."

Camille's short burst of laughter was a mocking sound. "Are you joking? The Broken Spur might be a little ratty on the inside, but the food is great. Makes me feel right at home like I'm in my own diner. And they make their milkshakes by hand one at a time. With real ice cream."

Chuckling, Emily-Ann affectionately patted Camille's protruding belly. "And the little guy is growing. He deserves the real thing."

"Darned right," Camille agreed. "So what do you say? I won't keep you for more than thirty minutes. I need to get back to the ranch soon anyway. Mom wants this new lipstick I picked up for her. Uncle Gil is taking her out to dinner tonight."

Emily-Ann's looked at her with interest. "Really? Is she calling it a date?"

Camille shrugged. "I don't know what Mom is calling the outing, but I can tell you that she's awfully excited about it."

"Aww, that's so romantic," Emily-Ann replied, then suddenly realized that kind of remark might not go over well with Camille. "Sorry, Camille. I spoke before I thought. You might not want to think of your mother having a romantic evening."

"Don't be silly," she said with a dismissive wave of her hand. "I've already told you that I want Mother to be happy. And if that means having Uncle Gil in her life, then that's okay, too."

"Not all children feel as generous toward their parent as you do."

Camille smiled wistfully. "How could I want to deny her the pleasure of loving someone when I have so much with Matthew?"

"True. And you don't have to worry about Gil being like Gorman, thank God," she said, then called over her shoulder as she started to her car, "Okay. Let me get my purse and we'll go to the Broken Spur. I'll have an ice tea while you enjoy *real* ice cream."

Camille drove the two of them to the far south side of town where the old Broken Spur building sat on the edge of the highway that led to Phoenix. The place was usually full of old cowboys and construction workers and today was no different, Emily-Ann decided, as she and Camille sat in a corner booth, sipping their drinks.

"Camille, I swear, each time I see you it's like your face is glowing. Have you found some sort of miracle moisturizer, or something?"

Camille chuckled. "When a woman gets overloaded with hormones, she not only cries, but she has much nicer skin. This glow will go away once I have little junior or baby princess."

Emily-Ann sighed. For the past few years she'd watched the Hollister women give birth to several babies and each time she'd been very happy for them. And when she'd heard that Camille was expecting Matthew's child, she'd been thrilled for her friend. Yet she'd never really allowed herself to dwell on the idea of having her own children. The notion had never seemed to fit her life. Not without a good man in it. But now, after making love to Taggart, she was imagining herself more and more with a baby.

"Actually, I'd better fess up," Camille went on. "Mother did want the new lipstick for tonight, but she also sent me into town on a nosy, fact-finding mission. And I agreed because I'm really curious, too."

Emily-Ann asked blankly, "Curious about what?

I didn't know anything new had been happening around here."

Her expression innocent, Camille stirred the straw through the creamy strawberry milkshake. "According to Isabelle something has been happening. She told Holt that Tag cooked supper for you the other night. And you know Holt, you'd have to duct tape his mouth before he could keep it shut."

Emily-Ann couldn't stop a pink blush from coloring her cheeks. "Well, no need to beat up Holt. It's not like we were trying to be secretive or anything."

Camille's blue eyes were suddenly sparkling with interest and she leaned earnestly across the tabletop toward Emily-Ann. "Good. I want to hear all about it. So does Mother."

Maureen had always been like a second mother to Emily-Ann, but she couldn't remember a time that the woman had actually been interested in her dates.

"Why is she interested? The dinner was—well, just a casual outing."

"Do you want your nose to look like a carrot?" She grimaced. "With fibs like that it's going to."

Emily-Ann shifted uncomfortably on the padded vinyl covering the booth bench. There was no way she could tell her friend that she'd experienced something with Taggart that had been totally magical and life changing for her. She'd not had any idea that having sex with a man could make her feel so wanted and loved and needed. She'd not known that she was capable of feeling that much pleasure or that much emotion. But she had. And two days later she still didn't know where their relationship was headed or what any of it might mean on down the line.

"Okay, I'll admit it was more than special." Shaking her head, she momentarily closed her eyes. "Camille, I never thought—well, can you imagine a man like Taggart cooking supper for me? If it hadn't actually happened it would be downright laughable."

"Why?"

Emily-Ann's eyes flew wide. "Why? Are you kidding? Think about it, Camille. I'm the girl that was fed a sandwich from a convenience store for her twenty-seventh birthday and I had to eat that meal sitting in the car in the parking lot because my date had an aversion to picnic tables. I've never been treated as nicely as Taggart treats me."

A wide smile came over Camille's face and she reached across the table and squeezed Emily-Ann's hand. "That's wonderful."

Emily-Ann let out a heavy breath. "I'm not so sure if it is or not."

"Now who's sounding like they've slipped a cog or two?"

"I realize that sounds crazy. But that's because you don't understand, Camille. When something or someone as good as Taggart comes along in my life I'm fairly certain I'm destined to end up a loser— again. He's not going to want to invest much more time in me. And he especially won't want to invest any true emotion."

"That's an awful thing to say, Emily-Ann. Don't you think you're doing Taggart a discredit by thinking that way?"

Emily-Ann sighed again. "I'm trying to be practical about this, Camille. He—uh—he's already told me he doesn't think he can make a long-term commitment to me—or any woman. You see, he—" Unsure as to whether she should say more, Emily-Ann paused and glanced down at the tabletop. "Well, let's just say he's not looking for love."

"Don't most men say those things? Matthew tried his best to run from me. But in the end he decided that marrying me was a chance he had to take."

Grimacing, Emily-Ann lifted her tea glass and drew on the straw. "Yes, well, Matthew had good reason to be gun-shy. He'd been through a divorce. And Taggart has good reason to be leery of loving again. He—" Pausing, she shook her head, then seeing Camille was waiting for her to continue, she said, "I'm not sure I should be repeating this. But he didn't ask me to keep it a secret."

"You don't have to tell me anything private about you and Taggart. Not unless you want to," Camille assured her.

The thought of what he'd gone through had continued to revolve through her mind, haunting her with images of his loss and pain.

Pinching the bridge of her nose, she said, "Maybe he's told Blake or someone in your family about this. I don't know. He didn't say. But he was married once—years ago. His wife and unborn child were killed in a car accident."

Camille looked genuinely stricken. "Oh, how completely horrible."

"Yes. And not only that, his mother died three months later. From what he told me, he was very close to her and losing all of them so close together has sort of warped his heart, I guess you'd say."

"No doubt. But time heals. We both know that. And none of that means he's incapable of falling in love again—with you," Camille argued. "After all, what man couldn't fall in love with you?"

The absurdity of Camille's question caused Emily-Ann to laugh outright. "Oh, sure. Men have been knocking down my door for years," she said with sarcastic humor.

"Well, you have one on your doorstep now. A good one. What do you intend to do about it? Mother happens to believe you and Taggart make a perfect match. Should I tell her that you think so, too?"

Emily-Ann groaned, then looked across the room to where a row of men sat at a worn bar eating pie and drinking coffee. The image reminded her even more of Taggart scarfing up the pecan pie that Reeva had made for him. He'd eaten the dessert with the same enthusiasm he'd made love to her.

Swallowing hard, she turned her gaze back to Camille. "Tell your mother that it's going to take more than a bridal bouquet for Taggart to fall in love with me."

The horses were tired, prompting Taggart and Matthew to pull them to a slow walk as they traveled the last half mile back to the ranch yard.

"The grass is looking good," Matthew said. "The cows are all settled where they need to be and the branding and vaccinating is all finished. I think it's about time Camille and I head back home to Red Bluff. You have everything under control here."

Taggart let out a cynical grunt, but his reaction had very little to do with being foreman of Three Rivers Ranch. He could truthfully say he felt confident about his job, with or without Matthew here to guide him. But as for his personal life, it was totally out of control.

Even if taking Emily-Ann into his bed had been the most incredible experience he'd ever had, it was still a stupid mistake on his part. He should've known that once he touched her, he'd only want more. He should've known that he couldn't just have sex with her, then walk away. No. She was meant to be made love to and he was very much afraid that's exactly what he'd done. Now his brain, his heart, his very being was consumed with her. And he didn't have a clue as to what he was going to do about it.

"I can't speak for Camille, but I'd be willing to say you'll be glad to get back to your own ranch."

This time it was Matthew who grunted. "For years, if anyone had told me I'd be looking forward to leaving Three Rivers for Red Bluff, I would've considered them crazy. Three Rivers was my very lifeblood. But things change. Most of the time in ways a man never expects."

Taggart understood that only too well. And in his own case, the changes weren't good. "Guess you're talking about your wife now," he said, as he absently flipped the ends of the split reins back and forth across the cantle of the saddle.

"Yeah. Nothing would mean much of anything without her and the coming baby. I'm building Red Bluff for them."

"Must be nice."

"Nice, hell. The feeling it gives me is impossible to describe." He glanced over at Taggart. "And frankly, I never imagined myself being this blessed. Sometimes it's scary because I never had much in the way of family. My mother died when my sister and I were young. After that we were sent to live with an uncle that was a real bastard. Finding the Hollisters and loving Camille is sometimes too good to believe. You understand what I'm trying to say."

"More than you could know, Matthew. My mother died, too, when I was in my midtwenties. And Dad—he's not worth talking about. I don't have a loving wife to share things with, but landing here on Three Rivers is more than I ever expected in my life."

"Yeah. I guess being here does feel pretty good to you."

Making his home on Three Rivers and being with Emily-Ann had changed his life drastically. And those good changes were scary. But he wasn't a timid little calf, afraid to follow his mama to greener pastures, Taggart mentally argued with himself. Sure, he'd suffered through some tragedies, but he'd come out on the other side a bit wiser and hopefully stronger. And a man couldn't go forward if he continually held on to the past.

"It feels damned good, Matthew," he finally replied.

For the next few minutes, the two men rode on down the well-trodden cattle trail in companionable silence until Matthew abruptly pulled his horse to a stop and climbed down from the saddle.

Taggart reined his buckskin next to Matthew's horse. "Anything wrong?" he asked.

"No. I'll be right back."

He walked a few steps off the trail and snapped off a long bough of blooming sage. After he climbed back into the saddle, he looked over at Taggart and grinned.

"Camille loves this stuff. It grows everywhere like annoying weeds, but she thinks it's beautiful and special. Go figure." He held up the branch with silver-green leaves and tiny purple blooms. "This will make her happy."

"You're a smart guy, Matthew."

The other man chuckled as he nudged his horse into a walk. "Not smart enough."

No, Taggart thought, a man could be a genius and still not be able to understand a woman. The tears he'd seen in Emily-Ann's eyes when they'd begun to make love had puzzled him. He'd kept wondering what she could've been thinking to put them there.

She hadn't been thinking, Taggart. She'd been feeling. Those tears had come straight from her heart. But you don't want to face that kind of truth. You don't want to think that Emily-Ann could feel that much for you. That would make everything more complicated and painful when it ended. Right?

Shoving at the nagging voice, Taggart glanced over at Matthew and the bough of sage he'd laid across the front of the saddle seat.

The foreman of Red Bluff was more like him than Taggart could've guessed. He'd not been born into wealth and from what he'd just said, his growing-up years had been far from easy. And along the way, he'd lost loved ones. Yet he'd found the courage to give his heart to a woman, to marry her and plan a future.

Could he be that brave? Taggart asked himself. Or was he going to keep on hiding his heart and hoping that Emily-Ann couldn't find it?

Chapter Ten

Emily-Ann leaned back from the computer monitor and rubbed her weary eyes. Ever since she'd gotten home from her outing with Camille at the Broken Spur, she'd been sitting at the tiny desk set up in her bedroom. That had been three hours ago. Now her eyes were burning and her shoulders felt like they were permanently locked in one painful position.

She was shutting down the computer and switching off a table lamp when her cell phone dinged with an incoming message.

Seeing it was from Taggart, she quickly grabbed up the phone and scanned the brief note.

Don't eat. I'll be there in thirty minutes.

Her heart tapping a rapid thud against her chest, she lowered the phone and stared unseeingly at the wall in front of her.

Taggart was coming to see her tonight? Only two days had passed since she'd gone to his place for supper. She'd not expected him to want to see her again this soon. What did it mean? That he was actually beginning to care about her? Or he was simply wanting another round of sex?

It was pointless to ask herself those questions. No matter the answers, she couldn't resist the man.

Focusing on the phone in her hand, she tapped a one-word reply.

Okay.

Thirty minutes later after pulling on a pair of faded blue jeans and a red peasant blouse, she dabbed on a small amount of makeup and added a pair of silver hoops to her ears before she hurried to the living room to pick up the clutter.

She'd barely had time to carry a couple of dirty cups and a stack of junk mail to the kitchen when she heard Taggart's footsteps on the porch.

When she opened the door, he was standing on the threshold grinning back at her. Dressed in jeans and a blue denim shirt worn through in several places, he was holding a sack in each arm. The scent of fried food wafted toward her.

"Is that chicken I smell?" she asked, as she motioned him into the house.

The grin still on his face, he moved into the living room. "Since we ate beef the other night at my place, I thought you might like a change," he told her.

After dealing with the door, she crossed to where he was standing. "You didn't need to bring food. I would've made something for you," she said, then chuckled. "Uh—but you were probably afraid I'd give you cold cuts again."

"I love cold cuts," he insisted. "I just wanted to treat you."

Seeing him again was causing bubbles of joy to dance around inside of her and she didn't think twice about rising on the tips of her toes and pressing a kiss on his cheek.

"I'm so happy you're here, Tag. And thank you for the treat—whatever it is," she said, then gestured toward the kitchen. "Let's take it to the table."

He started toward the kitchen and Emily-Ann followed along at his side.

"Sorry about the short notice that I was coming," he said. "I hope you didn't have other plans."

"You mean like stare at the walls?" she teased, then shook her head. "No plans. In fact, I just finished studying for the night. I'm all set for my chemistry test."

"I'm glad it's you and not me. I was fairly good with math, but chemistry usually got me confused. Now Doc can rattle off all those different elements and medicines used to treat animals like he's talking about what he likes for breakfast."

"Chandler is a brain, plain and simple," Emily-Ann said.

They entered the kitchen and he placed the large paper sacks on the table. "I stopped by the clinic before I headed over here and Doc removed the stitches from my arm. He also gave me a warning to go with the service," he said.

"Oh, what was the warning?" she asked curiously, while thinking Chandler had probably warned Taggart to stay away from her. Not that the veterinarian was a snob. He was far from it. And he truly was Emily-Ann's friend. But that didn't mean he thought she'd be the right woman for their new foreman.

"That I quit playing with Holt's yearlings," Taggart answered.

Emily-Ann laughed. "Good advice."

His expression suddenly changed from playful to coy as he reached inside one of the sacks and pulled out a bunch of white tulips mixed with some sort of vivid pink flowers she'd never seen before. The bouquet was beautiful and obviously expensive.

"For you," he said gently. "I hope you like tulips."

Clasping the bouquet with both hands, she stared

down at the blooms in stunned fascination. "I love tulips. I—"

Her words broke off as the tears clogging her throat made it impossible to speak.

Embarrassed by the overemotional reaction, she turned and hurried over to the sink. With her back turned to Taggart, she placed the flowers on the cabinet counter and attempted to wipe the tears that were suddenly rolling down her cheeks.

When she felt his hand come down on her shoulder, she sniffed and desperately tried to compose herself.

"Sorry, Tag. The way I'm acting you're probably thinking I never received flowers from a man before. And you'd be right. I haven't."

He didn't reply and, when his silence continued, Emily-Ann figured he was feeling worse than awkward. He was probably kicking himself for becoming involved with a woman who'd never so much as merited a bouquet of flowers.

Clearing her throat, she stepped away from the hold he had on her shoulder and walked to the opposite end of the cabinet to look for something to hold the bouquet. After a moment of digging around in a bottom shelf, she pulled out a pitcher made of blue knobby milk glass.

"I'll put the flowers in some water," she told him. "And then I'll set the table so we can eat. We don't want the food to get cold after you went to the trouble and expense of buying it."

She was chattering, but that was the only way she could handle his silence and keep her tears at bay at the same time.

Her attention focused solely on taking care of the bouquet, she filled the pitcher with water and dropped in the flowers. However, that was as far as she got before Taggart's hands were on her upper arms, pulling her around to face him.

"Forget the damned food," he muttered. "Forget about everything, but this."

He didn't give her time to utter any kind of question. Instead, he tugged her into his arms and fastened his mouth roughly over hers.

The contact of their lips was all it took to wipe everything from Emily-Ann's mind. All she could think about was making love to this man, who was quickly becoming everything to her.

Just as her taut nerves began to relax and her body sagged against his, he lifted his head and sucked in a ragged breath. "You don't have a clue as to how much I want you, Emily-Ann."

Her hands gripped the front of his denim shirt as she tilted her head back to look up at him. "But I thought—"

"You're always thinking too much," he interrupted.

Lowering her lashes, she looked up at him with

a properly chastised expression. "And talking too much," she said, unable to stop the corners of her mouth from bending upward. "Aren't you going to tack that on, too?"

"No." His smile a little wicked, his hands slipped to the rounded curve of her bottom and pulled her hips forward until they were snug against his. "I have other ways to keep you from talking."

Her arms slipped up around his neck. "I'd like for you to show me those—other ways."

"It'll be my pleasure, sweet Emily-Ann."

Taking him by the hand, she led him through the small house until they reached her bedroom.

"I don't think we need a light this time," she said as she urged him toward the double bed covered in a white chenille bedspread. "The streetlight shines through the slats of the blinds."

"I wouldn't care if we were in the blaring sunlight or the deepest blackest night, I'd want you just as much," he said.

"I'll be honest, Tag, I didn't expect to see you again this soon." Even as she said the words, her hands were reaching for the front of his shirt, pulling the snaps apart. "You've made me happy."

He pushed her hair aside and pressed a track of kisses up the side of her neck and onto her ear. "Mmm. I'll try my best to make you even happier."

Seconds ticked by as he showered kisses upon her face and lips, then down the creamy column of her throat. When his mouth finally reached the cleavage between her breasts, he lifted his head and went to work removing her clothes.

By the time he got down to her bra and panties, her breaths had gone short and rapid, while her heart was pounding, drumming out a rhythm that he and he alone controlled.

"Tag, I don't think you—you're not supposed to be making me feel this good," she whispered hoarsely. "It's decadent. And scary. And addictive."

He groaned. "It's not me that's making this magic. It's us. Together."

With her lingerie off and out of the way, he eased her onto the bed, then quickly shed his own clothing and joined her in the middle of the mattress.

She reached to wrap her arms around him and as his mouth found hers, his hands began a slow foray of her body, pausing at certain parts to tug and tease, until the fire inside her began to burn hotter than an Arizona wildfire. She did her best to reciprocate the pleasure by soothing her fingers over his broad shoulders, down his rib cage and onto his back.

Between them she could feel his hard erection pressing against her belly and the evidence of his desire emboldened her to give everything to him and take exactly what she wanted.

He continued to kiss her over and over and each time the connection grew deeper until she was certain their breaths had braided into one life-giving function. Thinking became nonexistent as her senses scattered like a covey of birds flying in every direction. All she knew was that Taggart wanted her and she wanted him with every cell of her being.

And when he finally rolled her onto her back and coupled his body with hers, Emily-Ann felt, for the first time in her life, that she was totally and truly complete.

Much later, after Taggart had gathered enough energy to open his eyes, he noticed the cover at the foot of the double bed was striped with artificial light streaming through the blinds. Alongside him, Emily-Ann was lying on her back, her breasts rising and falling as she slowly regained her breath.

Across the small room, on the wall directly in front of the bed, a partially raised window allowed the cool night air to drift over them. The breeze carried no scent of sage or juniper. And though he caught the sound of barking dogs and distant traffic, there was no bawling cows, nickering horses or wailing coyotes.

Next to him, Emily-Ann stirred and slipped an arm across his waist.

In a drowsy voice, she asked, "What are you thinking?"

"How different it feels to be in town." Which was true enough, he thought. But he couldn't tell her all the other things that were swirling around in his mind. Like how the simple touch of her hand turned him inside out and how being with her had become a very important part of his life.

"Hmm. Well, you're not a town guy," she remarked, then rose up on one elbow and looked down at his face. "I've been wondering something about you."

A wry grin slanted his lips. "What's that? If I've ever spent time in jail?"

She chuckled. "The possibility never crossed my mind. But I'll bet you'd look good in orange."

He couldn't help but laugh and when his gaze found her sweet face in the semidarkness, he felt everything inside him go soft and gooey.

"What have you been wondering?"

With her free hand, she trailed fingers up and down the length of his arm. "Where you learned about ranching? How you came to be a cowboy?"

He drew in a long breath, then blew it out in a rough sigh. "From my maternal grandfather and my father. When I was a little kid, my sister and I and our parents all lived with Grandad Walt on his ranch near Hereford. So I grew up learning all about being a cowboy and caring for livestock."

Her brows pulled together. "Oh. Didn't you tell me before that your father was a carpenter?"

"That was several years later," he explained. "See, Grandad Walt died suddenly and willed the ranch to his sister. So we all had to move out. When that happened Dad went to work on the Flying W."

She stared at him in wonder. "Your grandfather didn't consider leaving the ranch to his daughter—your mother? Seems like that would've been the logical thing. Especially with your whole family already living there."

Taggart snorted cynically. "Are you kidding? Grandad couldn't stand Dad. He only tolerated his son-in-law because of his daughter. And to be fair, he knew what my father would do with the place if it went to Mom. Dad would've wrung every dollar he could from it, then let it go to ruin. No, Grandad made the right choice."

Frowning, she said, "Wait a minute. Did you say your father went to work on the Flying W? Isn't that—"

"Yeah. The ranch where I worked before I moved to Three Rivers. Doesn't sound right, but it's true. Several years after they fired Dad, I wanted to get away from the monotony of the feedlot job and asked the family with the Flying W to hire me. I was fortunate. The Williamsons didn't hold it against me because of Dad's shiftless attitude. You see, he didn't like taking orders. Nor did he want to do anything that required him to get off his horse—like mending fences, repairing broken windmills, or whatever needed to be done on the ground."

"What a terrible waste—on your father's part, I

mean," she said. "Sounds like he had plenty of good opportunities and blew them."

Talking about his father's shortcomings had never been easy for Taggart, but he learned with Emily-Ann he didn't need to sugarcoat the facts. He could be honest and not have to worry about her being judgmental.

He said, "Well, selfish people tend to squander anything that's worthwhile."

"Hmm. Sad, but true." She eased her head onto his shoulder. "I witnessed plenty of squandering in my family, Tag, and I don't want to be guilty of doing it. Especially with you."

Sliding his hand against her back, he threaded his fingers in her long hair. It was still damp from the exertion of their lovemaking and when he lifted the strands to his lips, the scent was a reminder of all the soft and tender things he'd missed these past years.

No. He didn't want to squander this precious time with Emily-Ann, he thought. He wanted to hold on to it—to her—as long as this thing between them continued to hold together.

"You know, we have food waiting for us in the kitchen," he murmured.

"Mmm. And my beautiful flowers, too." She tilted her head just enough to allow her gaze to settle on his face. "Tag, the flowers—I didn't mean to cry. The tears came before I could stop them—because I was so touched that you thought of me in that way.

And I was thinking, too, that all through my mother's life, she never received a single flower from a man. She was a good woman. She deserved better—but I could only think that I didn't deserve better than her. Does that make sense to you?"

He tightened his arm across her back and drew her closer to his side.

"Sorry, but it doesn't make sense," he said gently. "You're a good woman, too. And you're not your mother. Just like I'm not like any of those guys who've disappointed you in the past."

She studied his face for long moments and then she asked, "Do you think we could forget about the food for a little while? Right now I need to kiss your lips. I want to make sure they really did say I was a good woman."

Cupping his hand at the back of her head, he drew her face upward until the tip of his nose was brushing hers. "Right now my lips are going to say the food can be reheated."

With a lusty chuckle, she curled her arm around his neck. "I can be, too."

The morning sun was just beginning to peep over the eastern hills as Taggart watched the cowboys form groups of two and three as they headed in different directions across the ranch yard. The work orders he'd just given the men for the day had all been received with smiles and good-natured jokes.

Since he'd taken over the job of foreman, not one had grumbled or griped about the task he'd assigned them. Taggart liked to think the men were cooperative because they approved of him being their new foreman. Yet he realized they'd all been handpicked by the Hollisters and most of them had been here on Three Rivers Ranch for years. Some even before Taggart had been born. They weren't the type of men to slough off or complain.

The thought caused his mind to drift back to the night he'd taken Emily-Ann the flowers and he'd talked to her about his father and the problems the man had caused his family. Something had happened to him that night. He'd felt a connection to Emily-Ann that was unlike anything he'd ever experienced before. It had filled him with warm contentment and a sense of homecoming. Now, more than two weeks later, he was still trying to figure out exactly what those feelings meant and how he was going to hold on to them—and her.

Walking over to the horse he'd saddled for his personal use today, he tried to put Emily-Ann out of his mind for the moment. He had work to do and she was coming out to the ranch to see him tonight. He'd let himself concentrate on her then.

Hell, he'd do more than concentrate, he thought. Once he had her in his arms, he wouldn't be letting her go until the wee hours of the morning.

And do you honestly believe having sex is all the

woman wants from you, Taggart? Could be that she's just like all other women. She might want to be wined and dined and taken somewhere other than to bed. But then, you don't really care about what she wants, do you? You say you don't want to be like the other men she's had in her life, but that's a laugh. You need to take a long look in the mirror and make yourself face the truth.

Doing his best to block out the caustic voice going off in his head, he got busy tightening the cinch strap on the saddle. With that task finished, he was checking the rest of the tack when the cell phone in his pocket pinged with a new message.

Thinking it might be Blake wanting him to stop by the office, he pulled out the phone and was a bit surprised to see a message so early in the morning from his sister, Tallulah.

To give you a heads-up—Dad has been coming around, asking for money. I haven't given him any. But he's making noises about coming out there to see you. Guess he thinks you're rich now. She ended the message with a heart emoji, along with a smiley face.

Hearing from his sister usually gave Taggart a happy lift, but this warning about their father was unsettling. Damn it. The man was a user and Taggart wanted no part of him. And he definitely didn't want the man making his sister miserable or messing up things here on Three Rivers.

"That frown on your face is about as deep as the Grand Canyon. Trouble this morning?"

Maureen's voice pulled Taggart out of his dark thoughts and he turned around to see the Hollister matriarch walking up to him. She was wearing her usual work attire of jeans and boots and an old gray felt hat pulled over her chestnut ponytail. A saddled bay horse followed close behind her right shoulder.

"No. Nothing that can't be fixed." He dropped the phone back into his shirt pocket and looked at her. "The men are just now heading out. Were you planning on joining some of them, or me?"

Smiling, she said, "Given a choice, I'll take you. I don't know what you had planned for this morning, but I thought we might take a long ride."

Questions immediately circled through Taggart's head. Normally Gil showed up with Maureen every morning and the two of them had been going out together to help with the ranching chores. But the man was clearly absent today.

"I can do that," he said. "Did you have a certain place on the ranch in mind?"

"I do. I want to ride over to water pump number nine."

Taggart stared at the woman and hoped the shock he was feeling didn't show on his face. "Maureen, I—are you sure? That's the place—"

Her lips formed a grim line. "Listen, Tag, you don't have to tiptoe around me. My sons think they

need to treat me like I'm a marshmallow or something. They're wrong. Do I look soft?"

"Not exactly." On the outside she was an attractive woman, but Taggart had already learned that on
the inside she was as tough as nails.

"Hell, I'm not going to fall apart if someone mentions Joel's name. Or says he was most likely murdered. I've lived with the reality of his death for
years now."

"Yes, but do you think it's wise for us to ride to
that area? Does anyone, other than me, know what
you have planned?"

She scowled at him. "No. And I don't intend on
telling any of them. I don't want to hear all their ar-
guments and excuses to try to stop me. As far as
anyone knows, you and I are going out to check on
a herd of cows. That's what I told Reeva when I left
the house this morning and that's what we'll tell anyone else if they ask. Got it?"

"Got it," Taggart assured her. "We're checking
on cows."

What else could he say? She was the owner of
the ranch. He didn't want to go against her wishes.
But the more he thought about it, the more he liked
the idea that she felt she could trust him. And if he
could help her, even if it was just to ease her curiosity about the area where her husband had met his
demise, it would be well worth the ride.

She wasted no time swinging herself into the saddle. "I have a canteen of water," she said. "Do you?"

"I have a couple of bottles in my saddlebags."

She rolled her eyes. "You young people. Those things burst at the drop of your hat. Plus they don't keep the water cool like a canteen. I'm going to make a point to buy you one."

Grinning, Taggart finished tightening his cinch. "Yes, ma'am."

Maureen chuckled as he swung his leg over the saddle and reined his horse alongside hers.

She said, "Forgive me, Tag. I'm sounding like a mother. Sometimes I just can't help myself."

"Don't worry. I can get used to it."

For the next two hours they rode in a southerly direction, occasionally alternating the gait of the horses from a walk to a long trot.

With the ranch covering miles in all directions, Taggart still hadn't seen all there was to see of the property. But last week, he'd ridden with Joseph over to water well number nine and he'd not forgotten how to get there. The deputy was always in hopes of finding new evidence and the two of them had searched several dry gulches before they'd finally given up and headed home.

Taggart was wondering if Maureen knew about their recent trip or any of the past trips her sons had made to this area of the ranch. So far during their ride, she'd not mentioned anything about the investigation the men had been making into Joel's death, but that didn't mean she was oblivious to what had been going on.

"I imagine you've been wondering why Gil didn't show up with me today," she said, as the two of them crossed a shallow stream shaded with willows.

"It did cross my mind," Taggart admitted.

"He had to go to Phoenix today on police business. They still ask for his help sometimes on certain cases. But he doesn't plan on making a habit of going down there. He'd rather be here on the ranch."

"He seems to like doing ranch work." And being with you, Taggart could've added.

"Ranching is what he was really meant to do," she said, then glanced over at him. "I think my children and most everyone who knows me has been wondering why I invited Gil to move into the ranch house instead of getting a place of his own."

"I've not heard anyone remarking on the subject," Taggart said honestly.

She let out a short laugh. "I'm sure the subject has been beaten to death by many, but that doesn't really worry me. There are reasons I feel this way. And no. Gil and I aren't having an affair, but we are growing close. Like you and Emily-Ann, maybe?"

Her question caught him by complete surprise. Not that she knew he'd been seeing Emily-Ann, but because she'd openly asked him about it.

Knowing his expression was worse than sheepish, he wiped a hand over his face and tried to give her a genuine smile.

"We have been spending a lot of time together. She's a special woman."

"I've always known it would take a special man to see that about her. I'm glad it's you, Tag."

What would Maureen think if he told her that he'd been doing more than seeing Emily-Ann? That he was having an affair with her? Most likely, she'd be highly disappointed in him. It was obvious that Maureen thought of Emily-Ann as a third daughter and she didn't want her hurt for anyone or any reason.

Not that Taggart planned to hurt her. But he was beginning to ask himself just how far their relationship could go. In spite of how happy she made him, he still couldn't let himself think in terms of forever. He'd already learned that there was no forever. Not for him.

His troubled thoughts must have shown on his face, because Maureen suddenly asked, "What's wrong? You look awfully glum for a man who has a special woman in his life."

Lifting his hat from his head, he swiped a hand through his sweaty hair. "I haven't told anybody but Emily-Ann about this, but I was married a long time ago. She and the baby we were expecting got killed in a car crash."

"I know."

Stunned, he stared at her. He couldn't believe

Emily-Ann had divulged something he'd told her in private. "How did you know?"

The smile she gave him was gentle and reassuring. "You don't think I would allow anyone to come in and take over the foreman job at Three Rivers without learning all about him first, now do you?"

So the Hollisters had done more than read his résumé, Taggart thought. Well, he should have already realized they would do a background check on him. They ran a multimillion-dollar business. They couldn't take chances on hiring someone who might end up being dishonest.

"Oh. Well, you never mentioned anything about it to me," he reasoned.

"There wasn't any point. And I wouldn't be doing it now but I think I've become somewhat of an expert at being a widow and I know the sort of things that are probably still going through your mind— even though it's been a long time since the tragedy."

Sighing, he absently stroked the sorrel's neck. "You can't forget, Maureen. Not entirely."

"Exactly. But you can move beyond it."

Curious now, he looked at her. "Is that what you've done with Gil?"

Before she could answer, he swiftly shook his head. "I'm sorry, Maureen. I'm being too damned nosy. Just forget I asked that."

"No. I'm glad you did ask it. My answer is that I'm trying. And that's what I hope you're doing, too,

Tag. With Emily-Ann. Moving forward. Unafraid. I think you both deserve that."

He could've told her he'd been hoping for the same thing. Hoping that one day soon, he would wake up feeling like a confident man. God only knew how much he wanted to be free of the past and to be able to reach out for the things he truly wanted. But moving on took lots of courage and strength and so far he'd not been able to find those things.

Glancing ahead, he noticed they were approaching an arroyo that was so deep that cattle and horses could only climb in and out at certain places.

"We don't have very far to go to the well pump now, Maureen," Taggart told her. "If you want to turn around and go back, I'll understand."

Shaking her head, she smiled at him. "I just gave you a talk about moving forward, Tag, and that's exactly what we're going to do."

She nudged her spurs into the horse's side and the bay took off into a long trot straight toward the arroyo.

Taggart realized Maureen wasn't going to give him the option of turning around. Like it or not, he had to follow. And he suddenly wondered if this long trip had actually been taken for her sake, or his.

Chapter Eleven

Later that same day, a few short miles before the turnoff to Three Rivers Ranch, Emily-Ann passed the entrance to the Bar X where Tessa and Joseph lived with their young son, Little Joe, and baby daughter, Spring. The youngest of the Hollister brothers, he'd been the first to marry and have children. Now the men were all married with growing families and so were their sisters, Vivian and Camille. One by one, Emily-Ann had watched them find love and happiness, the kind that tied two people together for the duration of their lives. And somewhere between the weddings and showers and christenings, she'd hoped and prayed that the same sort of love and happiness would come to her.

So far it hadn't happened, and though she'd allowed her hopes to rise when she'd first met Taggart, she was beginning to accept the fact that he'd been completely honest when he told her he wasn't looking for anything long-term.

This past month the two of them had spent every possible night they could manage with each other. And when she'd been lying in his arms, he'd never as much as mentioned the word *love*, much less coupled it with the word *future*. The two of them were simply living in the moment. And she had no idea how much longer this thing between them could last.

The reality caused her to push out a heavy sigh, but it was hardly enough to make her put her foot on the brake and turn the car around. No. Being with Taggart was something she couldn't resist. He made her feel beautiful and sexy and worthy. And for now she had to hold on to the hope that one day he might actually fall in love with her.

You ninny. When are you ever going to grow up? A man like Taggart isn't ever going to fall in love with you. The only kind of man you'll ever snag is one that's afraid of his own shadow, poor as a church mouse, or so slovenly you'll have to knock his feet off the furniture. This cowboy is temporary with a capital T.

Hating the nagging voice rattling around in her

head, Emily-Ann pushed harder on the accelerator. Taggart was waiting for her and right now that was all that mattered.

Taggart was late getting home. Through the darkness he could see Emily-Ann's car already parked in her usual spot next to a patch of prickly pear. The fact that she was here to greet him lifted some of the fatigue from his shoulders.

By the time he reached the steps to the porch, he spotted her sitting in the wooden swing. King was up in the seat, lying with his head on her lap.

"So much for King being a big, tough working dog," he joked. "It's no wonder he wants to stay here instead of the ranch yard—where he belongs."

Smiling, she stroked the dog's head. "With a name like his, he's supposed to be treated like royalty."

"Hmm. I think I'll change mine to prince." Grinning, he sauntered over to the swing. "Maybe I'll get more kisses that way."

"Hah!"

Easing the dog's head off her lap, she stood, wrapped her arms around Taggart's waist and planted a soft kiss on his lips. "Hello, Prince."

The sweetness of her greeting pushed away the troubling thoughts that had drifted in and out of his head all day and he gladly kissed her again. Just to make sure they didn't reappear to ruin this night for him.

"Sorry I'm so late. You should have gone on in the house. Have you been here long?"

"Not too long," she answered. "And don't worry, I've already been inside. I brought food."

Curving his arm around her shoulders, he urged her toward the door. Behind them, King lifted his head and whined in protest.

Pausing, Emily-Ann glanced back at the dog. "We could let him inside for a little while, couldn't we?"

"Are you kidding? He's a cur—a working dog. He's not supposed to be in the house. Doc would have a fit."

"I seriously doubt Chandler would throw a fit. Of all the Hollister brothers, he has the softest heart."

"You say that like you're sure."

She beamed a knowing smile at him. "I should be sure. I've known them since I was in third grade."

And that was a heck of a lot longer than Taggart had been acquainted with the Hollisters. Which made it no surprise that Maureen made no bones about wanting Emily-Ann to be happy and treated with respect. Taggart got the impression that Maureen believed his intentions toward Emily-Ann were honorable and he'd not said anything to make her believe otherwise. So now he could label himself a big hypocrite along with being a coward, he thought grimly.

Caving in to Emily-Ann and the dog, he said,

"Okay. Come on, King. I guess you can be a house dog for a little while."

The three of them entered the house and Taggart promptly excused himself. "I'd better go wash up before we eat," he told her.

"Take your time. I'll get things ready for our supper."

Short minutes later, when he entered the kitchen, he noticed Emily-Ann had set the table with paper plates. As she filled iced glasses with sweet tea, he sniffed the air with appreciation.

"Mmm. How did you know I'd been craving pizza?"

She placed the pitcher on the table. "You talk in your sleep."

Laughing, he walked over to the table and pulled out her chair. "Since when have I ever been asleep while we're in bed together?"

A pink blush stole over her cheeks and he was amazed that the intimate part of their relationship still had that much effect on her.

"Good point," she said with a chuckle.

After she was seated, he made himself comfortable in the chair angled to her right elbow. Emily-Ann promptly opened the lid on the pizza box and offered it to him.

"You must have had last-minute work to keep you late," she said. "I was beginning to think there was an emergency going on."

He placed two wedges of pizza on his plate, while marveling how the day had ended up pulling every ounce of energy from his body. Which didn't make sense. Most of the day he'd spent in the saddle, riding with Maureen, and the rest had been spent at the ranch yard sorting steers to be shipped to Red Bluff.

"No. Nothing like that. I was just running behind on everything that needed to get done. Maureen and I rode most of the morning and part of the afternoon—checking on cows."

She looked faintly surprised, but not nearly as surprised as Taggart had felt this morning when Maureen had approached him with her wishes.

"Oh. Did Gil go with you? I remember you saying he'd been going out every day, working with Maureen."

"No. Gil had to make a trip to Phoenix today."

She cast him a curious glance as she helped herself to the pizza. "I'll bet Gil has been looking into Joel's death. Did Maureen mention anything about it?"

He'd promised Maureen he wouldn't mention that the two of them had ridden to water pump number nine. And he would keep that promise. But he didn't want to lie to Emily-Ann, either. "Only in passing. She's aware that her sons have been investigating the matter. I get the impression she has her own ideas about Joel's death. I can see that Maureen isn't a vindictive person, but if it was ever revealed that Joel was murdered, she'd damn well want justice served."

"And who could blame her for that? Losing Joel was like sticking a knife in the heart of the family."

Taggart didn't make a reply to that and as long seconds ticked by without her saying more, he was relieved that she'd decided to drop the gloomy subject.

"You look exceptionally pretty tonight. That dress is nice." The green-and-white fabric formed a ruffle that fell just off her creamy shoulders. The top part of her hair was wound into a bun, while the rest hung loose against her back.

"Thanks. Actually it's a gift from Camille. She loves to buy me things even though I tell her not to." She looked at him with sad acceptance. "She tells me that she and Matthew are going to be leaving for Red Bluff next week. It'll probably be ages before I see her again."

"Maybe not. Matthew has TooTall to keep things going while he's away. They'll probably come in for a holiday or special occasion."

The smile she gave him was wan at best. "I hope so. Anyway, I can tell when we talk that she's missing the diner and her friends at Dragoon. Maybe they'll make the trip back up here for Sam and Gabby's wedding. That's going to be a very special occasion. Isabelle tells me they're going to throw a

big shindig on the Bar X and invite the whole countryside."

His sigh was heavy. "I'm not surprised. Weddings
seem to be important functions around here."

She looked at him as though she wanted to say
something, then quickly changed her mind. Was she
thinking it was about time she had a wedding of
her own?

*Don't be stupid, Taggart. Emily-Ann hasn't known
you long enough to fall in love with you, much less
decide she wants to be your wife.*

Maybe not, Taggart thought, as he fought against
the voice inside him. But when she held him, kissed
him, he felt as though she was pouring her heart out
to him. And he'd been just greedy enough to take it.
Or maybe he'd been misinterpreting all those sighs
and kisses and words of desire whispered in his ear.
A woman could enjoy sex without having her heart
involved. Could be she was beginning to think Taggart was a dead-end street and she wanted to travel
down a bigger and better avenue. One where she
could find a man more than willing to marry her.

Finally she said, "Weddings are very important—
to some people."

He didn't know what to say to that and after a
moment they both fell silent until she pushed back
her plate.

"One piece is all I can eat," she said. "You can
save the rest of it for your supper tomorrow night."

He'd never known Emily-Ann to be a finicky eater. "Are you feeling ill?"

"No." She smiled at him as though to prove it. "I'm fine. I just had a very busy day. I had to try to take a test between waiting on customers this morning. It was chaotic. I only hope I passed."

"I had a surprise this morning," he told her. "I got a message from my sister saying that Dad had been bugging her for money. He's threatening to come out here to Arizona."

Her brows lifted. "Threatening? That's a strange word to use in connection with your father."

"Well, if you knew him, you'd understand why I worded it in that way. He causes trouble wherever he goes. And he doesn't ask, he demands. I don't want to have to deal with him, Emily-Ann. And I certainly don't want the Hollisters to meet him."

She reached across the table and smoothed her fingertips over the fresh scar where he'd been bitten by the stallion.

"I wouldn't worry. I'm betting he doesn't have the money to make the trip out here. But he wants you to think he'll show up so that you'll send money to him. Just to make sure he stays away."

"You're probably right. And I can't be worrying about him now. I just don't want him harassing my sister."

She rose from the table and crossed the room to where the coffee machine sat at the end of the cabinet counter. As she began to gather the makings, she said, "Sounds like she's the one who needs to make the trip out here. A one-way trip."

"I've considered the idea of asking her to move here. But I need to get some things…settled before I do."

After she flipped the switch and the coffee began to brew, she walked back over to the table and rested her hands on the back of his shoulders. "What kind of things settled? Your job is secure. And you have a nice home here. You don't have anything else to settle—unless you're talking about your finances."

It suddenly dawned on Taggart that sometime during the past month they'd quit talking like people who were simply dating and started conversing like a man and wife. He couldn't rationalize how or why that had happened. Except that somewhere along the way he'd made a huge mistake. He'd slowly and surely allowed himself to get too close to Emily-Ann.

"I'm not concerned about that." He tilted his head around so that he could look up at her. "When the coffee finishes, I'd like to go to the living room. I need to talk to you about something."

Deep down, Emily-Ann had always known that sooner or later, she'd get the old "we need to talk" from Taggart. Yet she'd thought, or maybe she'd been hoping more than thinking, that she wouldn't hear those final words from him for a long, long while.

And why not? Everything had been going so great between them. If all the passion he'd showered on her this past month had been an act, then he deserved an award for the performance. But passion wasn't love, she realized. And love was the binder that held two people together. Not a set of sweaty sheets.

Emily-Ann carried a tray with their coffee and a saucer of Reeva's homemade cookies into the living room and after setting it on the coffee table, she eased down next to Taggart.

He looked unusually tired this evening and she wondered if spending most of the day with Maureen had stressed him out. Not that the woman was difficult to get along with. On the contrary, she was a joy to be around. But she and Blake were Taggart's bosses. He might've been feeling like he was under a microscope. *Anyway, what did any of that matter now?* she glumly asked herself.

Getting right to the point, she asked, "So what did you want to talk to me about?"

He reached for one of the coffees and took a long sip before he spoke. "I've been doing a lot of thinking about you and me. We've been spending a great deal of time together—both of us driving back and forth from here to Wickenburg. Which is hardly a short distance."

"I haven't minded." Her palms were so sweaty she had to wipe them on a napkin from the tray before she could pick up her coffee cup.

"I don't feel good about it, Emily-Ann. I worry about you driving in the dark on these lonely dirt roads. It isn't safe."

She didn't know where he was going with this. "I guess you're thinking about your late wife now."

He looked at her with something like surprise and then the expression turned to a glower. "No. I'm not thinking about her. I'm thinking about *you*—being safe."

"Oh. But surely you're not thinking you'll do all the driving to my place."

"No. I'm not. I'm young and healthy, but I don't think I could hold up to that pace and work, too."

Over the rim of her cup, she studied his face and tried to interpret the expressions she saw in his eyes and on his lips. He looked frustrated and lost and most of all weary. But from what? Was she doing this to him?

"Okay. So I guess this means you want us to slow down. To just see each other once in a while. Is that what you're trying to tell me?"

He looked at her and frowned. "Hell, no. What I'm trying to tell you is that I want you to move in with me."

Emily-Ann had never been so stunned in her life. For the past fifteen minutes she'd resigned herself to the fact that he wanted to end things. Instead, he was asking her to move in!

She must have stared at him far longer than she

thought because he finally scooted to the edge of the cushion and squared around to face her.

"Well? You're not saying anything. What do you think?"

"I wasn't expecting this from you." Dazed, she rose and walked across the room to where the main door had been left open to allow the cool night air to sift through an old-fashioned screen door. "If you want me to be completely honest, I don't like it."

Her throat was so thick she was surprised he'd heard the choked words. But he must have because he was suddenly standing directly behind her and so close that she could feel the heat radiating from his body.

"Why don't you like it?"

How could she begin to answer his question when she couldn't even explain the reasons to herself? She only knew that if she moved in with Taggart, she'd be giving up everything she'd ever wanted for herself.

"I—just don't think it's a good idea," she whispered, as the reality of his feelings were suddenly becoming quite clear to her.

His hands came down on her shoulders and for a second the emptiness inside of her wanted to turn and grab hold of him.

"You have something against a man and a woman living together—is that it?"

"No. It's probably the right choice for some people. Just not for me."

Awkward moments of silence began to tick away as she held her breath and waited for his response. Yet even as she clung to the tiniest hope that he'd say something—anything about loving her, she knew deep down that he was never going to have those kinds of feelings for her.

"I thought you liked being with me," he reasoned. "And I definitely want to be with you. I thought us living together here on the ranch was a good solution."

A solution to what? she wanted to ask. His urge to have sex whenever he wanted? Maybe that was enough for him, but not for her.

Her throat aching, she whispered, "Moving in with a guy has never been what I've planned for myself, Tag."

He tightened his hold on her shoulders. "A person can change their plans."

"Yes, and I can see I'm definitely going to have to change mine."

"What does that mean?" he asked.

Summoning up more strength than she ever dreamed she possessed, she turned to face him and then nearly wilted as her gaze met his. Confusion and disappointment swirled in the brown depths of his eyes.

She said, "It means that I think it would be best if we didn't see each other anymore."

He visibly flinched and she realized she'd surprised him. No doubt he'd seen her as too besotted with him to walk away. Well, she *was* besotted with the man, she thought sickly. More than that. She was in love with him. But no way would she ever admit that to him now. No, at least this way she could walk away with some shred of pride in herself.

"Are you serious?"

"Never more so," she said flatly. "You've made your feelings clear, Tag. And frankly, we're not on the same page."

A scowl caused his brows to form one dark line. "Am I supposed to understand that?"

Sighing, she reached up and gently touched her fingers to his dear face. For days after he'd given her the flowers, she gazed at them and allowed herself to believe they might have a real future together as man and wife—the whole family shebang. What a gullible idiot she'd been.

"No. I don't expect you to understand, Tag. And I'm sorry that you feel slighted. It's all my fault, really. When we first met, you made your feelings clear about love and marriage. I should've run from you then. But I didn't. So here we are at a dead end. That's all."

She hadn't thought it was possible for his frown to go any deeper but somehow it did. Taut lines ran from the corners of his mouth and eyes and furrowed his brow. He looked like a man in physical pain, but she knew that wasn't the case. Not over losing her.

A man had to love beforehand to experience that kind of loss.

"Love and marriage? Don't you think you're rushing things?"

His disbelief verged on the comical and the reality that he considered love and marriage to her a joke was all it took to have her backing away from him.

"Get this straight, Tag, I'm not asking anything from you. Now or ever! So relax. Go have yourself a good laugh."

She stalked over to the end table where she'd left her handbag when she'd arrived earlier this evening. After shouldering the leather strap, she walked back to the door with King trotting right on her heels.

"This is your way of solving things?" he asked, his voice incredulous.

She struggled to keep her lips from quivering. "There's nothing to solve. I'm glad for the time we spent together, but all good things come to an end. We both know that. But if you ever decide you want a cup of coffee and a pastry, you know how to find Conchita's."

She pushed past him and out the door. In spite of the pain ripping her heart and the tears swimming in her eyes, she put one foot in front of the other until she was down the porch and out to her car.

When she opened the door to climb in, she realized King had followed her and the sight of the whining dog was enough to cause a sob to slip past her lips.

Kneeling down to him, she cradled his face with both hands. "King, you can't come with me. You have to stay here on the ranch and hunt cows in the brush. That's your job. Tag will take care of you and someday—maybe—I'll see you again."

She dropped a kiss on top of the dog's head, then quickly climbed in the car and drove away. It wasn't until she was a quarter mile away from the house that she noticed King was chasing after her.

Blocking the dog and Taggart from her mind, she pressed down on the accelerator and headed the car onto the main road that would take her back to Wickenburg. Where she belonged.

Taggart stood on the porch and stared into the darkness where Emily-Ann's taillights had disappeared only minutes before.

What in hell had just happened? How could she just leave like that without giving him a chance to explain and reason with her?

Forget the past. Move forward. Hell! That's exactly what he'd been trying to do when he'd asked Emily-Ann to move in with him. But she'd taken the invitation as an insult. Maureen's theory on life was probably good for her, but it hadn't work for Taggart, he thought glumly.

He muttered a curse, then stuck two fingers in his mouth and let out a loud whistle.

"King! Come here, you damned traitor! There's no use chasing after a woman who doesn't want us!"

A couple of long minutes passed before the dog finally emerged from the dark lane and trotted up to the house.

As King approached the porch, Taggart started to give him a harsh scolding, but that plan was waylaid the minute the dog sat down next to him and let out a pathetic whine.

"Okay, boy," Taggart said, as he bent to pat the dog's head. "You're not in trouble. You'll just have to forget about her. That's what I'm going to do."

He turned and started back into the house and King determinedly trotted behind him. When they reached the screen door, Taggart hesitated for only a moment before he allowed the dog to follow him into the house.

The tray of coffee and cookies that Emily-Ann had carried to the living room were still on the coffee table. He picked it up and carried it to the kitchen where their meal of pizza was still scattered over the table and nearby cabinet counter.

Taggart began to clear away the mess, while wishing he could clear away the agony and confusion he was feeling.

Today, for the first time in years, he'd decided it was time to try to tear down the walls he'd built around his heart. Not just because Maureen had suggested he move on from the past, but because he felt like things between him and Emily-Ann had reached a point where snatching pieces of time here and there to be together was no longer enough. He'd thought having her move in would be the next logical step. Then he'd have plenty of time to get used to the idea of having her in his life for the long haul. He'd have a chance to decide if he really wanted to commit that much of himself to her.

And what the hell was Emily-Ann supposed to do while you sat around trying to make up your mind, Taggart? She deserves more than a trial run from you and you know it. So if that's all you can give her, then you got exactly what you deserve—a swift goodbye.

Damn. Damn. Taggart silently cursed as he tried to shut out the condemning voice in his head. Didn't he have a reason to be cautious? Didn't he have a right to think things through before he handed another woman his heart?

Yes, he did. But that didn't mean he had the right to take her to bed and expect that to be all she needed or wanted, he thought miserably.

Jamming the leftover pizza back into its box, he shoved it into the refrigerator, then got out his phone and punched his sister's number.

He was sinking into a chair at the table when she finally answered.

"Hi, Tag. How's my sweet brother?"

Sweet? Right now he felt as bitter as a green persimmon. "I'm fine," he lied, while wondering what he could do to get the clenched knot out of his stomach and the pain in his chest to go away. "I'm just calling to check on you."

There was a moment's pause and then she said, "I'm sorry if my text this morning caused you to worry about me. Everything is okay, Tag, really. I can handle Dad."

"Yeah, by tiptoeing around him like a Gila monster."

She sighed and Taggart could easily picture his sister with her dark hair hanging around her shoulders and her brown eyes full of warmth. Tallulah not only resembled their late mother, but she also possessed her soft heart. That was one of the reasons he didn't want her to have to deal with Buck O'Brien. She wasn't emotionally strong enough. Especially now that she and Trent had gotten divorced.

"He's not that bad—yet. But I'm thinking he's gotten into some kind of trouble that he doesn't want me to find out about."

Taggart gripped the phone, while wondering how much more his aching head could handle tonight. "What kind of trouble?" he dared to ask.

"I don't know anything for sure. It's just a hunch that he might be involved with some nasty loan sharks and they're breathing down his neck to be repaid. He seems more desperate than usual."

He groaned out loud. "That's just dandy. What's the old man going to do next, huh?"

"Who knows? Just be glad you're out there in Arizona, far away from the man, Tag."

He'd thought leaving the Flying W, and the demanding new owners, along with his shiftless father, would make his life free of stress and worry. Now he realized how ridiculous that sort of thinking had been. This rip between him and Emily-Ann was like nothing he'd ever endured. But he couldn't let himself think about her now. If he did, he might just break down and spill the whole pitiful mess to his sister.

"That's another reason I'm calling, sis. I've been doing some thinking. About you."

A teasing chuckle sounded in his ear. "Missing me already?"

"Sure I am. You're the only family I have."

There was a moment of silence and then he caught the soft sound of her sigh.

"You're the only family I have, too, Tag."

"That makes what I'm about to propose make even more sense," he told her. "I'd like for you to move out here, Tally."

"To Arizona? And live with you?" She sounded flabbergasted

"Yes, to Arizona. And yes, live with me for a

while. Until you get settled and then I figure you'd like to get a place of your own nearby."

"I'd definitely want that. Otherwise, we'd be trying to tear each other's hair out."

"You mean like we did when we were kids?"

"Exactly."

He could hear a smile in her voice, but the sound wasn't enough to lift the corners of his mouth. He felt like every cell in his body was frozen with pain and shock. Would this awful emptiness go away by tomorrow? Or would he have to wait a week or even months before he began to feel like a human being again?

"I'm serious, Tally."

"I understand that you're serious, Tag. But all my friends are here. So is my job at the real estate office. And—"

"You can get a better job here. That damned boss of yours is just using you. He makes bucket loads of money and pays you like you're the janitor instead of a secretary. He's a jerk and you're putting up with it."

A long stretch of silence passed before she finally spoke. "What in the world is wrong with you, brother? You sound like you're ready to coldcock somebody. Has something happened?"

Yes, something has happened, he thought. His whole world had just stopped spinning and no matter how hard he tried, he couldn't see any sort of happiness in his future.

"No," he said sharply. "Everything here is great."

"You could've fooled me. I'm afraid to hear what you'd sound like if something bad really had happened. Just proves to me that I'd rather stay here and be used by Mr. Graves than be growled at by my bearish brother."

Closing his eyes, he raked a hand through his tumbled hair. If Emily-Ann hadn't walked out on him, he would've already had her in bed by now. At this very moment she would've been kissing him, loving him in a way that no woman had ever loved him.

Love. Love. He never wanted to hear the word or have it enter his mind ever again, he thought bitterly. He didn't want to think that he'd just lost his one and only chance to know what real love actually felt like.

"I'm sorry, Tally. It's been a long, stressful day. I didn't mean to sound sharp. You're my favorite sis, you know."

She laughed then. "I'm your *only* sis. Remember?"

"Yeah, I remember. So will you seriously consider my invitation?"

There was another long pause and she finally said, "Yes. I will think deep and hard about it, Tag."

They talked a minute more and then Taggart finally ended the call and left the kitchen. When he entered the living room, he saw King pawing at the screen door.

The sight was like a knife slicing right through him and for the first time in years he was finding it hard to hold his emotions together. "Okay, so you want out. Now that Emily-Ann isn't here you don't like it inside. Well, just go." He opened the screen door and King shot onto the porch and down the steps like the devil was following him. "Go on back to Doc," he called after the yellow cur. "That's where you belong. And don't come back thinking she'll be here. She's gone."

And she won't be coming back.

The heavy weight of that reality settled on Taggart's shoulders as he shut the door and bolted it.

Chapter Twelve

"Emily-Ann, is that you?"

About to step out of the glass foyer and onto the wide sidewalk, Emily-Ann turned to see Camille bearing down on her.

Oh Lord, Camille was the last person she'd expected to run into here at the medical clinic. What was she going to tell her? That she had to visit the doctor because she couldn't eat? Couldn't stop crying?

Biting back a helpless groan, she squared her shoulders and waited for Camille to catch up to her.

"Camille, what are you doing here? Are you having a problem with the baby?"

Her friend quickly dismissed the question with a wave of her hand. "We're in fine shape. Matthew wanted me to have an extra checkup before we travel home," she explained, then laughed. "I think he's worried I'll go into labor while he's driving. He'll be pulling a trailer load of steers back with us and he doesn't think he can handle them and me having a baby at the same time."

Emily-Ann tried to laugh, but couldn't summon up anything that resembled a sound of amusement. She'd left the doctor's office in shock and the fog in her brain was still muddling her senses.

Camille peered closely at Emily-Ann. "What are you doing here at the clinic? Have you been sick or just having a yearly checkup?"

"Neither. I—uh, nothing serious. I've just been feeling a bit off, that's all." Deciding it would be pointless to hide the news from her closest friend, she grabbed Camille by the arm and urged her through the sliding glass doors. Once they were outside, she pointed down the sidewalk to a concrete bench shaded by the overhang of the building. "Do you have time to sit a minute?"

"Are you kidding? I'm not going anywhere until you tell me why you look like you've stuck your face in a bowl of flour."

They walked down to the bench and after both of them were comfortably seated, Camille leveled an anxious look at her.

"Okay, out with it," she demanded. "You were lying to me a minute ago. Something is seriously wrong with you."

"Something is wrong all right," Emily-Ann ruefully agreed. "With my head. I'm a stupid woman, Camille. There's no better way to explain the reason I had to visit the doctor."

Camille rolled her eyes. "You can't fix stupid at this clinic, Emily-Ann."

She groaned. "You're right. The doctor can't fix it. But he can certainly diagnose it!"

Camille must've decided that Emily-Ann's health wasn't in dire jeopardy because a perceptive grin suddenly appeared on her face. "Uh-huh. So what have you done? Spent too much money on something you didn't need and now you're getting ulcers worrying about it?"

The sound that burst past Emily-Ann's lips was something between a sob and a hysterical laugh. "How could I do that when I barely have enough to pay bills?"

Camille's expression softened as she reached over and gently rubbed the top of Emily-Ann's hand. "I'm sorry. I'm only teasing. I can see you're upset. Tell me what's going on with your health. Did the doctor give you a prescription?"

Emily-Ann pulled a small square of paper from her purse and thrust it at her friend. "Only this. I can buy them off the shelf."

Camille read the scribbled words, which promptly caused her mouth to fall open and her shocked gaze to fly up to Emily-Ann's face. "Prenatal vitamins! You're pregnant?"

Nodding, Emily-Ann fought at the tears scalding the back of her eyes. "Dr. Revere believes I'm about a month along. I don't know how it happened, Camille."

In spite of Emily-Ann's obvious distress, Camille laughed. "Of course you know how it happened. Every woman does."

Emily-Ann tried to clear the gravelly lump that had formed in her throat. "Well, yes, that part of it I know. I got too close to a long tall Texan! Obviously he was more potent than the pill I'm taking! That's my theory on the matter. The doctor seems to think the pregnancy occurred because I had a cold for a few days and that can sometimes affect the strength of the pill."

Her eyes twinkling with delight, Emily-Ann said, "When you two met at the party, I was fairly certain you and Tag were going to hit it off."

"Hit it off!" Emily-Ann practically shouted. "We've done more than that. We've created a baby!"

Camille's smile spread wider. "This is wonderful, Emily-Ann! Our children will practically be the same age—only a few months difference. They might both turn out to be redheads and grow up to be great friends, like us."

Camille made it sound like Emily-Ann had just been handed the best news a woman could ever receive. And it suddenly dawned on her that her friend was so very right. A child was a blessed gift. Plus, she'd always dreamed of having children. She had to feel happy about the pregnancy, even if it was an unexpected shock.

"That part would be nice," Emily-Ann agreed. "I only wish—oh, Camille, I don't want this baby to grow up without a father. I don't want my child to ever have to know that he or she wasn't important enough to deserve a full-time father."

Frowning, Camille squeezed her hands. "I don't understand. Don't you think Tag will be happy about the baby? I surely do. He has family man written all over him."

"Hah! Not a family with me, Camille." Shaking her head, she pulled a tissue from her handbag and dabbed it at her teary eyes. "I'm sorry. You couldn't know that Tag and I ended things a week ago. I haven't seen or talked with him since I was out at his house. But now—well, I'm going to have to face him with this new development. And I'm not looking forward to it."

Camille was silent for a thoughtful moment and then she said, "I wasn't aware that anything had happened between you two. Tag must not have mentioned it to Matthew or my brothers. But that's hardly a surprise. What little I've been around him, he doesn't do much talking about himself." She turned a questioning look at Emily-Ann. "So what happened? He's found someone else? Or he's tired of dating?"

Emily-Ann glanced around at the people going to and from the medical building to the large parking lot. This wasn't exactly the ideal place to be discussing something so private, but no one seemed to be paying the two women any mind. Most of them were probably dealing with their own troubles, she thought glumly.

She pushed out a heavy breath. "Nothing like that. Tag asked me to move in with him. And I—obviously, I refused."

"Oh. Move in," Camille murmured. "I see."

Bitter gall was spreading from her chest to the back of her throat, practically choking her. "No. I doubt you understand. So go ahead and tell me I'm an idiot for not grabbing what he offered. And maybe I am the biggest one to ever walk the earth—I don't know. But I am sure about one thing—I'm not going to be like my mother. I'm not going to live my life with a man who doesn't love me."

"Oh, Emily-Ann, this is—I don't know what to say. Except that if Tag wanted you to move in with him that certainly doesn't sound like a man who's tired of you. Or that he doesn't want to be involved."

Bending her head, Emily-Ann muttered, "You don't understand, Camille. He wants the convenience. It's nothing about having deep feelings for me. All the time we were together, he didn't say anything about caring for me—really caring. And then last week before I left, I finally got so angry I brought up the words *love* and *marriage*."

"And?"

"He looked like I'd thrown cold water in his face." Lifting her head, she shook it with grim determination. "No. I made the mistake of falling into the same trap my mother did. She believed she'd found love when actually all she'd been was a sex partner."

"Emily-Ann, I'm having a hard time believing that! Tag doesn't come off as that kind to me. How do you think he's going to react when he hears about the baby?"

Emily-Ann lifted her gaze to the cloudless sky. "I'm clueless there. I'm guessing he's not going to be a bit pleased. I imagine he'll be thinking I want to hook him into marriage." Her lips clamped tightly together, she looked at Camille. "Well, he's in for a surprise. I'd rather walk down the aisle with a jackass!"

Camille was clearly disappointed. "Why are you thinking like this?"

"I'll tell you why. All her life, my mother got nothing but crumbs from my biological father and then from the man she finally married. I'm not going to settle for crumbs, Camille."

"Damn it, Emily-Ann, you aren't your mother!"

"That's right. And I don't ever intend to be." Rising to her feet, she grabbed up her handbag. "I need to go. I took the afternoon off work to visit the doctor and now I have online classes scheduled. I can't afford to miss them."

Reaching down, she gave Camille a hand up from the bench.

Once she was on her feet, Camille said, "I think Matthew is planning on leaving for Red Bluff Sunday morning. Hopefully I can see you again before we go." She smacked a kiss on Emily-Ann's cheek. "I love you. Don't worry. You're going to have a baby and that's all that really matters."

Emily-Ann gave her a wobbly smile. "You're right. This little life I'm carrying means everything to me. And I'm not the only woman in the world who can be a good single mom."

"Now, you're talking." She gave Emily-Ann a parting hug. "Chin up. Everything is going to be fine."

Emily-Ann gave her friend a grateful squeeze, then hurried away before she could see the tears in her eyes.

"You don't have anything planned for tomorrow evening, do you?"

From his seat in the cushy leather armchair, Taggart glanced across Blake's office to where the man sat behind his desk, signing off on purchases for grain and fencing supplies.

After a long workday in the saddle, Taggart had

received a brief text from the man asking him to stop by the office to discuss plans for cutting the irrigated hay meadows. If the grass was ready, haying usually began the next month. But so far the two men had talked about everything but the hay. "Not unless you count doing my laundry and fixing myself something to eat."

"I can't help you with the laundry, but forget the cooking. Reeva will take care of that chore. I realize tomorrow night is Saturday night, but Mom has her heart set on you having dinner with us. It's a goodbye thing for Matthew and Camille."

Taggart wasn't decent company for anyone, but to make Maureen happy and to show Matthew his appreciation for all the support the man had given him these past six weeks, he supposed he could fake it and smile his way through the evening.

"I'll be glad to show up. Actually, I need to present Matthew with some kind of award for all the patience he's shown me since I arrived. He not only taught me lots of things about the ranch, but he also made me feel at home. I'm going to miss him."

"We're all going to miss him. And Camille—well, just when we get her back here on the ranch for a little while, she's leaving again." Leaning back in his chair, he linked his hands at the back of his neck and let out a long sigh. "But this time is different. She's happy and in love. And we don't worry about her anymore, because we know Matthew will take good care of her."

Take good care of her. There'd been times when Emily-Ann had been lying next to him that he'd wanted to hold her tight and promise he'd always take care of her, that he'd always be there for her no matter what the future held. But each time the promises had lodged in his throat. Because each time he'd realized no man can stop fate from stepping in and wiping away the things he loved the most.

Love. That awful night Emily-Ann had left his house, he'd vowed to never let the word enter his mind. But these past few days his mind had gone rogue on him. All it seemed to want to think about was love and how he'd lost his chance at having it, holding it and cherishing it.

Shaking away the bitter thoughts, Taggart focused his attention back to the present. "Yes, Matthew is a good man. He'll make a fine father, too."

Blake gathered the stack of papers he'd just signed and placed them on the corner of his desk before he glanced over at Taggart. "You know, you ought to invite Emily-Ann out to have dinner with us. She'll be wanting to see Camille before she leaves."

Blake might as well have thrown a bucket of ice on him, Taggart thought. He was so frozen by the man's suggestion that for a moment he couldn't speak. Finally, he managed to say, "I don't think that's a good idea. Uh—besides, it's your mother's party. It's her place to do the inviting."

And if Emily-Ann was going to be there, he didn't think he could bear it, Taggart thought.

Blake frowned at him. "Why wouldn't it be a good idea? I thought you and Emily-Ann were getting along great."

Too restless to remain in the armchair, Taggart got up and poured himself a cup of hours-old coffee and added several spoons of sugar. "We were. But things have changed. We're not seeing each other anymore."

A long stretch of silence passed before Blake finally said, "Oh. I'm sorry to hear that. I thought—"

Blake went silent again and Taggart slanted a curious glance in his direction. "You thought what?"

Leveling a shrewd look at him, Blake answered, "That you two might actually be getting serious about each other."

The pain in Taggart's chest was so unbearable he swallowed several gulps of the awful coffee before he could speak. "I don't know why you'd come up with that idea. I'm not a serious kind of guy. Not where women are concerned. Emily-Ann figured that out for herself. And—that's probably all for the best. No ties or broken hearts. You know what I mean."

His expression solemn, Blake continued to study him. "Yeah. I know what you're saying. You've already lost a woman you loved. You don't want to go through it again."

Taggart's eyes narrowed. "You've been talking to your mother."

"No. Why? Have you?"

There was no way Taggart was going to break his promise to Maureen and tell Blake, or anyone for that matter, that the two of them had ridden to water pump number nine. Nor was he going to tell him the personal things they'd talked about.

"Uh—no. I just thought—well, women kind of have an intuition about men—and she might have voiced her thoughts about me to you."

"No. But I read your background check before we ever hired you. I just never mentioned you're a widower because there was no point in bringing the matter up."

Taggart frowned. "But you think there's a point now?"

"I do. Because I hate to see you make a big mistake. One you might regret for the rest of your life."

Taggart swigged down the last of the coffee and tossed the foam cup into a trash basket next to the small refreshment table. "If you're talking about Emily-Ann, that's over. She wants more than I can give her."

"Guess you're talking about love and marriage now. Well, why shouldn't she want that for herself? Why should she settle for anything less?"

Moving in with a guy has never been what I've planned for myself, Tag.

Emily-Ann's words circled his weary brain, just as they had a thousand times since she'd walked out the door several nights ago. He'd hurt her terribly. He could see that now. But how did he go about trying to repair the damage? Would she even let him try?

With a heavy sigh, Taggart sank back into the armchair and dropped his head into his hands. "There's no use in me trying to act like I'm a cool piece of steel, Blake. I've been miserable without Emily-Ann. I guess—I didn't realize how much she'd come to mean to me until I—until she was gone." Lifting his head, he cast Blake a wry look. "That's the way it is with a fool, isn't it? He never appreciates what he has until he loses it."

Shaking his head, Blake said, "You're not a fool, you're just a little scared like every other man who's ever loved a woman. You've already learned the hard way that standing at the altar and saying your vows doesn't mean you get a guarantee with the marriage license. Regrettably, our mother learned the same thing. You think my brothers and I weren't afraid to take wives and have children? We all wanted to run like chickens. But we all had sense enough to know that living alone and miserable wasn't a good alternative."

Dear God, he'd been alone for a long time and during those empty years he'd believed that was the answer, the alternative to having his heart torn apart.

But Emily-Ann had shown him that living behind a guarded wall was not really living at all.

"I just wonder if Emily-Ann might give me a second chance."

Smiling now, Blake picked up the purchase orders, then switched off the banker's lamp on his desk. "I'll have Mom invite her. In the meantime, you be thinking about what you're going to say to her. Something meaningful and persuasive."

"You mean like I'm a heel and a jerk?"

Blake laughed. "That'll be a start."

Seeing Blake was shutting things down for the night, Taggart rose to his feet. "I thought we were going to discuss the hay meadows?"

He grabbed his Stetson from a hall tree and levered it on his head. "Oh that. We'll go over the hay situation later on."

Taggart shot him a suspicious look. "Damn it, Blake, did you call me in here to talk about Emily-Ann?"

Blake let loose a guilty laugh. "Look, Tag, you might as well get used to us poking into your private life. You're family now and we want everyone in our family to be happy."

Happy? Was there a chance that he could still find happiness with Emily-Ann? He could only hope.

The next evening in the den of the Three Rivers Ranch house, Emily-Ann sat in an armchair with a dessert plate filled with strawberry torte carefully balanced on her knees. Normally she loved the sweet dish, but tonight she'd only managed three bites before her jangled nerves made it nearly impossible to swallow anything past her tight throat.

Camille must have noticed that she was merely pushing the dessert around the plate rather than eating it, because she suddenly spoke up.

"Emily-Ann, would you like for Jazelle to fetch you a different dessert? You've hardly touched the one you have. You might like the pecan pie better."

Emily-Ann glanced over to a leather love seat, where her friend was cuddled comfortably next to her husband's side.

"No!" she blurted out, while thinking she'd never touch another piece of pecan pie as long as she lived. After sharing one with Taggart, it would never taste the same. "I—uh—this is fine. I ate so much for dinner that I really don't have room for dessert."

Maureen walked up on the group just in time to hear Emily-Ann's excuse for her lack of appetite. Now the woman ran a keen gaze over Emily-Ann's face.

"You ate like a bird," Maureen insisted. "And you look peaked, honey. Are you feeling okay?"

She shouldn't have worn this damned yellow dress, Emily-Ann thought. It made her appear even more washed out than she already looked.

"Sure, I'm feeling wonderful." Between bouts of

nausea and having every nerve in her body clenched in a viselike grip, she felt just dandy, she thought sickly. "And dinner was delicious. I'm just feeling a little blue at the idea of telling Camille goodbye."

"You can always come visit us," Matthew spoke up. "We'd be glad to have you."

"That's very nice of you, Matthew. Maybe after your baby gets here I can drive down for a visit. But only for a very quick one. You two are going to have your hands full without added company."

"Well, once baby Matthew gets here, she's definitely going to have to put up with her mother and her sister for a few days," Maureen said teasingly. "But we already have it in mind to shoo Camille off to the diner and keep the baby all to ourselves."

"Hah!" Camille laughed. "Baby Matthew. Who says?"

"TooTall," Matthew answered as if that guaranteed the gender of the baby would be male.

While the three of them continued to discuss the baby and TooTall's prediction, Emily-Ann couldn't help but notice how Matthew had his arm around his wife's shoulders and how the man kept darting loving glances at her. How would that feel, she wondered?

The question had her directing a furtive gaze across the room where Taggart, Holt and Chandler were standing near a wet bar, seemingly in deep conversation.

Thankfully at dinner, Maureen had seated Emily-

Ann several chairs on down the table from Taggart, which had made it much easier to avoid looking in his direction. And since then, she'd not once allowed her gaze to land on his handsome face. She couldn't bear it. Just being in the same room with him made her feel sick and stupid and humiliated.

So far tonight, she'd avoided facing him head-on, but at some point before the evening ended she was going to have to speak with him about the baby. Was he going to be angry? Was he going to accuse her of using her body to set a snare for him? Even if he didn't react quite that harshly, he was still going to throw some hard questions at her and how was she going to answer them?

Oh God, the mere thought of standing in front of him, telling him he was going to have a child, was enough to cause clammy sweat to pop out on her forehead and the base of her throat.

Certain if she didn't get some fresh air, she was going to throw up in front of everyone, Emily-Ann jumped up from the couch. "Please excuse me," she said, darting a frantic glance at Camille. "I, uh, need to step out for a moment."

As she hurried toward the French doors that led out to the patio, she noticed Camille starting to rise to her feet, but Maureen said something that caused her daughter to immediately sink back down on the love seat.

Thank God, Emily-Ann thought, as much as she

loved Camille, her frayed nerves weren't ready for a pep talk or sermon from her dear friend.

She didn't realize just how far she'd walked until she found herself standing by the cottonwood where she'd found Taggart the night of the party. Had she unconsciously sought out the spot, or was fate simply playing cruel tricks on her? It didn't matter, she decided. Nothing mattered now, except the child growing inside her. His child.

She was leaning against the trunk of the tree, allowing the cool air to wash over her when she heard a twig snap behind her.

Thinking Camille had probably come out to check on her, she turned with a weary sigh, then promptly gasped at the sight of Taggart walking out of the shadows.

By the time he reached her side, she'd managed to gather herself enough to speak. "What are you doing out here?"

"I could ask you the same thing."

"Getting some fresh air," she said stiffly, then turned her back to him and gazed blindly out toward the ranch yard in the far distance.

He said, "I guess you came to dinner because of Camille."

The familiar sound of his voice was like shards of glass raining over her. "And you're here because of Matthew."

"Yeah. We both had an obligation to show up for our mutual friends."

She heard him take a step closer and the idea that he might actually touch her sent her shredded nerves into chaos.

"You purposely followed me out here," she said in a strained voice. "Why?"

"I've been trying all evening to find a private moment to speak with you. When I saw you running out of the den, I decided to follow."

Had she actually been running? Lord, everyone in the room must be thinking she'd lost her mind. And they wouldn't be far off from the truth. For the past week and a half she'd done nothing but cry and throw up everything she put in her stomach. She'd reached the point where she hardly knew what she was doing or saying.

"Oh. Well, you've solved my problem. Because I've been wondering how I could talk to you—alone."

"Really? You haven't so much as looked at me tonight. I can't imagine you wanting to talk to me," he said. "You left the house more than a week ago and I've not heard a word from you. That doesn't sound like a woman who wants to talk."

Was it possible for a heart to split down the middle and still keep beating, she wondered? Because hers felt as though it was slowly and surely cracking.

"I've not heard a word from you, either. But then

I didn't expect to. You've made your feelings clear and I've accepted that what we had is over."

"Is it?"

Suspicious now, she studied his shadowed face. "I haven't changed my mind about anything, Tag. If that's what you're thinking."

"I don't want you to change your mind," he said flatly.

The pain in her chest was practically wiping out her ability to breathe and she had to turn her back to him as tears began to fill her eyes. "Oh. Well, that's that. So if you don't mind, would you please go back inside and leave me alone? I don't want to—continue this conversation—not tonight."

"Sorry, Emily-Ann, but I'm not going to leave you alone. Not until I say a few things that... I think you ought to hear."

Bending her head, she swallowed hard. "All right. Say them," she whispered.

His hands suddenly settled on her shoulders and all the familiar feelings of his touch poured through her like warm rain.

"I don't know where to start. So I'll just begin by saying I've been a complete jerk—an idiot. And I'm sorry. Terribly sorry."

Hope tried to enter her heart, but she immediately slammed the door on it. His being sorry didn't change the fact he wanted a bed partner rather than a wife.

"What do you have to be sorry about?" she mumbled the question. "Being honest?"

"But I haven't been honest," he admitted, then gently turned her so that she was facing him. "You've turned me into a habitual liar, Emily-Ann. Ever since I met you, I've continued to lie to you and myself. I've been telling myself I didn't love you. That I didn't need you in my life. Not as a wife or the mother of my children. But all along I knew I was lying and yet I was too much of a coward to face up to my real feelings."

She shook her head with disbelief. "Are you trying to say that…you love me?"

"Yes. But I'm butchering it up pretty badly, aren't I?"

A sob burst past her lips and then he was pulling her into his arms, holding her so tight that the side of her face was crushed against his chest.

"I'm hearing it, Tag. But I—"

"I know. You don't believe me. But I promise, Emily-Ann, I'll spend the rest of my life showing you just how much I love you. That is, if you'll let me."

Wedging her hands against his chest, she levered herself away enough to see his face. "I don't understand, Tag. You didn't want strings, or love or marriage. Why now?"

"Ask King. He'll tell you how miserable I've been without you. It only took me a couple of days to realize that my job, my home, my life meant nothing if you weren't with me."

The reality that he really did love her was beginning to set in and the joy that was pouring into her heart was healing the broken cracks she'd felt only minutes before. "And the rest of the days we've been apart?"

"I've been trying to figure out how to get you back—wondering if you could possibly forgive me." Reaching up, he stroked a hand over her hair. "I asked you to move in with me because—I was too afraid to ask you to be my wife. But I'm asking you now, Emily-Ann. Will you marry me?"

His declaration of love had been far more than she'd ever expected to hear from him. Now, he was proposing. It was almost more than she could take in. "Marry you!" she finally whispered. "Are you serious?"

He reached into the front pocket of his jeans and pulled out a velvet ring box. "I went to town yesterday and bought this because I knew you'd be here tonight. Ever since I've been praying you'll accept it."

When he flipped open the lid, Emily-Ann sucked in a sharp breath. The engagement ring was a large square-shaped diamond, flanked by two smaller emeralds and set in filigreed gold. It was far beyond anything Emily-Ann had ever dreamed a man might give her.

"Oh my! Oh, Tag, it's so beautiful! But it's too much," she protested. "A girl like me—"

"A girl like you deserves something beautiful," he finished.

Dazed, Emily-Ann watched him pull the ring from its velvet bed, but when he took her hand to push it onto her finger, she promptly shook her head and pulled back.

"I can't accept it, Tag. Not yet. Not until I tell you something you need to know."

Frowning, he dropped the ring into his shirt pocket. "Okay, what? That you don't love me? Well, I don't care. I'll love you enough for both of us."

She touched a hand to her forehead as her mind whirled with everything that had just happened. "I don't know how to tell you this, except to just come right out with it. You're going to be a father."

It was his turn to look flabbergasted. "A father! Are you saying you're pregnant?"

She nodded, still uncertain how the news of the baby was going to affect him. "About a month or so along. I guess it happened when we—uh—first got together. The doctor said my pill lost some of its strength because I had a cold, but that hardly changes the fact now."

He leaned back his head and let out a joyous shout. "A baby! Our baby!"

Smiling ear to ear, he lifted her off her feet and

whirled her around until she was laughing breathlessly.

"Are you really pleased, Tag?"

He set her back on her feet, then pulled her into his arms and kissed her for long, long moments. "Pleased? Oh, my darling, I couldn't be any happier."

Fifteen minutes ago, her heart was bursting with pain, now it was overflowing with joy. "I started to tell you when you first walked up. Now I'm so very glad I didn't. I'll always know that you wanted me to be your wife before you learned about the baby. I didn't want you thinking I'd gotten pregnant to snare you."

He pressed his lips to her forehead. "You got pregnant because you gave yourself to me. Because you put your love and trust in me. And I promise you, darling Emily-Ann, that I'll cherish you and our children the rest of my life."

Leaning her head back, she looked at him with starry eyes. "Children? As in plural?"

He chuckled. "You don't think we'll stop with one, do you? We have a long ways to go to catch up with the Hollisters."

Fetching the ring from his pocket, he slipped it onto her finger, then placed a soft, promising kiss upon her lips.

"Let's go tell everyone our happy news," he said.

She reached for his hand and just as they turned to walk back to the house, she began to laugh.

Pausing, Taggart asked, "What now?"

"I caught Camille's bridal bouquet at her and Matthew's wedding and ever since she's been predicting that I'd be getting married soon," Emily-Ann explained. "I'll never hear the end of this. She'll swear that the bouquet brought us together."

Laughing, Taggart tugged her on toward the house. "Come on, I'm going to go thank her for not throwing those flowers to anyone else but you."

Epilogue

On the last Saturday in June, the hot Arizona sun dipped behind a ridge of red, rocky bluff to spread a spectacular sunset of pink and gold over the huge crowd that had gathered at the Bar X to watch Gabby Townsend and Sam Leman exchange their vows of love.

The wedding ceremony was the second one Emily-Ann and Taggart had attended in the past three weeks, the first one being their own. Which had been a simple, yet elegant ceremony the Hollisters had given them at Three Rivers Ranch.

However, this wedding was far different from Emily-Ann and Taggart's. This event could only be described as a whopper of a shindig. People from every corner of Yavapai County and beyond had come to help the newlyweds celebrate. Now that the pastor had introduced the old foreman and the pretty artist as man and wife, the reception was in full swing. Champagne corks were popping in all directions and live music floated across the rapidly cooling air.

Joseph and Tessa had gone all out to help give their devoted foreman a wedding to remember. The backyard had been set up with rows of tables decorated with flowers and loaded with food and drinks of all kinds. Paper lanterns had been strung from tree limbs and crisscrossed the wide parquet dance floor. Folding chairs, along with bales of hay, were grouped strategically away from the dancing area for those guests who chose to sit rather than stretch their legs to the music.

"This isn't the sort of music I would've expected to hear at a ranch wedding," Taggart said, as he twirled Emily-Ann across the makeshift dance floor.

"Sam and Gabby wanted to dance to standards, so Isabelle searched until she found a band from Phoenix who could play them well. Personally, I love it," she said, her eyes twinkling up at him. "It's very romantic. Especially when I'm dancing with my handsome husband."

Smiling he rubbed his nose against her forehead.

"My beautiful wife will always be a romantic. I just feel bad that you didn't have this big of a wedding."

She laughed. "Are you kidding? I didn't want the whole county at our wedding! Besides, we were in a hurry and Maureen and Camille and Isabelle rushed like crazy to get our ceremony pulled off. It was beautiful and I have a stack of photos to prove it."

"I don't need a photo to remember how you looked that day," he whispered near her ear. "You were a heavenly dream in your long ivory dress and tiny flowers pinned in your hair. Come to think of it, you look mighty heavenly right now."

"It's the extra hormones from being pregnant. Camille says it makes us glow," she said with an impish grin, then added with a wistful sigh, "I wish she and Matthew could've been here tonight. They were planning to come, you know. But her doctor advised against it. The baby could come at any time."

"I'm sure they're thinking about everyone." The song came to an end and Taggart led Emily-Ann off the platform. "Let's go have some punch. We'll dance again in a few minutes. I don't want to wear you out."

"Something to drink sounds good," she agreed.

The two of them made their way to one of the quieter tables set up near a pair of Joshua trees. Once there, Taggart filled two glass cups with punch and handed one of them to Emily-Ann.

As he sipped the fruity drink, his gaze drifted over the heads of the guests to where Gabby and

Sam were being monopolized by well-wishers. "The music isn't the only thing that's surprised me this evening," he said. "I wasn't expecting to see Sam in a Western-cut suit. He looks downright dignified."

Emily-Ann nodded. "Very handsome for a man of his age," she agreed. "And the way he looks at Gabby—it's obvious he adores her. And she gazes at Sam—well, like he hung the moon just for her. It's an inspiration seeing them together."

He cast a wry glance at his wife. "Well, there's another couple here tonight that looks to me like they're very much in love."

Moving closer, she slipped an arm around the back of his waist. "You mean us?"

Taggart tightened his hold on her waist while thinking it was indecent to feel this happy. Being married to Emily-Ann and sharing their home together on Three Rivers Ranch was like finding heaven on earth. Now that they had a child on the way, he was eagerly looking forward to being the father he'd always wanted and needed, but never had.

So far, Buck O'Brien hadn't tried to contact him, but the old man continued to make life hard for Tallulah. Taggart and Emily-Ann were both trying to persuade his sister to move here to Arizona. The last time he'd talked to her, he'd gotten the impression she was close to giving in.

"Other than us," he said, then inclined his head

toward the far end of the dance floor where Gil was guiding Maureen into a slow two-step.

Emily-Ann's gaze followed Taggart's. "Oh, you're talking about Maureen and Gil. Yes, the more I see them together, the more I'm sure she's completely gone on the man. Which I think is okay with all her children, don't you? I know for sure that Camille doesn't object. But guys are kind of different when it comes to their mothers—they can be possessive."

"You mean since Joel is gone, the guys might need to protect their mother from assertive males?"

"That's close to what I'm trying to say. Not that I think Gil is assertive. Quite the opposite. He's very nice. He even stops by the coffee shop when he's in town and always leaves me a tip."

Since they'd married, Emily-Ann was still working at Conchita's and planned to keep her job until the baby arrived. After that, she was going to take time off to be a mother and finish her nursing degree. At least, that's what she had planned. Taggart couldn't imagine her giving up the coffee shop job completely. Not when she loved it so much. But that was her choice. All he wanted was for her to be happy and to know that he loved her and the baby utterly.

"Gil is a stand-up guy," Taggart said. "I just wish—"

"What?" she prompted.

"Oh, that the mystery around Joel's death could

be solved," he said. "I think it would help Maureen put losing him behind her once and for all."

Her eyes full of love and tenderness, she reached up and touched a finger to his cheek. "And what about you, Tag? Have you put your losses behind you?"

The smile he gave her couldn't have been more honest. "All I see, my darling wife, is the future. With you and me and our children."

He had just finished placing a soft kiss on her lips when Chandler strode quickly over to them and from the look on his face, he had good news.

"We just heard from Matthew. Camille has delivered her baby. A boy—Matthew Harrison Waggoner."

"Sounds like he's going to be a junior," Emily-Ann stated.

Chandler shook his head as he jerked out his smartphone and held it out for them to see the tiny baby swaddled in a blue receiving blanket. "Matthew is calling him Harry for Harrison and since that was our maternal great grandfather's name, Camille is happy with it."

"Are she and the baby okay?" Taggart asked.

"Matthew snapped this pic before they carried the baby off to the nursery. He says everyone is great and little Harry has red hair like his mother."

"Oh my!" Emily-Ann exclaimed, then sniffed as joyous tears filled her eyes.

Spotting them, Taggart asked, "Honey, why are you crying at this wonderful news?"

She dabbed a finger beneath both eyes. "Camille wanted our babies to both be gingers—like the two of us. Now if mine doesn't turn out having red hair, she'll be terribly disappointed."

Both men laughed loudly and then Taggart wrapped a reassuring arm around her shoulders and squeezed her close to his side.

"Don't worry, sweetheart, if this baby of ours doesn't turn out to be a ginger, the next one will be."

Chandler winked at Taggart and gave him a playful swat on the arm. "Welcome to the family, Tag."

* * * * *

COMING SOON!

We really hope you enjoyed reading this book. If you're looking for more romance, be sure to head to the shops when new books are available on

Thursday 2ND April

To see which titles are coming soon, please visit

millsandboon.co.uk/nextmonth

MILLS & BOON

Coming next month

BABY ON THE TYCOON'S DOORSTEP
Nina Milne

Isobel headed to the kitchenette, scooped powder into another bottle and handed it to Jake, waited whilst he poured the water in from the kettle.

Took it from him and stepped closer to demonstrate. Too close—she was way too close.

Focus. But not on his body, the sculpted forearms, the swell of his upper arms, the strong thighs. Not on his smell, not on the way his hair spiked up— This was a bad idea but for the life of her she couldn't figure a way out of it.

'Put your thumb over the top of the teat, so you're blocking the hole. Then you shake' Like this.' Her voice emerged squeaky…breathless…*ridiculous*.

He'd moved even closer to her now and his eyes held a wicked glint that ripped the breath from her lungs.

'So it's all in the wrist action,' he said dead pan and her gaze flew to meet his, in shock at the double entendre.

'I—'

Then he grinned and wiggled his eyebrows. 'Sorry I couldn't resist. Puerile but—'

'Yes,' she said, trying to keep a straight face. 'Definitely puerile.' But be that is it may she succumbed to a giggle, which morphed into a full-blown laugh. And in seconds he had joined in.

Now their gazes locked and she could feel the shift in the atmosphere, the swirl of desire, the fugue of need. They were even closer now. His scent tantalised; the warm smell of baby milk mixed with a hint of citrus clean sharp shower gel and a whiff of bergamot. Her head whirled and there was an utter inevitability about what happened next. She wasn't sure afterwards who initiated it, who made the fatal decision or whether it was a completely synchronised movement.

But one step took them closer and then she was in his arms and her lips met his and oh god it felt so good. His lips so familiar and yet so new, and her lips tingled as tremors of raw desire shuddered her body. Gentle, hesitant at first as if they both feared rejection and then the kiss deepened, intensified, sent a sear through her veins. His fingers tangled in her hair, she pressed her body against his wanting more, her pulse rate accelerated at his taste, his scent, the way his kiss could drive her to the edge of desperate need for more. Her body alight and craving more of him—of Jake—she wanted his touch, wanted the satisfaction her body knew and remembered.

Continue reading
BABY ON THE TYCOON'S DOORSTEP
Nina Milne

Available next month
www.millsandboon.co.uk

LET'S TALK
Romance

For exclusive extracts, competitions
and special offers, find us online:

 facebook.com/millsandboon

 @MillsandBoon

 @MillsandBoonUK

Get in touch on 01413 063232

For all the latest titles coming soon, visit
millsandboon.co.uk/nextmonth

MILLS & BOON
A ROMANCE FOR EVERY READER

- **FREE** delivery direct to your door

- **EXCLUSIVE** offers every month

- **SAVE** up to 25% on pre-paid subscriptions

SUBSCRIBE AND SAVE

millsandboon.co.uk/Subscribe

MILLS & BOON

THE HEART OF ROMANCE

A ROMANCE FOR EVERY KIND OF READER

MODERN

Prepare to be swept off your feet by sophisticated, sexy and seductive heroes, in some of the world's most glamourous and romantic locations, where power and passion collide.
8 stories per month.

HISTORICAL

Escape with historical heroes from time gone by. Whether your passion is for wicked Regency Rakes, muscled Vikings or rugged Highlanders, awaken the romance of the past.
6 stories per month.

MEDICAL

Set your pulse racing with dedicated, delectable doctors in the high-pressure world of medicine, where emotions run high and passion, comfort and love are the best medicine.
6 stories per month.

True Love

Celebrate true love with tender stories of heartfelt romance, from the rush of falling in love to the joy a new baby can bring, and a focus on the emotional heart of a relationship.
8 stories per month.

Desire

Indulge in secrets and scandal, intense drama and plenty of sizzling hot action with powerful and passionate heroes who have it all: wealth, status, good looks…everything but the right woman.
6 stories per month.

HEROES

Experience all the excitement of a gripping thriller, with an intense romance at its heart. Resourceful, true-to-life women and strong, fearless men face danger and desire - a killer combination!
8 stories per month.

DARE

Sensual love stories featuring smart, sassy heroines you'd want as a best friend, and compelling intense heroes who are worthy of them.
4 stories per month.

To see which titles are coming soon, please visit

millsandboon.co.uk/nextmonth

MILLS & BOON

HISTORICAL

Awaken the romance of the past

Escape with historical heroes from time gone by. Whether your passion is for wicked Regency Rakes, muscled Viking warriors or rugged Highlanders, indulge your fantasies and awaken the romance of the past.

MILLS & BOON
MEDICAL
Pulse-Racing Passion

Set your pulse racing with dedicated, delectable doctors in the high-pressure world of medicine, where emotions run high and passion, comfort and love are the best medicine.

JOIN THE MILLS & BOON BOOKCLUB